A PANORAMIC SAGA
OF AN INDOMITABLE AMERICAN
FAMILY—THREE GENERATIONS
OF PROUD AND GENTLE WOMEN
AND
THE MEN TO WHOM THEY GAVE
THEIR HEARTS.

THE VAN VRADENBURG WOMEN

1858—A pretty blonde schoolteacher is swept off her feet and into marriage with a handsome trapper . . .

1880—Their daughter pledges her life and her love to the Indian brave whose tribe kidnapped her as a child . . .

1910—Their granddaughter defies convention to follow her heart and pursue her career in central California.

A SPELLBINDING STORY OF
COURAGE, PASSION AND
ADVENTURE

TRAIL TO GLORY

MARILYN
MEREDITH

LEISURE BOOKS ∞ NEW YORK CITY

A LEISURE BOOK

Published by

Dorchester Publishing Co., Inc.
6 East 39th Street
New York, NY 10016

Printed in the United States of America

TRAIL TO GLORY

Preface

This is the story of three generations of a real family. Most of the facts are true, though many happenings had to be imagined, but it is as accurate as old records, letters, and the sometimes faulty memories of older relatives could make it.

Many thanks to my sister, Margie Turner, who researched the Van Vradenburg family; my parents, Genevieve and Murl Mitchell, for guiding me through Delano, the old homes and cemetery; Huberta Schmelter of Delano, and another descendant of the Van Vradenburgs, who helped with some of the later history, and for sharing *Where the Rail Road Ended: Delano, 1873-1973*, Delano Centennial Editorial Board, and *Delano, A Land of Promise*, Delano Historical Society.

Marilyn Meredith

BOOK I

1858
The Van Vradenburgs

Chapter 1

Mary could sense the note of frustration in the tall stranger's voice as he spoke to Mr. Graham, the storekeeper. "Is this all you have in the way of clothing for little girls?" The dress he held in his large hands was beribboned and heavily trimmed with lace. The child he was shopping for stood beside him.

Mary smiled as she thought how inappropriate the frilly dress would be for the six or seven-year-old girl. Her straight ginger colored hair had been hacked off unevenly into a straggly bob. Her plain face was smudged with dirt and her thin body was clothed in a shirt several sizes too large, and an ill-fitting pair of overalls, one strap falling off her shoulders, pant legs rolled up above skinny ankles. The only articles of clothing which seemed to fit were on her feet—a pair of Indian moccasins.

The man was handsome in a rugged sort of way. A leather hat was jammed over thick, dark brown hair which curled above the collar of his doeskin jacket. He wore fringed pants, also made of leather, not unlike those she had seen on the Menominee, Winnebago, and Fox Sioux Indians of the area. His skin was tanned from the sun, and though he seemed disheartened at the moment, laugh lines were etched at the corners of his dark eyes. Mary guessed he was a fur trapper. The town of Woodlake, Wisconsin had begun as a small fur trading post, with Oshkosh as its closest neighbor. Mary was curious what circumstances had brought the backwoodsman to the incongruous task of shopping for a child's clothes.

"Excuse me," she said, surprising herself by her boldness. "Perhaps I may be of assistance."

The man turned to look at her. His smile was wide, his teeth strong and white. "Ma'am, I'd be mighty pleased with any advice you can offer! My name is William Van Vradenburg. I'm a trapper by trade—though it appears I'll be seeking a different way to make a living now that I'm responsible for my sister here, Druscilla."

He stuck out one of his big hands and shook Mary's mightily. "The dresses she brought with her didn't last long out in the woods. Besides she's grown like a weed the past couple of months. Got the duds she's wearing now from a farmer with a passel of boys who felt sorry for the tyke. Afraid I haven't been any great shakes at raising this young 'un."

Mary responded to this outpouring with a smile, knowing instinctively the man wasn't usually so talkative. "I'm Mary Harrington, one of the school teachers here in town. How old are you, Druscilla?"

The girl, not happy to be the object of so much attention, hid behind her brother's leather-clad legs and murmured, "Seven, ma'am."

"Mr. Graham, don't you still have some of those ready-made chambray dresses like those Mrs. Otis bought for her daughters?" Mary asked.

While the storekeeper went to look for the requested items, Mary turned again to the trapper. "How long are you planning on staying in Woodlake, Mr. Van Vrandenburg?"

"If I can find a place for me and my sister to stay, I'd like to stick around at least until I find a plot of land somewhere. Guess I'll take up farming."

Now that she knew the relationship of the child to the man, Mary was curious to hear the rest of their story. "Mrs. Brady has an empty room," she offered. "Brady's Boarding House—that's where I live. When you are through with your business here, if you'd care to, you may come along with me and meet my landlady. We can see if her place would suit you. Three meals a day are included with the rent."

"That's mighty kind of you, Miss Harrington. Sounds like one solution to my problems."

Mr. Graham returned with a dress nearly the right size for Druscilla. Mary held it against her and assured Mr. Van Vradenburg she could alter it to fit in a matter of minutes. She also suggested he choose some material for another garment or two, so he could hire the local dressmaker to sew others.

After the purchases were made, Mary, with the tall stranger and his little sister, walked in the cool afternoon sunshine toward the boarding house. As they walked, Mr. Van Vradenburg told Mary he had become his sister's guardian the year before. His parents had died within days of each other in a cholera epidemic which had struck his hometown in Canada. Word finally reached him, and when he arrived at his parents' home, he discovered that Druscilla was being grudgingly cared for by elderly neighbors. He was obliged to take over her care. But the solitary life of a fur trader didn't lend itself to the proper upbringing of a young girl.

Reluctantly, he'd realized the adoption of Druscilla necessitated his choosing a new way of life. That, and his sister's desperate need for new clothes, had brought him to Woodlake. He'd left his horse and gear at the stable, planning to seek lodging after the purchases for Druscilla.

"The first bit of good luck I've had in days is meeting you, Miss Harrington," he said warmly as they turned into the yard of Mary's rooming house. He put his hand lightly on Mary's shoulder in a friendly manner. When Mary felt the warm pressure she was unable to control the blush which colored her cheeks.

"Come on then, Mr. Van Vradenburg," she said in a rush, hoping he hadn't noted her discomfort. "Let's step inside so you can meet Mr. Brady. I'm sure she'll be delighted to have someone rent that empty room!"

Mrs. Brady had been widowed several years before. Taking boarders into her large, two story home was her only means of support. It was as Mary had surmised; her landlady was pleased to have the woodsman and his sister move in. She even found a trundle bed tucked away in the attic to offer Druscilla.

The plump, gray-haired Mrs. Brady took over the settling of the Van Vradenburgs, and Mary told the man she was going to her own room to freshen up for the evening meal. Before she could turn away he took hold of one of her hands and said, "Thank you again for your kindness, Miss Harrington. I'll be looking forward to seeing you at supper." Mary was horrified to find herself

blushing again. She hastily pulled her hand away
and fled up the stairs.

In her own room, she sat on the edge of the bed
and put her palm to her warm cheek. "What on
earth has come over me?" she murmured. At
twenty-three, Mary considered herself a spinster.
She had dedicated her life to teaching and molding
the lives of other people's youngsters. Teachers
were not supposed to marry, or even keep company with the opposite sex.

To convince her own parents she should continue with her education after the usual few years,
Mary had professed a longing to be a teacher,
thinking up every possible argument why she
should enter the profession. She had not only convinced her mother and father, but also herself.
Consquently, Mary had never indulged in any
fantasies of a handsome prince on a white charger
sweeping her off her feet. Most of the men she met
were already married. The few eligible ones were
rough, raw-boned, smelly, and uneducated—
larger versions of the boys who were in her class
at school. They treated her with respect and
looked upon her with awe because of her vocation.
In any encounter she had with the male members
of the community, she had never once lost control
of herself as she had with Mr. Van Vradenburg.
Mary prided herself on her serenity and capability
to handle each and every human relationship as it
came along. Her surprising reaction to the
stranger's touch had put a slight tilt to her safe
world.

After washing and changing her dress, she stood
before the small mirror atop her dressing table
and surveyed herself. "Mary, you *must* take yourself in hand," she scolded her image. Her light
reddish-blonde hair was caught in a thick bun at
the nape of her neck, but no matter how severely

she wore her hair, its unusual color gave her a gay, frivolous appearance. Her blue eyes were a clear, pale shade, much the color of an early spring sky. Thick brown lashes accented them becomingly. Her nose was short and slightly uptilted, and no matter how carefully she protected her face from the sun, a light sprinkling of freckles scattered over the otherwise fair skin of her nose and cheeks. Overgenerous was her opinion of her lips, though they did have a definite, feminine outline.

The plain dress she was wearing was the same blue as her eyes. It was high-necked, long-sleeved, and the bodice accented her full bosom and tiny waist. The skirt flared over her many petticoats. Shaking her head in amazement, she realized she seldom took the time to admire her reflection. It was *most* unlike her! Meeting Mr. Van Vradenburg had caused her to act like a silly schoolgirl!

When Mary went downstairs for supper, she was unable to control the faster pace of her heart, or the smile which burst forth when she saw Mr. Van Vradenburg standing by his place at the table. His handsome face beamed as he greeted her with, "Miss Harrington, how splendid you look!" The other boarders peered up at her in surprise.

Miss Fannie Newton, an elderly spinster, appraised her and snorted, "Looks like usual to me!" Mr. Fintel, a drummer, somber and dour, allowed a half smile to flicker across his countenance, and quickly resumed slurping his soup. Druscilla, seated beside her brother, glanced momentarily at Mary, a tiny grin quivering on her lips, before she again concentrated on the contents of her bowl.

"Do sit down, Mary," ordered Mrs. Brady. "You are tardy. We've already had the blessing and have begun the meal."

Mary was glad to busy herself with eating. The

other boarders' attention was quickly diverted. As she began spooning up her soup she glanced furtively across the table at Mr. Van Vradenburg. To her chagrin, he was staring unabashedly at her while he ate, and he continued to do so throughout the meal. Each time she glanced in his direction, he grinned at her. Though Mary managed to eat most of her supper, she had no idea what any of it was.

When everyone had finished and began leaving the table, Mary cleared her throat and said quietly, "If you will all excuse me, I'll . . ."

Mr. Van Vradenburg leaped from his seat and rushed to her side. "I hope you don't have anything pressing to do. I'm not used to being cooped up like this, and after such a hearty meal—my thanks to the cook, ma'am—" he nodded in Mrs. Brady's direction and continued, "I was hoping you'd consent to taking a walk with me."

"I don't know, Mr. Van Vradenburg. I have some papers to correct, lessons to prepare, and there's Druscilla for you to tend."

"Don't you fret about Druscilla," he said. "She's been readying herself to bed right along." As if it had been rehearsed, Druscilla, her small hand covering a yawn, murmured to her brother, "I'm sleepy, William. I'm gonna go to bed."

"Good night, Sis." He leaned down and gave her a kiss on the cheek. "See, Miss Harrington, there's no need to concern yourself with Druscilla. Tomorrow is Sunday, so you don't have to worry about school either. I'd be mighty pleased to have the pleasure of your company."

"All right. I suppose a short stroll would be nice." Mary took her shawl from the hall coat rack. As she put it around herself, Mr. Van Vradenburg settled it into place, giving her shoulders a slight squeeze as he did so. He opened the front door and offered her the crook of his elbow. She slipped her hand through it and he placed his other hand over hers. It seemed a familiar gesture for him to make on such short acquaintance, but at the same time she felt comfortable and protected.

They walked for some distance in silence. He shortened his stride to match hers. Approaching the outskirts of town, where the trees grew closer together, Mr. Van Vradenburg pointed to a fallen log. "Why don't we sit and rest for a moment?"

Mary wasn't at all sure it was the proper thing to do, but it was dark, the last house was far away, and she was beginning to tire. Besides, he pulled her down beside him before she could protest.

"Mr. Van Vradenburg . . ." Mary began. She wondered why her heart was beating so furiously.

"Wait, Miss Harrington," he said, taking hold of one of her hands. "I have a request. Please call me William, and may I call you Mary?"

"I—I suppose that would be all right," she faltered.

"Mary, you are the loveliest woman I have ever seen!" He cupped her chin in his large hand.

"Mr. Van Vradenburg—I mean, William—thank you for the compliment, but I don't think you should be speaking to me this way!" Mary could feel the flush again rising on her cheeks. The man was much too forward! She knew she should express annoyance, perhaps even anger, but there was another equally strong, unidentifiable emotion troubling her.

"My remark wasn't meant as a compliment, merely a statement of fact. I'm thirty-one years old and I've traveled many miles and seen a pretty woman here and there. In my judgment, you are the best looking gal I've ever laid eyes on!" And with that he circled her waist with his hands, pulled her closer to him, and kissed her full on her lips.

Mary was so stunned that she didn't do anything at first. Her lips tingled under his, her body yielded against him. But in a moment she pulled herself away. The shock she was feeling registered in her voice as she exclaimed, "William, *please!* We only met a few hours ago! Your behavior is most unseemly!"

"Not unseemly at all! As to our short acquaint-ance, we will remedy that quickly. I don't have time for courting and all the folderol which goes along with it. I can't stay cooped up in a boarding house for long, certainly not long enough to do what others might consider proper courting. I knew you were the woman for me the minute I laid eyes on you!"

Mary nearly choked. "You've taken me completely by surprise, sir! You can't be serious!"

"My dear," his voice was tender, "I'm more serious than I've ever been in my life. I want you to be my wife."

In her best schoolteacher manner, holding her back straight and her chin high, Mary pushed him away. "Mr. Van Vradenburg, I am not planning on marrying. I have my career."

William smiled disconcertingly. Even in the dark Mary could see his eyes sparkle. "Young woman, that's all been changed! You had no way of knowing you were going to meet me. But now that we *have* met, it should be perfectly obvious to you—as it is to me—that you and I are going to be married." Again he gathered her into his arms, pulling her against his chest, pressing his lips to hers.

Mary's thoughts swirled in her brain. What was happening to her? The wonder of his kiss, the strong warmth of his arms around her, the way his body felt against her filled her mind. She could think only of the glory of this man. She relaxed in his embrace and forgot any arguments she might have offered.

Chapter 2

Over the next two weeks, Mary felt as though she were in a whirlwind. Sometimes she couldn't believe what was happening to her. At other times she wondered if she's lost her senses. Previous to meeting William, her future had been easily forecast. She knew she would grow old alone, and she'd been resigned to her lot. Now her well-ordered life had been turned topsy-turvy. What was she thinking of, to be making wedding plans with a man she scarcely knew?

But when she was with William all her doubts and fears disappeared. He took charge and made plans and it all seemed perfect. When he touched her, any remaining misgivings simply melted away. It was hard for her to believe how this stranger had affected her emotions, and that was what troubled her most. Was the strong physical attraction she felt for William affecting her judgment as well?

The teaching year came to a close and Mary handed in her resignation to the school officials, who were visibly shocked by her decision. Mrs. Brady, her landlady, reacted to the news in an entirely different manner. The large woman clapped her plump hands together and chortled, "Wonderful! He's the perfect mate for you. Thank your lucky stars he's saving you from becoming a dried-up spinster! The wedding will be right here in the front parlor . . ."

"You mustn't go to any trouble, Mrs. Brady," Mary protested.

"Oh, it won't be a bit of trouble. It'll be my pleasure to give you nice young folks a proper send-off!" Mrs. Brady happily charged ahead with her plans.

William purchased a wagon and outfitted it with farm implements and household supplies. Most evenings he and Mary sat on the front porch of the boarding house, discussing their future. William did most of the talking. His dreams were hard for Mary to visualize—they were all about raising crops and animals, somewhere far away from town.

The night before the wedding, William led Mary to the porch swing. After they were settled, he took her hand in his, announcing abruptly, "We're leaving right after the wedding supper."

Mary's stomach did a flip-flop as she turned to stare at her husband-to-bed. "Leave for where, William?"

His dark eyes stared off into the twilight shadowed yard. "I want the beginning of our life together to be out in the open . . . where there are no people, no walls or roofs. I don't want to start our marriage in a rooming house."

Frowning, Mary said, "Are you saying you want us to spend our wedding night outside . . . with the snakes and wild animals?" She was trying to keep the fear she was feeling out of her voice.

William laughed, a rumbling, somewhat reassuring sound. "You don't have to worry about snakes and wild animals, my dear, not when I'm around . . . and I will always be nearby. Don't fret, my sweet. You'll love it just as I do, you'll see!"

She knew he assumed she would be willing to accept his plan. "William, of course I'll do whatever you think best, but . . ."

"Well, then," he interrupted, "it's all settled! I'll finish packing the wagon tomorrow after the wedding supper, and as soon as we've said our goodbyes you, Druscilla and I can be on our way!"

Mary wished she felt as positive as William sounded, but she still had serious doubts. She squeezed his hand. "Please listen to me, William. I'm terribly afraid I'll be a great disappointment to you!"

He shook his dark, curly head. " Dear one, there is nothing about you that could possibly disappoint me."

"Hear me out, William, please!" She was beginning to feel desperate. Perhaps the whole idea was a mistake. They didn't know much about each other—they were from entirely different worlds! "I began teaching school as soon as I left home. I've always lived with the families of my pupils or in a boarding house. Someone else has always taken care of the cooking and household chores. Of course I helped my mother when I was a child, but I've had very little experience since then. I probably won't be the kind of wife you need or expect. William, I don't know the first thing about preparing a meal in the wilderness!" She felt that she might cry.

William laughed heartily, causing the swing to sway, and hugged her. "Is that what's bothering

you? Don't give it another thought! I know everything there is to know about living in the woods.
Remember, it has been my home for many years. I
can teach you, and you will love it as much as I
do.''

Again she wished she shared his confidence, but
there seemed to be no tempering his enthusiasm.
Before she could offer another argument, his
mouth sought hers. It was impossible for Mary to
think rationally when William kissed her. All she
was aware of was her own softness against his
hard, muscular body. While she was in his arms
she knew they were meant to be one, despite all
obstacles.

The wedding was a blur to Mary. The minister of
her church officiated and she became Mrs.
William Van Vradenburg in short order. The wedding guests shared in the bountiful supper provided by Mrs. Brady. Practical gifts of a feather-
bed, quilts, pots and pans, and dishes were
showered upon the newlyweds, along with
congratulations and best wishes for their future
happiness.

Then William helped Mary up to the seat of the
wagon, tucked a drowsy Druscilla in beside her,
and they rode out of town. Nearly two hours had
passed when William halted the horse. It was so
dark Mary couldn't really tell anything about their
surroundings except the shadowy shapes of trees.

''We'll stop here for the night.'' William set
about unhitching the horse. Then Mary watched her
husband fix a bedroll for his sister, tucking in the
sleeping child. He built a ring of stones, gathered
wood, and built a small fire. Spreading canvas on
the ground, he fluffed the feather mattress on top
and arranged their quilts.

Swinging Mary from her perch, he led her by the

hand to the makeshift sleeping arrangement. "Mrs. Van Vradenburg, our marriage bed awaits."

"What about Druscilla?" She nodded in the direction where the child was curled in her blankets on the other side of the campfire.

"Don't give her another thought. Once my sister is asleep she never wakes until morning."

"I'll just go after my nightgown," she murmured, turning toward the wagon.

"Lesson number one." William grasped her by the shoulder and began unhooking the fasteners on the back of her dress. "We'll strip to the skin. It will be far warmer sleeping that way."

"I've never slept without being clothed," she protested, shocked.

"Tonight will be the first time for many things, won't it, Mary?" he said quietly.

She could feel the heat rising to her cheeks, but she didn't object when he lifted her dress over her head. He removed her petticoats and corset as though he were unwrapping a fragile gift. Pulling the pins from her hair, Mary felt her thick, fair locks tumble around her shoulders.

When she was completely naked, William held her at arm's length and gazed at her. The glimmer of the fire glowed on her pale skin. Her breasts were high and full, her waist tiny, her hips flared to rounded thighs. He enveloped her in his arms, and she felt his large, work-roughened hands slide down her back.

"Mary, sweetheart, you are exactly as I had imagined," he whispered huskily.

She shivered involuntarily, partly from the slight chill in the evening air, and partly from a mixture of fear and anticipation.

"My poor darling. Are you cold, or are you frightened?" he asked. "Come, get into bed. Don't be frightened. I'll be gentle." William tossed the quilts aside and helped her under them. Quickly he dropped his own clothes in a pile and scrambled in beside her.

Putting her arms around her husband, Mary ran her fingertips down his back. She could feel the ripple of muscles under the smooth skin. She had never touched a naked man before.

Using his lips and hands, he touched and explored her entire body, causing her to tremble. A rush of love swelled within her, and at last she returned his caresses. William was gentle, and when he made them one, tears filled her eyes—not from the slight discomfort, but the overwhelming emotions she was experiencing.

"William, I do love you," she cried. "I'm so happy!"

Afterwards, when her head was cradled on his shoulder, William whispered, "I've been looking for you all my life, Mary."

She was warm and content as she cuddled close to the man who was now her husband. A million stars were overhead and night birds, frogs, and insects serenaded them.

"I didn't know love was so wonderful," she murmured.

He smoothed strands of her hair with his hand while he gazed at her. He gently kissed her eyelids, her nose, and traced the outline of her lips with a fingertip. With quickened breath, his lips brushed hers. His hands sought her secret places, and she felt as though she were on fire as once again he made her his.

In the morning, Mary woke with a start. The sun's early light was shimmering through the thick foliage of the trees. Druscilla was beside the fire helping William with the cooking. Mary sat with the quilt held around her shoulders and, embarrassed, reached for her clothes.

"Ah, my dear, you're finally awake." Amusement was in her husband's eyes as he watched her wiggling under the covers to dress.

"Mary!" Druscilla ran to her side. "Breakfast is ready! I cooked it."

The meal consisted of biscuits, bacon, and eggs, and Mary couldn't remember such simple fare ever tasting so good. Then the campsite was cleared quickly, the wagon repacked, and once more they were on their way.

Mary was surprised by the change which had come over Druscilla. The ginger-haired child was bubbling with chatter. Eagerly she pointed out interesting sights along the trail. "Look, Mary, there's a squirrel! Doesn't he have a bushy tail? . . . Did you ever see so many trees? William can tell you the name of every one, can't you, William? . . . What a pretty stream, could we stop here? . . . What are those funny little flowers called? . . . Oh, oh, there's a mama deer and her baby . . ." Druscilla seemed to blossom in the fresh air. The shy, silent little girl had been transformed into a gay, inquisitive, vivacious child. Town life must have intimidated her as much as it had her brother.

As they rode along, Mary rested her hand on Willima's leather-clad thigh, and from time to time he leaned over to nuzzle her cheek with his. Though Mary couldn't begin to imagine what the future held for them, she knew nothing mattered except having her new husband at her side.

With each passing day, Mary learned more about William and his many skills. When he made camp in the evening he seemed to know whether or not to expect rain. Sometimes, though there wasn't a cloud in the sky, William would carefully cover the contents of the wagon and would build a shelter with tree branches for them all to sleep

under. And the rain would come. William kept
them in good supply of wild game and fowl, and he
pointed out the edible plants and berries to Mary
and Druscilla.

After a week of travel, William stopped the
wagon in heavily wooded area abounding with
pine, juniper, and oak. A stream flowed below a
grassy meadow which rose to a hillock. William
paced the area, peering here and there, with
Druscilla trotting at his heels.

He returned to Mary, who had waited beside the
wagon, a broad smile on his face. "This is it, Mary.
This will be our home!"

"Yippee!" Druscilla cried, scampering off.

William encircled Mary's waist with his arms
and pointed to the small rise above the stream.
"There is where we'll build our cabin with a small
garden nearby."

"It's certainly lovely, but aren't we rather far
from any other people?" Mary asked apprehensively.

"We don't need people. We can go back to
Woodlake when we need supplies. But most
important now is for us to build our home."

Mary discovered muscles she didn't know she
had, and her hands became callused as she worked
beside William gathering rocks, helping to build a
fireplace and chimney, felling trees, and raising
their two-room cabin. By the end of summer it was
complete, along with a small outbuilding for their
horse, tools, and a large supply of firewood.

William fashioned their beds, a rough plank
table, and benches, using his ax and saw. Soon
their cabin looked like a real home. And Mary
knew there was going to be an addition to their
little family, though she hadn't yet revealed the
news to her husband.

The forest was beginning to take on autumn colors when William announced it was time for him to return to Woodlake for their winter supplies. "I can make better time and will have more room for my purchases if you and Druscilla stay here. Do you think the two of you can manage by yourselves?" he asked.

Putting her arm around Druscilla and smiling bravely, Mary answered, "Of course we can!" But inside she was fearful. It was a long way to Woodlake and there was no neighbor to call on for help. But she didn't let William know she had any doubts.

At dawn the next morning, William set off with horse and wagon, and Mary and Druscilla watched until he disappeared into the forest. As the day progressed it became warmer than usual, and Mary decided it would be a good time to do the laundry. She and Druscilla washed the clothes in the stream, and after they were all spread out on the grass to dry, Mary grinned at her young sister-in-law and suggested, "I've a great idea! Why don't we take a bath?"

Druscilla didn't wait to answer. She stripped off her clothes and ran into the icy water, splashing and laughing gleefully. Mary disrobed too, stepping cautiously from the bank. But soon she too was wet all over, even soaking her long hair.

While she was wringing out her curls, she heard a twig snap. Startled, she raised herself from the water, brushing her wet locks from in front of her face, and glanced about.

"Druscilla?"

"I'm here, Mary." The naked child was wading upstream.

Mary looked all around but saw nothing unusual. But the air suddenly seemed chilly, and the water was no longer comfortable. "Come, Druscilla, it's time we dressed," she called.

"Not yet, Mary," Druscilla argued.

"It's cooling off. I don't want you to get sick. This is no time for either of us to become ill. Do as I say, dear," Mary insisted. She glanced about uneasily. She was cold, and there was something else—something eerie. Quickly she stepped into her undergarments and pulled her dress over her head. As she slipped it into place she heard Druscilla let out a little squawk.

Standing no more than two feet away from her was a tall Indian, dressed in fringed leather pants and a shirt intricately decorated with beadwork. Taking a step backwards, Mary noticed that one side of his face was cruelly disfigured. The side which was unmarred was handsome, even aristocratic, but the cheek of the other was criss-crossed with raised purple and puckered scars, and the eye was nearly closed and blind. The good eye stared at her menacingly.

"Stop," he commanded, grasping her shoulder. His fingers dug painfully into her flesh.

"Please, you're hurting me," Mary gasped, terrified.

Druscilla came running and kicked at the Indian's shin with her bare foot. With his free hand he slapped Druscilla across the face, knocking her down. Druscilla lay crumpled, whimpering.

"Stop it, you fiend!" screamed Mary, hitting the Indian with her fists. "I'll call my husband and he'll kill you!"

"Your man not here," he said simply.

Mary tried to wrench herself from his grasp. "Leave us alone!"

"Be still. I will not hurt you."

"You already have," Mary gasped. The Indian released her shoulder and she dropped to her knees, gathering the sobbing Druscilla to her bosom. "There, there, dear. It's going to be all right," she reassured the girl, though she was not at all sure it would be.

The Indian leaned down and lifted a strand of Mary's hair. "Red like the flower the white man calls Indian paintbrush. When he returns, tell your man Half-face was here."

Mary stared wordlessly at him. He let her hair slip from his fingers and walked slowly into the trees.

When he had disappeared, Mary stood up shakily and pulled the naked and trembling Druscilla to her feet. "Come on, let's run!" she cried. Holding hands, they ran into the cabin. Once inside, Mary put the bar across the inside of the door, then leaned against it and shook uncontrollably.

Morning became afternoon, the shadows lengthening. Peeking out the windows, and seeing no sign of the frightening Indian, Mary said to Druscilla, "This is silly! Half-face, or whatever he calls himself, could come and get us any time he wanted. If he'd meant to harm us, surely he'd have done it be now. Let's gather the laundry, and prepare our supper."

Never catching sight of the Indian again during William's absence, Mary still felt his presence whenever she and Druscilla were tending to their outside chores.

Chapter 3

The sound of a horse and wagon approaching signaled William's return even before he came into sight. "Druscilla," Mary called, "It's William! He's home!" Holding up her skirts, she ran down the hill as William rode into view.

Druscilla dashed past her yelling, "William, William, we were attacked by *Indians!*"

Pulling the horse to a halt, the familiar buckskin clad figure dropped from the wagon. Mary threw herself against his broad chest. "Oh, I'm so happy you're finally back!"

Druscilla jumped up and down beside them, ginger-colored hair bobbing, chanting, "The Indians came to get us!"

William kissed Mary for a long time. When he released her, he scooped up his sister with one arm. "I'm mighty glad to be back! What's all this chatter about Indians?"

While Mary and Druscilla helped him unload the

wagon, they related what had happened. "So you see, we weren't exactly attacked, and he said, 'Tell your man Half-face was here.' Have you ever heard of anyone like that?" Mary asked.

William's mouth spread into a grin. "Half-face is a friend of mine! I wonder if he's still around."

"I wouldn't be at all surprised. I had the feeling he was watching us all the time. How can he possibly be a friend . . . he was so frightening!"

"And he knocked me down," Druscilla added, sticking her lower lip into a pout.

William raised a dark eyebrow. "You must have done something to provoke him. Half-face is usually a gentle person."

"He wasn't exactly nice to me either," Mary argued. "I know he was watching me bathe in the stream. And he hurt my shoulder; holding me so tightly when he talked."

"He hung onto you to keep you from running away. He's scary to look at, with his face scarred so horribly. But see here, my beautiful wife, I'm hungry and tired, and I could do with a cup of coffee. After I eat and rest a bit, I'll tell you all about my Indian friend. With any luck, now that I've come back, he'll visit again."

Over a second cup of coffee, William told his wife and sister how he'd come to be friends with the Indian. "Several years ago, when I was fur trapping, I was skinning and drying some pelts when I heard a ruckus nearby. It sounded like a very angry bear . . . and the horrifying screams of a man. I grabbed my rifle and ran.

"A huge bear was tossing an Indian around like he was a rag doll. He was fighting back with his bare h ands, but there was so much blood I knew he was losing the battle. I got off a good shot and killed the bear. The Indian was unconscious and one side of his face was a bloody mess. His eye had been gouged from its socket, and his cheek was ripped and hanging in strips."

Mary gasped at the gory description. Druscilla leaned her elbows on the table, her chin cupped in her hands, listening fascinated. William continued, "I carried the man back to my campsite, washed his wounds and poured the last of my whiskey over them. I tried to put the pieces of his face back together, but he was so badly mutilated I knew he would be horribly scarred. To tell you the truth, he'd lost so much blood, I wasn't sure he was going to live. I bandaged him and wrapped him in a blanket.

"He was unconscious for three days and three nights. When he finally came to, it was a while before he remembered what had happened to him. He spoke a bit of English and I understand a little of the Menominee dialect, so I was finally able to piece together the events.

"Half-face—which is what he told me to call him after he saw his reflection in the lake near my camp—said he'd been checking his bear traps when he came upon the bear which had shortly before pulled itself free from a trap. It leaped on top of him, knocking his knife from his hand. He figured it was the end of him when the bear started tearing at his face. He heard the shot I fired but that was all he remembered.

'It is the Menominee's way to trap bear in the fall, but they usually get the younger bears when they are fattened for winter," William explained.

"I've run into Half-face off and on over the years. He's a strong, kind, and gentle man. But he knows his scarred face frightens people. I hope he's still around. I'd like to see him again. But right now, I'd mostly like to go to bed. I've been riding day and night without stopping to sleep."

By the time Mary and Druscilla had washed and

dried the supper dishes, loud snores vibrated through the small cabin. Mary giggled. "That horrible noise seems like music. That's how glad I am he's home!"

"Me too," agreed Druscilla. "But I don't know if we'll get any sleep. He's so loud!"

"We must try. Scoot into bed, dear, and have a good night." Mary kissed the child on the forehead. Druscilla was soon settled in her bed in the corner near the fireplace.

Snuggling beside the warmth length of her husband, Mary was grateful he was home. Despite his snoring, she fell asleep quicker than she had on any of the nights while he was gone.

In the morning as Mary stirred the coals in the fireplace to start the breakfast fire, there was a banging at the door. She pulled it open a crack, peeking out. Half-face stood there, straight and imposing, his face shadowed.

"Your man here," he stated.

"Yes—yes, he is," she stammered, opening the door the rest of the way. "Come inside." She stepped back to allow him to pass.

William emerged from the small bedroom, pulling his pants on as he came. Smiling broadly, he threw his arms around the Indian. "Half-face, my friend! It's good to see you!"

"*Poso*, friend," greeted the Indian, the grin on his face as wide as William's. They hugged and pounded each other's backs.

"*Poso*," William returned in the Menominee language. "Come, sit, you'll share our morning meal."

"Wait." Half-face held up his hand. "I have a gift for cooking." He slipped outside, returning with a string of freshly caught trout which he handed to Mary.

"Thank you," she said, "they are beautiful." She

began preparing breakfast.

"I have presents for your women. I want to be friends," Half-face continued. Druscilla was helping Mary, but keeping a safe distance from the Indian, casting a wary glance in his direction from time to time.

"There is trouble," Half-face said seriously. "I watch you leave, I stay to make sure nothing happen." He then lapsed into his native tongue.

William translated for Mary as the Indian spoke. "There was a band of renegade Indians on the prowl . . . one from the Menominee tribe, a crazy misfit who had teamed up with deviants from other tribes . . . they were attacking lone settlers, killing their families and burning their cabins . . ." As an aside, William reminded Mary that back in 1854, Chief Oshkosh had negotiated a treaty with the white man's government, and the Indians were given a reservation to hunt on. The land was called Weesechosea, "a good place to live," but it was much too confining for the Menominees. The Indians had been accustomed to roaming and hunting wherever they wanted, and now were supposed to stay within the bounds of the reservation. Many didn't abide by the rule— including Half-face.

When Half-face had seen William riding off in his wagon and realized Mary and Druscilla were alone, he felt he should stay around, keep an eye on the women, protect them if necessary. When he had approached them they were so frightened that he continued watching from afar.

The Indian finished by telling William that the last time he'd crossed the trail of the renegades, they had been headed in the Van Vradenburgs' direction. He reached into his pack and commanded, "Little girl, come!"

With fearful reluctance Druscilla approached

him, stopping just out of arm's reach. Half-face held a pair of leather moccasins toward her. "For you. I am friend."

Druscilla's eyes widened; a smile played on her lips. The moccasins were made of soft doeskin. "Oh, thank you, they're beautiful!" she cried. Taking them, she dropped immediately to the floor and slipped them on her bare feet. "Look, they fit! They're so soft!" She jumped up, throwing her arms around the startled Indian's waist and hugging him.

Half-face grunted, untangling himself from the skinny girl's arms. "Now you." He held a multi-colored beaded headband out to Mary. "For paint-brush hair."

Mary accepted the intricately designed gift. "This is lovely, Half-face. Thank you. I shall treasure it always."

"Friend, your woman's hair like Indian paint-brush flower, a powerful love charm to look at every day. May your coming son also have Indian paintbrush hair. Make him have power of peace."

William glanced from Half-face to Mary, puzzled. "What do you mean, Half-face? I thank you for the good wishes, but what do you mean, 'coming son'?"

"When your woman bathe in stream I see she is with child."

Mary blushed at his announcement.

"Is this true, Mary? Are we going to have a baby?" William leaped from his chair and picked Mary up, hugging her tightly. "What great news!"

After the excitement died down, Mary said, "Tell me about the Indian paintbrush, Half-face. I know it's the bright red flower that blooms in spring and summer. But what does it mean to your people?"

William chuckled. "I'll explain it. The Indian

maidens believe the essence of the Indian paintbrush blossom contains a potent magical charm.
If it's sprinkled on a girl's sweetheart, love will be
forever."

Chapter 4

Half-face stayed with the Van Vradenburgs until the first heavy snowfall, informing them they need not worry about an attack from the renegade Indian band until spring.

"When it is time for your son to be born I will return," the Indian assured them after bidding them farewell. "*Poso,*" was his last word before he disappeared into the snow.

Mary's pregnancy progressed trouble-free. One night in late March when she and William were preparing for bed, they were startled by a knock at the door. With his rifle in the crook of his elbow, William opened the door cautiously.

"Half-face!" he shouted, admitting his friend to the room.

The stately Indian, wrapped in a bearskin robe sprinkled with snow, entered. "*Poso,* my friends. It is time!"

William turned and looked at Mary with a question in his eyes. She shrugged; she didn't know what Half-face meant. Time for what?

After an exchange of greetings and bits of news, Mary announced she was retiring. "I wait here for baby," Half-face stated, wrapping himself in his bearskin as he squatted near the fireplace with its dying embers.

So that was it! Half-face thought the baby was coming! Mary wondered what the Indian knew that she didn't. She mulled it over in her mind as she settled her cumbersome body under the quilts on the cozy feather bed. There had been no signs of labor yet, though the time was drawing near. She drifted off to sleep, barely aware of William when he leaned down and kissed her forehead.

A dull ache in her lower back awakened her. It was still dark. While turning awkwardly, an enormous pain circled from her back to her pelvis. A groan escaped her lips.

William woke, startled. "Mary, what is it?"

"I don't know how he knew, but Half-face was right. Our baby is coming. It's begun!" she whispered.

The remainder of the night had a strange dream-like quality. The pains came closer together, their intensity increasing. Time seemed to race by. Mary was only vaguely aware of William and Half-face, who spoke softly to each other as they tended her. She neither understood nor cared what the words were.

By midmorning her whole being was one paroxysm of agony with a sole intent—*push*. William murmured encouragement as he wiped the sweat from her brow. Gentle hands helped her, hands belonging to Half-face.

With an overwhelming force which strained all her muscles and strength to their limits, she pushed her child into the world. The infant's lusty cry brought her back from the black void she'd been slipping into. A girl, small and perfect, had been born to the Van Vradenburgs, and they called her Jestina.

As Half-face had predicted, trouble arrived with spring. William had gone into the forest to hunt for meat for their table; Mary had finished hoeing between the rows of the newly planted garden, and Druscilla was rocking baby Jestina in her cradle on the grassy knoll in front of the cabin. Mary started into the barn to put away the hoe when a dull thud overhead startled her. Looking up, she saw the feathers on the end of the shaft of an arrow, its head deeply embedded in the wood of the barn.

"Oh, my God!" she cried, dropping the hoe. Gathering up her skirts, she ran toward Druscilla and the baby. "Quick! Into the house!"

Mary snatched the baby from the cradle as five painted Indians on horseback burst from the woods. Their wild screams rent the air and filled Mary's heart with fear. With her free hand, she grabbed Druscilla's and fled with her and the baby into the cabin. Handing Jestina to Druscilla, she barred the door seconds before the Indians reached the front of their home. She raced to each of the windows, pulling shutters closed and fastening them. Her heart beat madly within her, almost as loud as the sound of the Indians battering against the door.

"May God protect us," she groaned. Heaving the table onto its side, she pushed it against the shaking wood of the door. Jestina was wailing. Druscilla tried to soothe her, but her voice was quivering with fright.

The sickening sound of splintering wood

announced the succss of the Indians' battering. Mary dashed to the hearth, snatching up her heaviest skillet. A brown hand poked through the gap in the door, reaching for the wooden bar. With all her strength, Mary brought the skillet down on the hand. A screech of pain and outrage came from outside, and the broken hand quickly disappeared.

A renewed effort was begun to break down the door. The pounding and splintering of wood was deafening, and the flint head of a tomahawk chipped at the widening hole. The shutters on one of the windows rattled as someone pushed against them.

Feeling strangely light-headed, Mary knew she had no defense against the savages. She turned to Druscilla and ordered her hoarsely, "Take Jestina into the other room."

Whimpering, Druscilla did as she was told, closing the door behind her. Mary took a stand in the middle of the room, the frying pan in one hand, her butcher knife held high in the other. As though in a trance, she watched as the front door was being destroyed at a frightening speed, and the window shutter shook with each renewed blow.

A brown face with a fierce grin suddenly appeared at the opening in the door. Terrified, Mary ran at it, swinging the skillet. The face started to withdraw, but not before she smashed the skillet's heavy bottom full against it, flattening the savage's nose. Blood spurted, and she heard an angry cry.

The shutter burst open and another Indian began climbing inside. Mary's fright turned to rage. Screaming as she dashed toward him, she raised the iron pan in an arc, the knife clutched tightly in her other hand. But before she reached him, a shot sounded. The Indian fell forward, hanging half into the room, blood spurting from a hole in his bare back. Another shot rang out, and a man screamed outside the cabin. She could hear the Indians shouting to each other. Then their voices faded, and she heard the sound of horses riding away.

Mary dropped her makeshift weapons and struggled to pull the table away from the door, moving it just enough to lift the heavy wooden bar from its slots. William pushed the shattered door open the rest of the way and stepped inside. She threw herself into his arms, sobbing against his chest.

He held her tightly and asked, "Are you all right? What about the baby and Druscilla?"

Mary gasped, "I thought we were going to be killed!"

"We have Half-face to thank for saving us again." He turned her toward the door and pointed. Their Indian friend was crouched low behind an outcropping of rocks, pointing a rifle in the direction of the fleeing marauders.

"I was stalking a deer when Half-face appeared beside me. He said the outlaw band had come into the area again, and he was uneasy for our safety. You can imagine how I felt when we came within sight of the cabin and spotted those savages battering down the door and window!"

"It was horrible!" Mary shuddered.

"We've cut them down. Two are dead and another is wounded. One rode off with a broken nose and a badly smashed hand. You did a good job of protecting our home and family."

Though Mary was no longer crying she continued to tremble, grateful for his strong arms around her. "Oh, William, I was so *scared!*"

Putting his large hands on her shoulders, he looked down at her, his face was solemn, dark eyes clouded. "Mary, we must move back to town. I don't think these Indians will rest until they've run us off or killed us. Half-face has offered to escort us in case of an ambush on the way."

"William, our beautiful home! I don't want to leave. Isn't there any other way?"

"I don't want to give in, but there's nothing else we can do. We're too isolated. We've been lucky so far that Half-face has been around to come to our aid. But he can't stay near us always. He has responsibilities to his tribe. I can't take the chance of something happening to us while we're asleep, or to you and our family when I'm away from the cabin. They will be even more determined to slaughter us now that we've killed two of their band!"

Chapter 5

The Van Vradenburgs once more packed their possessions into the wagon, leaving their empty cabin standing solitary amidst its lush surroundings. Mary shed a few tears as they began their retreat. She felt almost as though she were leaving a part of herself behind—her first real home, the birthplace of her first child. Fortunately they saw no sign of hostile Indians on their journey.

They lived in a small frame house in Woodlake for seven years. In April of 1860, their second year back in town, Mary gave birth to another girl, whom they named Desdemona Diana. In 1864, a third girl was born, called Eudora Josephina. By the spring of '65 William felt it was safe for them once again to leave the security of town.

He built another home, a larger one this time to accommodate his growing family. Their new home was located only three miles from Woodlake, and the following spring they moved in. This time they had neighbors less than a mile away, a comfort to Mary who was carrying her fourth child.

The Van Vradenburgs' new neighbors were the Fosses, a childless couple with personalities totally unlike those of Mary and William. Myrtle Foss was only a year older than Mary, now thirty-one, but appeared to be much older. Though Mary and Myrtle had little in common, the caustic woman was at least another adult for Mary to visit when she was lonely. Myrtle enjoyed tending to baby Eudora, though she was at times unreasonably strict with Jestina and Desdemona, expecting them to be quiet at all times.

Myrtle also disapproved of Druscilla's habit of dressing in boy's clothes. Though she expected the girl to dress and behave like a lady, she didn't feel it proper that Druscilla should enter into adult conversation, an attitude which didn't endear Mrs. Foss to her.

Mary had always treated her young sister-in-law as a friend, and now that the girl was fifteen, their friendship had grown even closer. Mary was able to understand Druscilla's growing animosity toward Mrs. Foss, but urged the girl to try to understand that though Myrtle was stern and set in her ways, she was a good woman underneath her ironclad exterior. Myrtle was quick to offer her services to Mary when the new baby came.

"I can help you, Mary," Druscilla argued. "We don't need that old pickle-puss around here!"

Mary was unable to suppress a giggle, but she shook her head and admonished her gently, "You mustn't be disrespectful. Myrtle can't help the way she is. And being married to a man like Hiram Foss would turn any woman sour!"

Hiram Foss was a hard-working, God-fearing man. His only interest, other than working the land, was studying the Bible and praying on his

knees for long hours. Even his appearance was
forbidding. He seldom smiled and his eyes glinted
sternly from behind the spectacles which were
usually perched on his long, thin nose. Prematurely iron-grey hair hung limply to his
shoulders and the lower half of his face was
hidden by a long scraggly beard which hung part
way down his chest. He always wore overalls and
flannel shirts which never quite fit—his bony
wrists hung below the cuffs. Because he walked
hunched over and with a shuffle, he looked like an
old man, though in fact he was several years
younger than thirty-nine-year-old William.

Mary patted her large belly and smiled at
Druscilla. "Honey, you are such a help to me that I
couldn't get along without you. But I've gotten so
much bigger during this pregnancy . . . and I'm so
tired all the time. I'm worried there might be
something wrong. I will feel better if Myrtle is
here to help out, and it won't be for very long. Try
to understand."

"I'll try, but I won't like it!" Druscilla huffed,
flipping her one long ginger-colored plait over her
shoulder. "Jestina and Desdemona aren't going to
like it either! I can just hear her now—'Mary, I
just don't know what *devil* possessed you to give
these girls such frivolous names . . . Jestina, Desdemona, Eudora . . . and Druscilla's no better! God
forgive me, sounds like names for fancy-women!' "
Druscilla did an excellent job of imitating Myrtle
Foss' high pitched whine, and Mary exploded into
laughter.

Mary did find Myrtle's constant badgering
about her choice of names for the girls trying. But
she usually smiled at Myrtle until she wound
down and thought of another subject to pontifi-
cate about. Despite her criticisms, Mary was
grateful to Myrtle for her lessons in quilt making,

and for sharing her secret for baking the lightest, most delicious loaves of bread, and for teaching Mary new ways to preserve the game William brought home in abundance. Mary always gave some to the Fosses. Myrtle's homemaking knowledge was extensive, and her willingness to share that knowledge more than made up for her constant badgering. And when she allowed chubby two-year-old Eudora to climb into her lap, the harsh lines around her mouth would soften and her voice was almost a coo as she talked to her sweet 'Dora,' as she called her.

When the pains began, announcing the impending arrival of Mary's and William's fourth child, Mary was down in the root cellar checking her food supplies for winter. She tried to ignore the low backache and the cramping, for by her calculation it was too soon for the onset of labor, so she continued rearranging the footstuffs. It was a satisfying job to inventory their abundant supply of preserved or dried fruits and vegetables in orderly rows on the shelves, the salted meats, and the root vegetables stored in bins.

She had nearly finished when the pain struck again. Despite the coolness of the cellar, perspiration beaded on her upper lip. Awkwardly, she climbed up the ladder into their main room and onto the wooden planks, pausing to catch her breath.

"Mama," cried four-year-old Desdemona, dropping to her knees beside Mary. "What's the matter, Mama?"

Trying to smile, Mary reassured her, "It's all right, sweetheart. It's time for mama to have the new baby." She smoothed Desdemona's shiny, dark brown hair, noticing the child's blue eyes were wide with fright.

"Druscilla!" Desdemona called. The older girl

TRAIL TO GLORY   49

came from the children's room with Eudora in her
arms, set the child down and ran to Mary's side.

"Mary, what is it?"

With Druscilla's help Mary was able to struggle
from the floor into a chair. By this time, Jestina
had joined them, jumping up and down anxiously,
red curls bobbing. Baby Eudora peered from one
distraight face to another and began to wail.

"Please, girls, quiet down," Mary said quietly.
"Jestina, run outside and fetch your father. He's
probably in the barn now. Tell him the baby is
coming and to please go fetch Mrs. Foss." Jestina
ran outside, shouting for her father.

Mary continued to give directions. "Desdemona,
tend to Eudora. Play with her, and try to stop her
crying. Druscilla, keep an eye on the stew cooking
in the fireplace and make some dumplings to go
with it. You'll have to put supper on the table
tonight. When William returns with Mrs. Foss,
feed the girls and yourself. I'm going to bed." The
pains were now coming regularly, and Mary
walked slowly into the room she shared with her
husband, praying desperately that Myrtle would
arrive in time.

All she could think of was her anguish when
Myrtle burst into the room. Her mousy brown hair
was skinned into a tight knot at the back of her
head. From beneath her heavy, dark brows, her
sunken grey eyes peered with concern. Thin lips
were pursed tightly together.

"Thank God you're here, Myrtle," Mary
groaned. The relief she felt allowed her to put all
her energy into the birthing of her child.

"Not a second too soon, from the looks of
things," Myrtle muttered. "That babe is mighty
impatient."

Within minutes Myrtle held a tiny infant in her

arms. "It's another girl, Mary. This time give the child a decent name!"

Mary watched as Myrtle bathed her newest daughter and wrapped her in warm flannel. An intense pain, every bit as unrelenting as the ones that had brought her baby into the world, took her by surprise, and she moaned.

Myrtle frowned. "What is it?"

"It can't be . . . but it is . . . another labor pain!"

"William!" Myrtle screamed. "William, get yourself in here this instant!"

Myrtle unceremoniously thrust the newborn into William's arms as he ran through the door. "Here, hold your daughter!"

"What's going on?"

Myrtle ignored his question, announcing, "Here comes another one! Praise the Lord, William, you've been blessed with twins!"

The second infant was a boy.

After the excitement had subsided, both babies were tucked in beside their mother. Myrtle gazed with pride at Mary. "Well, who'd ever have thought it! Two perfect babes!"

William knelt beside the bed and gently kissed Mary. He took her hand in his, and there was great love in his eyes as he looked at her and his twins. "They are beautiful, Mary . . . and so are you!"

Too tired to speak, Mary smiled at her husband. It was so wonderful—she could feel the warmth from the tiny bundles on either side of her—and Mary fell asleep.

Chapter 6

They named the twins William and Wilhelmina, but William was soon dubbed "Willy." Myrtle clucked her tongue and said, "Finally give a child a sensible name and then you turn around and shorten it! As for Wilhelmina—! However do you dream up such frivolous names?"

Mary ignored her friend. Her daughters were fascinated by the twins, and Mary had all the help she could use to care for them. Myrtle came often; Mary suspected she wanted to be near the new babies. Even Hiram made excuses to come along with his wife, casting sly, admiring glances at the twins.

Willy was a strong and lusty boy, favoring his father's look. His dark hair already curled. Wilhelmina's also showed signs of curls, but it was a fiery shade of red. She was smaller than her brother, and quieter.

All of the children were healthy. Druscilla,

Jestina, and Desdemona attended school in Wood-lake when it was possible for them to get there. During the worst part of the winter when the trail was impassable, Mary tended to their schooling herself.

The Indian problem seemed to be over. No news of raids reached them. Half-face came to visit several times, reporting that no one in his tribe had heard from the Menominee member of the renegade band.

The last word they had of their Indian friend was of his death. A young Menominee brave rode into the Van Vradenburgs' land. When Mary spied him riding up to William who was working near the barn, her heart skipped a beat, but it quickly became apparent that it was a friendly visit. In a few minutes the Indian left. William returned to the house, and Mary knew by his slumped shoulders and sadness in his eyes, that the news was bad.

William told Mary Half-face had died of an illness several days before. Shortly before his death he'd requested that William be informed. "He was a good friend, Mary," William said. "I will miss him."

Mary put her arms around her husband and held him tightly. Though her own heart was sad-dened, she knew William's mourning was deeper than she could imagine. Besides herself, Half-face was William's only true friend. Hiram Foss con-sidered himself a friend, but he was too stiff and reserved for William to feel any warmth toward him. Half-face and William had laughed together, showing their affection for one another with great bear hugs. Yes, William would miss his Indian friend.

Another summer had passed. The days were

cooler. The twins were now two years old. Mary paused in her daily chores to peek at them while they took a midday nap. The chubby pair were sleeping soundly at each end of a small rope bed, Willy sprawled on his back, arms and leg spread wide, dark brown curls damp with perspiration. Wilhelmina was curled in a ball, bottom in the air. Her face was hidden by her copper-colored curls.

The older girls were all in school, except for Eudora, who was still too young. No longer requiring an afternoon nap, she was in the main room of the house stirring a batch of biscuits. Before Mary returned to her young helper, she opened the front door and looked across the yard at William, who was chopping wood.

At forty-one, he looked much the same as when they had married—tall and straight, well-muscled, his curly hair dark, thick an unruly, though there were a few more lines at the corners of his eyes from squinting in the sun. He worked from sun-up to sundown as always, tending to his animals and crops, fishing and hunting, or any of the other myriad of chores which faced him each day, yet he always had enough energy at the end of the busy day to enjoy a romp under the quilts at night.

The sound of hoofbeats brought her back to the present. She wondered who could be coming. It certainly wouldn't be the Fosses in the middle of the day—unless there was trouble. Several horses were approaching. William had stopped chopping wood, holding the ax in midair.

Mary's heart pounded wildly as Indians on horseback burst into her line of vision. Her first inclination was to run to William. Instead she made herself turn from the terrifying sight, step back inside and close the door quietly.

She ran into the children's room, scooping Willy and Wilhelmina under each arm, carrying them as she ran into the main room. Dumping them in squalling heaps on the floor, she kicked aside the braided rug which covered the trap door to the root cellar and yanked it open.

"Quick, Eudora, climb down the ladder!" she cried.

Eudora's eyes were big and puzzled. "Why, Mama?"

"Now!" Mary commanded. Eudora ran to the opening and scrambled down the ladder. Mary carried the crying twins down one at a time, depositing them on the hard packed dirt floor.

"Be quiet!" Mary snapped. They stared in astonishment at their mother, and sniffled softly, swallowing their sobs.

Climbing back up to the room, Mary closed the trap door and covered it again with the rug. She ran to the door. Putting her ear against it, she could hear the Indians galloping and screaming. Unable to bear the uncertainty, she opened the door a crack.

The scene before her caused bile to rise in her throat. One Indian lay sprawled near where William had been chopping wood, the ax imbedded deep in his skull. William, one foot tied by a rope, was being dragged around the yard by an Indian on horseback. His head was covered with blood; his body jerked convulsively. Another Indian galloped madly in a wide circle, holding what had been William's scalp high above his head, laughing maniacally. Blood dripped from the grisly prize and ran down the savage's arm.

"Oh, my God," Mary moaned. She stared at the horrifying tableau, not caring if the marauders saw her. Her husband was dead. Hate filled her. She wanted to run outside, to try and avenge his death, but knew she would be unable to do anything. If the Indians saw her they would kill her too. She had to think of the children—they had no one left but her to care for them.

Trembling, she pushed the door shut. As she climbed down the ladder into the cellar, she arranged the rug so it would fall over the trap door when it closed. Collapsing onto the dirt floor, she gathered the three children to her, her arms tightening around the small bodies.

Wood splintered overhead and floor boards creaked. The Indians were inside the house. Mary held the children more tightly, making quiet shushing sounds. Upstairs, her dishes and pots and pans were being thrown to the floor. Her emotions were torrential—hatred for the Indians who had murdered her husband and were now ransacking her home; panic that they would discover her and her babies' hiding place; and deep, almost unbearable grief.

All at once Mary realized everything was quiet. She remained huddled with her arms around her children for a long time while she gathered her courage to climb the ladder. Sternly instructing the twins and Eudora to stay where they were and not make a sound until her return, she pushed the trap door open a mere sliver, terrified the Indians might be waiting. But she saw nothing but overturned furniture and household goods scattered about. She scrambled up into the room.

Disregarding the mess, she knew she had a dreadful task to perform. She must do something with her husband's body before she brought the children up from the cellar. After scanning the yard to make sure it was deserted, she ran to William's body.

She put a hand to her mouth to stiffle a scream of anguish. His dark eyes stared sightlessly, though they still seemed to reflect the pain and horror of his last minutes of life. His once handsome face was contorted in a grimace of death. Mary squeezed back the tears which stung her eyes, swallowed hard, and began dragging William by his feet into the barn.

Tears streamed down her face as she stumbled back to the house, obscuring her vision. Suddenly she tripped over the body of the dead Indian. She kicked at it in fury, realizing she couldn't leave the body outside for the children to see. For a moment she wondered why the Indians hadn't taken their fallen member with them as they usually did. But, she surmised, if the Indians were outcasts from several tribes, they were no longer observing tradition.

Grasping the ax handle, she yanked hard, freeing the blade from the back of the Indian's head, and tossed the ax aside. She tried not to look at the smashed skull, the black hair matted with blood, but then she realized that she had seen the man before. His nose had been broken and had healed crookedly. It was the same Indian she'd hit with a frying pan so long ago! With a certain grim satisfaction, she pulled him by the ankles through the dirt, depositing him next to William inside the barn.

Exhausted, she hurried back to the house. Tossing aside the rug, she opened the trap door. Peering up at her were three pairs of large eyes. She attempted a smile, but the attempt was a dismal failure. "Oh, my darlings," she moaned.

"What happened, Mama?" asked Eudora. "Where's Daddy?"

Mary couldn't answer. She helped Eudora up the ladder, then carried the babies out of the cellar. Collapsing onto the plank floor, she held her three youngest children close to her, unwilling and unable to move. When Druscilla, Jestina, and

Desdemona came in from school they found Mary and the children.

Druscilla, shock apparent on her face, cried out in alarm, "Mary, what's happened?"

"We were attacked by Indians." Mary took a deep breath, interrupted by a ragged sob. "William is dead. Please—go to the Fosses—let them know what has happened."

Chapter 7

Mary threw down the hoe in disgust. She blew at the lock of red-gold hair which fell across her eyes and shook her head. She'd been working in the garden all morning. Her muscles ached from the effort, and she was still a long way from doing all that was necessary. She and the children had made it through the winter months because of her well-stocked root cellar, but they had nearly exhausted the supply of food.

Peering at the few remaining chickens in the yard, she knew they had already eaten more of them than they should have, but there wasn't much meat for the table these days. Her youngsters were outgrowing their clothes, but she was too busy and too tired to make new ones.

It was time to prepare the midday meal, but she didn't even know what that possibly would be. As she headed toward the house she heard an approaching horse and wagon. It was Hiram and Myrtle.

Myrtle ran to Mary and kissed her dryly on the cheek. "I had hoped we might see you and the children in church this morning," was Myrtle's greeting. "You've stayed away far too long."

Knowing better than to offer an excuse, Mary kept her mouth shut. The children came running at the sound of the visitors, and Myrtle appraised each one from head to toe, shaking her head.

"Mary, these youngsters look like ragamuffins!" Myrtle chided.

"Yes, I know."

"Well! Give me a hand. I've brought all the fixings for a nice dinner. Hiram, you see what you can do about that barn of Mary's. I'll send one of the girls after you when we have food on the table."

Mary was surprised to see Hiram dutifully head toward the barn, hammer in hand. She knew it went against his beliefs to work on the Sabbath— so she was doubly grateful.

The children gathered around the wagon, eagerly taking the covered pans and dishes as Myrtle handed them out. Mary felt bitterness, knowing how hungry they were and how little she could provide. She followed Myrtle and her happily chattering brood into the house.

The somber woman immediately took over, ordering everyone about and criticizing Mary. "Stir up the fire, Druscilla. The stew needs heating. You there, Desdemona, set the table. Jessie, take those apple pies and start slicing them.

"Mary, it's time you took yourself in hand. You've mourned long enough for William. You must begin to care properly for yourself and your family. These young'uns are a sight—not only are their clothes in rags, but they all look half starved!"

Something snapped inside of Mary. With her eyes brimming with tears and her voice quivering with anger, she answered, "Stop mourning William! I haven't had time to mourn William! Why I haven't even thought of William for days! I'm so tired I can barely think. And as for my children—you're right, they haven't had enough to eat—nor have I, for that matter. We're all hungry, and I don't know what we're going to do . . ." She put her head down on the table and let the tears come.

Myrtle stepped over to Mary, awkwardly patting her on the shoulder. "Now, now, Mary, you mustn't cry. I know it's been difficult . . ."

Raising her head, Mary sniffed and said, "Myrtle, I can't do it all by myself! There are too many mouths to feed. And I don't know how to do all the things William did." Jestina was staring at her from over the pie she was cutting, knife dangling in her hand, while Desdemona lowered the stack of plates she was holding onto the table. Druscilla stood in front of the fireplace wiping her hands on her trousers, and even the twins stopped playing to listen in wide-eyed wonder.

"Of course you can't!" Myrtle said gently. "If there is anything Hiram and I can do, just tell us. You know we'll do anything for you and the children!"

The sincerity in Myrtle's voice sparked an idea in Mary, an idea that drove away her desperation. Taking hold of Myrtle's hands, she stared intently and asked, "Would you? Would you truly do anything?"

Myrtle swallowed hard and answered, "Yes, yes! Of course I would."

Taking a deep breath, and not looking at any of

her children, Mary queried, "Myrtle, will you take my three oldest girls and raise them like they were your own?"

Mary ignored her offspring who were obviously shocked by their mother's startling question. But she couldn't ignore Druscilla who elbowed Myrtle aside to stand directly in front of Mary. The girl's square jaw jutted out in defiance, her face burning with anger. "Not me, Mary! I'll move out before I'll go live with Myrtle Foss!"

"No, dear, of course not," Mary soothed. "You're nearly eighteen, and I suspect you'll be marrying soon. Perhaps you would have done so already if you hadn't known how desperately I need you."

Druscilla's cheeks turned an even brighter crimson, and she turned away. Mary knew her sister-in-law was thinking of Henry Graham, the general store owner's son. He was only a couple of years older than Druscilla, and they had attended school together. For quite a while his interest in her had been obvious, and ever since he had taken over the running of the store, he had been more and more forward with his attention to Druscilla.

Though Druscilla hadn't encouraged her would-be suitor, Mary felt sure it was because of her and the children. Druscilla hadn't the time to be courted, but her seeming lack of interest hadn't dampened Henry's ardor.

Myrtle, who had been trying to digest her friend's surprising proposal, sank into the nearest chair. She rubbed her squinty eyes, stammering, "I . . . I hardly know what to say! How could you possibly give up your own children?"

"It won't be easy—but it's better than watching them starve, isn't it? I must consider their well-being first, so I don't have any choice, do I? So . . . will you do as I've asked?"

"Oh my! I'd love to! Children to care for—it's all Hiram and I have ever wanted. Oh, I'll take such good care of them. But I have to ask Hiram!" She oohed and aahed all the way out the front door, pausing on the threshold to beam. For a moment, Myrtle's face was transformed, the hard, pinched lines softened to the radiance of her smile.

When the door had closed behind Myrtle, Druscilla knelt beside Mary, pleading, "Oh, Mary, you can't give Jestina, Desdemona, and Eudora to that old woman! They'll hate living with her! We can manage somehow! There has to be another way!"

"Mama, please . . ." Desdemona cried as tears streamed down her face. "I can't bear the thought of leaving you."

Eudora was sobbing too hard to say anything. The twins, not really understanding but feeling the strong emotion of the moment, howled in unison.

"Hush now, all of you," Mary said sternly. "You must listen to what I am about to say." She went to her three oldest children and put her arms around them. "We can't keep going on the way we are now. We don't even have enough to eat, but I can probably get along with only the twins to provide for. I have to decide what is best for all of us. Myrtle will take good care of you girls. She and Hiram can give you the things I'll never be able to afford. And you'll still be close. I can come to see you often, and you can visit here, after all."

Jestina smiled bravely. "Mama is right. We'll do just fine at the Fosses. And we'll have each other."

Hiram readily agreed to the plan, and the girls were moved, along with their beds and few belongings, the following day. Mary, along with Willy and Wilhelmina, visited her children often, and the two older girls often walked over to see Mary, bringing gifts of food.

It was on these visits that Mary heard how the girls were truly faring in their new home.

"She has so many silly rules, it's horrible," Desdemona complained.

Jestina, older and always more complacent, defended Myrtle. "Oh, it's not so bad. She just wants us to keep everything neat and tidy. You really shouldn't grumble. We always have plenty to eat . . . and Mrs. Foss is making you a new dress."

Desdemona stuck out her lower lip and crossed her arms over her newly developing bosom. "You know what's the worst of all? She calls me Minnie! Minnie is an ugly name. I hate it!"

Hugging her daughters, Mary consoled her with, "I know how you feel, darling, but you'll always be Desdemona to me."

Jestina said, "What difference does it make. Mrs. Foss calls me Jessie, and she's shortened Eudora to Dora, but we don't mind. She's very kind about most things."

"But I *do* mind!" Desdemona snapped. "I don't think old Mrs. Foss is kind at all. She's mean and hateful."

Jestina smiled at her mother. "Minnie . . ."

"Don't call me that ugly name!" Desdemona snapped. "I'm Desdemona!"

"All right, then. Desdemona and Mrs. Foss clash from time to time, but it's usually Min . . . Desdemona's fault. If she'd only bend a little, try to see Mrs. Foss's side once in awhile, I'm sure they could get along."

"I'll never be able to get along with her!" Desdemona retorted, stamping her foot impatiently.

Mary hugged her daughter, brushing her lips

against the child's forehead. "I'm afraid you'll have to try a little harder, my dear. I can't make any other arrangements. I can barely scratch together enough to feed those of us left here, so we must all be grateful for the generosity of the Fosses."

Druscilla, who had come in from feeding the chickens just in time to hear Desdemona's last statement, said, "I know exactly how she feels. I'd never be able to live in the same house with that woman!"

"Hush, Druscilla," Mary admonished. "Desdemona has to live with Myrtle, and she must try to get along with her."

Desdemona soon learned that all her complaints about Myrtle Foss fell on deaf ears. Mary knew her daughter often sought out Druscilla, the only one who would sympathize with her. But before the year was over, Desdemona had lost her one ally. Druscilla married Henry Graham and moved to Woodlake.

The years passed uneventfully, marked only by the twins contracting the usual childhood illnesses. The summer and fall of 1871, Willy and Wilhelmina's seventh year, was extremely dry with the whole of Wisconsin being plagued by both brush and forest fires.

Early one fall morning, Mary woke to an unusual crackling sound and an eerie glow on the bedroom wall. "Oh, my God, it's a fire!" She leaped from the bed and ran to the front door. The sky was black with smoke, and it hurt to breathe. Ashes and glowing embers floated through the air. Though the fire was still contained within the surrounding forest, Mary feared a spark would ignite the barn or the house.

Aghast at the disaster confronting her and her family, she stood in the doorway peering at the threatening scene, already feeling the heat of the fire. Willy and Wilhelmina, clad in their night-dresses and barefoot, ran to her side.

"Mama, what is it?" Willy stared outside, wide-eyed.

"A forest fire—and it seems to be headed this way," Mary answered dully.

Wilhelmina squeezed her eyes shut, grabbed a handful of her mother's nightgown and began to wail.

"Children, listen to me, you mustn't cry. You have to be grown up and help me. We've got a lot to do to keep our house and barn from burning!"

Wilhelmina stopped crying abruptly, and looked up attentively at her mother. "What can I do?"

"Since the barn is nearest to the woods we'd better move the cow and horse to a safer spot. That's first!" They led the animals behind the house and tied them to a fence, then made several trips to salvage some of the tools.

With more black smoke billowing around them, it was hard to breathe. Grey ash rained over every-thing, and sparks ignited small fires in the dry grass and weeds. The twins dashed about throwing dirt on the flames.

As Mary scooped water into a bucket from the horse trough, intending to throw it on a sliver of flame inching along the side of the barn, a pair of large, masculine hands firmly took the bucket away from her. She looked up into the long, homely face of Mr. Cromer, an acquaintance from town.

"I'll do it, Mrs. Van Vradenburg. Fetch some quilts from the house, wet them down, and we'll put them on the roof."

Mary hadn't heard him ride into the yard over the roar of the fire, but she certainly was grateful for his help.

By the time she returned with an armful of quilts, Mr. Cromer had doused the flames threatening the barn. They worked side by side the rest of the morning, wetting quilts and blankets and spreading them on the roof of the barn, then keeping them damp with water from the trough.

It was midafternoon when Mary noticed a distinct change in the direction of the wind. Squinting toward the forest she thought the fire was no longer moving toward them, and the spark and ash shower had appreciatively lessened. She glanced questionly at Mr. Cromer, who was also staring toward the trees.

"The worst may be over," he stated, pulling a large bandana from his hip pocket and mopping his face. His efforts merely smeared the black soot which clung to his sweat-dampened skin, making himself even dirtier than before.

Mary giggled, then glanced at herself and laughed even harder. There she was, in the middle of her yard with a near-stranger, clad only in her sooty nightdress. Her hair was flying about wildly, and she supposed her face was as dirty as Mr. Cromer's. "Oh, what a sight I must be!"

Willy and Wilhelmina, startled by the sound of their mother's sudden gaiety, stared at her. "Mama?" questioned Wilhelmina.

"It's all right, honey. Everything is going to be just fine!" Smothering her giggles, she put one hand on a dark head, one hand on a head full of copper curls, and pulled her children to her.

"I'm hungry," Willy stated, wiggling out of his mother's grasp.

"Me too!" Wilhelmina echoed.

Mary agreed. "And so am I. If you think it's safe

now, Mr. Cromer, perhaps we can wash up, and I'll fix us something to eat.''

"Don't be going to any trouble for me, ma'am,'' Mr. Cromer muttered.

Mary thought she detected a slight blush on his blackened cheeks. "Now don't be silly. We're terribly grateful to you for your help. Why, who knows—we might have lost our home if you hadn't been here! You come along into the house, and after you've cleaned up, you can change into some of my husband's clothes I have packed away. They may be a bit large, but I'm sure they'll do for now. Come along.''

Mary took the protesting man by the arm, while Wilhelmina grabbed his hand. As Willy ran ahead, they escorted him inside. It took several buckets of water, but finally everyone was clean and dressed in fresh clothing. With the children's help, Mary prepared a meal.

"Won't you have some more biscuits, Mr. Cromer,'' Mary asked, when they had nearly finished.

"No, thanks, I have had my fill.''

"We can't thank you enough, Mr. Cromer, for all the help you gave us,'' Mary said. "How did you happen to be out this way?''

"I noticed the smoke and remembered you and the children live out here. Figured you could use a little help.''

"And thank goodness you did. I don't think we could have managed without you, sir.'' Mary smiled gratefully, and this time she could see a distinct blush on his cheeks.

"Mr. Cromer, I'm afraid I really don't know too much about you.'' All she really knew was a polite gentleman who often crossed her path in town.

"Oh . . . well, there's not much to know. I work at odd jobs here and there . . . do a fair amount of carpentry . . . build furniture and the like . . . built a house or two in my day."

He almost choked on a swallow of coffee when Mary asked, "Are you married, Mr. Cromer?"

"No, ma'am, never been so fortunate as to find a woman who'd have me," he answered shyly.

Mr. Cromer certainly wasn't as ruggedly handsome as William had been. He appeared a few years older than Mary, with sandy hair beginning to recede from his forehead and ears poking out from the wispy strands which hung to his collar. A bushy moustache covered his upper lip, but when he smiled he explosed large teeth while his eyes squinted into slits. He was shorter and of slighter stature than William had been, but perhaps he wasn't as homely as she had first thought. Actually he was quite pleasant looking.

Mr. Cromer began to squirm uncomfortably under Mary's appraising gaze, pushing his chair away from the table and standing. "Ma'am, thank you kindly for the meal. It sure was tasty. Time I headed for home." He backed towards the door.

"Thank you again, Mr. Cromer." Mary followed him and took hold of one of his hands. Again his cheeks flamed. Amused, she added, "Please, do come visit us again."

Mr. Cromer grinned widely and squeezed Mary's hand before he pulled it free. "And thank you, ma'am. I was going to ask if you minded if I came and peeked in on you from time to time."

"Why, Mr. Cromer, you're more than welcome—anytime."

Andrew Cromer became a frequent visitor to the Van Vradenburg home. On his first visit after the big fire, he brought news that the town of Poshtige had been wiped out by a huge conflagration which killed more than a thousand people.

Sometimes when Andrew visited, he helped Mary with her many chores, while other times he brought her gifts of food—a wild turkey, a ham, a bushel basket of fruit—or wooden toys he'd made for the twins. Mary was comfortable around Andrew and came to depend upon his help, content with his companionship.

At least once every six months Andrew, in his own shy way, made an oblique suggestion that they marry. But his proposals were always so roundabout, liberally accompanied by coughs and throat clearing and fiery blushing, Mary would laugh and casually change the subject.

Though she cared for Andrew, she didn't feel the love for him she had had for William. And even though William had been dead for several years, she still felt like she was his wife.

In the spring of '76, Jestina—as her mother still called her, though Jessie to everyone else—was married. The small wedding was held in the Fosses home. The groom was a young man named Harold, and the newlyweds left almost immediately to homestead land in South Dakota. And despite much protesting from Myrtle, they took fourteen-year-old Eudora with them.

Desdemona, at sixteen, was now the only one of Mary's daughters left with the Fosses. She also had been invited to accompany her married sister and husband, but confided to her mother that she felt obligated to stay with Myrtle. The poor woman was devastated by the loss of Jessie and Dora, and Desdemona feared for her guardian's mental, if not physical, health.

In '78 Mary and Myrtle both received letters from Jessie informing them of the birth of her first child, a daughter she called Lottie. Mary, though a grandmother, was still being actively courted by Andrew Cromer, but she was sure he'd given up the hope of actually ever winning her hand in marriage.

The twins, now in adolescence, looked even less like twins than before. Willy was a wonder! As soon as he'd been able to toddle behind his mother he'd helped with the chores. The bigger he grew, the more help he was. Often he told Mary, "I'll always be here to help you, Mama."

Wilhelmina didn't care much for the outside world. As soon as she learned to read, curling up anywhere with a book was her idea of true pleasure. She loved school since it meant even more books.

Seemingly unaware of her looks, Wilhelmina promised to be a beauty. Her skin was fair, her eyes a strange shade of blue which appeared lavender in certain light. She was slim and graceful, beginning to round out with feminine curves. But her hair was her greatest asset. Wilhelmina called it a nuisance and difficult to untangle, but wonderous was a better description. It was long, thick, and fell into tight, springy ringlets which escaped the ribbons used to tie it back. The color was brighter than her mother's and shinier than a new copper penny. When Wilhelmina walked through town people turned to stare, but she seemed unaware of all the attention.

Chapter 8

It was an early summer day. Mary discovered she was out of sugar after beginning to mix a batch of cookies, and she had planned to have them ready for Andrew and Willy when they returned from fishing.

"Wilhelmina, I'm going to ride over to the Fosses and borrow some sugar." Mary wiped her hands on the corner of her apron. She smiled as Wilhelmina mumbled an "uh-huh," while continuing to read her book as she sprawled on her stomach on the worn braided rug near the fireplace.

"The least you could do is sit in a more ladylike position," Mary admonished. Wilhelmina's answer was to turn a page. Mary shook her head, still smiling and left the house.

The ride to the Fosses was enjoyable, as the weather was perfect, with many wild flowers in bloom. Upon arriving, she drank the cup of coffee which Myrtle offered and talked about the girls, now all married and raising their own families. She then borrowed the needed sugar and returned home. She'd been gone a little more than an hour.

Entering the house, Mary noticed Wilhelmina's book open on the rug. "Wilhelmina," she called. There was no answer, but her daughter couldn't be very far since Willy had taken one of the horses, and she the other one.

While the cookies were cooling on the table and the minutes stretched by, she started to feel uneasy about Wilhelmina. She peeked into the bedrooms and found them empty. Stepping out into the yard and shading her eyes with her hands, Mary gazed about. There was no sign of life except for the chickens scratching in the dirt.

Panic overcame her, and she gathered her skirts and dashed into the barn. Flinging the door open she screamed, "Wilhelmina!" But only her own voice echoed back at her.

She brushed her hair from her eyes and rushed back out into the yard. "Oh, God, please," she moaned. There was terror in her heart.

"Wilhelmina!" she cried out over and over again, until her throat hurt and her voice was hoarse. Dashing madly about, she looked every which way for her daughter.

"The root cellar! That's it, she's down in the root cellar!" But when she climbed down the ladder into the cool darkness, there was no one there.

Then she heard horses and knew Andrew and Willy had returned. Before Andrew could dismount, Mary rushed to him, throwing herself against his leg. Tears streamed from her eyes, as she sobbed, "Andrew, something has happened to Wilhelmina! She's disappeared!"

"Now, now, Mary, calm down. Let me get down, and tell me what the trouble is."

When he was standing on the ground, Mary collapsed into his arms. "I can't bear it. She was here when I left—and when I returned she was gone! Someone has taken her—I know it!"

"Mary, come inside. I think you need to sit down." Andrew patted her consolingly. "Tell us exactly what happened."

"I'll go look for her, Mother," her son offered.

"No, Willy!" Mary shouted. "You stay with me! I don't want anything to happen to you."

Once inside, Andrew managed to quiet Mary enough for her to relate the simple events of the morning. After she finished, Andrew suggested, "Maybe she went for a walk."

"No, she would never do that when she had a book to read. And you can see, she wasn't half through that one." She pointed to the abandoned book laying open on the rug.

"I'll get some men from town and we'll search the woods," Andrew suggested.

"It won't do any good. She's gone!" Mary was devastated. Wilhelmina had been snatched from Mary just as William had been. She didn't know what had happened to her daughter, only that she was sure it was something dreadful.

"No, Mama, don't say that," Willy cried, tears glistening in his eyes.

"Everyone I love seems to be taken away from me."

Willy sobbed and threw his arms around his mother's waist, burying his head in her lap. "I promise I'll never leave you!"

Andrew placed his hand on Mary's shoulder. "I'm going now. We'll find her. Don't you worry, we'll find her."

A search party was organized, and they combed the part of the forest surrounding the Van Vradenburg home for two days. No one found any trace of

Wilhelmina—or any clue to her whereabouts.

There was much speculation in town as to what had happened to the girl. Some thought she had been carried away by gypsies; others thought perhaps she'd run off with a handsome lover. "She was always a strange child, filling her head with romantic notions from all those books."

"Probably took a walk in the woods and lost her way. Never did pay no mind to where she was headed."

"Some hungry bear attacked her and hauled her off to his den."

"It was Indians what took her. All that wild, red hair of hers is probably hanging from some Indian's belt."

Fortunately Mary heard none of these conjectures, though her own suppositions were just as grim. When each day came to an end without news of her daughter, she knew she would never see her again. She went through her every day chores apathetically. With the loss of Wilhelmina another spark had been extinguished within Mary's spirit.

Nearly a month had passed.

"Is there any news?" Mary greeted Andrew with her usual question, though she had little hope.

"No, I'm afraid there isn't."

Staring blankly at the wall, Mary was surprised to hear Andrew ask, "Willy, would you mind leaving your mother and me alone for a bit?"

She was curious—how unlike Andrew—and she turned to look at him. Willy raised an eyebrow in a silent question. She nodded, and he went outside, closing the door behind him.

"Mary, I have something important to ask you." Andrew spoke quietly, taking her hands into his. "It's the same question I've been asking right along. But this time I want you to consider it carefully before you answer me."

This gentle man had become a dear friend, and she smiled encouragement at him as he continued. "You and me . . . we get along pretty well. We're neither one getting any younger, and it's lonely for me living by myself . . . must be lonely for you too. I had an idea, maybe, if you and me got married, we could move away from here. I was thinking . . . how about if we went to South Dakota where your daughters, Jessie and Dora, are? Wouldn't it be nice to see them again? Jessie told you in her letters it's real pretty there. You could get acquainted with your grandbabies. Mary, I'd be so pleased if you'd just let me take care of you for the rest of your life. What do you say?"

She was amazed at this lengthy discourse, since Andrew seldom uttered more than one sentence at a time. She patted Andrew's hand, smiling at him through unexplainable tears. "Andrew, I'm very fond of you—I think you know that. But how can I move to South Dakota? What about Wilhelmina? What if she should come home and I'm not here?"

Andrew hugged her. "Oh, Mary, I know you can't help hoping, but I don't think she's ever going to come home again. You'll have to face up to it sometime, my dear. If she was anywhere to be found she would have been discovered by now."

He was putting into words what she had been feeling, but hadn't been brave enough to even acknowledge to herself. It was as though if she gave up hope she was giving up her daughter. But he was right, and she knew it. "Yes, I know, Wilhelmina is lost."

Tears streamed down her face, yet somehow she was able to smile. "Yes, Andrew, I think I will marry you . . . and, yes, let's do move to South Dakota. I'd love to see the girls, and my grand-babies!"

"Mary!" Andrew gasped. "I can't believe it. You've just made me the happiest man in the world!" He held her tightly and whirled her around the room. He kissed her and ran to the door calling for Willy.

When he stopped inside, Willy looked anxiously from Mary to Andrew. "What's the matter?

"Nothing's the matter, son. Your mother has just said she'll marry me. I'm going to be your stepfather!"

Willy admired Andrew as he would a father, and a wide grin replaced his frown.

"I'm glad you're so pleased. We have some other news," Mary added, "and I hope you take it as well."

Mary became Mrs. Cromer. She, Andrew, and Willy said their farewells to Desdemona and the Fosses and headed towards South Dakota to Jessie and Eudora.

BOOK II

*The Children:
Jessie and Eudora*

Chapter 9

Jessie was the first one of the girls to adjust to living with Myrtle and Hiram Foss, and she didn't mind being called Jessie at all. Sometimes the other girls at school had teased her about having the name Jestina. More than once an uppity classmate had said, "You don't even have a real name—your mother musta made it up!"

Always good at homemaking chores, she was a great help to Myrtle, who showered her with praise. Mary had always accepted her help matter-of-factly.

To be fair to her mother, Jessie realized she was just too busy to spend time handing out compliments. But in all honesty, Jessie was happier in the spotlessly clean, orderly household of the Fosses. She looked forward to eating the plentiful food she helped Myrtle prepare, and together they had made several practical dresses for herself and her two sisters. Jessie was quite content.

But she did have a nagging guilt about her mother. She wondered if she should be missing her more than she did. The only thing she did miss was the off-hand physical affection which her mother gave so naturally and which Myrtle Foss found impossible.

But her mother visited often, and Jessie enjoyed those visits—and the hugs and kisses which came with them. In between times, Jessie would shower her affection on her little sister, Eudora, the younger girl who was having a difficult time adjusting to her new home.

Jessie knew Desdemona would never be content with her new circumstances. She and Mrs. Foss clashed often over the most ridiculous things—as far as Jessie was concerned. Mrs. Foss would call out, using the name Minnie, and Desdemona wouldn't answer. How ridiculous! All Desdemona had to do was respond, and she and Myrtle would have gotten along better. Instead, because Desdemona was so hard-headed and stubborn, Mrs. Foss thought her an ungrateful child. Jessie knew Desdemona wasn't ungrateful—only very different from the older woman. Where Myrtle Foss was practical, Desdemona wasn't interested in necessities. She would do what had to be done, but her mind was often on the beautiful and frivolous things of life. Jessie could only sigh and shake her head when she thought of her sister. She understood her, but there was no way to explain her to Myrtle Foss.

Jessie expected to stay with the Fosses forever. She envisioned herself repaying them for their generosity by caring for them in their old age. But this dream was dissipated when she met Harold Robbins.

Jessie had accompanied the Fosses on a shopping expedition to Woodlake. She was in the general store visiting with Druscilla when a young man entered, and Druscilla called out, "Harold, come over here. There's someone I'd like you to meet."

Built sturdy, though not much taller than Jessie, Harold had a shock of unruly, cornsilk hair. His light brown eyes, flecked with yellow, inspected Jessie with open admiration.

"Harold, this is Jessie," Druscilla introduced. "We were brought up together like sisters. Harold Robbins here fancies himself to be a gold miner."

"A gold miner? Where would you find gold hereabouts?" Jessie asked.

Harold grinned. "I'm trying to get a stake together and then I'll be heading for the Black Hills of South Dakota. The gold there is just waiting for someone to gather it."

Always sensible, Jessie commented, "I doubt if it's that easy."

Harold's smile broadened, and Jessie spied a dimple dancing in his smooth cheek. "You're most likely right about that. But heading for South Dakota is what I've been aiming to do, and I've nearly saved up enough to get going."

"Good for you," Jessie said, admiringly. Druscilla had her arms crossed, a strange expression on her face as she watched the newly introduced couple get acquainted.

"Well, I'll probably be here a while longer," Harold added tentatively. "Have you got a beau?"

Jessie was surprised to feel her cheeks flush. "No, of course not. I'm only seventeen."

"Oh . . . but Mrs. Graham has told me how grown-up you are for your age."

Jessie flashed a reproachful look at Druscilla, but was really grateful she had been described in such a manner to this most forward, yet somehow appealing, young man.

"Anyway, what I am wondering," he continued, running his fingers through his fine, cornsilk hair, "is if I could come and see you while I'm still around?"

As the Fosses entered the store, Jessie spoke loud enough for them to hear. "Yes, indeed, I'll be happy to see you from time to time, but of course I must have the permission of my guardians, Mr. and Mrs. Foss."

Myrtle and Hiram could never deny the usually compliant Jessie any of her infrequent requests. Besides—Harold Robbins, with his apple red cheeks and innocent brown eyes, promised to be a suitable beau for their Jessie. However, they didn't realize the romance would progress with the rapidity with which it did.

Harold fell head over heels in love with Jessie on their first afternoon together. He had never seen anything so beautiful as the round-faced girl with her auburn hair pulled into a simple bun on top of her head. The clean, soap and lavender smell which surrounded her affected him in a way he couldn't explain. He only knew the gold in South Dakota wasn't worth anything compared to the treasure he'd discovered in Wisconsin.

By his second visit he knew he would marry Jessie. Aware that it was too soon to broach the subject—he did so anyway. As they sat together on the front porch of the Foss home, pretending to watch the sun set, Harold reached over and lifted Jessie's hand from her lap. Holding it like it was a fine piece of porcelain, he blurted out, "Jessie, will you be my wife?"

Surprise showing on her placid face, Jessie looked directly at a blushing Harold and answered, "Yes, I would be honored to be your wife."

Harold pulled Jessie to her feet, war-whooped, a 'yipee', then hugged her and kissed her hard on the lips.

The Fosses, along ith Desdemona and Eudora, spilled out the front door, startled by Harold's cry.

"Mr. Robbins, what is the meaning of this vulgar display?" Hiram demanded.

Harold tried to pull away from Jessie, but she kept her arms tightly around his waist. "Harold and I are going to be married," she announced.

"Oh, my," Myrtle gasped.

Desdemona put her arms around her sister and Harold, kissing Jessie on the cheek. "Congratulations, Jestina." Eudora jumped up and down and clapped her hands.

"Settle down, settle down!" scolded Myrtle, two lines creasing her forehead. "Tell me what your plans are. Will you live hereabouts? Jessie told me you had plans to be a gold miner—but of course that is no life for a woman!"

"Well ... ah ..." Harold stammered. Everything had happened so fast, he wasn't sure of anything. "I've heard tell of free homestead land out th ere in South Dakota. If Jessie's willing, I think we'll claim some of that."

"You mean you'll be leaving?" Myrtle gasped. The color drained from her already pasty face, and she appeared ill. "When do you expect all this to take place?"

Harold looked to Jessie for help. Only moments ago he'd been a bachelor with a future full of unknown adventure—and perhaps, treasure. Everything had changed so quickly he'd had no time to think things through.

Obviously Jessie was more able to think clearly under stress. She smiled confidently at him and answered Myrtle. "We'll go wherever Harold wants to go . . . and I think that will be as soon as possible!"

Jessie turned to her sisters. Desdemona was smiling and appeared to be delighted, but tears were beginning to cloud twelve-year-old Eudora's eyes at the thought of losing Jessie, who had been like a second mother.

But Jessie had already made another decision. "We'll be taking my sisters with us, won't we, Harold?"

"What? Oh, surely not! How could you take my whole family away from me?" Myrtle moaned, looking even more ill than before.

Harold was quite numb. He hadn't even digested the fact that Jessie had actually consented to marry him. Everything which came after that was falling on deaf ears. He probably would have agreed to anything Jessie suggested at this point.

Eudora started jumping up and down again, squealing, "Oh, goody, goody." She hung onto Jessie's free arm. Everyone knew that Eudora loved Jessie more than anyone else, even more than her real mother. She had transferred all her affection from Mary to Jessie after they had come to live at the Fosses. Jessie had become her security.

Desdemona took a step nearer to Myrtle Foss. "Thank you for you invitation, Jessie, but I guess I'll stay here with Mrs. Foss."

One of Jessie's red eyebrows raised in surprise at her sister's answer.

"Whatever you decide, of course," Jessie said. "But the invitation will be open until we depart."

The wedding took place in a week. After tearful farewells, the newlyweds, along with Eudora, set off for South Dakota in a wagon packed with their meager belongings.

The haste of the wedding and the immediate

departure did not allow for a proper honeymoon, and Harold was painfully aware that a wedding night shared by his wife's twelve-year-old sister was not going to be easy. "Where are we going to sleep?" Eudora asked innocently, looking over the wooded area Harold had picked to spend their first night.

"Well," Harold began, his face turning pink, "why don't we put your bedroll right here by the fire and we'll just sleep over there under the trees."

"I can't sleep all by myself," Eudora wailed. "I'll be afraid!"

Jessie cast a sharp look at her new husband. "Of course you can't sleep all by yourself. Harold and I will sleep right here beside you."

"I just thought . . ." Harold began.

"It doesn't matter what you were thinking, dear. Who knows what wild animal might be lurking behind the trees. The only safe way is for us all to be together!"

Harold nodded his head. "Yes, of course you're right, dear."

After Eudora and Jessie were tucked into their bedrolls and had settled down, Harold pulled off his shirt. He stood on one foot, then the other, finally crawling into bed with his trousers on. He wiggled and squirmed so that Jessie whispered, "What on earth is the matter?"

"I'm trying to take off my trousers," he answered.

"Oh," Jessie said, wondering if all men were so foolish as to wear their trousers to bed, only to wiggle out of them afterwards. When he finally was still she opened her arms to him. As he pressed himself close to her, she felt happy and proud. Harold was going to be a good husband—she felt loved and protected.

When she felt his hands fumbling at her bosom,

she ignored it, thinking he was merely trying to settle into a comfortable position. But when he tugged at her night dress and his hand slid up the inside of her thigh, she was shocked.

She pushed his hand away and hissed, "Harold Robbins! Whatever do you think you're doing?"

"I was only . . . after all, it *is* our wedding night . . . we *are* husband and wife," he stammered.

"Indeed! But this is hardly the time or place for such goings on, sir! My baby sister is barely three feet away, and if you should wake her I would be mortified. I'm afraid we'll just have to wait until we have proper accommodations with the necessary privacy." And with that she turned her back to him.

Jessie didn't know what Harold had expected on their wedding night, but she didn't plan on finding out while her bed was the ground.

Awakening once during the night, she felt Harold pressed against her, his warm breath exhaling regularly on the back of her neck. Becoming aware of the strange noises of the night, she was grateful for her husband's proximity.

They were not alone on the trail. Many others were traveling to South Dakota, lured by the promise of gold and the offer of free land. Two young men, near the age of Harold, passed them on the road. One of them—skinny, pimply faced, with a straggly mousy brown moustache—swept his dirty hat from his head and bowed from the waist while still atop his horse.

"Howdy, ma'am," he said to Jessie, his horse dancing beneath him. "The name's Gar Fielding."

His friend snickered and whoaed his horse to a stop. "Don't mind my friend, ma'am. He fancies himself a ladies' man."

Jessie peered up at Harold who was riding on

the wagon while she walked beside it for a spell. Harold's brown eyes sparked with anger as he stared fiercely at the strangers. In a voice much lower than normal, her husband said, "My name is Robbins, and this here is my wife, Mrs. Robbins."

"Oops! Pardon, Mr. Robbins," the man called Gar said. "Natural mistake. Saw the little girl up ahead and figured you to be the brother of the ladies. Why your misses here looks too young to be a married woman."

Jessie raised her round chin haughtily. "We were only married a few days ago."

"Newlyweds!" The other man exploded into laughter. "Come along, Gar, they have no need for our company." They rode off, their horses kicking a fog of dust into Jessie's and Harold's faces.

Jessie spit dirt from her mouth, while Harold coughed and sputtered, "Good riddance. Those two are nothing but trouble."

The following day they were joined by more compatible fellow travelers. The Stovers were a family of three, though an addition was expected. Frank Stover was a bull of a man, with a "take charge" personality.

"Travelin' alone?" he asked while strolling alongside Harold who was walking beside his wagon. Before Harold could answer the man introduced himself, continuing with, " 'Tain't safe to be travelin' alone. Here tell there's been some Injun trouble here and there. 'Spect we'd best join forces. I'll send my Liz up to introduce herself to your womenfolk."

Harold and Jessie exchanged glances, but neither had time to comment before a tight-faced woman walked up beside Jessie. "The name's Liz Stover. Frank didn't think to ask for yours."

Jessie smiled. Liz reminded her of a younger version of Myrtle Foss. "We're the Robbins. I'm

Jessie, this is Harold, and riding on the wagon is my sister, Eudora."

"Pleased to meetcha, I'm sure." Liz bobbed her head, sunbleached top knot wobbling. "Good luck we happened along just now! We can team up together—safer that way. Indians 'tain't 'zactly friendly hereabouts."

Jessie frowned at Harold. Frank and Liz Stover were the first to mention any upsetting news about Indians, and Harold just shrugged, ignorant of the situation.

Liz continued without a pause. "We've a little boy back there in our wagon. 'Nother will be along soon." She patted her rounded belly. "How about yourself . . . had any luck yet?"

The question was embarrassing, certainly not one that should be asked by a stranger. "No . . . ah . . . well . . . we haven't . . . ah . . ."

"Never you mind, dear," Liz assured her. "It won't be long now, I'm sure. You're a right healthy looking girl, and that young husband of yours . . . well, you know what I mean!" She poked Jessie hard in the ribs with a sharp elbow.

With a ribald wink and grin, Liz said, "Well, folks, guess I'd best be heading back to my wagon. My little boy'll be hollerin' for his lunch soon. Nice talkin' to you."

"Friendly folks," Harold commented.

"Uh huh, though a bit forward, I'd say." Jessie had been embarrassed by Liz's remarks. The woman may have had the same plain features and worn her hair severely pulled back from her face like Mrs. Foss—but that was where the resemblance ended!

The sun was dropping close to the mountain tops when they stopped to set up camp among the spruce and juniper trees. The Stovers pulled their wagon alongside. The men tended to the horses while the women built a fire and began cooking. Jessie was glad to be busy, allowing little time for conversation with Liz.

After the meal, Jessie and Liz washed dishes, while Eudora played with the Stover's toddler, Little Frank.

"I hear somebody comin' up the trail," Frank hollered, pulling a rifle from his wagon. He walked toward the edge of the clearing, Harold right behind him.

Jessie, hands full of cooking gear, paused on her way to the wagon. She listened apprehensively. When she heard Frank call out "Howdy, folks," she relaxed.

The newcomers had obviously been invited to share the campsite. Two horse-drawn wagons, preceded by a horde of children—Jessie counted seven—were pulled into the area. A tiny man with a long, greying beard jumped from the first one. He effortlessly swung down the woman who'd been riding beside him. She was no taller than he, but round as a barrel.

The woman had black hair, parted in the middle, with braids wound around her head. She smiled at Jessie, her eyes disappearing into half-moons above her plump cheeks.

"Hello there. I'm so glad your husband signaled to us. I was ready to stop hours ago. But Jack— that's my husband—always has to try for that extra mile!" Her voice was as merry as her smile, and she accented the end of her sentences with a gay laugh. The laughter came often, seeming to bubble up from somewhere deep inside the rolls and layers of fat.

"I'm Jessie Robbins, and that's my husband over there—Harold. The little girl playing with the toddler is my sister. And he belongs to her," Jessie added gesturing toward Liz.

Angular, except for the round belly, plain-faced Liz joined them, wiping her hands on her apron. "We're the Stovers. Liz, Frank, and Little Frank. I'm afraid I didn't get your name."

The woman chortled, flesh jiggling. "I didn't give my name for you to get. I'm Fanny Tressler, and that's my huband, Jack, and together we produced this brood of young'uns."

"Hey, Ma, I'm hungry," a boy of six or seven whined.

"This here's Jasper. Won't try to name 'em all off. You'll run into 'em soon enough. All right, son, fetch your brothers and sisters, and if you hop to it, we'll have supper ready in a jiffy!"

Without lifting a plump finger, Fanny sat on a log supervising the preparation of the meal. Boys and girls of different sizes dashed back and forth between the wagons, fetching and carrying. In what appeared to be chaos but turned out to be a well rehearsed routine, a huge repaste was prepared, cooked, and eaten in record breaking time. While the Tresslers were all sitting together, Jessie counted heads. There were nine children in all. The oldest was a boy of eighteen or so, and the youngest, Jasper.

Finally the camp settled down, the only light that of the flickering camp fire. The younger children had been put to bed, and the older ones, along with the grownups, were gathered around the fire.

Liz and Fanny were both talkers, and Jessie knew it was useless to try and join in. Besides, the men's conversation interested her more. She leaned against Harold's arm and listened.

"Haven't had no trouble with Injuns myself," Frank commented, "but sure heard tell of some real nastiness."

Jack Tressler drew on his pipe, puffing out a cloud of smoke which circled around his teeth, and offered, "Yep, I heard they wiped out whole wagon trains right off this here trail!"

Jessie heard her husband take a deep breath before he said, "I haven't seen any sign of Indians since we've been traveling. Have either of you fellows?"

The oldest Tressler boy, Jamie, spoke, "We've been seein' smoke signals back and forth right along."

Jessie felt cold, goosebumps on her arms. Jack and his son, Jamie, and Frank began to swap tales of atrocities performed by the Indians in horrifying detail.

"Yep, a friend of mine rode up on a real mess. A whole family had been massacred. Them savages hacked off parts of those poor folks's bodies— arms, legs, and heads were scattered everywhere!" Jack described.

His son chimed in, "Even cut open the man's belly and had his guts spread out all over the place!"

Frank added, "I seen a mess like that once. Friends of mine, they was, too. Everyone of them killed dead, their scalps cut clean off their heads. I can tell you, I got no use for them murderin' savages. I'd be happy to have one cross my path so's I could send him to his happy hunting ground!"

Jessie was beginning to feel sick to her stomach. All this gruesome talk about Indians killing made her think about her father. "Harold, I'd like to go to bed now."

He jumped to his feet and helped Jessie up. "Good idea. We've got another long day ahead of us. Night all."

Wishes for a good night were extended all

around, and the Robbins headed for their wagon. "Newlyweds you know." Jessie recognized Liz's voice, followed by a low rumble of laughter. Jessie felt the heat rise in her cheeks and was grateful for the darkness.

Harold had made their bed on one side of the wagon and Eudora's on the other. It was a warm night, and Jessie decided against wearing her flannel nightgown. Instead she stripped down to her shift, leaving her dress and petticoats on the wagon seat.

Lying under a single blanket, Jessie turned to Harold. "What is all this talk about Indian attacks? Those men are scaring me. You know my father was killed by Indians."

Harold slipped his arm under Jessie's neck and she settled her head comfortably on his chest. His hand rested lightly on her hip, and she found his nearness comforting.

"Yes, I remember. But I don't know any more about the Indians than you do, Jessie . . . but I do know men. They like to exaggerate, boast, and tell a tall tale. I figure that's what Frank and Jack were up to mostly."

Jessie's voice seemed tiny when she said, "I do hope you're right."

Harold hugged her tightly. Jessie felt strangely vulnerable, perhaps for the first time in her life. She'd always been the strong one, the comforter, but now she pressed herself against the length of Harold's body, her lips touching his neck and feeling the strong pulse beat of his heart.

Her own heart quickened and she felt a yearning deep inside. She wished Harold would kiss her and imagined what it would feel like if his hand touched her breast.

The sound of her husband's even breathing told

her he was asleep. She sighed, pressed closer to him, and within the circle of his arm she finally slept.

The beauty of the black hills was not lost on Jessie. The small wagon train passed through canyons, the sides of which were multi-hued, disappearing into blue and purple shadows at their depths. Above them were rugged rock formations, formidable sentries to the land they were entering. Towering ponderosa pines, spruce, and juniper abounded.

An idea formed in Jessie's head as she noticed the unmistakable silhouettes of Indians high on the hilltops. It was obvious the progress of their travel was being closely watched. But despite the repeated warnings of Frank and Jack, they were allowed to pass undisturbed. Jessie thought she understood the Indians' fierce defense of their beautiful land which once had belonged only to them and was now being taken over by the white man.

When she attempted to voice her thoughts to Fanny and Liz, Fanny merely laughed and Liz was shocked and said so over and over. "Why, Jessie Robbins, whatever are you thinking? This isn't the Indians' land! They're only savages, after all. They don't even till the soil—or stay in one place long enough to call it home. This land belongs to the government! All the Indians know how to do is steal and kill. What makes you think Indians have feelings? I never heard such foolishness in all my born days!"

After that Jessie kept her conversation limited to simple things—the weather, recipes, and the like. She no longer attempted to express any serious thoughts which came into her head. And never would she have discussed the one topic which troubled her the most—her unconsummated marriage.

She knew she would be ridiculed. So instead she kept all her questions inside, whirling incessantly around her brain.

What would it have been like if she hadn't turned Harold away on their wedding night? What could she do to let him know she was ready? What would it be like? Would she like it? Why couldn't Harold see the agony she was suffering?

Chapter 10

The Robbins parted company with the Stovers and the Tresslers on the outskirts of Deadwood City. "You couldn't pay me to set foot in that city of sin," Liz declared righteously. "We aren't settling anywhere near any no good gold miners!"

As they rode into town, Harold felt as though he'd been insulted since he'd almost been a gold miner himself.

Jessie felt no pangs of regret as she waved good-bye. The incessant empty laughter of Fanny, and the know-it-all callousness of Liz had begun to wear on her nerves.

"Aren't we ever going to see them again?" Eudora asked, as all three of them crowded together on the wagon seat.

"Will you miss all the Tressler children and Little Frank?" Jessie asked, immediately regretful because Eudora had lost her playmates.

But Eudora's answer was a surprise. "No,

Jessie. The Tresslers were all so silly—always playing pranks and making jokes. I'll miss Little Frank some . . . but Mrs. Stover always made me look after him. I'm glad we're back to just the three of us.''

"Me too, Dora." Jessie laughed, hugging her sister.

Harold added, "And I'm also glad we're on our way again . . . alone."

Riding into Deadwood was an experience none of them would ever forget. Nothing in their respective pasts had prepared them for what lay ahead. Though it was nearing sundown—suppertime, a quiet period in most towns—the main street of Deadwood was teeming with life. The dusty road which ran through town was bordered by wooden sidewalks, and people of all descriptions, mostly male, dashed up and down, back and forth. Others on horseback or in wagons, clattered up and down the street.

Crudely lettered signs hung on the buildings— if they could be called buildings. They were little more than huts, the signs testifying to the kind of business inside. There was an assayer's office, a few boarding houses, a general store, and the rest seemed to be saloons.

"Wonder what's going on?" Harold queried. "You and Dora wait here and watch the wagon. I'll try and find us a room to rent for the night."

Jessie and Eudora waited as instructed, but pretty soon they were attracting undesired attention from the town folk. A group of men gathered on the wooden walkway and in the dust in front of their wagon. For a long while no one said anything—they just stared. Jessie slid a protective arm around her sister and stared straight above the heads of the men in front of her.

"Jessie?" Eudora whispered. "What do they

want? Why are they looking at us like that?"

"I don't know. Be quiet and pretend they aren't there."

A foul-smelling, rat-faced man stepped up next to the wagon. "Hey! Hey there! What you two girlies doin' settin' up there?"

Another, his courage coming from the bottle he was holding, leaned against the wagon and extended a free hand. "Why don't you step on down here? We'll show you a good time!" The rest of the men began to press closer, laughing and shouting ribald remarks.

Two loud explosions scattered the crowd. Jessie and Eudora clung to each other in fright as they watched a tall, thin figure walking toward them, holding a smoking revolver in each hand.

"What the hell are you fools standin' around gawkin' at? Git back to whatever orneriness you was up to before." The rough voice sounded strangely feminine.

The man slowly backed away, disappearing into the open doors of the saloons along the way. Jessie stared at their rescuer and realized it was a woman! Dark wispy hair was caught up under a battered heat, the angular body clad in stained, rough buckskins.

"Thank you very much for stepping in like that." Jessie kept her arm around her sister. "I don't know what harm might have come to us if you hadn't come along just then."

Their rescuer spat a stream of yellow tobacco juice into the dust of the road. "Oh, them dudes are purty harmless. Too liquored up to bother ya much. What in tarnation are the likes of you two doin' settin' up there all by yerselves? This ain't the safest place for two refined females like yerselves to be alone! More gold's been discovered between here and the town of Lead, and everyone's gone near crazy!''

Jessie sat up as straight as possible. "We are not alone, ma'am. My husband has gone to find us rooms to spend the night."

The woman put her hands on her narrow hips and guffawed. "There ain't been an empty bed in Deadwood for weeks, honey! We're full up with prospectors and speculators."

"Oh, dear," Jessie moaned. "I had so hoped we could get a good wash and sleep in a real bed tonight."

"Hey, I got an idea! When yer man gits back, you can all come to my place. How 'bout that?"

"Oh, no, we couldn't possibly—that would be an imposition." Jessie shook her head. She wasn't at all sure she even wanted to accept the strange woman's hospitality.

"Damn it, honey, don't be silly. I'm tellin' ya, there ain't a bed to be had in the whole of Deadwood. And even iffen there was, the likes of you wouldn't want to sleep in it. I'm a purty fair cook, and I got me a nice bed I'd be glad to give up for you and yer man, and I'd surely enjoy the company."

"Well, ma'am . . . ah . . . we'll see what Harold says when he returns." As she finished her sentence she could see Harold's bright corn silk hair as he threaded his way through the crowded street, a dejected slump to his shoulders.

"Look, here he comes now," she said, pointing him out.

When her husband reached the wagon, Jessie explained, "Harold, this kind lady has offered us the hospitality of her home."

Harold's face brightened instantly, though his eyes clouded a bit at the sight of the strangely garbed female leaning against the wagon.

She leaned forward and grabbed Harold's hand,

shaking it vigorously. "Howdy, pleased to make your acquaintance. My name is Martha Jane Clary, but folks hereabouts mostly call me Calamity."

"Yes, well, how do you do, Miss Calamity," stammered Harold. "I'm Harold Robbins, my wife, Jessie, and my sister-in-law, Eudora."

"Well, climb on up, Harold," Calamity directed. "Scoot over and make room for me and I'll just drive these here horses to my place."

Eudora climbed over the seat to perch atop the loaded wagon, while Calamity, true to her word, took the reins with an accomplished hand. Hollering "Giddyup," she drove through town, shouting obscenities at pedestrians and other wagons that didn't move out of the way fast enough to suit her.

Calamity's small frame house was located just outside Deadwood, and upon arrival, she jumped from the wagon and began unhitching the horses. "Well, don't just sit there, Harold. Git on down here and lend a hand. Sooner we get these horses tended to, sooner I can get a fire goin' and some food cookin'."

Harold had never been given orders by any woman, except maybe his mother, but since Calamity seemed used to being the boss, he only raised an eyebrow but went along with her.

Inside the house, Calamity tossed her fringed jacket onto one of a huge pair of antlers that was fixed on the wall, then unbuckled her gunbelt and slung it over the other antler. With her hands on her hips she barked out more directions.

"Harold, you take that bucket and go out and pump me some water. Eudora, you can set the table. Jessie, peel me up a mess of potatoes for frying. A friend of mine happened by today with a nice big chunk of venison. I'll hack it up and fry the pieces." Calamity was a fast worker, and the meal was soon on the table.

The venison steaks were tender and tasty, and Calamity had cooked them with herbs unknown to Jessie. The potatoes were golden brown and crispy fried. Calamity had also diced a few carrots and a summer squash, boiled them tender and served the mixture with a huge dollop of fresh butter melting on top. Jessie had mixed togeter some baking powder biscuits and baked them in Calamity's black stove. Not much talking except for "Please pass the . . ." went on while the Robbins and Eudora and Calamity consumed the meal.

"Mighty tasteful even if I do say so myself." Calamity lit a lamp in the kitchen and poured everyone another cup of coffee. "What brought you folks to Deadwood?"

"To be honest, I was kind of hoping to get in on the gold rush," Harold explained, casting a guilty glance in Jessie's direction. "I know I said I'd given up the idea—Jessie and me were going to find land to homestead—but when we got on the road I heard everyone talking about gold and it stirred my interest again. I kind of thought we could stick around here for a bit, and I could maybe try my hand at prospecting. But now that I see how crowded Deadwood is—and how wild—I guess it's no place for us."

"Yer dern tootin', Harold! This here's no place for the likes of Jessie and Eudora. You'd best get back to yer idea of homesteading. There's some right purty land south of here. You folks oughta head that way."

"That's what we'll do. We'll head out first thing tomorrow morning," Harold stated.

Eudora curled up on the bearskin rug in front of the stove and was soon fast asleep. While Jessie worked beside Calamity washing the supper dishes, she questioned their hostess about her own life in Deadwood.

"I've been around here for nigh on to two years," Calamity explained. "Came here with a gentleman friend by the name of William Hickok. Bastard up and got married on me awhile back. But we had a great time while it lasted."

Jessie studied Calamity and realized the woman was much younger than she appeared. Because she was tall and slim with sharp angles and had bold, almost masculine features, with her hair pulled back she could easily pass for a man. But her skin, though tanned by the sun, was smooth and free of wrinkles. Jessie guessed that in all likelihood Calamity was about the same age as she.

When the chores were done Jessie, and then Harold, bathed in a large oaken barrel in the privacy of the kitchen. After their baths, Calamity entertained them in the parlor with tales of her past.

Jessie asked how she'd come by the name of Calamity. "Now I don't rightly 'member when I first got called Calamity, but let me tell you, I've lived up to my name!" She laughed heartily. "Now it seems everytime I go into a saloon the men all holler, 'Here comes Calamity!', so I have to put on a show."

She leaped from her chair, whooped, and drew make-believe pistols, pointing and shouting, "Bam, bam, bam—and that's the end of a lamp, or a mirror, or a row of bottles. Why I've filled up more empty saloons thataway. Draws a crowd every time!"

She told them she was born on a farm in Missouri and had come west with her parents in '63. She left home at a very young age to serve as a scout for General Cook.

"That was a great time! No one even suspected I

was a girl—until I made the mistake of skinny-dippin' one day with the troops. Some durn scallawag went and told the General I was a female—and that was the end of that!''

Coyly, she related how she met Wild Bill Hickok in the hills of South Dakota where, as she put it, "We were more than friends for a time." They came to Deadwood, and being his constant companion, she'd gained notoriety as the sidekick of the colorful lawman. Unfortunately his unexpected marriage earlier in the spring had put a damper on their friendship.

"Folks, it's getting mighty late and if yer planning on an early start in the morning, you best get bedded down." She blew out the lamps, threw herself down on the horsehair sofa, propped her boot-encased feet on the wooden arm, and promptly fell asleep.

Harold and Jessie groped their way in the dark to the bedroom, amazed by their unusual hostess. A thought struck Jessie as she climbed into the fourposter, and she voiced it aloud. "This is the first time we've been in a real bed together, Harold."

Her husband leaned over and gave her his usual 'good night' peck on the cheek. Jessie put her hand behind his head and held him while she pressed her lips against his. When she released him, he gasped.

"Jessie?"

"Well, it *is* a real bed, after all. It's time we made our marriage real, don't you think?"

Harold pulled away from Jessie and leaped from the bed. At first she was afraid she'd offended her husband by her boldness, but she soon realized he was merely stripping off his long johns. Jessie pulled her nightgown off over her head.

When Harold slipped back under the light coverlet, Jessie pushed her plump, naked body against him. She could feel him tremble. Putting her arms around him, she held him tightly, her large breasts pressing against her husband's broad, hairy chest. Her round tummy fit perfectly into the indentation of his stomach.

"I love you, Jessie," Harold murmured. He leaned over and kissed her neck, carressing her shoulder, then slipping down to her firm breast. His hands and lips worked in unison exploring the curves and crevices of her body, and Jessie was overcome with intense emotions she'd never known before.

She eagerly welcomed Harold when he thrust himself inside her. The quick unexpected pain caused her to gasp, but as Harold moved rhythmically, Jessie was surprised when the pain was replaced by pleasure—a pleasure which grew until it exploded. When Harold collapsed against her, Jessie felt a warm satisfaction, a sense of comfortable well-being filling her soul. She kissed Harold's damp forehead, hugging him tightly.

"Oh, Jessie," he whispered hoarsely.

"I know, Harold, I know," she murmured, stroking his back.

He held her in his arms, and in minutes Jessie knew he was asleep. But it didn't matter. What she had just experienced was wonderful! She hadn't anticipated anything like it. Being married was going to be so much more than what she had expected. With a smile turning up the corners of her mouth, Jessie fell asleep.

Chapter 11

The Robbins had no difficulty following Calamity's directions to the beautiful valley she had described. It was the perfect setting for their home. There were plenty of trees to provide lumber for building, and a stream meandered through the fertile, green meadow brightened by berry bushes and wild flowers.

Harold registered their homestead in the town of Hill City, which was four miles south, and that was where they started to shop and soon made friends.

Rumors of Indian uprisings led by Sitting Bull and Crazy Horse led to Harold being pressed into service as a part-time deputy sheriff. It was the end of June before the gruesome details of the massacre of Custer and his troops by the Sioux and Cheyenne reached them, and Harold and Jessie discussed moving into Hill City for safety.

But even before they had decided, word was

brought to town that most of the warring Sioux had been driven into Montana by the Army, and the remaining Indians had signed a new treaty with the government. And they heard that even Sitting Bull had fled all the way to Canada.

The warm summer was spent building their house and a barn. Harold was a good carpenter, and the house he built, with Jessie and Eudora's help, was of his own design—ruggedly spacious and built upon a knoll overlooking the valley. It had a large center room and kitchen, with two bedrooms on either side.

Jessie questioned the need for four bedrooms. "We'll soon fill them all with children," was his answer, "and I'll probably have to add a few more."

She wasn't as sure as he. Despite frequent and enjoyable lovemaking her menstrual period arrived with annoying regularity. Jessie prayed she wouldn't be like Myrtle Foss—never able to bear children. She'd always had little ones to care for, and now that Eudora was nearly full-grown, Jessie felt a longing for a child of her own.

Harold had perfect faith they would be blessed with children in due time. He often discussed plans for a future that included sons and daughters. Jessie kept her doubts to herself.

One morning she awakened to the familiar warm stickiness between her legs and she began to cry. Harold rolled over and peered at her in alarm.

"Whatever is the matter, Jessie? Are you sick?" He put the back of his hand against her forehead.

"No, no, it's nothing like that," Jessie sniffed. "I'm just disappointed and sad."

Harold kissed her soundly. "What on earth have you to be disappointed or sad about? Our new house is nearly done. We live in the most beautiful valley in the world. We're healthy and we love each other."

Jessie wiped her eyes, attempting a smile. "I know, but my monthly time was a few days late and I hoped I was finally expecting. But it was all for nothing!"

Shaking his bright, blond head, he asked, "Is that all? We've got plenty of time. We're going to have lots of babies—you'll see."

"Maybe not. Oh, Harold, what if there's something wrong with me, and I can't have children?"

Harold laughed. "Now you're being ridiculous. I've never seen a woman who was so perfectly formed for motherhood. Look at your hips—they're made for bearing children. And those breasts—molded for babies." He leaned over and cupped one of her large breasts. "Yep, just right for babies. Now stop being such a worrier. It's time for us to get up and get started with our chores. I'm hungry!"

Jessie never brought the subject up again, even though she didn't share Harold's optimism, and he never seemed to notice when she had her monthly period. His only comment was, "It's nature's way."

Jessie wished she could be as unconcerned and blissful, but all she could do was yearn for the tiny baby she wanted so badly.

The house was finished, as was the barn, before the onset of winter, at which time Harold concentrated on the interior during the inclement weather. The first snow arrived in February as did their first overnight guest.

Gunshots echoed through the valley, bouncing off the hills. Jessie and Harold glanced at each other in alarm, as he grabbed his rifle from over the fireplace.

"Ooooh, be careful," Jessie cried fearfully. She ran to the door, watching her husband walk to the edge of the wide porch and rest the rifle on the top step.

A familiar voice cried out, "Yahoo! I knew this just had to be yer place!"

"Calamity! Calamity Jane!" Harold shouted. "Come on out here, Jessie. It's our friend, Calamity!"

Jessie dashed onto the porch as the other woman climbed the few steps. "What a grand surprise! You must be frozen! She dusted snowflakes from Calamity's leather-clad shoulders.

"Wouldn't turn down a chair by the fire! Could you tend to my horse, Harold? She's plum tuckered out." Calamity hoisted a bulky saddle bag over her shoulder and followed Jessie inside.

Carefully setting the bag down, she stood with her long legs wide apart and surveyed her surroundings. She took in the high, heavy beamed ceiling and the massive stone fireplace with its raised hearth and polished walnut mantel. Collapsing in the rocking chair in front of the fire, she stretched her legs towards the warmth of the flames.

Sighing contentedly, she raked the saddle bag to her side with a swift movement of her booted foot. Flipping back the cover she removed a bottle which Jessie knew must contain some form of alcohol. Calamity opened the cap, pressed the bottle to her lips, and took a long swig. She recapped it, wiped her mouth, and glanced at her hostess who had settled in the wing back chair.

"Pardon me, Jess, would you care for a swallow?" Calamity held the bottle in Jessie's direction.

"Oh, goodness, no!"

"Nothing warms your insides better on a cold day," Calamity said, tucking the bottle back into her pack.

"What brings you our way, Calamity?" Jessie asked.

"Wanted to see you folks, mostly. Just been travelin' around lately, here and there. Happened to remember you when I spied this pretty valley. Spotted the house and just knew it had to be yours."

The front door burst open, a flurry of snow preceding a well-bundled Eudora. She ran to Calamity and kissed her on the cheek. "Hello, Calamity! Harold told me you were here when he put the horse in the barn. He'll be in in a minute."

Calamity straightened herself in the chair, grasping Eudora by the elbow and examining her from head to toe. "Well, girlie, you've grown up since the last time I seen you. You'll be having to chase the boys away from this gal soon, I wager."

Eudora giggled, while Jessie smiled in agreement. Grown-up, yes, but a long way from being a temptation to young men. Two scraggly, dark copper braids hung down from her knitted hat, bony wrists stuck out from the sleeves of her dripping coat, and feet encased in sopping shoes seemed far too big for the rest of her skinny frame.

"You are wet through and through!" Jessie exclaimed. "Put on some dry clothes immediately and come warm yourself by the fire. I have a big pot of stew on the stove, and that's just what we all need on a night like this!"

Before the dishes had been cleared from the table, Calamity left the kitchen, returning with her whiskey bottle. She topped off her half-full cup of coffee with the amber liquid. "Anyone else?"

Harold and Jessie shook their heads in unison,

so Calamity set the bottle on the table and hunched down into her chair. Intermittently sipping at the mixture in her cup, she related the sad tale which Jessie suspected was the cause of her drinking.

"Last summer I lost the best friend I ever had—Wild Bill Hickok. After Bill's marriage he showed every sign of settlin' down. One night while having a friendly little game of poker in a saloon in Deadwood, he made the mistake of settin' with his back to the door. Can't figure that one out—he knew better'n leaving his back exposed like that. Being married must've softened his brain!

"There he set payin' no mind to nothin' but his hand, when some no count, do nothin' by the name of Jack McCall crept up behind Bill firing a bullet right into his brain. And he didn't have no reason at all, 'cept I guess so's he could say he was the one what killed Wild Bill Hickok." Calamity brushed a tear from her eye, jumped up from her seat, grabbed the bottle from the table, and strode into the main room.

"Jessie, why don't you go after her," Harold suggested.

"No, I think she'd like to be alone for a bit. Eudora and I will do the dishes. Why don't you sit for a spell, and let your food settle. When we're all through here will be time enough to join Calamity."

Calamity was back to her old self—the bottle hidden away in the saddle bag—when the family joined her in front of the fire. Her spirits had lifted—or she was covering up well—for she entertained them with her ribald stories far into the night.

She was up early in the morning, and after a hasty breakfast, she saddled up, despite Jessie's invitation to stay on indefinitely. "Thanks anyway, but I got to be movin' on. I'll think of you people often, but I can't never stay in one place very long. I need to find an honest way to make a livin' for myself. One of these days I'll surprise you and drop in again for a visit."

But she never did. The Robbins never saw Calamity Jane again. Calamity became somewhat of a celebrity, and news of her came to them from time to time. She went on the stage billed as "The Famous Woman Scout of the West," and she appeared for a time in Buffalo Bill's Wild West show, putting on riding and shooting exhibitions. But they also heard that Calamity's drinking kept causing her problems.

Before spring came Jessie realized that her dreaded menstrual time was overdue, but she said nothing to Harold. There was no need for both of them being disappointed.

"Come outside and take a look at the garden," Harold suggested after breakfast. It was a warm spring day; everything was green and fresh, with tiny blossoms appearing on the flowering bushes and trees.

"See, Jessie, everything is coming up that we planted. This is rich, good soil. We can grow anything!" He gestured to the neat garden plot, leafy green sprouts poking through the reddish brown dirt in even rows.

He turned to her and took hold of her hand. "Jessie, isn't there something else beginning that you haven't told me about?" His blue eyes twinkled, and the corners of his mouth twitched as he tried to suppress a grin.

Jessie nodded. "Yes. I think we're going to have a baby—at least, I dearly hope so."

"I knew it!" Harold shouted, twirling Jessie around.

"Careful!" Jessie warned. "We don't want to do anything that might harm the baby."

He hugged Jessie carefully. "See, I told you that you were meant to have babies, that we only had to be patient. It'll be so great to have a son."

Jessie pulled away. "Wait a minute, Harold. It might be a girl, you know."

"It doesn't matter—boy or girl—we're going to have plenty of both!" Harold was ecstatic.

"What made you guess, Harold? I wasn't going to tell you for awhile."

"Aw, c'mon, honey, you *are* my wife. It's been a mighty long time since you've had your bleeding time. And look at you! I didn't think it was possible, but you're breasts are bigger than ever. And your belly, it's as round as can be. I'd have to be blind not to have noticed."

Jessie stared pensively in the direction of the green hills. She wrinkled her forehead.

"Now what's the matter?" Harold asked.

"Nothing really. I just kind of wish Mama was here. I know all about taking care of babies but I don't know a thing about having one."

Harold put his arm around her shoulder. "Don't you worry about that at all! I've been talking to old Doc Porter. He delivers all the babies hereabouts, and when I'm in town next I'll tell him the good news. I'm sure he'll be glad to stop out here and answer any questions you might have."

But Doc Porter didn't give Jessie much reassurance. He had come to visit just as Harold promised. He arrived in a fine, black buggy, drawn by two dappled grey horses. Jessie's first thought —as she watched the doctor climb out of his conveyance with tremendous effort accompanied by loud grunts and groans—was that the doctor took much better care of his horse and buggy than he did himself.

The physician's white, wiry hair was in much need of grooming, growing straight out from his head every which way. A nearly white beard straggled down his chest, boasting stains of past meals. He wore a wrinkled and soiled baggy suit, and his shoes were so dirty it was impossible to tell if they were brown or black.

"Mrs. Robbins," the unsightly man huffed. "I'm Doctor Porter. Your husband asked me to look in on you."

"Do come in, Doctor. It was very kind of you to stop by." Jessie held the door open.

The smell of alcohol and perspiration assailed her nostrils as the doctor stepped by her into the house. "Take a seat, sir. May I bring you some refreshments? I just took a pound cake out of the oven, and there's a fresh pot of coffee on the stove."

"You wouldn't have any spirits in the house now, would you?"

"No, I'm afraid not," Jessie apologized.

"Guess I'll settle for a cup of coffee." The doctor was overtaken by a coughing fit, hacking and wheezing into a crumpled, yellow handkerchief he pulled from the pocket of his suit jacket.

Jessie brought him his coffee, holding it until his spasm subsided. His apparent unhealthy condition did nothing to inspire confidence. He dabbed at his watery eyes and dripping nose, cleared his throat, stuffed the wadded handkerchief back into his pocket, and reached for the cup and saucer. After taking a sip, he balanced the saucer on his knee.

"Mr. Robbins tells me you are expecting. When do you think you will deliver?" Dr. Porter's eyes were small, the yellow-brown irises surrounded by white crisscrossed with spidery red lines.

His bulbous nose was also marked by a woven design of broken blood vessels.

"I think in the fall—most likely October."

"Well, you certain are the picture of health, my dear. Just remember you are eating for two now!" The doctor chuckled, triggering another paroxysm of coughing.

Jessie peered anxiously at the coffee sloshing about in the china cup. "Is there anything I can do?"

He shook his head and mopped at his eyes and mouth again with the soiled handkerchief. When he was finally able to speak he continued as though he'd never been interrupted. "You need plenty of rest, of course. When the time comes, just have Mr. Robbins fetch me. I've delivered every baby that's been born in these parts for the last ten years."

Jessie thought the reason must be because he was the only doctor. She was relieved when he climbed back into his buggy and rode off. Remembering that she had been delivered by an Indian, her sisters by her father, and the twins with the help of Myrtle Foss, she decided maybe she wouldn't need too much help to bring a child into the world. "I'll have Dora watch the doctor carefully. Then she can do whatever needs to be done when I have other children."

Jessie's pains began early. It was a beautiful autumn day. The hills were colored golden yellow, deep red, and rust brown, and there were late squashes and pumpkins on the vine, still to be picked. She stepped out onto the front porch, clad only in her nightdress and knitted shawl.

The pain had awakened her before anyone else was stirring, and she had known immediately that it was the beginning of labor. She put her hands on

her distended belly. It was hard. Rubbing it, she
thought of the baby who would soon arrive.

"Jessie, is something the matter? What are you
doing outside so early?" Harold, bare-chested and
buttoning his trousers, stepped out on the porch.

Jessie ecstatically clutched her belly as she
turned to face her husband. "Harold, it's begun."

"The baby? Oh, I'd better wake up Eudora. She
can ride by Dr. Porter's on the way to school."

Jessie clutched Harold's arm. "No, please, I
want *you* to fetch the doctor. I'd like to keep Dora
home with me today."

"Well, if that's the way you want it . . ."

"Let's go inside, Harold. It's too chilly out here
for you without a shirt." In the house, she added,
"Finish dressing and go for Dr. Porter. I'll have
breakfast ready for all of us by the time you
return."

"Breakfast? Shouldn't you go back to bed?"
Harold asked.

"Don't worry, dear. I'll go to bed when it's
time." She gave him a playful shove. "Hurry now
and get dressed, or you won't be ready for this
baby."

Jessie woke her sister and explained what was
happening. " . . . and I want you to stay with me
every minute."

"Oh, I will," Eudora promised, "but I don't
know a thing about delivering babies."

"I'm not so sure the good Dr. Porter does either.
But I want you to keep an eye on him. Watch
everything he does very carefully."

"Whatever you say, Jessie," the young girl said,
her eyes round with anxiety.

"Dress quickly now, I'll need your help making
breakfast—and getting everything ready for the
baby." Jessie's pains were coming regularly,
about every twenty minutes, but they weren't

particularly uncomfortable yet. She set about breakfast as quickly as possible in her very pregnant condition. She put the coffee pot on the stove, fried the bacon, scrambled a dozen eggs, and made a batch of biscuits. After dishing up a plate of food for herself, she put the pans onto the warming shelf.

She was buttering a second biscuit when Eudora finally joined her. "Oh, you've already cooked breakfast."

"Yes—and nearly finished eating mine. I want you to dish up Harold's and the doctor's breakfast as soon as they arrive. But don't hang around in here. Leave the dishes. You can do them later. I don't want you to leave me alone for an instant!"

Jessie hurried into her bedroom and put clean rags on the bed over the sheets. Even though she had been young when the twins were born she remembered the process had been messy. Glancing at the cradle in the corner she checked it once again—the flannel blankets and the tiny clothing she had sewn with the tiniest of stitches. She refolded and smoothed the triangular scraps of flannel which were stacked on her commode.

A sharper pain squeezed around her pelvis area reaching to the small of her back. When it finally subsided it left the remnant of a dull ache. "Hmmm," she thought, "he or she must be getting anxious."

She crossed the main room and went once again into the kitchen. Another pain began. She clutched the back of the chair, gritting her teeth and holding her breath.

"Jessie? What is it?" Eudora looked up from her breakfast with alarm.

"Ummm, just another pain dear . . . but it's getting close to the time. I hope Harold returns with the doctor soon."

Just then they heard the sound of horses in the yard. "That must be them now," Eudora cried, running from the room.

Jessie could hear her calling, "Thank goodness you're finally here!" but couldn't understand what the doctor answered.

Harold burst into the room. "Jessie? Shouldn't you be in bed?"

"I'm on my way," she answered. "I was merely waiting for you to get back with the doctor."

Dr. Porter trailed in behind Eudora. "Well, well, well, and how are you doing? Still up and about, I see."

"I'm going to bed right now," Jessie said, regretting the sound of annoyance which crept into her voice.

Dr. Porter put a liver-spotted hand with ragged, yellow fingernails on her distended stomach. "Pains coming pretty close together now, are they?" Jessie nodded her head and bent over as a pain wracked her whole body.

"Nice hard contraction," Dr. Porter commented, his hand still pressed on her belly. He turned and gazed greedily at the pans of food setting on the warming shelf over the wood stove. "Is that our breakfast?"

"Oh, yes." Eudora sprang into action, setting the table and dishing up the food.

Dr. Porter pulled out a chair and sat. He tucked a napkin into the collar of his shirt and began shoveling food into his mouth while he talked. "Sit down and eat, Mr. Robbins. With a first baby you never can tell how long it will take. You just give me a call, young lady, when I'm needed." He never glanced in Jessie's direction.

Eudora put her arm around Jessie's waist and helped her toward the bedroom. Jessie's progress was slow, the pain never leaving her, merely intensifying spasmodically. When this happened she had to stop and cling to Eudora. Sweat beaded on her brow.

Jessie finally reached her bed. Always practical, she hiked her nightdress up over her plump buttocks before climbing into bed. "No sense staining a perfectly good nightgown."

Instructing her sister, her voice coming in ragged bursts, she said, "Pull off my good quilt, please, and fold it up."

Suddenly Jessie called out, "It must be nearly time. I can feel the baby's head. Run for the doctor!"

Eudora scampered from the room, and Jessie was consumed by another pain. She grunted and heaved, fearful her child would be born when no one was with her.

Eudora appeared at her side, eyes huge with fright. "He won't come yet. Says there's no need. He'll be here when he finishes his coffee."

"We'll have this baby without him then." Jessie spoke breathlessly. Her whole being was thrust into the task, muscles strained, pelvis bone stretched to the breaking point. A watery substance burst from her.

"Oh, oh, oh, oh," Eudora cried. "Something's happening!"

Jessie was unable to speak. She was unaware of the guttural sounds coming from her throat, and though she could feel a tearing, she now was above the pain. She was only aware of the task at hand—pushing the baby out into the world.

"Oh, Jessie, I can see it's head!" Eudora didn't sound frightened any more. One last great push and Jessie knew it was done. Then she was still, momentarily conscious only of her own breathing.

"Look," she heard Eudora say, and she opened her eyes. Her sister was holding a tiny, wiggling baby—a girl, red all over, mouth open wide. The high pitched squall was music to Jessie.

Happy tears blurred her vision. Dr. Porter burst through the door and snatched the infant away from Eudora. "Never expected it to be over so quickly!"

"Remember, Dora, watch the doctor," Jessie whispered.

She must have drifted off to sleep because the next thing she knew her daughter was tucked in beside her, all clean and sweet smelling, wrapped tightly in a flannel bunting. Her heart flooded with love.

"Ah, Jessie, you're awake." Harold stepped to the side of the bed and kissed her. "How are you feeling?"

"Wonderful," she said. "I've never been so happy. Isn't she the most beautiful baby you've ever seen?"

Harold beamed. "Most beautiful baby . . . and most beautiful mother. I'm sorry about the doctor. I know he wasn't much help to you."

"Doesn't matter. From now on Eudora will deliver my babies," Jessie announced. "Now tell me—what are we going to name this pretty little girl?"

Chapter 12

"And what does Myrtle Foss have to say?" Harold asked.

Jessie unfolded the letter and tucked it into the envelope. She held it against her bosom and sighed. Whenever she received mail from home, which wasn't often, she felt a pang of homesickness. She would dearly love to see the Fosses again —and of course, her own mother.

"Mr. and Mrs. Foss are all alone again. My sister, Minnie, has married a carpenter by the name of Julius Bailey. Hiram is complaining of rheumatism, but my mother and the twins are doing fine. My, my . . . how I would love to see them all again."

Jessie was expecting her second child. Lottie was nearly two and a half. A joy to her mother, father, and aunt, she was spoiled by them all. When she didn't immediately become pregnant after weaning Lottie, she lavished all her affection on her daughter, sure that no more children would follow.

It was hard not to be a doting parent to such a wee charmer. Lottie's dark curls bounced all over her head, and her brown eyes sparkled with both mischief and pure innocence. She had a tiny, turned-up nose, and a rosebud mouth which puckered for many generous kisses. Jessie found it impossible to punish Lottie. Whenever the child transgressed, she would throw her arms around her mother's neck, planting a wet kiss on her cheek. And any thought of punishment Jessie might have harbored disappeared.

Even Eudora was under her niece's spell, and she couldn't do enough for her. She sewed new clothes for Lottie's rag doll, baked cookies for her, and took her for long walks in the woods.

Eudora had come in from school and taken Lottie on just such a walk right before Harold arrived from town with the mail.

"Your mother would be as crazy about Lottie as we are. It's a shame she isn't here to enjoy her first grandchild . . . and the one coming," Harold mused. "You know, I've been wondering how Lottie's going to take to this new baby. She may be jealous."

Such a suggestion was irritating to Jessie. "She'll be nothing of the sort! I was the first child too, you know, and I never resented my younger sisters and brother. I dearly loved them all."

Harold nodded his head. "Oh, I'm sure she'll love the new baby . . . but I don't think she'll be able to help feeling a bit put out. After all, we've made her the center of our lives."

With some difficulty, Jessie heaved herself out of the rocking chair. She had gotten much heavier with this pregnancy, and she felt more awkward. She rubbed the small of her back, which always seemed to ache. "There's enough room for two in the center!" She disappeared into the kitchen to avoid any further comments from Harold.

It was time to start supper, but spying Eudora walking hand in hand with the delight of her life, she sat down in the chair by the window, resting her plump elbows on the sill and watched them skip and hop their way to the house.

Lottie, beginning to wave as soon as she noticed her mother, pulled away from Eudora and ran to the back door. Scampering into the kitchen she flung herself into what was left of her mother's lap. The child covered Jessie's face with kisses, her tiny arms around her neck.

Jessie squeezed back, settling Lottie on her knees. "Did you and Aunt Dora have fun on your walk?"

"Oh, yes, Mama. We saw a big squirrel. He ran up a tree and he jumped over to another one!" Her round, dark eyes sparkled with animation.

"Tell your mother about the baby birds," Eudora prompted as she entered the kitchen.

"We saw a whole nest full of baby birdies. We even watched their mommy feed them." Lottie clapped her hands and giggled.

Jessie remembered the conversation she had held with Harold earlier. "Wouldn't it be fun if *we* had a baby?"

Lottie screwed her heart-shaped face into a frown. "We don't need a baby."

Eudora knelt beside Jessie's chair. "Oh, I think it would be lots of fun to have a baby. It would be just like a real, live doll!"

Lottie slid off her mother's lap. Pouting, she crossed her arms and stamped her foot. "Don't need another doll!"

Eudora frowned at Jessie. Jessie shook her head, and held a cautioning finger to her lips. With a great deal of effort Jessie stood. "Come, Lottie, sit here in my chair. Mama's going to fix you a very special dessert tonight, and you may help."

She put a bowl full of wild berries in front of the child. "I want you to pull the leaves and stems off. Aunt Dora will help you."

Jessie pushed her daughter's harsh words into the corner of her mind. Lottie was so perfect in every other way, she knew she would be a loving sister for the new baby.

When the birth waters gushed down Jessie's legs as she was hanging up the wash, she was more surprised than anything. By her calculations it was at least two weeks too soon! Since she experienced no pain, she finished hanging up the last load.

"Guess you'll be bringing in the wash by yourself this afternoon, Dora," Jessie said. Her sister was watering the garden with rinse water from the tub.

"Is it the baby?" There was a half anxious, half excited tremor in Eudora's voice.

"My water broke a few minutes back. Nothing else so far, but I better make things ready."

Eudora blocked Jessie's way. "Should I get Harold and tell him to go after Dr. Porter?"

Jessie put one hand on a plump hip and the other atop her protruding belly. "Absolutely not, Dora! You delivered Lottie without any help from that rummy doctor. All he was good for was cutting and tying the cord. And you said you paid good attention when he did that."

Eudora shook her head nervously. "I did, Jessie, but it's been two and a half years. I'm not sure I remember exactly."

"You'll remember just fine! As good as that silly doctor. He's probably got his brain so pickled by now he doesn't know as much as you!" Jessie patted her sister on the shoulder. "I think Harold's cutting wood behind the barn. Why don't you take Lottie over to him and hurry on back."

The pains soon began with great intensity. Jessie wasn't able to accomplish too much in the way of preparation, because it was impossible to remain on her feet. She changed clothes and lay down on her bed. The pain seemed to focus in her lower back making it impossible to lie flat, so she curled up on her side.

When Eudora entered the bedroom, she asked, "Jessie, do you think you should lie that way?"

"I don't know. But my back hurts terribly. I'll turn over when I feel the baby coming."

But she wasn't able to turn when the time came —she didn't have the strength. She hurt so badly that she couldn't open her eyes. She could hardly think. She felt Eudora pull her over onto her back, then she thought she heard people talking.

Harold said, "Maybe I better get Dr. Porter after all. He'll know what to do."

"Nooo!" Jessie screamed. "Eudora can do everything. Let Eudora do it." The pain engulfed her, tore at her, and she lost consciousness.

When she finally awoke the room was dark. She heard a mewing sound and felt a light weight on her arm. Feeling with her free hand she lightly touched the fuzz on the top of the baby's head. She nuzzled the velvety, smooth cheek with her nose.

"Jessie, are you awake?"

"Yes, Harold. Is the baby all right?"

Harold lit a lamp and brought it close to the bed so Jessie could see. The infant didn't have much hair. It was plump, with round cheeks—a much bigger baby than Lottie had been.

"It's another little girl, Jessie."

"Oh, dear, you must be disappointed. I know you were hoping for a boy this time."

"I'm not disappointed, just terribly grateful you and the baby are all right. For a time we really didn't know if either one of you would make it."

Jessie knew this had been a more difficult delivery than her first, but Harold's words made her fearful for the infant beside her. "Tell me the truth, is there something wrong with my baby?"

Harold sat on the edge of the bed, taking hold of Jessie's hand comfortingly. "The baby came bottom first. She was stuck. You would have been proud of your sister. Somehow Dora managed to move the baby around until she was able to pull her out by her arm. If it hadn't been for Dora, I'm afraid we'd have lost you both."

"The baby, Harold—tell me about the baby." Jessie knew there was something dreadful.

"It's her arm. It isn't right. Your sister thinks she may have pulled the baby's arm out of its socket."

Jessie raised herself. Quickly she unwrapped the infant, slipping the sleeves of its kimono off. At first glance she could see no difference in the child's arm. But when the cool air touched the baby's skin, she wriggled, raising her left arm above her head—the right arm was motionless, a slight discoloration around the shoulder. Jessie touched it lightly with her finger. She kissed the bruised spot. "Poor little baby. We can't call you baby forever—have you thought of a name, Harold?"

"My mother's name was Ethel, and there's something about the baby that reminds me of my mother," her husband said.

"Ethel, yes, that's a fine name for you, sweet baby." Ethel answered with a few lusty howls.

Jessie, with love mingled with pity, noted

though Ethel was now actively squirming, her right arm remained limp at her side. With tears stinging her eyes, Jessie offered her breast to her daughter—and the cries stopped.

"Maybe if we massaged her shoulder . . ." Jessie began.

"We'll do whatever we can," Harold agreed.

Eudora brought Lottie in to see her mother and her baby sister early the next morning. Jessie was sitting up in bed and her first born scrambled up beside her.

"Are you sick, Mama?" Lottie asked.

"No, honey, I'm just tired. Look, I have a surprise for you. Here's your sister, Ethel." Jessie held out the sleeping infant for Lottie to see.

"Ugh!" Lottie spat. "She's ugly. I don't want her."

"Lottie, for shame!" Eudora scolded.

"It's all right, Dora. Lottie will come to love Ethel. She's just feeling a little put out," Jessie said, speaking more calmly than she felt.

"No, I won't love her. Never, never, never!" Lottie slid off the bed and ran from the room, dark curls bobbing.

"I'll go after her."

"No, wait. She'll come around—you'll see. It's not in Lottie's nature to be so hateful," Jessie said optimistically, hoping her words might make it so.

"She's such a sweet thing." Eudora leaned close to the baby. "I'm so sorry about her arm, Jessie. I'd give anything for that not to have happened. But Jessie, I just didn't know what else to do. You were straining so hard to push her out, and she wasn't coming the right way. I knew I had to help somehow. I just grabbed and pulled . . ."

Jessie patted her sister's arm. "It's all right, Dora. Harold told me all about it. He said if it hadn't been for you, Ethel and I would have died. Look, let me show you what I've been doing with her."

Jessie opened the infant's clothing and gently massaged the tiny shoulder. Then she slowly moved the healthy looking but lifeless arm up and down. "If we keep exercising it, someday it will be fine."

"Oh, Jessie, I do hope so."

Jessie faithfully worked on Ethel's arm, but there was no noticeable change. Unless Jessie was holding the limb, it fell limply at Ethel's side.

Lottie's attitude toward her sister didn't improve either. The first time she noticed Jessie nursing the baby, she stood and watched for a time. She asked, "Why are you doing that?"

"I'm feeding the baby, dear. Just like I did with you. This is the only way she can eat," Jessie explained.

Lottie thought for awhile, her sweet face seriously posed, then said, "Don't feed her anymore."

"Why, I have to feed her. If I didn't, she would die."

Lottie nodded her head solemnly. "That would be good. Then we'd be like we were before. It was better without Ethel." She twirled on her toes, her dark ringlets bounced, and she skipped from the room.

A few days later, as Lottie lay on her tummy, her chin propped up by her hands, she watched Eudora massage and work on Ethel's damaged arm. "Why are you doing that?"

"I'm trying to make the baby's arm better. You know it was hurt when she was born." Eudora often massaged and exercised Ethel. Jessie suspected it helped her sister's feeling of responsibility for the infant's defect.

"If she isn't right, why do Mama and Papa want to keep her?" Lottie peered at her aunt pensively.

"Lottie!" Eudora cried. "You mustn't talk that way. They want to keep her because they love her, just like they love you."

Lottie didn't say anymore. She just stared at her baby sister with large, solemn eyes.

When Eudora related the episode to Jessie, she added, "I think we should keep an eye on Lottie when she's around the baby."

Jessie was aghast by Eudora's unspoken implication. "How can you even hint at such a thing? Lottie may be jealous of Ethel, but she would never, never consider harming a hair on Ethel's head!" How could Eudora even think such a terrible thing about sweet Lottie?

But that very evening she began to have the tiniest of doubts herself. Jessie was suddenly aware Ethel's mealtime was long overdue. Her breasts were full and uncomfortable, and she wondered why the baby wasn't making any fuss. She finished sewing the patch on Harold's overalls before setting her mending aside.

"I can't imagine why Ethel isn't hollering for milk," she commented to Harold.

Walking into the bedroom, Jessie heard a strange, muffled cry. Looking in the cradle she was horrified to find a fluffy, down pillow laying on top of the baby. "How on earth did that get there?" She snatched it away.

Ethel's face was bright red, her mouth gasping for breath, her good arm waving. After a good swallow of air, she let out a tremendous bellow. Jessie scooped the baby from the cradle, holding her comfortingly to her bosom. "Poor baby," she murmured, rubbing her back.

Dashing into Lottie's room next door, she found

her daughter lying on her side, hands tucked under her head. With dark lashes casting shadows on smooth, pink cheeks, her face was as innocent as an angel's. Jessie backed out of the room and shut the door quietly.

Sitting in her rocking chair she began nursing Ethel, cooing and petting the child soothingly while her mind raced madly. Could her sweet Lottie have put the pillow on top of the baby? Certainly neither Harold nor Dora did, and it couldn't have gotten there by itself. But—Lottie? Was she really that jealous of her sister? From now on she would keep a good eye on both children. Nothing further was going to happen!

The days and weeks turned into months, and finally a whole year passed without incident— and Jessie relaxed her guard. Ethel was beginning to walk, and Lottie seemed to be taking a real interest in her sister's progress. She would sit for many minutes coaxing Ethel to take a few steps into her arms. The toddler was brave, and though she could only break her fall with one hand, she always tried again after every spill.

Jessie was in the kitchen shelling early peas and listening to her daughters play together in the front room.

"Good, Ethel, keep coming . . . oh, oh, watch out . . ." Lottie said. They both laughed, and Jessie guessed Ethel had taken a tumble.

"Come, little sister, try again. That's good. Lottie's right here. Come on . . . that's it . . . oh, oh, down she goes." And there was more laughing.

"Up on your feet . . . Lottie will help . . . big girl . . . you're doing so good . . . come this way . . ."

Jessie raised her head to listen. The voices seemed farther away—too far away. She put the bowl of peas on the table and stepped into the other room. The girls weren't there and the front door was ajar.

Feeling a wave of foreboding, Jessie lifted her skirts and ran as she hadn't in years. She heard a bumping sound and darted through the front door, afraid of what she might find.

Ethel lay in a crumpled heap at the bottom of the porch stairs. Lottie stood beside her. Jessie could have sworn her oldest daughter was smiling —but when she spied Jessie, tears filled her large eyes, and she appeared tiny and frightened.

"The baby fell!" she sobbed. "I was walking backwards. I didn't know we were so close to the steps. I tried to grab her, Mama, but her bad arm was closest to me!"

Jessie knelt beside Ethel and carefully turned her over. Her forehead was bleeding as was one of her knees, but she was breathing, and her eyelashes fluttered when Jessie cradled her in her arms. Her eyes opened wide and she cried, "Mama!"

"Hush, sweetheart, Mama is here. You're going to be just fine," Jessie assured her. To Lottie she added, "Go into your bedroom and wait for me. I'm going to tend to your sister, and after that you and I are going to have a talk."

Without a word, Lottie turned and ran into the house. Jessie was angry and frightened. She cleaned the baby's cuts, then checked for other bruises. When Ethel was sufficiently calm, Jessie put her on the floor with her wooden toys and went to Lottie's room.

The girl sat on her bed, her eyes wide with bewilderment. "What's the matter, Mama?"

"You know what's the matter, young lady! You either pushed her or deliberately let your sister fall down those stairs. She could have been killed! Is that what you were hoping for?"

"No, Mama, I didn't mean for her to get hurt," Lottie cried. Her bottom lip quivered, her eyes bright with tears.

"Lottie Robbins, I'm telling you here and now—there will be no more of this. You will never again do anything to harm your sister! Do you understand me?"

Lottie nodded her head. "Yes, Mama."

"To make sure you do remember, I'm going to give you your first—and I hope your last—spanking."

Jessie sat on the edge of the bed, placing Lottie across her lap. "I didn't think I would ever do this to you." She soundly whacked Lottie on her round buttocks three times.

Lottie didn't make a sound, but her face was streaked with tears when Jessie set her firmly down on the floor. "Now, young lady, it's over, and we will never speak of this again."

"You aren't going to tell Papa?" Lottie asked.

"No, I'm not. And I expect this is the very last time anything like this will happen. Am I right?"

"Yes, Mama."

Lottie never received another spanking—and she never harmed Ethel again. Perhaps, after a few other shenanigans over the years, a spanking or two might have slowed her down—but then again, it might not have helped at all.

Chapter 13

"Oh, no! How terrible! Oh, my poor sister! My mother must be going out of her mind!" Jessie was reading a letter from Wisconsin which Harold had handed her minutes before.

"What is it?" Harold asked. "Which sister? What on earth happened?"

"The letter is from Minnie. She says Wilhelmina —she must be, let's see, sixteen now—has disappeared!"

"What do you mean disappeared? Was she kidnapped, wandered away, what?"

Jessie shrugged and sniffed. "Minnie writes there wasn't a trace of her though they searched everywhere, even in the forest. She says poor mother is having a hard time accepting it. Oh, Lord, it's hard to believe!"

Jessie stared at the letter for a few moments longer, adding, "Minnie says mother is being courted by some man by the name of Andrew

Cromer—and from the way things look, they might get married. He must be very special for mother to even consider marrying again."

"She probably needs someone to lean on. No telling how the shock of Wilhelmina's disappearance has affected her," Harold commented. "How is Minnie and her family?"

"That's the good news. Her son and daughter are fine, Roy is already three, and Beulah Belle a year. I'd dearly love to see her children." Chuckling, she held the letter out for Harold to see. "Look how she signed it—Desdemona Diana. No one but our mother has called her anything but Minnie for years. She never gives up."

Harold put down the newspaper he'd been reading. Whenever Jessie received a letter from home she was overcome by homesickness and would start reminiscing about her childhood. Harold would quietly listen to her often-told stories, willing to do nearly anything to make her happy. Jessie knew that in his eyes she was still the pretty, though plump, girl he had married. In reality Jessie had gained weight with each pregnancy and had been unable to shed any of it. And it didn't help that she was an excellent cook who enjoyed her own cooking. Her face was rounder, she had a double chin, and a thick layer of fat covered her entire body. She tired easily, huffing and puffing after any exertion.

Fortunately Eudora was finished with school and was at home full time to help with the girls and the chores.

Eudora didn't mind helping around the house. She always had felt closer to Jessie than Myrtle Foss—or even her own mother for that matter. And she loved her nieces as much as if they were her own—especially Ethel. She would always have a soft spot in her heart for Ethel because she felt responsible for the girl's deformity. Desite countless hours of therapy on the child's arm, it still hung limp and useless at her side. She was only able to lift it a few inches. It looked the same as her other arm, so her affliction wasn't noticeable until she tried to do something which needed two hands. Eudora's heart went out to Ethel everytime she watched her struggle.

But Jessie had decided—and Eudora went along with her decision as best she could—that Ethel must learn to do for herself. It was remarkable how well the girl learned to manage with only one healthy arm.

Eudora's life centered around Jessie and the family, but she did have other interests which went by the names of Charlie, Alvin, Gus, and Terrence. Eudora had become the most sought after belle in the whole of Hill City and the surrounding countryside. The aforenamed gentlemen vied for Eudora's attentions, and she had myriad invitations for weekend events—square dances, picnics, buggy rides.

"How do you ever decide who to say yes to, when those four fellows invite you to the same functions?" Jessie asked her sister.

Eudora patted her dark, red hair which was arranged in a stylish pompdour and smiled coquettishly. "I choose by the occasion rather than the suitor!"

Puzzled, Jessie asked, "What do you mean?"

"Though each is nice enough, I suppose, I'm not overly fond of anyone. After all, I've heard stories all my life about how our father swept mother off her feet. And it's always been obvious to me that you and Harold were truly meant for each other. So, I'm not about to accept second best. The perfect mate is out there somewhere, and I'll come across him eventually. Meanwhile, there certainly is no reason I shouldn't enjoy myself in the interim!"

She knew that neither Harold nor Jessie would understand her reluctance to accept her suitors' many times repeated proposals of marriage. Charlie was a big, rugged, sheriff's deputy, quite handsome, and a most charming escort. Alvin, tall and dark, had a mysterious air about him, though only a clerk in the bank. Gus, a bit older, was a widower and had a small farm on the south side of Hill City. Though heavier set, he was the lightest on his feet and was always her choice when the occasion called for dancing.

Terrence—or Terry, as she usually called him—was the town blacksmith and by far the most fun. Light-hearted and poetic, he could make a walk on a moonlit path the most romantic of endeavors. Weighing them one against the other, she supposed Terrence was in the lead—but not quite enough to make her say 'yes' to him.

And whenever she tired of the persistence of her usual beaus, there was always someone new to come along and try his luck with the unattainable Miss Van Vradenburg. Her aloofness served to keep her life entertaining, while waiting for her true love to materialize.

The years flew by. Jessie was delighted to discover she was pregnant once again. Maybe this time she would have the boy she was so sure Harold desired. Lottie seemed to have accepted Ethel's presence, though mostly ignoring her while Ethel, on the other hand, idolized Lottie and followed her everywhere. Whatever Lottie did or said, Ethel copied her, much to Lottie's disgust.

Eudora continued her various flirtations, though never getting any closer to an engagement

as far as Jessie could tell. Jessie was afraid her
sister's suitors eventually would tire of the
competition and Eudora's indecision, leaving
Eudora an old maid without any prospects for
marriage.

Jessie sat on the front porch with her swollen
feet propped up on a stool. Both of her daughters
were napping and Eudora was off picnicing with
Terrence and several other couples. Harold was in
town doing his duty as deputy sheriff, so Jessie, all
alone, was indulging herself after a busy Saturday
morning of housekeeping and baking. She'd just
eaten a piece of fresh chocolate cake, washed
down with a cool glass of milk, and was enjoying
the cool breezes wafting across her porch.

She realized she must have been dozing when
she was awakened by the sound of horses and
wagons. Wondering who was coming, she hauled
her off-balance body from the chair and waddled
to the porch railing. Squinting, she peered in the
direction of two approaching wagons pulled by
teams of horses. A man and woman walked beside
the first wagon, and another man was riding on
the seat of the second.

She couldn't believe what she saw! "Ma! Ma! Is
it really you?"

The woman running toward her wasn't much
different from the mother she had left behind. Her
hair was still a light red, her sweet face had a few
new lines, and her figure was slim as ever. She
seemed agile and full of energy as she quickly
covered the distance separating them. Jessie carefully stepped down the porch stairs, leaning
heavily on the railing to counterbalance her huge
stomach.

"Jessie, oh, my Jessie," her mother cried as she
reached for her daughter. She hugged her tightly
and kissed her. "Oh, how are you, my darling

girl?"

Tears of happiness flowed freely down Jessie's plump cheeks. "I'm wonderful! But what are you doing here?"

"We've come to live," Mary stated. The first wagon stopped near the porch. Mary held out her hand to the man leading the horses. "Darling, come meet my eldest daughter, Jestina, though everyone calls her Jessie these days."

"I've heard a lot about you," the slight, rather plain man said. "I'm glad to finally meet you."

"Jess, this is my husband, Andrew Cromer."

"Minnie wrote and told me you might be marrying soon. I'm very pleased to meet you, Mr. Cromer. Well . . . we can't stand out here all day. Mr. Cromer, you can take the horses around back to the barn, and just leave the wagons wherever you see fit for now," Jessie directed.

"There's someone else you should say hello to, Jessie. Don't you recognize that young man?" Mary asked.

The tall youth stepped forward. He had outgrown his clothes—his homespun shirt stretched tautly across broad shoulders, his cuffs were three inches above his wrists, and overall bottoms exposed his ankles. He pushed back a straggly lock of dark brown hair and grinned. "Jessie . . . it's me, Willy."

"Willy, Willy. I didn't recognize you at all. How you've grown!" Jessie held her brother against her bosom and when she released him, her eyes were again spilling tears. "I can't believe you're all here. Please, come inside. You must be tired and hungry, and I'm anxious to hear all the news from home!"

Jessie was overjoyed when she realized her mother and stepfather planned to settle nearby if there was available land. The closer the better, Mary indicated, and Mr. Cromer agreed. When Harold returned home later that afternoon he and Mr. Cromer walked to a flat knoll less than a quarter of a mile away, and it immediately was declared a suitable location for a new home.

While Andrew Cromer and Willy built a small house to Mary's specification, Mary took charge of her daughter's household. Mary had been living under her daughter's roof only two days when Jessie gave birth to her third child. Eudora again midwifed for Jessie, and a fat, healthy boy made an easy entrance into the world.

Harold was delighted. After admiring his son, he kissed Jessie and said, "We'll call him Eugene. My best boyhood chum was called Eugene, and I've always hoped for a son I could call Eugene."

When Mary brought in her granddaughters to view their new brother, three-year-old Ethel peered at the wrapped bundle and smiled happily. She ran a finger over the infant's plump cheek. "Hello, baby brother."

Lottie, now five, sniffed and cast a haughty eye in the infant's direction. "Not another one! May I go out and play now?" She ran from the room without waiting for an answer.

"Goodness, what's the matter with her?" Mary asked.

Jessie sighed. "She was the ideal child—when she was the only one. She's not very fond of the idea of sharing life with a brother and sister."

"I've heard of children having that problem. I was fortunate—you all accepted each other quite well. In fact, Jessie, you were extremely fond of your younger sisters and Willy and were a great help to me with the little ones. I'll give Lottie some special attention; perhaps that will help," Mary said.

Mary took her oldest granddaughter under her wing, teaching her to crochet and enlightening her about different herbs and wild flowers. Whatever the chore Mary involved Lottie. And all the time they were together Mary entertained Lottie with stories of the earlier days.

The Cromers moved into their new home before the autumn leaves fell to the ground, and very soon a path was worn between the Robbins' and the Cromers'. Lottie spent more time dashing between the two houses 'than anyone else, dreaming up different excuses to visit her grandmother.

Jessie was grateful her mother was so close—not only because she had missed her during the time they had been separated, but also because she wasn't feeling well. She hadn't gotten back to normal as fast as usual after the birth of her son.

Eugene was nearly three months old and Jessie still hadn't taken over the household chores. It was all she could do to tend to her son's needs. Thankfully, she had Eudora to rely on for the cooking, cleaning, and washing, and her mother to keep Lottie occupied. Fortunately, Ethel was no trouble. More often than not the child sat at Jessie's feet, playing quietly with her rag doll.

For the first time in her life Jessie had no appetite, and when she did eat, often it would all come back up. She knew she was losing weight because her clothes fit loosely, but since basically she was still heavy, no one else noticed.

Discussing her condition with her mother one chilly afternoon, she explained, "I don't know what's wrong. I'm so tired all the time, and I can hardly keep anything in my stomach. I'm really concerned about my milk. Poor little Eugene—I wouldn't want him to suffer."

Mary glanced over at 'poor little Eugene' asleep in his cradle. His cheeks were fat as a squirrel's stuffed with acorns and they glowed a healthy pink. He slept like any well-fed, contented infant. "I wouldn't bother worrying about Eugene," Mary chuckled. "But your problem disturbs me. Maybe you'd better get the doctor out here to take a look at you."

Rolling her eyes heavenward, Jessie sighed. "Dr. Porter? Sakes alive, he wouldn't be able to help me. He can't even help himself. Harold tells me the poor man has nearly drank himself to death. Probably be a blessing to him as well as the town when he does pass on. Then we can get a decent doctor!"

"I wonder, Jessie . . ." Mary hesitated. "Could you possibly be pregnant?"

"Of course not, it's much too soon." Jessie was appalled by the idea. "I've always had two or three years between my babies."

"But there's no rule saying that's the way it always is," Mary commented.

"Well, I know, Mother, but . . ."

Mary lifted an eyebrow and interrupted. "Have you and Harold been intimate since Eugene was born?"

Jessie blushed. What a question for a mother to ask her daughter! Then she remembered a night when Eugene was merely a month old. Harold had awakened in the night and watched her nurse their son, and when she'd retuned Eugene to his cradle and climbed back into bed, Harold had cuddled her in his arms, telling how happy he was to have her for a wife. He had kissed her and murmured words of love, and before either one had time to think, they had made love. And that wasn't the only time!

Mary smiled at Jessie. "You don't even have to

answer. I can tell by the look on your face. Have
you missed a menstrual period?"

"I haven't even had one since Eugene was born,
but that isn't unusual while nursing . . . is it?"

"Under ordinary circumstances, no, but you
sound like you have all the symptoms to me."

"Maybe you're right." At first Jessie frowned at
the idea, then she laughed. "Can you imagine?
That means in less than nine months I could have
another baby. And to think that not very long ago I
was worried I might never have a child!"

Mary leaned over and patted her daughter's
knee. "I'd be willing to bet money you're
pregnant!"

Irwin was the name Harold chose for the little
brother who was born when Eugene was merely
ten months old. Jessie's health immediately
improved after Irwin's birth, and luckily for both
boys she had a more than ample supply of milk.
Her appetite returned, along with her energy, and
she was soon hustling and bustling about the
house.

Harold was proud as could be of his growing
family.

Eudora waited for the man of her dreams while
tantalizing the eligible bachelors of Hill City.

Ethel was happy to be big sister to two baby
boys.

Lottie was as disgusted with Irwin as she had
been with Eugene. But his arrival was easier to
bear because she now had her grandmother. And
luckily for her, she was the only one allowed to
walk alone to her grandmother's, and she did so
quite often.

And by the time Irwin was three months old,
Jessie knew she was pregnant again. "Goodness,
now that I've gotten a good start, it doesn't look

like I'm going to be able to stop," Jessie joked to Harold.

It was as though she marked time by the birth of her children—the most important and recurrent event in her life. To the rest of the community, more significant than Jessie's children, was the railroad coming to the Black Hills.

But to her mother, the most disturbing incident was the note she found on Willy's bed.

Jessie heard her mother crying before she even reached the house. "Something is wrong with Grandma!" Lottie shouted in alarm, holding the door open wide.

Jessie was shocked by her mother's appearance. Tears streaked Mary's face, her body heaving with sobs. Jessie put her arms around Mary and led her to a chair. The distraught woman collapsed into it, burying her face in her hands.

"Mother, please, try to calm down. Tell me what has happened. Is it Mr. Cromer? Has something happened to him?"

Mary shook her head and gasped, "It's Willy. He's disappeared, just like Wilhelmina."

"Oh, no!" Jessie cried, clasping a hand to her mouth. "Could he have been kidnapped?" But she couldn't imagine anyone being able to kidnap a tall, well-built boy of nineteen like her brother Willy—nor any reason why someone would want too.

Mary sighed raggedly, pulled a folded piece of paper from the pocket of her apron and handed it to Jessie. "Read it for yourself."

Jessie read it aloud. " 'Dear Mama, I know I promised I'd never leave you, but that was when there was only the two of us. Now you have Andrew, and Jessie, and Dora, and all the grandchildren, so you don't really need me anymore. I want to go see some new places and make my fortune. I'll be back one of these days. Don't worry. If you need me, I'll come home and take care of you. Love, Willy.' "

Handing the letter back to Mary, she said, "Well, Ma, after all, he's nearly a man."

"It's just like Wilhelmina all over again," Mary moaned.

"Aw, Mama, it's not the same at all. He knew you'd carry on this way—that's why he had to sneak off. He'll be back before you know it. You'll see."

Mary couldn't be comforted. When Harold returned from town she insisted he turn right around and go back to see if anyone had noticed Willy. Andrew went along with him, and they returned with the news that Willy had been seen riding in a wagon with a farmer headed south earlier in the day. Mary wept another round of tears before she finally got herself under control.

"Well! That's enough of that nonsense. Since there's nothing I can do about my boy, I guess I'll just take my Lottie home with me. Let's make a cake," she suggested to the girl who was watching her expectantly. "And, Lottie, why don't you pack your night clothes? I think this would be a good night for you to sleep over at your grandmother's."

Lottie flashed a pleading look at Jessie. Jessie never could turn Lottie down—and her mother certainly needed love and companionship this one night. But one night stretched into two, then another, and another, until Lottie was staying at her grandmother's all the time.

"Don't you think we should put our foot down and make Lottie come home?" Harold asked finally. "She *is* our daughter, after all."

"Oh, Harold," Jessie argued, "what is it hurting? And it does seem to be good for both of them. Lottie is filling the empty place in mother's life left by Willy, and Lottie needs to be a special person to someone—and she is certainly special to mother. It even seems to have improved her disposition. Now, when she comes to visit, she at least is friendly to Ethel and the boys. That's a great improvement over her past behavior."

Harold sratched his still bright, corn silk hair. "Well, when you put it that way . . . it just seems a bit unnatural for my own daughter to have left home at the tender age of eight!"

Chapter 14

Lottie gave the new baby her name. Of course Jessie and Harold had picked out a proper name—Cassie June. But Cassie June was born prematurely, while Jessie had the house torn apart for spring cleaning.

During the required viewing of the newest sibling, Lottie sniffed and laughed disdainfully. "This one is surely the worst of the lot. She looks more like an insect than a baby."

She squinted at the tiny, red, wrinkled infant. "Hi, Cricket." Though probably caused by gas, the baby's tiny mouth turned up at the corners, a big dimple dancing in her cheek.

"Would you look at that, Lottie?" Jessie hugged her oldest daughter. "She likes her nickname. Cricket is what we'll call her."

Lottie made a face at the baby, rolled her eyes, and stomped from the room. Jessie knew Lottie well enough to know she meant the name Cricket as an insult. But somehow, Cricket seemed to fit. Though she was tiny, she was perfect in every way, and apparently healthy. Mary had warned Jessie that premature babies were more susceptible to illness and that Cricket would have to be raised with special care.

Jessie watched Cricket as closely as possible with two other lively toddlers in the house. She was grateful for Ethel's placid nature and her desire to be helpful, since Jessie was well aware that she couldn't keep up with Eugene and Irwin by herself—they were into one mishap after another.

One way day, Eugene and Irwin both fell into the oak tub filled with soapy water. Fortunately Ethel had a watchful eye on them when they pulled a wooden box over to the tub and stood on it. At first the boys had been content to merely watch leaves sailing in the bubbles. When they both leaned over to retrieve their makeshift boats, Ethel watched horrified as first Eugene, then Irwin, slipped headfirst into the water.

Ethel ran to the tub. Reaching in with her good left arm, she scooped Irwin out, dumping him unceremoniously onto the grass. Next she retrieved Eugene, gave him a good shake and scolded, "You stay away from the wash tub! You both might have drowned. Be a good boy, Eugene, and set an example for your little brother!"

Jessie stood at the kitchen door, listening to her young daughter scolding the boys. There was no need for any explanation. The boys' dripping dark hair and the wet streaks staining the front of Ethel's dress told the tale.

A few days later Ethel had to fetch Jessie to help rescue Eugene. How the boy had reached the branches of the oak tree was a mystery, but reach them he had. Unfortunately, once he'd climbed up into the tree, his bravado deserted him and he began to howl. Irwin had run for Ethel, but Ethel was unable to climb the tree because of her bad arm—and neither could Jessie.

Jessie stared up at her young son as he dangled from one of the upper branches, arms and legs clinging tightly. She stood with her hands on her thickly padded hips and surveyed the scene. "You've certainly fixed yourself this time, young man! I can't climb that tree to rescue you!"

"If we get the ladder . . ." a very worried Ethel suggested.

"And which one of us is going to climb up it? You, with only one working arm, or me, who would probably break the first rung I stepped on? No, neither one of us can climb a ladder, and since your father's in town, guess the only thing left is to go for Mr. Cromer. Ethel, run up to your grandmother's and let Mr. Cromer know we need him. Let's just hope your brother can last that long."

Eugene renewed his howling, with Irwin echoing him. "Oh, hush, Irwin," Jessie said after awhile. "Eugene is going to be fine. I just hope both of you have learned a lesson from this."

Andrew arrived and plucked Eugene from his perilous perch. The boy was subdued the remainder of the day but was back to his tricks by nightfall.

Eugene never seemed to learn from his exploits. Instead, he went on to bigger and more dangerous adventures, often with disastrous results. In an attempt to slide down the peaked roof of the barn, he tumbled off the edge and fell to the ground, breaking his leg. At least that kept him safe and quiet for a time.

The leg had barely healed when he shot a hole in his big toe while hunting with his father's gun without parental permission.

The barn was a near casualty when he accidently dropped a candle in the hayloft. Harold was able to put out the fire before too much damage had been done. What was Eugene doing in the hayloft in the middle of the night? "Trying to catch an old owl that lives up there" was his explanation.

Jessie seriously wondered if Eugene would survive his childhood.

In 1888 Jessie gave birth to another girl. This one they called Dessie, and she was as robust at birth as most of the others had been. Cricket at two was still fragile looking, though surprisingly healthy. So far she had not contracted any serious childhood disease and Jessie no longer worried unnecessarily about her.

All her worry was directed toward her mother. Mary, slim all her life, had developed a protruding belly. Old Doc Porter, who had fallen into a drunken stupor one night and never awakened, had been replaced by a younger man. Dr. Sinclair was tall, painfully thin, and had beady eyes which peered through spectacles perched on his beak of a nose. So it was Dr. Sinclair who was called to examine Mary.

Jessie and Andrew waited outside Mary's bedroom door. When the doctor stepped out, he didn't appear particularly happy, though Jessie couldn't think of a time she had ever seen him look particularly happy.

"Well?" Andrew asked. "Is it serious?"

"Yes, it's very serious," Dr. Sinclair said in his deep, almost ominous voice. "Mrs. Cromer has an extremely large growth in her lower intestines—a tumor of some kind. There is nothing I can do for her right now. As times goes on, when it begins to cause her discomfort, I can give her something to ease the pain. I'm sorry . . . there really isn't anything else."

"Doctor," Jessie grabbed his arm, "are you telling me my mother is going to die?"

Dr. Sinclair gently removed Jessie's hand from his arm and nodded his head sadly.

Jessie was shocked. She glanced at Andrew, and saw a film of tears over his eyes and a vein in his forehead bulging. Jessie groped for her stepfather and clung to him, neither one noticing the doctor slip quietly from the house.

"What on earth is all the crying about?" Mary stood in the open doorway of the bedroom.

"Oh, dear, didn't Dr. Sinclair . . ." Jessie began.

"Tell me that I'm dying?" Mary finished. "In a round about way he did, but I find it difficult to believe such news when I feel so well. And I'm certainly not about to lie down and give up because some whippersnapper says I'm going to die! Where's Lottie?"

"I told her you were sick, and she would have to stay at home from now on," Jessie explained.

"You just go right back home and send the child up here to me! If I truly am dying—which I don't believe for an instant—please don't deprive me of my darling Lottie!"

"Whatever you say, Mama."

Two nights later, Jessie and Harold were awakened by pounding on their bedroom door. Jessie first thought Eugene was up to something, then she recognized Lottie's voice.

"Mama, please, can I come in?"

Lottie entered, carrying a lantern, clad only in a nightdress. Her feet were bare, and her dark curls were ashew with stray wisps hanging into her face. "It's grandma!" she cried. "I think she's dying! She wants you and Aunt Dora to come right away!"

"Has Mr. Cromer gone for the doctor?" Jessie asked, hoisting herself out of bed.

"She says she doesn't want the doctor; she only wants you and Aunt Dora. Please hurry!"

Sending Lottie to wake Eudora, Jessie only took time to put on her shoes and wrap a shawl around her shoulders. She brushed her lips against Harold's forehead and met her sister and oldest daughter in the front room.

Walking as fast as she could, Jessie followed along behind Eudora and Lottie. "Oh, Mama, please hurry faster," Lottie pleaded, the light from the lantern illuminating the path which led to the Cromer house.

"Lottie, you and Dora run on ahead. The moon is bright, and I know my way." Relieved to be able to rush ahead, Dora took her niece's hand and they broke into a run.

Jessie slowed to a more comfortable waddle, and as she walked she prayed. "Dear Lord, please don't let my mother suffer." She hoped she would reach the house in time to tell Mary once again how much she loved her.

When Jessie entered the house, she heard voices coming from her mother's and Mr. Cromer's bedroom. Pushing open the door, she was shocked by what she saw.

Lottie was huddled expressionless in a chair in the corner of the room. Mr. Cromer had a silly grin on his face. Mary, whom Jessie had expected to find near death, was sitting propped up by pillows, a strangely euphoric smile on her lips.

Eudora had a small bundle in her arms which she held out to Jessie. "Well, Jessie, come meet our baby brother!"

"Baby brother? What are you saying?" Jessie was unable to comprehend what she was seeing or hearing.

Awkwardly, she accepted the offered bundle and gazed with amazement at the brand new infant. "Is this . . . are you saying . . . Mother . . . you had a baby?"

"Isn't it the funniest thing you ever heard of? I started having some pain right after supper. I figured it was the beginning of the end. After a while I realized there was something very familiar about the pain and told Andrew that if I didn't know better I'd have thought I was in labor. Andrew decided we better bring you girls here, sent Lottie over and Eudora arrived in time to help bring my little tumor into the world."

Jessie stared at her mother, then at the baby in her arms, then back at her mother again. "I . . . I . . . don't know what to say!"

"You could say you're glad I'm not going to die! And you might congratulate Andrew and me on the birth of a fine son!" Mary held her arms out for the baby. "And what shall we name him, Andrew?"

After returning the infant to her mother Jessie shook her head. It was so surprising! She heard Mr. Cromer say, "Let's name him Perry. I've always liked the name."

Remarkable! Jessie had a baby brother named Perry!

Eudora said, "I'm going home now, Mama, but I'll come back first thing in the morning and give you a hand."

"That's nice, dear. Good night, daughters." Mary dismissed them offhandedly, not looking up from the bundle in her arms.

Jessie and Eudora were nearly halfway home when they heard someone running behind them. "Wait for me." It was Lottie, and she was carrying a full burlap sack. "I'm coming home, Mama."

"Oh!" Jessie was surprised once again. "Don't

you think your grandmother will miss you?"

"Grandma won't even notice I'm gone," the girl said bitterly. "Not with that ugly baby to take all her attention."

Harold was sitting in the main room, waiting for news. His face lifted in a broad smile when he saw Lottie with her sack of belongings. "Lottie! What's happened? Are you here for a visit?"

"I'm home for good," Lottie mumbled, disappearing into her bedroom.

Harold frowned. "That doesn't mean your mother has . . ."

"You'd never guess what it means—never in a million years!" Jessie exclaimed.

"You tell him all about it. I'm going to bed." Eudora disappeared into her room.

Harold took hold of Jessie's plump elbow and steered her into the kitchen. "I've got fresh coffee on the stove. Let's have a cup while you tell me whatever the big mystery turned out to be."

Sipping her steaming coffee, Jessie began, "There's no mystery to it. It's shocking, that's what it is. I guess Dr. Sinclair is not any better than old Doc Porter. Mother didn't have a tumor at all—she was pregnant! She just had a baby! Can you imagine that? My mother, at the age of fifty-three, had a baby! I have a baby brother—Perry."

Harold's mouth dropped open. Slowly, the corners of his mouth pulled up, and a rumble of laughter spilled out. "Oh, my, that's hilarious. Poor dear, and all this time she thought she was dying and she was pregnant instead!"

"I don't think it's all that funny." Jessie stood, staring out the kitchen window into the blackness of the night. With her back still turned, she added, "I think it's disgusting."

"Disgusting? What's disgusting?" Harold asked.

"Well, it means that my mother and Mr. Cromer

have been . . . well, you know . . . I hadn't thought
that they still would be . . . .after all, I thought they
were too old to . . .''

Harold started laughing again. ''Oh, Jessie,'' he
chortled. ''We'll see if you feel the same when
you're fifty-three!''

''Harold Robbins! Please! Everyone is going to
know about my mother now. It's downright
embarrassing!''

Chapter 15

"After all, Dora, you're twenty-five! If you don't get married soon you'll be an old maid!" Jessie reiterated often. She had seen Dora's suitors give up one by one, and go off to marry someone else.

"Oh, Jessie, you didn't really expect me to marry any of those fellows, did you? There wasn't a suitable husband in the bunch!" Eudora patted a spit curl that hung over her forehead. She was going off to a dance in Hill City with a man Harold had introduced her to.

Jessie talked to her sister's reflection in the mirror before which she was primping. "You're far too choosy for your own good, young lady. Each and everyone of those former boyfriends of yours—who you called too fat, too old, too ugly, too ignorant or too poor—was quickly snagged by some other girl."

Eudora got up from the stool in front of her dressing table, fluffing the skirt of her party dress.

"How do I look?" She twirled around. The shiny blue, chambray dress was cut a bit decollete, revealing a hint of a full bosom, and was nipped in tightly to her small waist with a gathered skirt falling in gentle fullness over the flare of her hips. When she took a step, the tiniest bit of lacy underskirt was revealed.

"Maybe Harold's friend, Mr. Burleigh, will find me enchanting and sweep me off my feet." Eudora grinned wickedly over her shoulder at her sister and swept into the front room with a rustle of her skirt.

Harold and Mr. Burleigh both jumped to their feet, with Mr. Burleigh offering his hand to her. "Ah, Miss Van Vrandenburg, how delightful you look this evening."

Roscoe Adelmar Burleigh was a tall, rangy sort of man. His sun bleached hair was damp combed off a broad forehead, and his deep set, blue eyes crinkled when he smiled. A drooping moustache perched on his upper lip, beneath a long, thin nose. His mouth was wide, his smile exposing a full set of healthy looking teeth, and his strong chin was divided by an interesting cleft. Eudora didn't put him into the handsome category, but he was pleasant enough looking, and he seemed to be fairly intelligent. She decided Mr. Burleigh did have possibilities.

She smiled demurely and held out her hand. "Mr. Burleigh, good evening."

A smile spread across his face, the blue eyes crinkling in admiration, and he took Eudora's offered hand. "You look lovely, Miss Van Vradenburg." He helped Eudora on with her cape. "I guess we're ready. Good night, Mrs. Robbins, Harold."

"Have a good time," Jessie said.

Outside, Roscoe boosted Eudora up onto the

seat of his borrowed wagon. "Since we're spending the evening together, why not call me Roscoe, and I'll call you Eudora."

"That's fine . . . except Dora will do. That's what everyone except my mother calls me."

"Dora it is." Roscoe pulled himself easily into the wagon, and settling himself beside her, they were on their way.

Roscoe wasn't a bashful man, and he told Eudora all about himself on the way to the dance. He'd studied law in New York, fought in the Civil War, and had been a scout for Custer for a short time. He was glad to be a civilian once again and liked his new job as a deputy for Hill City.

When they reached the large barn where the dance was being held, Roscoe turned to Eudora and said, "I'm surprised you aren't married, a fine looking woman like you."

The brash comment embarrased Eudora, and she felt herself turn crimson. "I haven't found anyone who suited me—not that it's really any of your business!"

"Hmmmm," was all he said. He gripped her waist and swung her to the ground. "Hurry along, now. I can hear the band has already started to play!"

Holding her hand, he pulled her through the open doors of the barn and she had to do a running step to keep up with him. The place was crowded with couples Eudora knew, with a few strangers scattered here and there. Roscoe put his arm around her, guiding her onto the dance floor, and Eudora was pleasantly surprised to find he was an excellent dancer, light on his feet and easy to follow. Twirling and leading her all over the room, they danced until the musicians stopped to rest.

"Oh, my, that was fun!" Eudora cried breathlessly. "But, oh, let's find a place to sit, please!"

Roscoe found her a spot on a plank bench, but before he could sit down beside her, someone called out, "Hello there, Roscoe."

Eudora looked up to see one of her old beaus, Charlie, shaking hands with her escort.

"Hi there, Dora," he said. "Going to try your hand at breaking the new deputy's heart, eh?"

"Why, Charlie. I'm going to do nothing of the kind!" Dora declared.

Charlie elbowed Roscoe in the ribs. "That's what she says! You watch out for her. She has the reputation of being the worst heart breaker in the whole county—and I know from experience!"

Dora glared at Charlie, wondering what had gotten into the big, loud-mouthed goon. She was relieved when he spotted someone else. "Oh, there's an old buddy of mine I haven't seen in a coon's age. I gotta go, but do heed my warning, Roscoe—watch out for this gal."

"Oh, what a silly man," Dora groaned.

"I don't know . . . maybe friendly would be a better word. It was right neighborly of him to alert me to your ways," Roscoe teased. "After all, I'm not looking for a broken heart."

Eudora sighed loudly. "He's ridiculous! I never gave him any reason to feel the least bit heart-broken. I went out with him a few times, and that's all!"

"And you obviously found him unsuitable—as you put it—and discarded him. The poor chap is still suffering!"

"Oh, piffle! He's suffering so much he's married to Annabelle over there, and they're expecting their second child." Eudora pointed to a small woman, midway through a pregnancy, visiting with a group of ladies.

"Ah, but he had to take second best. And from the envious glances I've been receiving from several of the men here this evening, there seems to be a bunch of broken hearts littering your past. But it's no wonder . . . you are certainly the finest looking female here!"

"Sir, you are teasing me," she reproved.

"Yes, I admit that I am," he chuckled. "I like the fire in your eyes when you're annoyed. But I was speaking honestly about your being the best looking gal here."

"Goodness . . . well, thank you." Eudora, who usually felt in command with her flirtations, suddenly felt at a loss. The music began, and she jumped to her feet. "Let's dance some more."

Roscoe didn't tease her anymore that evening. When he brought her home, escorting her to the door, he remarked, "I'd like to call on you again—with your permission, of course."

"Yes, of course."

He shook her hand, turned, and leaped down the stairs of the porch. Eudora stared after him, surprised by his abruptness. "I had a lovely time," she called out as he rode off.

Roscoe Burleigh became a regular visitor at the Robbins home. Eudora wasn't sure whether he came to visit her or her sister and brother-in-law. He ate Sunday dinner with them when he wasn't working, and he lavished compliments on Jessie's cooking, when she prepared special treats for him.

After one of these gigantic meals had been consumed, Roscoe would disappear with Harold and Andrew to the front porch. The children would play, while the women took care of the dishes.

On one of these Sundays, while Jessie washed and Mary dried and Eudora stacked, Mary asked, "Has he proposed yet, dear?"

"No, and I'm not sure he intends to," Eudora

answered sharply.

Jessie, with her hands in the sudsy water, commented, "My little sister has no patience. She was spoiled by her other suitors who fell all over themselves trying to please her. But they were all country boys. Roscoe is different; he's educated and well traveled and a little harder to please."

"He's certainly different," Eudora agreed. "So far he's the only man I would marry, and he hasn't even hinted at a proposal. There are times he treats me like we were already married—like right now. Here I am, cleaning up after dinner, and there he is, out on the porch swapping tales with all the men. He's hardly said more than 'hello' to me."

Eudora pouted as she vigorously wiped a large pot. When Jessie momentarily left to settle a dispute between Eugene and Irwin, Mary took pity on her daughter. "Why don't you step out on the porch and see if you can't tempt Roscoe into taking a walk."

"But there's still a lot of dishes . . ."

"Go ahead," Mary urged. "I'll get Lottie to come in and take your place, and besides, we're nearly done here. I'm sure the babies will be waking soon and Jessie and I will be busy with them for a while. Go on."

Eudora pulled off her apron and hung it on a door knob. Glancing at herself in the mirror hanging in the main room, she tucked up a corner strand of hair escaping from her pompadour and slipped outside onto the porch. Roscoe was seated alone on the porch swing, and Eudora slid in beside him. He smiled abstractedly in her direction, but kept his attention on the conversation.

"I didn't figure we'd have any more trouble from Sitting Bull when he came back to these parts. I heard he was living quietly on the

Standing Rock Reservation," Harold commented.

Roscoe smoothed his droopy moustache with his long fingers, and stated, "Everyone thought Sitting Bull would probably end his days peacefully, but I've heard things have gotten badly out of hand."

"So what is it that's happening?" Andrew asked.

Roscoe hung his arm casually over Eudora's shoulder while bringing Harold and Andrew up-to-date on the Indian situation. "It seems there's this Paiute Indian by the name of Wavoka who's started some sort of religious carryings-on. They call it the Ghost Dance, and it's spread all over the Sioux nation. Supposedly this Wovoka was born in Nevada and his father was a prophet. When his family was killed by soldiers, settlers adopted him and he lived for years like a white man—went by the name Jack Wilson.

"The story goes he was sick with a fever—nearly died—and he had a dream. In this dream he was lifted to the sky, the Great Spirit talked to him, and he saw all the Indians who had died living a happy life. The Great Spirit taught Wavoka some songs and this new dance. He told him to teach the Indians to end their fighting and lead good lives— and they would never be sick, or go hungry, or grow old."

Harold hunched his shoulders and frowned. "So what's the problem?"

Roscoe squeezed Eudora's shoulder and continued, "The problem is they get all worked up when they do this Ghost Dance, so wild that the authorities have outlawed the practice of the whole religion. The Indians do the dance and chant anyway, and when the soldiers try to arrest them, the fighting breaks out. Indians are killing the white man again—and vice versa."

"I don't see why they don't let the Indians go

ahead and do what they want. What's wrong with a little dancing and singing? How can it hurt anything?" Eudora interjected.

Roscoe stared at her directly. "What it's hurting, my dear, is the law. The Indians are breaking the law. And once the dance had been outlawed, the soldiers had to enforce the law, didn't they?"

"I guess so," Eudora agreed reluctantly, though the whole situation sounded stupid to her.

Continuing, Roscoe said, "I guess it's an impressive dance, and I hear the Indians have made special buckskin dresses to wear—blue and red with fancy painting on them."

"Roscoe, why don't we go for a walk?" Eudora suggested quietly.

"What?" Roscoe frowned, but then quickly smiled. "Oh, sure, why not. Excuse me, but the little lady has requested the pleasure of my company."

Roscoe and Eudora walked side by side without speaking until they reached a favorite spot of Eudora's on the bank of a stream which meandered through the vale. There was a large, flat rock that provided a natural seat, with an overhanging willow tree to shade it.

"This is my special place," Eudora said while arranging her skirt as she sat down on the stone.

"It's not quite as pretty as usual though. It's been so dry this year, and the stream isn't nearly as full." South Dakota was into its second year of drought, but fortunately for the Robbins and the Cromers, the underground spring which fed their wells continued to flow freely. Other people in the area were less fortunate and were beginning to suffer the effects of the drought.

Roscoe stood directly in front of Eudora, his hands resting on either side of her. "It is lovely," he said, though not taking his eyes from her face.

Eudora, feeling uncomfortable under his scrutiny, suggested, "Perhaps we should start back."

"Don't be in such a hurry," he said. "I'm trying to find the right words to say what's in my heart."

Endora's own heart leaped as Roscoe took her hands. "You know I have deep feelings for you."

Eudora hadn't known that at all. She, of course, hoped he had similar emotions to her own, but she wasn't about to voice this and interrupt him.

"I'm planning on our marriage—however there are some things I must attend to first."

Eudora rankled at this presumptuous statement. "Don't you think you should ask how I feel about the idea first?"

Roscoe grinned. "I already know how you feel. You're ready to get married—maybe even more ready than I am—and I know I'm the first man you've wanted to marry."

"Is that so? You do have your nerve, don't you?" She jerked her hands from his grasp and slid down the rock, intending to walk home. But before she was able to take a step, Roscoe grabbed her shoulders, pulling her against him.

"No, I don't think I have a lot of nerve. I was just speaking the simple truth. I'm interested in you, and it's obvious you feel the same about me. I want us to marry, but it isn't quite time yet. The only reason I'm telling you of my intention is so you won't get tired of waiting and maybe do something foolish."

Before she could argue, he pressed his lips hard against hers. She fought against him at first, but quickly realized she was finally where she'd had been dreaming about for weeks—in Roscoe's arms. She relaxed and returned his kiss, savoring the taste of his lips.

Roscoe pushed her away, abruptly. Eudora blinked in surprise. "Whatever is the matter?"

Roscoe smiled quizzically. "Nothing, my dear, nothing at all. But we can't carry on this way— not with our wedding still somewhere off in the future."

"Oh." Eudora's voice was tiny. "But I don't understand why we have to wait."

Roscoe cupped her chin in his palm and stared into her eyes. "I have plans, my dear Dora, and that's all that's necessary for you to know at the moment. Don't fret, because it all ties in with our future together. Now I think it's time we returned to your family. Why not make the announcement of our engagement to them?"

Roscoe held her hand, and she ran to keep up with his long strides. Though happy, she was somewhat mad—he was so damned condescending! If he truly wanted to marry her, why on earth couldn't he reveal his plans? It was her life too, wasn't it? She had half a mind to tell him to forget the whole thing, but she remembered how his strong arms felt as he held her against his hard body. She'd been kissed before, many times, but never before was a kiss so thrilling.

They reached the house to find the whole family seated on the porch, enjoying the late afternoon breeze. Roscoe stood at the bottom of the stairs, his hand around her waist, and in his deep voice, announced, "We have some exciting news. Eudora has consented to be my wife."

The air was filled with good wishes and congratulations, though no one seemed particularly surprised. Mary asked the inevitable question: "When are you planning on tying the knot?"

Eudora glanced at Roscoe, curious as to his answer. He ruffled his straight, blond hair, smoothing it to the side with his fingers. "We've decided to wait a bit. Give us a chance to become better acquainted. Also I have some business to take care of first."

Eudora found herself getting riled again that she had no say in the decision to wait. If it was up to her, she'd be married as soon as possible. What an exasperating man! She glared at him, but he didn't even notice as he settled himself into an empty chair. She felt her cheeks burn, but her fiance didn't cast another glance in her direction until he was ready to take his leave.

Roscoe thanked Jessie for the meal, told Harold he'd see him in town on Monday, bid everyone else goodbye, then took Eudora's hand and led her away from the porch. All sorts of sharp comments popped into her head.

But when he finally looked her straight in the eye, he was grinning in his endearing way. He hugged her tightly and brushed his lips against her ear. All thoughts were dashed from her head except that she loved him and wished he would hold her forever.

The embrace was all too short. He pulled away, grinning again. "I'll be by in a day or two," he said, swinging himself into the saddle of his horse and riding away.

Eudora stared after him, watching until he disappeared. Her longing again turned into irritation when she realized he hadn't even given her an opportunity to voice her opinion. She stamped her foot and growled. "Oh, that man!"

"What's the matter, Aunt Dora?" She was surprised to see Ethel standing beside her, holding two-year-old Cricket by the hand.

"Nothing, dear." Eudora laughed.

"Mr. Burleigh is a real nice man," Ethel said.

"Yes, he is," Eudora agreed. "Why don't I give

you a hand getting Cricket ready for bed? Then we can round up Eugene and Irwin and get them settled. After that I'll play you a game of checkers —would you like that?'' Eudora scooped up tiny Cricket and carried her into the house.

Chapter 16

The winter took its toll on Jessie. Though there was little rain and the snow fell lightly, it had been bitter cold. Jessie complained of dizzy spells and shortness of breath, spending many afternoons resting. Some days she could barely climb out of bed. Lottie, now thirteen, had to take over more of the household chores, and Eudora was teaching her to cook.

"You know, Lottie, one of these days Roscoe and I will be married, and you're going to have to help your mother with all the chores," Eudora explained.

Lottie tossed her curls and sniffed. "If Mama wasn't so fat she wouldn't be sick all the time!"

"I'm sure Jessie's weight has a lot to do with her poor health, but the fact is, she isn't well and has to have lots of help."

Lottie made a face. "I'll do anything but take care of the brats."

Eudora hugged Lottie. "I know you will, honey. And that's fine because Ethel loves to take care of your brothers and sisters."

Lottie did do a good job helping, but she did it grudgingly. "When I grow up I'm going to marry a rich man and have servants," she often bragged to her sister. "And I won't have any children!"

She kept the boys busy too, ordering them around, and they knew she'd whack them if they didn't obey. She had them scrubbing floors, cleaning lamps, washing dishes, and churning butter. Cricket and Ethel helped with the dusting, sweeping, and folding the wash.

As soon as the weather turned warmer, Lottie had the boys put the garden in order for planting. She kept them so busy they didn't have time to get into much trouble.

The wild flowers were blooming profusely when Roscoe finally told Eudora the time had come for their marriage. He surprised Eudora by visiting on a weekday afternoon and asking her to take a stroll. Myriads of blossoms brightened the meadow, and Eudora recognized bluebells, forget-me-nots, Lady slippers, and larkspur.

Roscoe stopped beside a tall pine and held her by the shoulders. Eudora knew she'd never forget how the sun made a halo of his golden hair, or the way his blue eyes twinkled, or the funny way his mouth pulled to one side under the drooping moustache when he smiled. "I have wonderful news! I wanted to be the first to tell you—that's why I came by."

"What is it? Goodness, don't keep me in suspense."

"I've been appointed the new sheriff of Hill City," he announced proudly.

Eudora mirrored his smile. "Oh, Roscoe, that is good news. I know how much you wanted the job."

The sheriff of many years had retired, and the job had remained unfilled until the circuit judge could come to appoint a new one. There had been quite a bit of speculation as to whom the new sheriff would be. Some thought Charlie Tankersly would be chosen as he had been a deputy the longest—except for Harold. But Harold was only part-time and wanted it to stay that way. Others thought Roscoe should be the new sheriff because of his education in law and his past experience as a soldier. Obviously the judge agreed.

Roscoe's smile disappeared, and he said seriously, "Do you know what this job means?"

Eudora shook her head.

"It means, my dear, that you and I can finally get married! I now have the kind of job befitting the husband of Mrs. Eudora Burleigh!"

Those were the very words Eudora had been longing to hear. But instead of being overjoyed, she was dismayed, tears stinging her eyes. "Roscoe, I can't marry you right now."

"What do you mean?" Roscoe searched her face for an answer. "I know your feelings for me haven't changed."

"It has nothing to do with how I feel," Eudora gasped. "It's Jessie!"

"What has Jessie got to do with whether or not we get married? I know she approves of me . . ."

Eudora interrupted. "It's nothing like that. It's Jessie's health. Somedays she can barely get around. I can't leave her and all the children now—they need me too much!"

"But you have to live your own life too."

Eudora smiled through the tears which were spilling from her eyes. "I would like to more than you'll ever know, but I have an obligation to Jessie. She brought me up and means more to me than my own mother."

"That's the answer—your mother! She can give Jessie a hand," Roscoe stated.

Eudora rested her head against his chest and sighed. "No, that can't be. Remember mother's house is nearly a quarter of a mile away. Eugene and Irwin cause one catastrophe after another, and though Lottie is learning how to care for the house, she is, after all, only fourteen. And Ethel, bless her—the oldest eleven-year-old in the world —cares for Cricket and Dessie as well as any grown person could. But as far as my mother is concerned, she has her hands full with my little brother, Perry."

Roscoe absently stroked Eudora's back and kissed her temple. "We're going to get married . . . and soon. Don't you fret. I'll figure out something."

Pulling slightly away from Roscoe, Eudora said, "Don't you dare say anything about this to Jessie. She would be so upset if she knew she was standing in the way of our marriage!"

"No, of course I won't . . . but I will come up with a solution, you'll see."

They returned in time to see Eugene come flying around the corner of the house. Irwin, who had been sitting on the ground, jumped to his feet, and with his head turned to look over his shoulder, ran full blast into Eugene. Eudora gasped, Roscoe shouted a warning, but it was too late.

The impact of the two boys' heads slamming together was sickening. Silence prevailed momentarily, then Eugene and Irwin dropped to the ground, their piercing shrieks filling the air.

Eudora and Roscoe covered the space separating them from the boys in seconds. Roscoe scraped up Eugene, and Eudora gathered Irwin into her arms. Eugene's eye was swelling shut and discoloring at an alarming speed, while blood spurted from his nose. Irwin had a lump growing on his forehead, his lower lip was puffing, and blood poured from a jagged wound.

Jessie appeared on the porch. "Oh, my Lord," she cried, "what have they done to each other now?"

"I think it looks worse than it is," Roscoe assured her. He carried Eugene inside the house, Eudora right behind with Irwin, both boys wailing at full capacity. Roscoe shouted over the din, "Once we clean them up we can see how bad it really is."

Even after washing away the blood, the boys' injuries were alarming to view. Eugene's eye was completely shut, grossly swollen and a deep purple. Irwin's forehead looked like a goose egg was jammed under his skin and was oddly discolored. His lower lip, still oozing, was puffed out in a lopsided pout.

Eudora fixed cool compresses for them, and once they quit crying, they began to enjoy the attention. Cricket was staring at their misshapen faces in bug-eyed fascination, while Dessie joined the hullabaloo by crying in her cradle. Jessie fussed and petted, and Ethel brought in a plate of freshly baked cookies and cups of cool milk. Only Lottie afforded them disdainful glances, continuing about her business.

Once the excitement was over, Eudora walked onto the front porch with Roscoe and said, "See? That's an example of what I was telling you. Those boys are always doing something disastrous. I just can't desert them."

Roscoe smiled at Eudora, his blue eyes twinkling. "I understand. But don't worry, I've already got an idea turning in my head."

As promised, Roscoe didn't mention Eudora's reluctance to marry and leave home to Jessie,

however, it soon became obvious that he and
Harold had discussed the subject.

Early one morning Roscoe appeared with a load
of lumber piled high in a newly purchased wagon.
Eudora was alerted to his arrival by the squeals
and hollers of Eugene and Irwin. As she stepped
onto the porch, the boys were yelling questions at
Roscoe who was still in the wagon.

"What's all the wood for, huh?" Eugene asked.

Irwin shouted, "Is that for us?"

"Is my Paw gonna build something?"

"Hold on, boys, I'll explain in a minute. Come on
down here, Dora. You're just the one I was looking
for," Roscoe instructed.

Eudora peered curiously at Roscoe and did as
he bid. "Whatever is all this for?"

"My dear, it's the beginning of our home," he
said proudly.

Eudora frowned. "But you know what I told
you."

"Yes, indeed I do. But our house is going to be
built right over there." He gestured to a nearby
clearing, edged with oak and spruce trees.

"I'm not sure I understand . . ." Eudora began.

"It's all quite simple. Harold suggested we build
our home in that spot. It's certainly a perfect
building site, don't you agree?"

"Yes, I guess so, but . . ."

"And you must admit, you'll certainly be close
enough to keep an eye on all the children, and lend
a hand to Jessie when necessary, won't you?"

Eudora was amazed. All she could do was nod
her head.

Roscoe continued, "Well, quit arguing—unless
there's some other reason why you can't marry
me." He paused, waited for her to say something,
and when she didn't, added, "Climb on up here
beside me and we'll go take a look. You can tell me

what you'd like your house to be like."

Eudora discovered another facet of Roscoe's personality while the house was being built—he was a perfectionist. The raising of their home took longer than Eudora had expected. Roscoe had to oversee the pounding of each and every nail, so building could only go on when Roscoe wasn't working. And now that Roscoe was the sheriff, that wasn't very often. The construction of Eudora's home was a slow process, and the marriage continued to be delayed.

Finally, by the end of 1889, the house was completed. Eudora and Roscoe were married by Roscoe's friend, Judge Wilcox, on New Year's Eve in Jessie's living room. The witnesses were Jessie, Harold, their children, Mary, Andrew, and little Perry.

Eudora wore a light blue, satin dress of her own making, with a lace scarf borrowed from Jessie over her copper curls. She held Roscoe's hand and found it hard to believe it was finally happening. All the children surrounding them were dressed in their Sunday finest with their faces scrubbed pink. Jessie and Harold stood on either side of them. Eudora scarcely heard Judge Wilcox's phrases; she clung to Roscoe's hand, her legs feeling wobbly.

The words "I now pronounce you man and wife" were the only ones that registered. It had finally happened! She faced Roscoe, who embraced her and kissed her for a long, wonderful time.

When he finally released her, the room seemed to explode with happiness. Everyone was kissing and hugging them, wishing them a long, happy life together.

Eudora would remember Jessie's two oldest daughters the most. Lottie, looking quite beautiful and grown-up, with her dark curls caught up with a ribbon, offered her congratulations, adding, "I'll be married soon too. You'll see."

"Oh, Lottie, you don't even want to consider such a thing. You're scarcely more than a child," Eudora said.

"I'm expected to do a woman's work."

Eudora put an arm around her. "Honey, I'll be near, and I'll help you. You aren't going to be left with it all." Lottie's mouth wavered in a half-smile, and she slipped out of Eudora's hug. Eudora knew her niece doubted her words.

Later, Ethel, with her right arm hanging limply at her side, kissed Eudora on the cheek. Her big eyes glowed with excitement. "Aunt Dora, you're the most beautiful bride, and when I grow up I want to be a beautiful bride just like you."

After the youngest children were fed and put to bed, Jessie and Mary served a midnight feast, and both the marriage and the New Year were celebrated together. When all had eaten and drunk their fill, Eudora began to clear the table.

Jessie stayed her sister's hand. "Not tonight. This is one time you won't be helping with the dishes. I'm sure your new husband has other ideas how the rest of the night should be spent."

Eudora blushed at her sister's words. Glancing at Roscoe, she knew by the look on his face he'd overheard, and she blushed even more. Roscoe stood, putting his hand possessively on Eudora's waist.

"Mrs. Burleigh, I do believe it's time we excused ourselves and returned to our new home," he proclaimed.

Eudora bowed her head to hide her flaming cheeks. She heard her sister and her mother tittering, while Harold guffawed loudly.

Eudora found herself clutching Roscoe's hand

tightly as they ran into the cold night and across
the yard to their house. The warm glow of a lamp
in the window spilled out across the bare ground.
Reaching the front door, Roscoe scooped Eudora
into his arms and carried her over the threshold
into the living room.

He swung her around, and she saw a dizzy swirl
of her furnishings. Kicking the door shut, he
carried her into their bedroom and set her on her
feet. "Mrs. Burleigh, I have yearned for this night
for so long. I'd like to help you undress."

She felt silly. She was perfectly capable of undressing herself, but perhaps it was something
bridegrooms did, so she turned and allowed him
to unhook the back of her dress. He gently turned
her to face him again and slipped the gown over
her arms and down to the floor. She stepped out of
it, and he carried it to the chair, arranging it carefully over the back. He unfastened each of her
petticoats, placing them on top of the dress.

He helped her out of her camisole top and lacy
drawers as carefully as if he were unwrapping the
tissue from a porcelain figurine. She stood still,
totally nude, while Roscoe stepped back, letting
his eyes wander slowly over her body.

He gasped and she wondered if he was pleased—
or perhaps disappointed—by what he saw. She
knew she probably was not the first naked woman
he had ever seen. Maybe she didn't measure up to
the others!

Silently, he continued to stare, but started shedding his own clothing with much greater haste
than he had taken with hers, leaving everything
where it fell. He had a bit of a struggle with his
boots, causing Eudora to giggle. His body was pale
in the faint glow from the lamp, though his chest
was covered with curly, brown hair. But as he
leaned over to pull at his boot, his lean buttocks

shone pink.

With his boots finally off, he lifted her into his arms as before, placing her gently on their new feather bed, then getting in beside her.

When he took her into his arms, he pressed the length of his body against her, and Eudora sighed with happiness. She felt so right to have her bosom soft against his muscular chest, their legs intertwined. Though Eudora came to her nuptial bed a virgin, she had been eagerly anticipating this night and came to her husband with great expectation.

Gentle and tender, Roscoe made Eudora truly his, and she was satisfied and surprised by her own feelings. When it was over she rested her head on his shoulder, caressing his cheek with her fingertips.

He spoke for the first time since he'd begun undressing her. "Eudora, I hope you are half as happy to be my wife as I am to be your husband."

Relief came over her, and she released a sigh. "Thank goodness. I've been so afraid when you didn't say anything that somehow I was a disappointment to you."

Roscoe laughed so hard he shook the bed. "A disappointment? Oh, my dear, far from it! You were so much more beautiful than I had imagined, I couldn't find the words to express my feelings. And how about you? Was my lovemaking terribly strange?"

Eudora giggled, kissing Roscoe's earlobe. "I'm afraid you might think me loose if I told you my true feelings."

Roscoe raised himself on his elbow and gazed at her sternly. "That is something we must get straight from the beginning. There must be no secrets between us. We should always be honest with one another. Agreed?"

"Oh, yes, that sounds like a fine idea."

"Tell me, then," Roscoe urged, "what did you think about the consummation of our marriage?"

"Jessie warned me about what to expect . . . she even told me it could be fun. She said it might hurt a bit at first, but if I'd relax, I'd enjoy it."

"So . . . did you?"

"Oh, yes, it was wonderful. Could we do it again?"

Roscoe laughed joyously and squeezed his new bride. "Oh, Lord, thank you for blessing me with a wife like my Eudora!"

But she was unable to comment further, because his mouth covered hers, and his hands caressed her body—and she no longer remembered what it was she wanted to say.

Chapter 17

In January of the following year, Roscoe and Eudora's marriage was blessed by the birth of a daughter, Hazel May. To the Burleighs, the tiny girl, with her auburn curls, was the culmination of their perfect love.

With some effort, Eudora managed to run both her and Jessie's households. With the older children in school, Jessie was usually able to care for her two toddlers and Eudora's Hazel, while Eudora took on the heavier chores.

Eugene and Irwin seemed less accident prone. Both boys had become hunters, having accompanied Harold, Roscoe, and Andrew on numerous forays for deer, elk, and wild turkey. On their own, the pair fished the various streams throughout the valley, catching brook and rainbow trout, a welcome addition to the dinner table.

Hearing her sister's scream, Eudora snatched

up three-year-old Hazel and ran toward Jessie's house.

Eudora dashed through the front door, stopping short when she saw all of Jessie's children peering into one of the bedrooms. Fearing the object of their silent stares, Eudora pictured her sister unconscious—or worse. She set Hazel on the floor, pushed Ethel and Eugene aside, entered the bedroom shared by Lottie and Ethel, and was surprised and relieved by what she saw.

Jessie was very much alive, standing in the center of the room, tears streaking her puffy cheeks, while shaking her head from side to side.

"Whatever is going on here?" Eudora cried.

"She's gone! Someone must've stolen her, just like our sister, Wilhelmina," Jessie wailed.

"Lottie? It's Lottie who's gone?" Eudora's eyes darted around the room. One of the beds was disarranged, the other neatly made. Eudora stepped to the wardrobe and saw that there were obviously clothes missing. She yanked open the dresser drawers and found half of them empty.

"These drawers are Lottie's?" Eudora asked Ethel.

The girl stepped inside the room and answered, "Yes, Aunt Dora." Ethel rummaged through the clothes remaining in the wardrobe and peered into the empty drawers. "None of Lottie's clothes are here."

"That tells me something—whatever she did, wherever she went, she had time to pack," Eudora surmised. "Is the made-up bed Lottie's?"

Ethel nodded, and Jessie wailed.

"She probably left last night after everyone was asleep. You didn't wake up, or hear anything, Ethel?"

Ethel hung her head. "No, ma'am."

Eudora patted her niece's shoulder. "Don't be

upset. It isn't your fault. No doubt Lottie was very careful not to wake you. But at least, now you know, Jessie, she wasn't kidnapped. She obviously left on her own free will."

"But why would she do that?" Jessie cried. "She has a good home, and we all love her."

Eudora put her arms around her sister in an effort to comfort her. "I certainly don't have the answer."

"I bet she went to find a rich husband," Ethel offered in a meek voice. "She was always saying one of these days she was leaving to find a rich man."

"Oh, oh, oh," Jessie moaned. "My heart is palpitating so that I think I'm going to faint." Her puffy face was drained of color, and her forehead was covered with beads of perspiration. She leaned heavily against Eudora.

"Do you think you can make it into your bedroom?" Eudora was alarmed by the unhealthy pallor of her sister's skin. Jessie nodded, fanning at her face with her plump hand.

"Ethel, run and get some cold compresses," Eudora ordered. The rest of the children stepped aside, frightened into an unnatural quiet.

Eudora helped Jessie into her room, and the overweight woman collapsed on the bed. Her breath came in shallow gasps, her eyelids fluttering. Ethel ran in with the dampened rags, and Eudora instructed her to put one on her mother's forehead and one on each wrist.

Going into the main room, Eudora grasped Eugene's shoulders and asked, "Do you think you could ride into town, find your father and tell him we need Dr. Sinclair?"

"Yes, ma'am!" The eleven-year-old dashed from the house.

Eudora turned to Irwin, instructing him to run

up the hill and fetch his grandmother. Taking hold of Cricket's and Dessie's hands, Eudora said, "Girls, I want you to be real quiet now and keep Hazel entertained. You can do that, can't you?"

The girls, now eight and six, nodded solemnly, and each of them went to either side of their three-year-old cousin and led her off towards the kitchen. Eudora rushed back into the bedroom where a worried Ethel ministered to her mother.

"How is she?" Eudora asked.

"She's breathing real funny, Aunt Dora," Ethel said.

"Mother will know what to do," Eudora said more to herself than to her niece. "Why don't you fan her? Maybe the breeze will help her catch her breath." Eudora wasn't sure if it would help, but it couldn't hurt. Ethel picked up an oriental fan from the top of the dresser, waving it vigorously over her mother's head.

Mary finally burst through the door. "What's been going on here? Irwin said something about Lottie running off, and Jessie collapsing . . ."

"That's about the way it is. I sent Eugene to town after Harold and the doctor," Eudora said.

Mary rolled her eyes. "Hope the boy doesn't dillydally. He never was one to follow instructions."

"I think he will this time," Eudora explained. "He was pretty upset by his mother's attack—and so are all the rest of us."

Stepping to the bedside, Mary slapped Jessie's wrists one at a time, keeping her eyes on Jessie's face, but there was no reaction. Lifting her eyelids gently with her thumb, Mary inspected her eyes. She made a clucking sound with her tongue. "She's just too fat! All that blubber around her heart doesn't do her a bit of good!"

Eudora asked, "Where's Irwin?" They didn't

need to have another lost child.

"I left him with Perry. Told him to keep an eye on the baby for me. And Andrew can keep an eye on both of them."

Though it was obvious Mary didn't have any more idea what should be done for Jessie than Eudora did, her mother's confident presence was a comfort and made waiting for the doctor a bit easier.

When Dr. Sinclair arrived and listened to Jessie's heart and felt her pulse, he announced solemnly, "Her blood pressure is dangerously high. She must rest. I'll leave some medicine—she should take a teaspoonful before meals."

Eudora noticed Harold standing in the doorway, his hand resting on Eugene's shoulder. Her brother-in-law, usually a placid, easygoing man, had a deep crease on his forehead, and his eyes were shadowed with worry. "Why is she so still?"

"She's asleep. The shock she received didn't help her condition any, and in the future, you all must take care not to upset her. Any bad news might cause her to have another attack like this. But the best medicine for her right now is rest."

After the doctor left, Mary put on a pot of coffee and coaxed Harold and Eudora into the kitchen. "What good is it going to do Jessie for us to watch her sleep?" she asked.

Eudora absently began wiping down the kitchen surfaces, while Harold paced back and forth. "How can I keep Jessie from worrying about Lottie? The foolish girl! I can't imagine what got into her to run off like this."

Mary shrugged her shoulders. "Nothing new got into Lottie—she's always been a strange child. She has too much spirit . . . and to be frank, she was stifled around here."

"Mother!" Eudora scolded.

Mary ignored her daughter. "Lottie wasn't meant to be cooped up in a house all day, doing household chores and tending to the little ones."

"And what else is a young woman supposed to do?" Eudora asked sharply.

"There isn't much else, to be sure, but Lottie needed the chance to see that for herself." Mary poured them each a cup of coffee. "Now, you two, set a spell and drink your coffee."

"Poor Jessie, she'll never get over this! She'll worry and fret about Lottie and never get well," Harold moaned.

Mary patted her son-in-law's shoulder. "Oh, she'll worry and fret a bit, it's true, but pretty soon the pain won't be so bad and she'll realize she has to go on living. There's other's who need her. That's just the way it is. Life continues, no matter what."

Eudora knew her mother was speaking from her own experience and what she had gone through when Wilhelmina had disappeared. "There are certainly plenty of youngsters still around to keep her mind occupied. Harold, did you see Roscoe to tell him what happened?"

Harold swallowed a mouthful of coffee. "Yes, Eugene found us together in the sheriff's office. Roscoe is checking around now to see if he can find out anything about Lottie."

Roscoe managed to gather several reports concerning Lottie. Mr. Pratt reported he saw her board the evening train, heading east. Old Mrs. Attebury was sure she'd seen a young lady of Lottie's description waiting for the early morning train that was westward bound. The owner of one of the hotels stated he's seen her ride off in a wagon with one of his guests, a salesman named Jones. One of her school chums, Lila Mae Guthrie, reported she'd been looking out of her bedroom window along about midnight and was surprised to see her dear friend perched atop a horse, clinging to a mysterious stranger. She was unable to describe the man as they had galloped past at great speed. But Lottie she could recognize anywhere!

Roscoe was unable to verify any of the accounts.

A year passed before any word was heard from Lottie, and then it came in the form of a letter. Surprisingly, Lila Mae Guthrie's account had been the accurate one. Lottie had met a gambling man who was passing through Hill City, and she had easily convinced him to carry her off with him when he departed. They were married, and now Lottie was the mother of a baby girl.

They heard from Lottie at irregular intervals from then on. The letters announced the birth of a series of daughters, six in all. She also had a series of husbands—at least five. What became of the former husbands was never explained.

Jessie did survive Lottie's departure and soon didn't have the time or energy to waste thoughts of Lottie, for another problem developed. And it came from a most unexpected source!

Chapter 18

"Mother, I'd like you to meet David Catlow."

Jessie glanced up from the peas she was shelling. Fourteen-year-old Ethel had come into the kitchen leading a skinny youth by the hand. "Why, hello there, young man."

"How do you do, ma'am." The lad's voice hadn't completely changed and squeaked a bit. He had sandy hair, a shade lighter than Ethel's, hanging in straggly wisps to his frayed collar. Narrow shoulders were covered by a worn shirt, and faded overalls fit snug on his thin frame.

"David's family just moved into the old Rathbun place near the forks. I've asked him to stay for super. Eudora says there's plenty, and I knew it would be all right with you." Ethel looked at Jessie, then immediately back to David.

There was something about the way these two children were gawking at each other that made Jessie nervous. "Well, of course, Ethel. You are always welcome to invite your friends for dinner."

"Come on, David." Leaving, Ethel called back over her shoulder, "We'll be back in time for supper. We promised Eugene and Irwin we'd meet them down by the pond."

Jessie watched Ethel and her friend run off, hand in hand. She was both amused and concerned. Dear little Ethel! She had rather expected this particular daughter might never have a beau because of her handicap, but she seemed to have charmed her young friend completely. Ethel had always been over shadowed by Lottie's striking good looks, but Jessie realized Ethel had matured with hardly anyone taking notice. She was fine boned, graceful and feminine. Shiny wings of honey-brown hair flowed from her high, pale brow, and her heart-shaped face was sweet and angelic.

Frowning, Jessie hefted herself up from the chair. Carrying the bowl of shelled peas, and the basket of pods, she waddled her way into the kitchen where her sister was busy at the stove. Jessie sank into a chair.

"Eudora, what do you know about Ethel and this friend of hers, David something or other?"

Eudora wiped her hands on her apron and shrugged. "I don't know anything about him at all. She only introduced him to me a few moments ago."

"Me, too. But she doesn't act like she just met him, does she?"

"No, I guess not. But Jessie, I can't help wondering how she did meet him. The girl is always busy helping or tending to the little ones—except of course when she's in school."

"That's it!" Jessie exclaimed. "School. He's a school chum!"

At the dinner table it was obvious all the

children were quite well-acquainted with David. And it came out they had all met him in school, and not a one seemed surprised Ethel had invited him to dinner.

But Harold was as disconcerted by Ethel's new friendship as Jessie had been. "Your father is Barret Catlow?"

David nodded, his mouth being full.

"I met his father in town, last spring, right after they moved in. David's father is a carpenter, Jess," Harold commented.

"Have another piece of chicken, David," Jessie offered.

"No thanks, ma'am. It's mighty good, but I'm pretty full." David smiled at Ethel who sat across from him, and she smiled back.

"Do you have brothers and sisters, David?" Jessie asked, in an effort to keep the conversation going.

"Just brothers, ma'am. They're all older than me."

"What do you plan to do when you grow up?" Harold asked.

"I figure I'm already grown, but what I'm going to do exactly . . . well, that depends on Ethel."

Jessie held her fork in midair and stared at David. Her apprehension was escalating. "Whatever do you mean? How could what you're going to do in any way depend on our little girl?"

"Because, Ma, David and I plan on getting married," Ethel stated.

"What on earth!" Harold exploded.

"Ethel, for goodness sake, you can't be serious," Jessie cried. "You're both children!"

Eugene leaped from his chair, hollering, "Hey! Great! David will be a swell brother-in-law!"

Irwin cheered and whistled, while Cricket and Dessie clapped her hands and oohed and aahed.

"Quiet, please!" Harold commanded. "Ethel, surely you're joking!"

"No, I'm not, Father. I'm very serious." Ethel turned to Jessie. "Mother, surely you understand. I don't feel like a child—I've never felt like a child—and certainly no one has treated me like a child for years. Seems like I've always been mothering babies."

Jessie was only able to manage a squeaky, "Oh." Her heart quickened a beat, and it was becoming visibly harder for her to breathe.

Harold rushed to her side, knocking his chair over in the process. "Jessie, please, don't get upset. We'll deal with this. Everything will work out fine."

Ethel ran around the table to her mother. Pressing her cheek against Jessie's, she pleaded, "Please don't get sick now. Try to understand. You're always told me over and over how grown-up I am, and that you can count on me to think things through, not to do anything foolish. Isn't that so?"

"Yes, Ethel, but I just lost Lottie a while ago, and I don't think I can bear to lose another child in such a short period of time," Jessie said, frantically trying to stay calm.

"I already explained that to David. And I told him you needed me here to help run the house and take care of the children. And since David doesn't have a job yet, he's agreed we should live here with you." Ethel got everything out in one breath and beamed at her mother.

Jessie felt overwhelmed. "I see."

Harold patted Jessie's shoulder. "It seems like you young folks have everything all planned."

"Yes, sir, we do." Ethel returned to her seat, smiling at David.

"I can't help thinking about the fact that Ethel is

only fourteen. And how old are you, son?" Harold asked.

"Sixteen, sir."

Harold continued, "Sixteen is pretty young to be getting married."

Ethel opened her mouth to speak, but Harold held up a cautioning hand. "My biggest concern here has to be your mother. We all know she mustn't be upset or worried. So, to keep life calm and quiet around here, I'll agree to the marriage."

Jessie gasped, her hand flying up to her open mouth. She could hardly believe her husband's words. He squeezed her shoulder. "Jessie, I have to do what's right. Our daughter and her young man aren't going to change their minds, so why should we waste our energy arguing with them? And besides, this time we aren't losing a child, we're just gaining another one."

Again the other children set up such a cheer that it was obvious how much they all liked David Catlow. Jessie breathed deeply, trying to minimize all her worries. There were worse things that could happen to Ethel, and it was apparent Ethel and David were, at the least, infatuated with each other. Jessie had never seen her usually quiet, placid daughter so animated.

Later Jessie and Harold learned that David and Ethel had been meeting daily all summer and that the younger children had been aware of it but sworn to secrecy.

After the fall harvest, a small wedding was held in the front room of the Robbins home. It was attended by nearly all the members of Ethel's family, along with Mr. and Mrs. Catlow and their three older sons. Ethel and David began their marriage life in the room Ethel previously had shared with her sister, Lottie.

It wasn't long before David was totally accepted

by Jessie and Harold as a part of the family. Jessie was even grateful to David after a short while—he'd added a new dimension to Ethel. She now bubbled with a new radiance that transformed her into a lovely young woman.

Chapter 19

In the spring, a welcome visitor came to the valley. When Eudora heard a horse trot into her front yard, she came around from the side of the house where she had been hanging up clothes, four-year-old Hazel clinging shyly to her skirt. A tall, slim man, dressed in an expensive looking suit with ruffles at the collar and cuffs of his shirt, swung down from his saddle.

Eudora peered intently at the handsome stranger, realizing there was something familiar about him. "Willy . . . is that you?"

She put out her arms and he ran to her and gathered her into an embrace. "Yes, 'tis me all right, your wandering brother. And who pray tell is this darling girl?" He released Eudora and lifted Hazel into his arms.

"That's my daughter, Hazel. But, Willy, where have you been? What have you been doing? Are you married?"

Willy gave Hazel a kiss and a squeeze before setting her back down. "Hey, not so fast, Dora. I've come to visit, and I know I'll be asked all the same questions again and again. If it's all the same to you, I'll wait and answer them one time around. Tell me, how is mother? Let's see, she must be nearing sixty. Is she well?"

"Mother is doing fine. She and Mr. Cromer are very happy together." Eudora stifled a giggle. "But there's something you don't know Willy, something that is going to surprise you very much —we have a seven-year-old half-brother named Perry!"

"Are you saying our mother had another baby? Isn't she a bit old for that sort of thing?"

"Not too old, obviously. Nobody was more surprised than she. But she's truly enjoying Perry, and Mr. Cromer dotes on him."

"Well, well, well," Willie chuckled. "Tell me, is there anything else I should know before I greet the rest of the family?"

"Jessie's oldest girl, Lottie, ran off, and the next oldest, Ethel, is married. She and her husband live with Jessie and Harold. Jessie hasn't been well the last couple of years. She's terribly overweight . . . and to be frank, she looks older than Mother. You'll be able to see for yourself, since here comes Jessie now."

Jessie huffed and puffed her way across the short distance separating her house from Eudora's. "Willie . . . is that really you?" Her four youngest children impeded her already slow progress by leaping and running around her, talking and asking questions concerning the handsome stranger with their Aunt Eudora.

"Hush, children, hush," she scolded. She was panting heavily by the time she reached Willy. Throwing her arms around him, Jessie embraced her brother. "I knew it was you. You were always the best looking of us all," she exclaimed after she caught her breath.

When Jessie besieged Willy with the same questions Eudora had, he shook his head and laughed. "I'm not answering a single thing until everyone's together! Come sit on Eudora's porch. Rest yourself, and introduce me to all these wonderful children!"

Addressing himself to the boys and girls who gathered around him, he said, "I'm your Uncle Willy. Will you tell me your names and how old you are?"

Jumping up and down, the children all began babbling at once. Willy raised his hand for silence. "One at a time, please. Let's start with you." He pointed at the tallest boy.

"I'm Eugene, and I'm twelve."

"I'm Irwin, and I'm eleven."

"My name is Cassie June, but everyone calls me Cricket. I'm nine-years-old."

"And as pretty as an angel," Willy commented. "Who are you, little one?"

"Dessie . . . seven."

"Well, well, what a nice group of children—and not a redhead among them! Guess little Hazel got all the red hair for this generation." He patted the top of the toddler's head. "Jessie, Dora, we'll have plenty of time to catch up later, but now I'd better go see Mother."

Mary was working in her vegetable garden when Willy arrived. She instantly dropped the basket she was filling and ran to her son.

"My boy! My boy! Perry, come quick—your big brother, Willy, has finally come home. Andrew! Andrew! Come see who's here!" Tears of happiness streamed from Mary's eyes.

Willy jumped from his mount and embraced her. "Mother, please don't cry!"

Andrew Cromer came running from the field in back of the house, arms outstretched. Willy noted the years had begun to show on his stepfather; his gait was slower, and his hair and beard had silvered.

But when Willy held his mother away to inspect her, he exclaimed, "Mother, I can't believe it. You're just as pretty as ever!"

Eudora had been right—Jessie was older looking than their mother. Mary's red hair had a few strands of grey, but her skin was smooth, with the exception of a few lines around her eyes. And she was as slim as she had been when Willy left home.

She too questioned him about his life over the years, and he again asked that the answers be given when the entire family was together.

In the evening, after the supper dishes were cleared away, all the Robbins, Burleigh and Cromer family members gathered in Jessie's front room. Mary, in a firm voice, said, "Now, Willy, it's time to satisfy our curiosity!"

Willy laughed. "First, it seems quite strange to be called Willy again. I'm simply Will Vradenburg to anyone I meet these days. And Mother dear, and my sweet sisters, no, I'm not married. I've had a few close calls, but luckily I've managed to escape thus far."

Willy reached into his vest pocket and pulled out a deck of cards which he shuffled expertly several times, fanning them out on the table before him. He knew his mother would take notice of his hands, smooth and uncallused, and the several rings which adorned his long fingers. He knew his clean, manicured nails were in sharp contrast with the hands of the rest of the men in the room.

"I'm a gambling man. I make my living with a deck of cards," he announced. Mary gasped.

"Now, Mother," Willy admonished, "don't be upset. I'm an honest gambler. Those who aren't don't last long, and I plan to be around for a long time."

He entertained them throughout the evening with tales of his adventures and the many big cities where he had plyed his profession.

The children remained fascinated by their exciting uncle, but as his sojourn passed, Eudora realized though her brother told many anecdotes about others, he never really revealed anything about himself. They knew little more about him at the end of his visit than they had when it started. But questioning Willy didn't help, since his answers were evasive and indirect. Eudora finally gave up, deciding to be satisfied that he appeared to be healthy and prosperous.

He stayed a week, becoming obviously more restless and anxious to move on. When he made his departure, his family gathered to bid him farewell. He hugged and kissed each of them, saving his mother until last. Mary's eyes brimmed with tears.

"Don't stay away so long this time, Willy. Keep in touch, let us know how you are," she pleaded.

After embracing her, he flung himself onto his saddle. "Goodbye all. I'll return again one of these days. Thanks for taking such good care of Mother, Pa." Will was the only one of Mary's children— with the exception of Perry, of course—who called their stepfather, Pa. After one last wave, he galloped off in the direction of Deadwood City.

Chapter 20

When Willy had been gone nearly a month, Ethel's young husband, David, was felling trees with Harold, swinging the ax with all his might. Suddenly, as the head hit the tree, it broke from the handle, glanced from the trunk, and embedded itself into David's thigh.

Harold ran to the fallen boy. The sharp blade had severed an artery, and blood pumped from the wound. After pulling the ax head from David's flesh, Harold yanked off his shirt and tied it above the deep gash. He scooped the unconscious lad into his arms and carried him to the wagon, placing him on the bottom.

Harold urged on the horses at top speed, the wagon bumping and banging, but mercifully David remained unconscious.

In front of his house, Harold jumped from the wagon, shouting, "Jessie! Jessie! Get out here, quick!"

She came to the door. "What's all the ruckus about, Harold?"

"It's David—he's been hurt—it's bad—call Ethel —she'll have to get Mr. Cromer to ride to town for the doctor." Harold gathered David into his arms and started up the porch stairs.

Ethel burst through the door and ran to Harold. She stared at her husband. His face was ashen, his pants bloody, the flesh of his wound glistening raw through the gash in his trousers. She clamped her hand over her mouth, muffled a scream and staggered against the porch railing.

"Ethel, get Mr. Cromer to ride to Hill City and bring the doctor here," Harold said as he headed toward the open door.

"I'll go!" Ethel said fiercely. She unhitched the horse, and with her good arm pulled herself onto the animal's bare back grabbing hold of the reins and galloping off.

The doctor arrived at the house several minutes before Ethel, her horse being too spent to ride back at the same breakneck speed. When she slid from her perch Dr. Sinclair was standing on the porch.

"Doctor, how is he? Will he lose his leg? Why aren't you inside taking care of him?"

"Ethel, I have bad news. There was nothing I could do for your husband. He was already gone by the time I got here."

"No!" she screamed. "It's not possible. David! David!" She wrenched herself from the doctor's grasp and ran into the house.

David was on the kitchen table. She flung herself on top of him. "David! David! I'm here. Wake up."

Jessie tried to pull her away. "There's nothing more anyone can do, Ethel. He's dead."

"No! No! He can't be!" Her cries became

screams, but she released her hold on her husband's body and Jessie was finally able to lead her into the bedroom.

They could hear her sobs the rest of the day and most of the night, but by morning she was quiet, solemnly joining her family for breakfast, staring out through red and puffy eyes. She never glanced into the main room where David's body had been put into a hastily built coffin.

The preacher came the following day for the funeral. The minute that he closed the service with "Amen," Ethel jumped on the back of the horse. With her light brown hair loose and flying, she galloped toward town, not returning until sundown.

She became a familiar sight as she continued her bareback rides, her skirt billowing behind her and her long hair whipping in the wind.

Ethel never again mentioned her husband. It was almost as though her marriage had never been, that part of her life had never happened. She was no longer the vibrant, sparkling Ethel who had been David's wife, but she didn't return to being the quiet, placid Ethel of her childhood either. The new Ethel was sullen, noncommunicative, depressed, and she would flare up at anyone with unprovoked anger.

After a year of living with the radically changed young woman, the entire family heaved a sigh of relief when Ethel announced she was marrying a storekeeper in town by the name of Shoemaker. Ethel didn't invite anyone to the wedding which was held in Hill City rather than the family home. Jessie prayed Mr. Shoemaker really cared for her daughter and had the patience and understanding to live with her, and Jessie continued to worry and fret about her because Ethel never came to visit after her marriage. She simply withdrew from her past.

In September of 1899, Eudora gave birth to her second daughter, another redhead who she named Vera, and the following year Ethel had a boy and finally began coming home for visits. The first time Ethel and Mr. Shoemaker arrived their infant son was only three weeks old. Ethel waltzed into Jessie's living room holding her son with her good arm.

"Mama, I've brought your grandson to see you," she announced proudly, depositing the baby in Jessie's lap.

The infant squirmed, his lips puckered, and a small cry escaped. Jessie smiled and picked him up. "He's a lovely little boy, dear."

"I named him David. He's the most beautiful baby ever!" Ethel stepped to her husband's side and tucked her good arm possessively under his. "We knew you'd be proud of him."

Eudora and Mary both dropped in while Ethel was there and when the Shoemaker's departed, Mary commented, "Ethel seems to have regained some of her old self."

Jessie nodded. "Thank goodness! I wonder who is responsible for the welcomed change—Mr. Shoemaker or the new baby?"

Eudora added, "The baby is adorable . . . but can you imagine Ethel naming him for her first husband?"

"Well, Mr. Shoemaker doesn't seem to mind," Jessie answered. "Though I must admit it does seem a bit unusual."

After totally shunning her family for a year, Ethel became a steady visitor, dropping in on Eudora, Jessie, and Mary with unfaltering regularity, two evenings a week and every Sunday. She put baby David on display, even foisting him on the other children who complained mightily outside her presence. Ethel's sole topic of conversation was her son—his angelic looks, his growth, his likes and dislikes, his intelligence, and his precious antics.

Soon both Jessie and Eudora dreaded the visits; they were nearly bored to tears by Ethel's constant bragging. Fortunately, Mary was more patient with Ethel, sitting quietly and smiling while her granddaughter droned on and on. Mary cuddled the baby and murmured in his ear. After all, he was the first great-grandchild Mary could enjoy, since Lottie had never made a visit home with her children.

The year David Shoemaker turned two, Mary and Andrew made an announcement which shocked everyone. "We're moving to Kansas," Andrew said simply, after a family dinner at Jessie's.

"Oh!" Jessie cried in dismay. "But why? Most of your family is right here!"

Quietly, Andrew explained, "Mary and I have discussed it, and we've come to the decision we'd like to move on."

Everyone began talking at once. The men questioned Andrew, and he smiled, saying, "We're getting on in years, and we'd both like to see a bit more of the country."

Jessie couldn't hold back her tears when she hugged her mother, and Eudora kissed her on the cheek and told her how much she would miss her. Mary kissed them both, and said, "And I shall miss you, too, but you both managed before I got here, and I know you'll do fine after I'm gone."

Ethel had listened and watched the proceedings

while holding cherubic David on her lap. She suddenly lashed out at her grandmother. "How can you leave me and my son like this? You're being selfish and cruel! You don't love us after all —you've been pretending the whole time! If you truly loved us, you couldn't desert us this way!" Her voice had reached a high pitch. Mr. Shoe- maker left his chair and went to her side, plucking nervously at her sleeve.

Mary reached across the table to her grand- daughter, but Ethel shrank from her touch, eyes flashing with hatred. Mary sighed. "I'm sorry you feel like that, Ethel, for I do indeed love you and David, very much. But I also love my husband and my own son, Perry. I must do what is the best for the three of us."

Ethel leaped from her chair, knocking it over in her haste. David cried out at the unexpected move- ment. "Come, Samuel, it's time we went home." Ethel marched from the house, her head high, ignoring her son's wails as she carried him in the crook of her good arm.

Mr. Shoemaker glanced apologetically at his in- laws, shrugged and mumbled, "Sorry." He hurried after his wife.

Mary, Andrew, and Perry went home soon after. While the women cleared the table and the two husbands sat in front of the fireplace, they all discussed what had transpired.

"Did Andrew mention to either of you before tonight that he planned to move?" Jessie asked her husband and Roscoe.

"Not in so many words," Harold began thought- fully, "but he'd expressed several times the concern he felt about Ethel's dependency on Mary."

Jessie nodded. "And it was truly something to worry about. Lord knows, Ethel certainly proved it with her outburst. I can hardly believe she's the same girl we raised! Andrew has good reason to take Mother somewhere away from Ethel."

"That's part of the reason, I'm sure. But I think there's more to it than that," Roscoe put in. "You know Perry is a very intelligent boy. I was talking to his teacher the other day, and she said for eleven, he's a wonder. He's ready every book in the school, and he does all his work with ease. She said it was a shame there isn't special schooling available for Perry. Now I've heard schools in Kansas are more progressive, and I have a hunch they're moving for Perry's sake, too."

Eudora nodded. "You're probably both right, but we'll certainly miss them." She smiled broadly. "Maybe at least we'll get a rest from Ethel now!"

The Cromers left in early summer. Though everyone missed them, Ethel felt her grandmother's absence the most. She tried to focus on her child, but she was tormented with thoughts about her grandmother. Why did she desert her and her son? Once again Ethel isolated herself— and there was no one to bring her out of her depression.

After three days of rain, the clouds finally parted and the sun shone through. David, who was nearly perfect in Ethel's eyes, was dangerously close to receiving his first paddling. Constantly under his mother's feet because of the inclement weather, he always seemed to be in the way, making messes and chattering incessantly.

Ethel had just finished scrubbing the kitchen floor on her hands and knees, when David ran across it and picked up Ethel's favorite potted plant, an amaryllis which had just begun to bloom. "David! Put that down!"

The pot slipped from his pudgy fingers, crashing to the floor and smashing into tiny pieces, dirt exploding across the shiny surface. Ethel snatched David off the floor with her one good hand and held him at arm's length. "You've been saved by the sun, dear child. You're going out to play even if it *is* muddy!"

Depositing him on the still soggy grass, she returned to the house. He often played outside. Samuel had built a four foot high picket fence around the yard, and the latch on the gate was much too difficult for David to open. Though she expected him to be covered with mud when he came in, it would be worth it to have a few moments of peace.

While she swept up the mess he'd made, she heard David laughing and she couldn't help but smile. It had been as hard for him to be cooped up, as it had been for her. She took advantage of the time alone to clean out a closet, and after everything had been sorted, dusted and rearranged, she realized she hadn't heard her son for awhile.

Opening the front door, she called, "David." There was no answer, and she stepped out onto the porch. "David, don't tease Mama." But again there was no answer, and her son was nowhere to be seen.

Alarm rose within her, and running down the steps, she screamed, "David, David," over and over as she dashed about the yard, peering under bushes, searching here and there.

When she realized her son was not to be found, she started to howl. It was a piercing, agonizing sound, which brought the neighbors running. Ethel was nearly incoherent, but when they finally realized what had happened, someone ran for Mr. Shoemaker at his store, also fetching Roscoe Burleigh as sheriff.

When Roscoe returned home that evening he related the tragic details of David's disappearance. "We searched everywhere and could find no trace of the boy. The only clues at all were some hoof prints in the yard, which leads me to suspect someone rode in there, picked up David and carried him off. But none of the neighbors remember seeing any stranger . . . and I'm afraid there isn't anything else to go on."

Eudora shook her head sadly. "How is my poor sister taking it?"

"Not well at all, as you probably guessed. You know how the sun rose and set on her child. I suggested she come home with me so she could stay with Jessie for a few days, but she just screeched, 'No, I won't go anywhere. And you tell Mama not to come! I don't want to see anyone!' When I left, one of the neighbors was there, but Ethel had shut herself up in her room."

Eudora found herself keeping a closer watch over her two redheaded girls in the following days, and most of the parents in Hill City did the same with their children.

Ethel finally began making appearances around town, and to the relief and surprise of the family, periodically visited her mother. She usually came alone, riding on the back of her horse. Ethel never mentioned her son. The few times one of her brothers or sisters unwittingly mentioned his name, Ethel had glared with such venom the child had fled from the room.

Jessie felt great compassion for her daughter. The wide-eyed girl, with one nearly useless arm, had suffered greatly in her nineteen years. Jessie wished there was some way she could comfort Ethel, but the girl was impossible to reach.

As Ethel was leaving after one of her visits, the whole family had accompanied her out onto the covered front porch. "Don't you think you should stay until the rain lets up a bit?" Jessie suggested. A sudden thundershower was pouring down relentlessly.

"I don't mind the rain," Ethel snapped, walking into the deluge.

Suddenly a bolt of lightning flashed out of the sky, striking Ethel. She dropped like a stone. The children screamed, and Jessie cried, "Oh, my God!"

Harold was the first to reach his daughter. Her eyes bulged from their sockets, staring straight ahead, and he thought she was dead. But a low moan came from her slack lips, and her eye lids fluttered. "Wha . . . what happened?"

"Thank God!" Harold gathered the bewildered girl into his arms and carried her into the house, placing her on the settee. Her concerned brothers and sisters gathered around her.

"What the devil are you all staring at?" she growled, sitting up. The children took a step back. Jessie sat beside her daughter, smoothing the hair from her forehead. "Try to be calm, Ethel. We're all worried about you, my dear. You were struck by lightning!"

"Don't fret yourselves, because I'm just fine! Let me up, and I'll be on my way!" she snapped.

"You mustn't go anywhere yet. The storm is as bad as before, and you should rest," Jessie cautioned.

Ethel leaped up, stamped her foot and marched to the door. "I said I was going!"

"Honey . . . please," Jessie called after her.

"Let her go," admonished Harold.

Ethel became stranger and more unpredictable than before, and people gossiped about her latest antics. Jessie and Harold were grateful Mr. Shoemaker was such a patient man.

Chapter 21

The turn of the century brought changes in the lives of Eudora and Jessie. In fact, Eudora's was altered drastically when the year 1900 had barely begun.

Harold Robbins was the reluctant bearer of the dreadful news. Coming home unexpectedly, instead of putting his horse in the corral as was his habit, he tied it to a tree in his sister-in-law's front yard.

"For goodness sake, Harold, why on earth . . ." She stopped talking when she noticed the somber expression on Harold's face and stepped aside so he could enter the house.

"Where are the girls?" he asked in almost a whisper.

"In the kitchen. We were eating lunch."

"Please sit down, Dora. I have some very bad news."

She perched on the edge of the nearest chair.

Searching Harold's face with desperation, she hoped what she suspected was not true.

"Roscoe's dead," Harold stated.

Eudora's breath came in shallow gasps. Tightly grasping the chair, she felt if she let go she would shatter into a million pieces. "How?"

Harold rested a comforting hand on her shoulder. "He was gunned down in the line of duty —preventing a bank robbery. He shot one of the would-be bandits, but the other one got away after killing Roscoe."

Eudora nodded slightly. She rose, and with a voice which seemed to come from faraway, said, "I must tell the children." She moved across the floor numbly, and when Harold spoke, she couldn't understand the words. It was as though all the blood had been drained from her body, and nothing was left but an empty shell. All meaning was gone from her life.

In the kitchen, nine-year-old Hazel broke into her grief. "What's the matter, Mama?"

Blood seemed to course back through her veins as she looked from her oldest daughter to little Vera, who was only three. Despite their red hair, she could see Roscoe in both girls. Hazel had her father's wide, blue eyes, and she held her chin high in the manner he had held his. And when Vera smiled, one corner of her lips was often higher than the other, a duplicate of her father's lopsided grin.

All her pent-up emotion broke though, washing over her while she gazed at her daughters. Her eyes spilled over with tears, great sobs racking her body. The girls ran to their mother, clinging to her; they were crying also, though they didn't know why.

When Eudora finally gained some control, she told them in a straight forward manner their father had been killed, and their cries became howls of great pain. Eudora regained her composure while consoling her girls. She realized though Roscoe was gone, he had left her a legacy—two daughters who would always remind her of him.

When Roscoe was buried in a grave near Ethel's husband, David, Eudora watched the proceedings dry-eyed—there were no tears left to shed. As she watched her two small daughters, so solemn and sad, bidding their father a final goodbye, an idea came into her head and she turned it over and over.

When she was finally alone in the evening, she took up pen and paper and composed a letter. In the morning she hailed Harold as he left for work and asked him to post it. Then she waited patiently. Now there was something to look forward to.

Jessie's eyes filled with tears at the news. Though Eudora was sympathetic toward her older sister's feelings, there was nothing she or anyone else could do to change her mind. Her plans were made.

"But if you leave I won't have anyone," Jessie moaned.

"That's not true! You have all your children—and most important, you still have Harold. Without Roscoe, I just can't go on living here. I'm stifled; I feel like I can't breathe," Eudora explained.

The answer to her letter had arrived that afternoon. After reading it, and rereading it, she had rushed to Jessie's to break the news. The letter was from Jessie and Eudora's other sister, Minnie, who now lived in California. Minnie and her husband, Julius, were extending an invitation for Eudora and her girls to move out there with them.

Eudora planned to leave as soon as she could sell her household furnishings, pack the rest of their belongings, and purchase the railroad tickets.

Jessie held her plump arms out to Eudora and enveloped her sister, squeezing her tightly against her mammoth bosom. "Oh, Dora, I'm going to miss you so! You've been much more than a sister to me. I love you as much as I do any of my children!"

Eudora could smell the sweet mixture of her sister's face powder and toilet water and was overcome with emotion. Most probably she'd never see Jessie again—California was so far away —and Jessie had always been a mother to Eudora. "Oh, Jessie, I do love you," she sobbed. "And I'm going to miss you dreadfully. But, I must go. I can't stay here and be happy without Roscoe."

Jessie, who seldom left her home, went to the train station, accompanied by all her children, to see her sister off. She stood uncomfortably on the wooden platform, supported on either side by her tall, teenaged sons, Eugene and Irwin. Dry eyed, but filled with repressed emotion, she kissed her nieces for the last time—Hazel first, then Vera.

Eudora, tears streaming down her face, pressed her cheek against Jessie's, squeezing her tightly for a moment. Her "goodbye" was little more than a strangled sound. Taking both girls by the hand, she marched toward the train. Harold followed with her carpetbags.

The entire Robbins family waved after the train until it was no longer visible. Then Harold put his arm around Jessie's plump shoulder. "Come, my dear, it's time we went home."

Jessie didn't trust her voice. She merely nodded her head, walking laboriously toward the wagons, and wished she had the recovery power of her children. Cricket and Dessie had wept gallons, but their tears had dried quickly, and soon they were

chattering and giggling about goodness knows
what. Even the boys, who had been sad-eyed and
long-faced, had brightened at the last of the train.

Jessie finally managed to throw off the cloak of
melancholy which had settled around her after
Eudora's departure. It was impossible to remain
blue while surrounded with such delightful
children as the four remaining at home. Eugene
and Irwin had both become responsible and,
fortunately for all concerned, less accident prone.
However they still were both pranksters, delight-
ing in teasing each other and their sisters. Cricket,
at fifteen, showed promise of great beauty. Still
appearing fragile, she was a strong though
feminine girl with large, dark eyes and prominent
cheek bones and not an extra ounce of fat. Cricket,
and her thirteen-year-old sister, Dessie, were
capable of running the entire household.

Dessie had a pleasant nature and tended to be
slightly overweight. Harold said she reminded
him of Jessie when she was a young woman,
though much sillier than Jessie had ever been. She
never uttered a cross word, and whenever things
didn't go quite the way they should, Cricket and
Dessie would simply collapse into giggling fits.

It was also obvious both girls would not lack for
suitors. Already a parade of young admirers
visited the Robbins home under a varied assortment of excuses. So far neither girl displayed any
serious interest in all the attention. Usually, after
politely dismissing some young man, the sisters
would roll their eyes and point out the poor soul's
lack of redeeming attributes, punctuating their
comments with conspiratorial laughter.

But Jessie knew one day a young man would
come along who would fulfill all the requirements.
She was glad that that day seemed to be a long

way off, and she would not have to give up another of her loved ones yet.

"Mama, Mama, please wake up!" Cricket was bending over Jessie.

The pale light of the moon filtered through the lace bedroom curtains dimly lighting her daughter's face. "What is it?" Jessie asked, heaving herself up to a sitting position.

Cricket's answer was a groan as she doubled over in pain. Jessie lowered her legs over the side of the bed and stood, putting one arm around Cricket's slim body and feeling her forehead with her free hand.

"What is it?" Harold asked.

"Cricket is burning with fever! And she seems to have a belly ache. While I help her back to bed, would you fix a hot water bottle, please?"

Harold went into the kitchen to heat some water while Jessie helped her daughter back to her bedroom. When she was tucked in, Cricket drew her knees up to her chest, groaning loudly.

Startled, Dessie sat up in the other bed. "What's wrong?"

"Your sister has eaten something that disagreed with her, it seems. Try to go back to sleep," Jessie urged. She pulled a chair to the side of Cricket's bed and sank onto it. Stroking Cricket's fevered brow, she listened to her moaning while shaking her head in concern.

Harold came into the girls' room carrying the hot water bottle wrapped in a towel. "Thank goodness." Jessie took it from him and placed it against Cricket's abdomen. "Now maybe she'll get some relief."

Jessie and Harold returned to their own bed but had hardly settled themselves when a cry of pain came from Cricket. "I'll have to stay with her,"

Jessie declared. "You go on back to sleep."

Her daughter seemed quieter with Jessie beside her, stroking her forehead and murmuring soothing words.

Jessie woke with a start to see dawn's glow lighting the room. She squinted at Cricket and gasped in alarm. The girl's face was stretched into a grimace of pain. Though asleep, her eyes flickered beneath eyelids so discolored they appeared bruised. Her cheeks were sucked in, her jaw clenched tightly. Placing the back of her hand against Cricket's forehead, Jessie was horrified— it was burning hot.

Hurrying as fast as she was able, she woke Harold. "Cricket is worse. Will you please bring me cool water." Jessie sponged her daughter from head to toe with the basin of water Harold had brought, but it didn't help.

Not waking fully, Cricket complained of stomach pains. Jessie refilled the hot water bottle and held it against her daughter's belly, which seemed to be distended and hard to Jessie's touch.

Jessie waddled into the kitchen where Harold and the boys were eating the breakfast prepared by Dessie. Harold put down his fork when he saw Jessie. "I can tell by your face she's not any better."

"I'm afraid she's worse. I'm going to give her a dose of castor oil—perhaps she's terribly constipated—but it might be a good idea for you to go after the doctor to be on the safe side."

Without finishing his breakfast, Harold put on his coat and left. Eugene and Irwin exchanged worried glances, and Dessie stared wide-eyed at Jessie. The children were well aware of their mother's poor regard for professional doctoring, so for her to ask for Dr. Sinclair signified the gravity of Cricket's condition.

Jessie felt helpless and desperate and wished Dora or her mother were near. The castor oil had no effect—if anything, the pain worsened—so Jessie prepared an herbal tea and forced a few drops through Cricket's dry, cracked lips.

Jessie became frantic. She had never felt so much at a loss, as she watched her fragile daughter twist and writhe in her bed.

By the time Dr. Sinclair walked through the door, Jessie had tried every home remedy she could think of but Cricket's condition had worsened. The doctor, peering over the spectacles perched on the hook of his long nose, harumphed and cleared his throat. He took Cricket's temperature, and raised one eyebrow to an alarming height when he peered at the reading. Reaching under the covers he pressed the tips of his skinny fingers on her taut flesh, then stood silently, shaking his head from side to side, until Jessie thought she would go crazy.

Finally, unable to contain herself any longer, she touched the physician's elbow and asked, "Doctor, can you tell me what ails Cricket? What can we do for her?"

Dr. Sinclair appeared startled, almost as if he had forgotten Jessie was in the room. "Oh . . . yes . . . Mrs. Robbins. I must operate. Your daughter's appendix—it must come out at once!"

Jessie tried, unsuccessfully, to swallow the huge lump which had formed in her throat. She stood up, even though she was feeling light-headed. "What can I do to help?"

Dr. Sinclair began digging in his black bag. "I'll need an assistant."

Jessie's head was whirling. "I'll do whatever is necessary."

The doctor reached out and grasped Jessie's wrist. "You're in no condition to help. Send in your oldest son, and bring me some clean rags and fresh water."

Jessie forced herself to leave the room. Taking deep breaths to keep her head clear, she had to support herself on the small Parson's table in the front room.

Dessie ran to her mother. "Mama, Cricket is going to be all right, isn't she?"

"Help me to a chair, please." She grabbed Dessie's arm, feeling even weaker than she had moments before.

Eugene and Irwin ran to her side and supported her until she reached a chair. Squeezing Eugene's hand, she said, "The doctor must operate. He's asked for you to help. Do you think you can?"

Not speaking, the tall boy pursed his lips tightly, nodding his head. Jessie released his hand, and he turned and disappeared into Cricket's room. Jessie instructed Dessie to gather clean rags and sent Irwin for water, which they handed through the doorway to the doctor.

Jessie and her children waited, their eyes fixed on the closed door of the bedroom. The minutes dragged by. She wondered where Harold was—he must have been detained in town. Irwin stood beside his mother, his hand resting on her shoulder, while Dessie sat on the floor, with her head leaning against Jessie's knees.

The bedroom door suddenly was flung open, banging hard against the wall. Eugene burst through it, pausing for a moment, his eyes bulging from their sockets. He ran past the waiting group and out the back door. Dessie jumped to her feet, started after her brother, paused and turned to her mother.

With tremendous effort, Jessie heaved herself to her feet. Fearfully, she forced herself toward the open door. But before she could reach it, Dr.

Sinclair stepped out, wiping his hands on a bloody towel.

One look at the doctor's somber face was enough to tell the tale. "Cricket's gone, isn't she?" Jessie asked.

The doctor nodded. "I'm sorry. I'm afraid I was too late to do any good. The appendix had already ruptured and burst—the poison was everywhere."

Shoving her fist into her mouth to stifle a scream, she put her other arm around Dessie who was weeping loudly. Dr. Sinclair took off his glasses and polished them with a clean corner of the soiled rag.

Putting a heavy hand on Jessie's shoulder, he said, "Give me a moment to tidy up a bit and collect my bag, and I'll be on my way. I'll break the news to Harold when I get back to town."

Jessie nodded; she was numb. She couldn't believe her little girl was dead. She dreaded going into that room, where she would have to accept the horrible reality that Cricket was gone.

When the doctor left, Jessie finished the walk she'd begun. Stepping to the side of the bed, she saw Cricket's body was covered with a sheet. A pile of putrid smelling, bloodied rags were scattered on the floor. The pail of water was a sickening pink with her daughter's diluted blood.

Turning back the corner of the sheet, Jessie stared at the heart-shaped face. In death the pain was gone, the features relaxed. Jessie's chin quivered, her sight blurred with tears. She stroked the smooth cheek and forehead, now cool to the touch. Though the face was the sweet, familiar one of her daughter, the essence of Cricket was gone. Her child was no more. Jessie collapsed to her knees and put her head on the bed, muffling the sobs in the mattress.

*   *   *

Jessie found that time didn't help the pain caused by the loss of her child. The days dragged by, and she filled them, making herself busy—and life went on. Oddly, despite her suffering, Jessie's health improved. She resumed more of her household chores, many of which she hadn't done in years, and it was a welcome change. Time passed faster when she could keep herself occupied.

There was another concern to engage her mind. Eugene's personality had been considerably altered since Cricket's death, and it was more than a brother's mourning for his sister. He was no longer the cheery, happy-go-lucky boy he once had been.

"It's as if he became a man overnight," Jessie told Harold one night after they had gone to bed.

"When Cricket died Eugene discovered his own mortality. Such a discovery can age a boy in a hurry," Harold commented.

Jessie remembered Cricket's final day and Eugene's flight from the house. "I think it's even worse than that. Whatever he witnessed while he was in Cricket's room helping the doctor had a powerful effect on him."

Stroking Jessie's plump arm, Harold said, "You don't want to know the details. Eugene told me all about the operation and what he saw when the doctor opened Cricket's stomach. It was sickening. It was all Eugene could do to hold back his breakfast until the doctor told him he was no longer needed. He wasn't even aware Cricket had died. He only knew he had to get outside because he was going to be sick."

"My poor, poor boy," Jessie murmured softly.

"It was truly a harrowing experience. But I don't think Eugene can be called a boy any longer. He earned his way to manhood that day." Harold kissed Jessie. "I think we should try and sleep now, my dear."

Chapter 22

It was 1903 when Harold brought home the news Calamity Jane had passed away in a town called Terry, a few miles from Deadwood, leading them to reminisce about the beginnings of their marriage.

"Oh my, how grown-up I thought I was, and really I was so uneducated in the ways of the world." Jessie laughed.

With eyes full of love, Harold said, "I wouldn't have had it any other way. You've been the best wife a man could have."

Jessie felt warm and happy inside. "Thank you, my dear, and I can't complain about you as a husband either. We've had some good times together, haven't we?"

They sat quietly side by side on their porch swing, occupied by their own memories.

After a short time Jessie heard the sound of a horse and wagon approaching. "Were we expecting anyone? The children wouldn't be returning so early, would they?" Eugene and Irwin had escorted Dessie to her first barn dance that September evening.

Harold stood and squinted into the dark. Jessie pulled herself up and stood beside him, clutching his arm with trepidation. "Oh, you don't suppose something has happened to the children?" She couldn't control her growing panic.

Harold patted her hand. "Now, Jessie, don't get upset before we know who it is."

Unreasonable as it was, Jessie's anxiety increased. "After all, Harold, whoever it is most certainly is coming here."

"We'll know in a moment." Harold stepped from the porch to greet the driver of the buggy as it rolled to a stop.

"Obie Jefferson," he called out, "what brings you all the way out here?"

Obie, a friend from town, smiled through his grey-black whiskers. "Got a surprise for you folks," he said, as he climbed down from the buggy seat. A stylishly dressed young woman, with a hat of feathers and bows perched high upon a smart, curly hairdo, stepped gingerly from the back seat, leaning lightly on Obie's offered arm. She turned and helped a girl of around six jump to the ground. The child was wearing a white dress with row upon row of ruffles and a blue satin ribbon tied high around her middle. Dark curls bounced around her heart-shaped face.

Recognition struck Jessie as she stared at the familiar features. "It can't be . . ." she began. She took a faltering step and paused. A smaller version of the first little girl was lifted from the carriage by Obie. The ruffles and ribbon were the same, but the curls were golden.

Obie flashed another grin above his scraggly

beard and reached inside and pulled out another child, smaller still, the curls a strawberry blonde. He did this two more times with tinier little girls, until he reached inside and brought out an infant wrapped in a knitted shawl which he handed to a startled Harold.

"Told you I had a surprise!" Obie laughed heartily. He set two large carpetbags on the porch. "I'll bring the trunk around in the morning." He drove off, leaving the elegant woman with her five daughters standing in a row.

The woman chuckled musically, stretching out her gloved hands toward Jessie. "Mama, it's me— Lottie!"

Jessie opened her arms in welcome, squeezing Lottie to her bosom, tears of happiness spilling down her cheeks. "Gracious, child, I didn't expect we'd ever see you again!"

Lottie stepped away from her mother and signaled to the row of girls. "These are my children. Girls, your grandma and grandpa." The girls all bobbed a curtsy.

"My, my, my," was all Jessie could say. The girls, who had been quiet, ran to Jessie, jumped up and down, and chattered in an unintelligible hulla-baloo.

Jessie's heart burst with love as she reached out and patted and touched the five little bouncing grandchildren surrounding her. "Oh, my little darlings, come along inside. I'm sure you must all be hungry."

For the next hour Jessie was occupied with the children. She prepared thick sandwiches of leftover biscuits and slices of ham, poured out cups of milk, and served oatmeal cookies with raisins. She instructed Harold where to set extra beds, which Lottie made up.

While Jessie tended to the children, she learned

their names and a bit about each of them. Myra
was the oldest, and most favored her mother,
though she was much fonder of her siblings than
Lottie had ever been. Several times Myra left her
snack to check on the infant, Eileen, who was
sleeping in an old cradle brought from the barn.
She watched over each of her sisters like a mother
hen.

"Be careful, Darla, you're going to spill your
milk . . . Hester, wipe off your moustache . . .
Grandma, Eula can't eat a whole sandwich . . .
Don't squirm in your seat, Pearl." It was hard to
believe such a grown-up child was no more than
six.

Pearl was five, her curly head a light blonde. She
wiggled and squirmed, more interested in her new
surroundings than the food in front of her.
Hester's hair was strawberry blonde, Darla's a
deep auburn. For four and three, the tiny girls
were quite well-behaved. Eula, with her honey-
colored hair, reminded Jessie of her own
daughter, Ethel, both in looks and behavior, and
she hoped the sweet child wouldn't turn out to be
as strange as her aunt.

Lottie entered the room, announcing "Time for
bed, girls, come along," and the children dutifully
slid from their chairs and followed their mother.
Jessie tagged along to help the girls shed their
clothing and put on their night dresses. With a
great deal of pleasure she kissed and tucked in
each of her granddaughters.

Jessie finally scrutinized Lottie as she sat in the
kitchen, sipping coffee and bringing them up to
date. Lottie had removed the frivolous hat and
elegant gloves, and her dark hair was loosely
rolled in a fluffy pompadour, spit curls carefully
placed on her pale forehead and in front of her
ears. Lottie didn't show her twenty-six years,

though Jessie noticed her daughter used cosmetic to accent her eyes and to add color to her lips and cheeks. She was amazed by Lottie's tiny waist after six pregnancies.

"Isn't that so, Jessie?" Harold asked.

Jessie realized Harold had been talking to her and she hadn't heard a word. "I'm sorry, dear, but I'm afraid I wasn't listening."

Harold chuckled. "I was just telling Lottie she and the children are welcome to stay as long as they want."

"Oh, yes, of course."

Lottie smiled, and Jessie could see the child she once had been. "I imagine you'd like to know what prompted this visit."

"Whatever the reason, we're just glad you're here," Jessie said.

Lottie patted her mother's hand. "My husband . . . Eileen's father—ran off and left me penniless. I had no where else to go."

Harold stared into his nearly empty coffee cup. "Despite how you may have felt about us when you left, Lottie, we loved you then, and we love you still. No matter what your circumstances we will always be here for you to visit, or to make your home with us—whatever you need."

"Oh, Lottie," Jessie exclaimed, "You don't know how nice it's going to be to have the house full once again!"

Lottie frowned. "Yes, I've been meaning to ask where everyone is. I didn't see any lights at Aunt Dora's. And did everyone else get married?"

Jessie exchanged a glance of sadness with Harold. "Your Uncle Roscoe was killed in a gun fight."

"Oh, no!" Lottie cried. "Poor Aunt Dora!"

Jessie continued. "She and her daughters moved to California to be near your Aunt Minnie. Eugene

and Irwin have taken Dessie to a square dance
tonight and will be returning shortly. What a
surprise you'll be to them!''

Lottie peered quizzically at her parents and
asked, ''What about Ethel and Cricket? What has
become of th em?''

''I'm sure Ethel will make an appearance as
soon as she hears of your arrival. But I think I
better fill you in a bit on what all has happened to
Ethel since you left. She's not the same person you
left behind,'' Jessie stated.

''Life hasn't been kind to Ethel,'' Harold explained, ''and your sister has been affected by all
her troubles . . .''

''What on earth happened to her?'' Lottie asked
impatiently.

Jessie took up the tale. ''She married soon after
you left—quite happily, in fact. Her husband was
killed in an accident and she began to withdraw
from the world. But despite her strange behavior
she married a fine man within the year. She had a
son she absolutely doted on—and he was stolen
right out of her front yard, never to be seen
again!''

''Glory!'' Lottie gasped. ''My poor sister! I would
positively die if anything happened to any of my
six babies!''

''That's not all,'' Harold added. ''She was also
struck by lightning and somehow survived with no
noticeable damage . . . that is . . . she's not quite
right.''

Lottie shook her head. ''I'm not sure anyone
would be normal after all that.'' After pondering
the sad story for a moment, she asked, ''What
about Cricket? You haven't so much as mentioned
her.''

Jessie couldn't bring herself to tell about
Cricket's fate and turned pleading eyes to her

husband. Harold understood and began, "Cricket's gone. She died of a ruptured appendix —there wasn't anything anyone could do. She was only fifteen, the sweetest angel child there ever was."

Eyes glistening with tears, Lottie said, "She was a pretty little thing. I'm so sorry I didn't get to see her again."

The three sat silently around the table sharing a moment of grief, then Lottie spoke again. "I'm almost afraid to ask . . . what about Grandma, is she well?"

"We hear from your grandmother quite regularly. She says she's as healthy as can be and very happy, though I still don't understand why they had to move." Jessie poured them all another cup of coffee.

Lottie laughed drily. "I didn't forgive Grandma for having Perry until I was married and had a child of my own. I had been convinced Grandma loved only me, until that baby was born. Oh, how I hated him! Seems like I spent my whole childhood being pushed aside by one baby or another."

Jessie wondered if Lottie still resented her brothers and sisters, and said, "You were our first-born, and we were never happier than when you came into our lives. We loved you so much, and that love didn't diminish when your sisters and brothers came along."

Lottie sprang from her chair, hugged Jessie and pressed her cheek against her mother's. "I know, Mama. I understand that now."

Pacing the floor, she held a hand against her forehead and spoke in a voice filled with emotion. "It took me a long time to realize it though. I foolishly looked for the love I thought I had lost in my husbands. Unfortunately, because I was foolish, I went from one unsuitable man to another." She chuckled. "And here I am, husbandless again, and the mother of six children."

The conversation was interrupted by Eugene, Irwin, and Dessie bursting through the kitchen door, bubbling over with gaiety.

"Ma, you should have seen Dessie," Eugene boasted. "She was the absolute belle of the ball . . ." His voice trailed off when he spotted Lottie.

"It's really me, Eugene. Your prodigal sister is home at last," Lottie announced.

Dessie dashed across the room, flinging herself with youthful exuberance at her older sister. "Welcome back."

"Well, I must say, you've certainly all grown up," Lottie commented wistfully.

Chapter 23

"You were certainly right about Ethel," Lottie whispered to her mother. "She doesn't even look the same. If it wasn't for her bad arm I'd suspect someone was marquerading in her place."

When word of Lottie's return had reached Ethel, she had immediately mounted her horse and galloped over to the Robbins home.

Ethel marched into the house, barely acknowledging her mother or sister's presence. Instead she asked, "Are these all the children?" Her face broke into a smile the like of which Jessie hadn't seen since before the disappearance of Ethel's son, David.

Kneeling beside the cradle, Ethel cooed at baby Eileen, then inspected each of the others carefully, almost as though she were looking over items to purchase. She fingered the different colored curls, caressed a dimpled elbow, stared intently at the small, puzzled face, then finally standing, spoke to Lottie. "You are most fortunate, sister. Your daughters are beautiful—perfect in every way, it seems."

She turned to the children. "I am your Aunt Ethel, and I will be coming to visit you often. Come here. I've brought you each a sweet." She dug into her reticule with was fastened to her waist and brought forth hard candies which she handed out to her delighted nieces.

"Now, girls, let's all go for a walk—with your permission, of course, Lottie." The girls had been won over by the candy and now clamored to accompany their aunt.

Myra, the oldest, only slightly more subdued than her sisters, asked, "May we, Mama? A nice walk would be ever so lovely."

Lottie, still bemused by her much changed sister, shrugged. "Of course, go ahead. It'll give you all a chance to get acquainted."

The girls, except for Eileen who continued to nap, skipped around their aunt, vying as to who would hold her hand. Ethel took on a totally different demeanor with the children than that which she faced the adult world. Her features softened, her usually wildly darting eyes calmly focusing on the small faces around her. Her lips, habitually pursed in a narrow line, relaxed into an open smile. Even her body underwent a change. Ordinarily she held herself stiffly; in the company of the children she bent gracefully toward each little girl who spoke to her.

The musical sound of Ethel's laughter echoed in Jessie's surprised ears as the group departed from the house. "My gracious, I can hardly believe what I've seen and heard! My granddaughters have caused a magical transformation. They've done for Ethel what no manner of kindness extended by family or friends was able to achieve."

Eileen began to stir in the cradle, and Lottie lifted her out. "I'm glad for that. The children certainly seem to take to her."

Ethel returned nearly every day to visit with her nieces, most often bringing gifts for all of them, but it soon became obvious she was partial to two-year-old Eula. Though all the presents she distributed were nice, Eula's were different, more expensive. When the other girls got hair ribbons, Eula received a silver brush. If the gifts were new bonnets, Eula received a matching pinafore.

Lottie and Jessie discussed Ethel's latest peculiarity. Lottie said, "I don't understand why she's favoring Eula. It's so obvious that I feel I should speak to her about it."

Jessie frowned. "Oh, don't say anything just yet. The girls are all delighted with their gifts. And Eula is too young to lord it over her sisters that she's receiving more. This new outgoing Ethel is such a relief; let's not do anything which might change her back."

Lottie agreed to let things go—for a little while, anyway.

Lottie and her six daughters had been living with Jessie and Harold and their family for three weeks when Ethel made her outrageous request. After sending the girls outside to play with the new wooden toys which had been the gift of the day, Ethel confronted Lottie.

"Lottie, I want you to give Eula to me."

Jessie stared in disbelief at her second born child, her knitting needles dropping into her lap.

Ethel stood defiantly, her one good hand on her hip, a determined look on her face. Jessie glanced at Lottie who had been mending the children's clothes. Her face had turned pale under her powder and rouge as she stared at her sister in disbelief.

"You must be out of your mind, Ethel!" Lottie snapped.

The allegation surprisingly had no effect on Ethel. Her voice was steady as she explained, "Lottie, you have six girls—you'll never miss one."

"My heaven's, Ethel, I certainly would!"

Ethel continued as if Lottie hadn't said a word. "It isn't fair, you know. I don't even have one child. You can let Eula come be my little girl."

Lottie closed her eyes for a moment, pressing her hand to her forehead. "People don't just give away their children, no matter how many they have."

"Grandma did," Ethel stated smugly.

Jessie jumped in. "That was a matter of necessity. She couldn't afford to feed us all."

"Well, Mama, you let Lottie go to live with Grandma for a time," Ethel argued.

Lottie nearly screamed, "But that was what I wanted! Eula's only two and she can't make a decision like that for herself!"

Ethel knelt in front of her sister. "Please, Lottie, I don't expect you to decide today. I only want you to consider it. Think about the benefit to Eula. I could give her so much more than you'll ever be able to."

Lottie's eyes snapped. "No, Ethel, and that's all there is to it!" She leaped to her feet, almost upsetting Ethel. She snatched up her mending and flounced off to the bedroom, slamming the door behind her.

"I didn't expect her to be upset." Ethel was genuinely surprised.

Jessie resumed her knitting, concentrating on the indigo yarn as her needle slipped under each stitch, her finger lifting and winding the yarn.

"You must understand, Ethel," she explained gently, "that was a startling request."

Ethel paced across the floor in a masculine manner. She whirled about and cried, "But I thought she would think it was a grand proposition! She has so many children and no means of support. I thought she'd be grateful to have one less!"

Jessie controlled her voice while she explained, "It was a generous offer, but a mother doesn't ever want to give up a child. And I'm sure little Eula would be terribly upset if she was taken away from Lottie." Jessie's knitting needles clicked swiftly.

Ethel leaned over her mother, putting her face inches from Jessie's. "You told me you were sad to leave your mother, but your new clothes and the good food in the Fosses' home made it easier."

Jessie put her knitting in her lap and held Ethel's disturbed face in her hands. "I was a big girl when I left my mother. And we never had quite enough to eat, and our clothes were shabby."

Ethel tried to pull away, her countenance darkening with frustration. Jessie held on to her. "Listen dear, I have an idea which might be satisfactory to both you and Lottie."

Ethel's expression changed to eagerness. "Tell me, quickly."

"Why don't you invite the girls one at a time to your house for an overnight visit? I'm sure Lottie will agree to that. It would be fun for you as well as the children."

Delighted by the proposition, Ethel clapped her hands and smiled. "Goody! Listen. I'm going to go home right now and get David's room ready. Tell Lottie I'll be back tomorrow to fetch Myra."

"But . . ." Jessie began, but Ethel had already disappeared. Jessie was worried she wouldn't have such an easy time convincing Lottie, but surprisingly, Lottie hadn't been as hard to persuade as Jessie feared.

At first she had been a bit reluctant, questioning, "Is Ethel capable of caring for a child?"

Jessie assured her. "Ethel was an ideal mother. I'm positive your children will be quite safe in her home. Having your daughters visit in this manner might be exactly what Ethel needs."

Lottie still wasn't totally convinced. "I don't know. I'm not willing to jeopardize my children's safety in any way in an effort to cure my sister of whatever it is that ails her."

"Of course, you must do whatever you think best. However, I know Ethel would never harm a hair on any child's head. The girls are my grandchildren, after all, and I have no doubts about them going to visit Ethel."

Lottie pondered her mother's arguments, then finally said, "I'll agree. But only because she asked to have Myra first. I still have some doubts about her motives, but since the girls seem to genuinely like her, I'm sure they'll enjoy their visits."

Lottie's daughters came home from their overnight visits enthusiastically bubbling over with news of how they had been entertained. They told of trips to the ice cream parlor, playing with a miniature snow scene under a glass dome, viewing impossible scenes which looked real through something called a stereoscope. Even sleeping alone in a room filled with toys one didn't have to share was a new and exciting experience.

When it was finally Eula's turn to visit her Aunt Ethel, she departed with enthusiastic anticipation, and Lottie kissed her goodbye without the least trepidation. The following day when Ethel usually returned the children, she failed to arrive. Lottie voiced her growing anxiety to Jessie.

"What do you suppose is keeping them?"

Busily kneading bread dough, Jessie asked, "What time is it?"

"Nearly three."

Jessie pounded and rolled the white dough on the floured tablecloth. "I wouldn't start worrying yet. Ethel may have had unexpected company, or perhaps there's problems with the buggy. There are any number of reasons they might be late."

"Yes—and one of them is she might not be bringing Eula back at all!" Lottie charged.

Jessie shaped the dough into loaves, put them into pans and slid them into the oven. "Don't create a problem before there is one, dear."

Myra ran into the kitchen and announced, "Mama, Eileen's awake."

"I'll tend to the baby now, but I won't be able to relax until Ethel arrives with my Eula."

It wasn't Ethel who arrived about an hour later, but an apologetic Mr. Shoemaker, Ethel's husband. Lottie met him in front, having heard the approach of the wagon. "Where's Eula?"

"She's still at home with Ethel, who sent me over to tell you we're keeping her one more day. The ice cream parlor was closed yesterday and today, and Ethel didn't want to slight the child." Mr. Shoemaker blurted out the explanation without pausing for breath.

"I see," Lottie said, "but she *is* planning on bringing her back at the usual time tomorrow?"

The middle-aged man, his hairline receding halfway up his head, wiped at his bald spot with his hand, obviously uncomfortable. "Oh yes, ma'am, that's the plan, I'm sure."

Jessie, who'd been listening from the doorway, called to her son-in-law, "Get down from there,

Mr. Shoemaker, and unhitch your horse. Eugene and Irwin are both busy out back somewhere—give them a holler and they'll water him for you. Come on in and have a cup of coffee with us. I have some fresh baked bread and a nice slice with some of my berry preserves will taste mighty good!"

Mr. Shoemaker was either enticed into the house by Jessie's tantalizing offer, or he simply didn't know how to turn it down gracefully. Once inside, he seemed happy enough to sample the freshly baked bread and the hot coffee.

"Is Eula having a good time?" Jessie asked.

"Oh, my yes," Mr. Shoemaker answered enthusiastically. "Ethel has a marvelous way with children."

Lottie, who was leaning in the corner with her arms crossed snapped, "That's fine as long as she remembers just who the children belong to."

Jessie ignored her daughter. "Yes, Ethel has always been fond of little ones. Even when she was a child she always looked after her younger brothers and sisters."

Mr. Shoemaker, never one to make idle conversation, finished his coffee and stood. "Thank you for the refreshment, Mrs. Robbins, but I must get back to the store—I promised my hired help I'd only be absent for a short time. Good to see you again, Lottie."

Before he could take his leave, Lottie clutched his arm. "Remember now, Mr. Shoemaker, you tell Ethel we'll be expecting her and Eula early tomorrow afternoon."

"Uh . . . yes, ma'am, I sure will."

Again Lottie was disappointed. And this time no one even came to give them word about Ethel and Eula. Lottie became more and more agitated as the afternoon sun began to sink behind the hill.

Dessie took over the care of Lottie's other children while Lottie spent her time peering out the door. Finally Eugene offered to ride to town and fetch Eula.

"Would you really? Oh, Eugene, that would be wonderful!" Lottie gave her younger brother a hug.

Her spirits were immediately lifted as Eugene set off on his mission. "Would it be all right if I baked a cake for Eula, as sort of a homecoming present?" she asked Jessie.

"That sounds like a marvelous idea," Jessie responded. She knew the waiting would be easier if Lottie was busy.

By the time Eugene returned it was nearly dark. Much to Lottie's disappointment and apprehension, he was alone. "Eugene! Where's Eula? Has something happened to my baby?"

"Calm down," her brother said. "There's nothing to be upset about. The doctor said she'll be fine in a day or two."

"The doctor!" Lottie shrieked. "My baby's sick?"

Eugene put a hand on Lottie's shoulder. "She has an ordinary case of the sniffles—nothing to be worried about. She has to stay in bed a couple of days, that's all."

"I knew it! I should never have let her go. If she's sick she should be right here where I can tend to her."

Jessie put a comforting arm around her daughter's shoulder. "I'm sure there's nothing to worry about, but perhaps, after supper, your father will drive you back to town and you can check on Eula yourself."

But Harold brought home an unexpected gust for supper. "Mr. Lounsbury, I'd like you to meet my wife, Jessie."

"Pleased to meet you, ma'am. Be obliged if you'd both call me by my given name—Evren."

Evren Lounsbury was a head taller than Harold. His shiny dark hair was slicked back, and surprisingly blue eyes gazed out from beneath straight, black brows. A small, well-trimmed moustache adorned his upper lip, and his smile easily revealed healthy teeth in a tanned and weathered face. Because he was dressed in a suit of expensive material, Jessie was surprised when she shook his hand—it was a hard working hand, callused and strong.

"Evren here was traveling west by rail. Unfortunately the train was boarded by bandits, and Evren was relieved of his purse. He stopped here to wire ahead to his home and have some money transfered to our bank," Harold explained.

Evren added, "And your kind husband, upon hearing of my penniless plight, offered me a meal and a bed for the night."

"And you're most welcome to both, certainly," Jessie agreed. "Come join the family around the table, as we were just about ready to serve when you arrived."

Introductions were made all around, and Jessie noted with amusement how Evren's gaze lingered when he was presented to Lottie. He didn't seem a bit dismayed when it was pointed out that the four little girls sitting at the table, as well as the infant in the cradle, all belonged to Lottie.

But Lottie barely acknowledged Evren's presence. Turning to Harold she asked, "Pa, could you drive me into town tonight right after supper?"

Harold frowning somewhat at the request, shrugged and said, "I suppose I could if it's really important."

"I found out today Eula is sick. I'd like to go to

Ethel's and check on her," Lottie explained.

"Excuse me, Harold, but I have an idea," Evren interjected. "If you'll allow me, I'll be more than happy to drive your daughter to town. Give me a chance to repay a bit of your fine hospitality."

"Now that would be most generous of you," Harold said. "It would allow me to go ahead with some chores that need doing."

Evren flashed a gleaming smile across the table at Lottie, who appeared to notice him for the first time. Her rouged lips smiled demurely, and her lashes fluttered. Through the meal, though Evren participated in the conversation, his eyes seldom strayed from Lottie.

Eugene inquired as to Evren's occupation. "I own timber in Oregon," he explained. "I have logging camps and a lumber mill."

Lottie raised one arched eyebrow, her interest obviously piqued. She was now returning Evren's stares, exchanging smiles and meaningful glances.

When the meal was done, Evren put his napkin beside his plate. "That was a delicious meal, Jessie. I think Lottie and I should be getting on our way if she's to see her youngster before bedtime."

"Irwin, give Mr. Lounsbury a hand hitching up the wagon," Harold instructed.

"I'll fetch my shawl," Lottie said. When she returned it was obvious she also had freshened her make-up and combed her hair. An aura of violets floated about her.

"I'm ready now," she chirped, slipping her hand into the crook of Evren's arm. "I can't tell you how grateful I am . . ." drifted back to the table before the front door closed on them.

Dreamy-eyed, Dessie cooed, "Ooooh, Mr. Lounsbury is so handsome."

Jessie laughed. "Your sister seems to agree with you." She began clearing the table with Dessie's help.

"Mr. Lounsbury and Lottie make a perfect couple."

Jessie shook her head. "My goodness, girl, let's not rush things!"

Eugene, who was eavesdropping, commented, "I bet Lottie's not nearly as worried about Eula now."

"For shame, young man," Jessie scolded, though the same thought had crossed her own mind.

In the days ahead, Jessie's and Eugene's supposition proved true. Lottie continued to make attempts to retrieve her daughter from her sister, but Ethel always thwarted her with plausible reasons why Eula should remain in her home. "Oh, dear, we have a dress fitting tomorrow." "We planned a picnic with the neighbors, and you wouldn't want to disappoint her now, would you?" And so it went—and Lottie pressed less and less.

Lottie's main interest was no longer Eula. Evren Lounsbury had postponed his departure, and it was obvious to all that he was concentrating all his efforts on winning Lottie's heart. What ensued was a romantic, whirlwind courtship. Jessie hoped Evren's motives were as honest and love motivated as they seemed, since she didn't want her daughter hurt. Evren showered his ladylove with store-bought candies, lacy handkerchiefs, a new hat which looked as though it was part of a spring garden, a cameo on a velvet ribbon, and finally, a gold ring encrusted with diamonds and rubies.

"It belonged to his mother," Lottie said proudly, holding her hand out for Jessie to see. Lottie had come into her parent's bedroom after an evening spent with Evren to announce her engagement.

"It's truly beautiful, dear. But are you sure he's the man for you? After all, you haven't been too wise in your choices before."

"Oh, Mama, he's so different from any of my husbands! He loves me, and he loves the girls, and after we're married we're all going to Oregon." Lottie was ecstatic.

Jessie kissed her daughter. "He does seem to be a very nice man and certainly appears to be smitten. I wish you every happiness."

"I already am so happy I could bust!"

Lottie made several more requests for Eula's return, but plans for the wedding taking precedence, she rationalized her failure to Jessie. "Ethel is Eula's aunt, after all. She does seem to love her, and no one can fine fault with the way she cares for her. Eula seems happy there, and she doesn't even act like she misses me or her sisters." Lottie was torn emotionally, her desire to remarry and follow her new husband overpowering her need to reclaim her child.

Another wedding was held in the large front room in Jessie and Harold's home. All the family members were present with the exception of Ethel and Eula. After the ceremony had begun, Mr. Shoemaker arrived, sitting shamefacedly, uttering a few words of apology for Ethel's and Eula's absence, then fleeing.

Lottie and Evren, accompanied by Lottie's five daughters and all their belongings, boarded the train leaving for the west the following morning.

Ethel was an outstanding mother to her adopted daughter, Eula. Some thought she hovered too much over Eula, never allowing her out of sight, but those aware of Ethel's past found this quirk understandable. Ethel's whole personality also changed for the better.

She became friendly to her neighbors and was soon a popular member of Hill City society, entertaining family and friends often—a most gracious hostess. Her wild horseback rides about the countryside were forgotten, and her once wild hair was tamed by regular visits to the hairdresser. She dressed in the latest fashion, and the other women looked to her as the leader of *haut monde*.

Jessie saw her oldest son, Eugene, marry. He became the father of two daughters, his wife dying after the birth of the second. He then moved home with the two little girls, and Jessie once again had children to care for. Eugene and the girls moved out when he remarried nine years later, and he and his new wife had eight more children.

Dessie married the fire captain of Hill City. A large wedding was held in the Presbyterian Church and as the highlight of the society season, it was presided over by her Aunt Ethel.

Irwin died of tuberculosis while still a young man.

News from California brought word that Jessie's younger sister, Eudora, died of dropsy at the age of fifty-seven.

Jessie Van Vradenburg Robbins, despite the problems of overweight and high blood pressure, outlived her husband and several of her children. She traveled to Smith Center, Kansas, to care for her mother until Mary's death at the age of ninety-four. Jessie lived to be a very old lady herself and died peacefully in her sleep.

BOOK III

Wilhelmina

Chapter 24

The girl was beginning to stir. The medicine man went over to where she slept on the pile of bear skins. Her eyes flickered open, but Wamedayin saw them cloud over with fear. He reached out to pat her reassuringly, but she cringed from his touch.

"Who are you?" he asked in the language of the white man.

She frowned. "I . . . I don't know, " she whimpered. When she attempted to sit up, a look of pain crossed her face, and she dropped back onto the bed.

"Be still," Wamedayin cautioned. "You have big bump on back of head. Rest. Wamedayin will send someone with food."

The girl did as told, wondering who she was and what could have happened to her. Looking around she saw the room had a door and two windows, that it was neat and clean with several baskets piled against the wall. There was a sweet, sugary scent in the air, and she realized she was ravenous.

A few minutes passed before a young Indian maiden entered with a bowl of food. She thanked the girl, who didn't understand, only handing over the bowl and leaving. Though not recognizing the ingredients of the meal, she ate greedily—it was delicious.

Soon after she had finished, the medicine man returned. She had been able to pull herself up to a sitting position despite a dull throb in her head.

"You feel better now?" Wamedayin asked.

"Yes, yes I do, thank you."

"Do you remember anything?" he asked.

"No, I can't seem to think. What happened to me? How did I get to this place?"

"I only know small part. Two braves from here were out hunting and came upon three strangers from another tribe. You were thrown over one of their horses. When our Indians came near, you were dropped to the ground, and the strangers rode off. Our braves brought you back to our village. Since you do not remember your name, we must think of another to call you."

The girl shook her head. "I just can't seem to remember what I was called before . . ."

"Never mind. The girl who has been helping me care for you has already given you a name. Perhaps you will like it," the old Indian said.

The initial apprehension the girl had felt upon first awakening in a strange place in the company of an Indian had faded completely. The man's broad, brown face was a network of wrinkles, his black eyes intelligent and kindly. She felt safe with him.

"I am Wamedayin, medicine man for this tribe. We are the Menominee Indians. We live on this land called *Weesechoseh*. It means a good place to live.

"Many years ago there was a great hunter in our tribe called 'Half-face.' He had a friend, a white man with a woman who had hair like yours." Wamedayin reached out and held a strand of the girl's light red hair. "Half-face came back and told us stories about this man and his woman. He called her 'Indian Paintbrush' because the color of her hair made him think of the red flower the white man called by that name."

Wamedayin smiled, exposing blunt teeth stained brown by tobacco. "Indian paintbrush flower very important to our young maidens. The essence of the flower contains a powerful love charm, and a young maiden who sprinkles it on her sweetheart will have forever lasting love. What do you think? Do you like Indian Paintbrush for a name?"

The girl, having enjoyed the story, nodded her head. "Oooh, that hurt. But yes, Wamedayin, I would like to be called Indian Paintbrush."

"Good," the old man said. "I go now. Owaissa will bring you more suitable clothing, then will be taking you to her dwelling. She is the youngest daughter left at home—all others have married. They have room for you, and you are welcome to stay until the time comes when you remember who you are and where you come from and are able to return to your own people."

Owaissa brought a set of clothes to Indian Paintbrush and offered them shyly.

"Thank you." Indian Paintbrush inspected the unfamiliar articles. "I suppose I'm expected to put these on." She glanced at the Indian girl hoping for suggestions, but Owaissa only stood patiently and smiled.

Indian Paintbrush pulled off her dirty and torn dress and dropped it to the floor. Owaissa stared with interest at the strange undergarments. Indian Paintbrush unhooked the waistband of her petticoat, letting it fall, and stood in her pantaloons and camisole.

Owaissa giggled when Indian Paintbrush pulled the buckskin leggings on over the bunched material of the pantaloons. She realized immediately they were not meant to be worn over underclothing such as she had on, but modesty prevented her from removing the pantaloons.

Owaissa handed her a shirt of soft woven material which she put on over her camisole, followed by a deerskin tunic which hung down to mid-calf. She knew the Indian clothing would feel more comfortable without her undergarments, but she wasn't ready to part with them. Her shoes and stocking were a different matter—she was quite happy to toss them aside. The soft leather of the moccasins encasing her feet was a comfort she'd never experienced before.

She smoothed the sides of the tunic and twirled in front of Owaissa. "How do I look?" she asked.

Owaissa nodded and smiled. Leaning over, she scooped up the discarded clothes and said a few words unintelligible to Indian Paintbrush, then made a motion with her free hand to follow.

The Indian maiden led the way through the village to her family's rectangular hut, made of bark. Her mother and father stood beside the doorway to welcome her, and Owaissa said the name for Indian Paintbrush in the Menominee tongue, introducing her to her parents.

"Wakuwa," she said, pointing to her father. No taller than Indian Paintbrush, he was a stocky man, dressed in the usual male garb of long shirt, breech cloth, and leggings of deerskin. When he didn't smile, Indian Paintbrush was a bit wary of his stern demeanor, but later she would come to realize Wakuwa merely was a quiet, thoughtful person.

Owaissa called her mother, "Nita Anobi," and Indian Paintbrush felt drawn to the older woman immediately. Her short, plump body was clad in a tunic gaily decorated with multicolored beads and porcupine quills in an intricate geometric design. Her round face was unlined, her eyes squinting merrily and her mouth smiling widely as she chatted on to her houseguest. Though Indian Paintbrush couldn't understand the words, the tone was friendly and gay, making her feel welcome.

Owaissa and her mother, Nita Anobi, led Indian Paintbrush inside the hut. Owaissa tucked her new friend's belongings in a corner under a buffalo robe, and Indian Paintbrush knew it was to be her bed. Owaissa and her mother conversed for a few minutes, all the while looking and pointing at Indian Paintbrush.

Owaissa took hold of her hand, leading her back outside to meet some of the members of the village. Indian Paintbrush was taken to several huts and introduced to various elders of the tribe.

She met women who were cooking and weaving, then leaving the village, she passed other women tending the new crops. Indian Paintbrush recognized corn and squash seedlings, later learning the strange leaves she couldn't identify were of the tobacco plant, a most important crop.

Owaissa broke into a run when she spied five young girls gathering berries, pulling along Indian Paintbrush behind her. Her introduction to Owaissa's friends was less formal than the previous ones, Owaissa chattering merrily, her sentences punctuated with laughter.

The Menominee girls circled around Indian Paintbrush, staring curiously. One of the girls plucked a long red curl, stretching it out straight, then letting it spring back to its original curl. The girls covered their mouths with their hands and giggled, while Indian Paintbrush nervously patted her unruly hair.

The Menominee maidens' straight, shiny black hair was arranged neatly in braids hanging down their backs, each individually decorated with leather beaded thongs or colored woven material. Indian Paintbrush envied their smooth, dark skin; hers was so terribly fair and freckled easily. They all had large, dark eyes, and she knew her own blue ones must be a curiosity.

The girls returned to their work, and Owaissa handed Indian Paintbrush a basket. She happily helped gather the berries, though she felt lonely and left out as she listened to the young women's gay chatter, unable to understand any of it.

Indian Paintbrush went with Owaissa each day as she joined her friends with their chores. They helped in the fields, gathering wild berries, roots, herbs, leaves, and tree bark. Owaissa's mother showed Indian Paintbrush how to cook the main staple of their diet, wild rice, along with many different kinds of fish, fowl, and meat. Though very little was familiar to Indian Paintbrush, it was tasty, and the menus varied. The only item in the Menominees' diet she found surprising was the heavy use of maple sugar. The sweet liquid was used on food like others would use salt—and it took a bit of getting used to.

Owaissa's mother was an artist at weaving and beading, and Indian Paintbrush was fascinated by the beautiful friendship bags Nita Anobi and other women of the village fashioned from bark fiber and buffalo hair. These bags were much desired by men of other tribes and were used by the Menominees as an item of trade to obtain broadcloth, which they used to make more friendship bags and ornaments to wear over the shoulder.

All of the items were heavily beaded, and Indian Paintbrush spent many afternoons stringing the small colorful beads for Nita Anobi. The older woman would weave them on her loom and sew them onto the broadcloth. Indain Paintbrush hoped Nita Anobi would teach her the next steps of the craft so she could make the beautiful Menominee garments, but she was frustrated because she couldn't make herself understood.

Being unable to understand or speak the language of the people made Indian Paintbrush desperately lonely. Even though she was sur- rounded by friendly faces most of the time she had no satisfactory means of communication.

The worst time came when she had her menstrual period. When she was finally able to make Owaissa understand what was happening, the girl had taken Indian Paintbrush to a hut set apart from the rest of the village. Several other women, young and old, were gathered around the outside of the hut. Owaissa spoke to the women, motioning to Indian Paintbrush to remain with them. The women smiled at her, attempting to make her welcome, and though no one could explain, it became obvious that when a woman had her monthly bleeding she was segregated from the rest of the village. Indian Paintbrush thought it a strange custom.

The other women and girls didn't seem to mind. They were free from most of their chores, only having to do a bit of cooking and housekeeping. Though it was a boring time for Indian Paint- brush, the others seemed to be enjoying them- selves, chatting and gossiping.

The confinement intensified Indian Paint- brush's loneliness. She became miserable and the few days of voluntary segregation seemed interminable. But she came to a major decision— somehow, she would learn the Menominee language.

Since the only person in the village able to speak English was the old medicine man, Wamedayin, she decided to go to him for help. She knew he was always busy caring for the sick and injured, but if she could make him see how lonely she was and offered to help him, maybe he would agree to teach her. Just being able to visit with someone would be heavenly.

As soon as she was able to leave the menstrual hut, she sought out Wamedayin and found him in front of his own home sorting through a collection of leaves, roots and bark.

"*Poso*, Indian Paintbrush. How are you finding life in our village? How are you getting along with Owaissa and her family?" he asked, after she greeted him.

"It's so wonderful to hear words I can understand," she began. "I've been so lonesome . . . and unhappy. Don't misunderstand, everyone has been kind to me. I love Owaissa, and her parents treat me like I'm one of their own. But I can't even thank them for providing me with a home. I want so much to be able to talk to everyone. Could you, please, teach me your language?"

Wamedayin placed a hand on her shoulder and stared at her pensively. He asked quietly, "Indian Paintbrush, have you remembered anything of your former life?"

She shook her head. "No. I have a flash of memory, but it's never anything I can put my finger on . . . or even explain. It's more like the vague remembrance of a dream. I don't think I'm ever going to know who I was."

Wamedayin smiled at her. "I understand. I had

thought you would be back with your own people long before this and there would be no need for you to learn our language. But perhaps your home will always be with us. Who can say? Yes, I will teach you."

"Oh, Wamedayin, thank you," Indian Paintbrush squealed, kissing the old Indian's leathery cheek. "And what can I do to repay you?"

"You may assist me in my work. I can use a young, energetic person to help me."

Throughout the summer, Indian Paintbrush was instructed in the Menominee language and learned the ways and customs of the village. Even before her lessons formerly began, she had learned a few words. She knew *poso* was a word of greeting, and Wamedayin explained it could mean either hello or goodbye, depending on how it was accented. At first it was difficult for her to remember the more unusual words, but soon it became easier, and she found herself communicating with the villagers.

Wamedayin also instructed her as to what herbs and roots to use for various problems and how they should be prepared. The blackberry root was boiled for tea to treat diarrhea and catnip for babies' colic. "But remember," he cautioned, "no treatment will work unless the patient believes in my power as a medicine man." He explained to her that he received his power from Manitou, the Great Spirit, and Wamedayin always made a tobacco offering to Manitou in the name of those to be healed.

More and more Indian Paintbrush began to feel an integral part of the community, almost looking forward to the time she would have to go to the menstrual hut on the edge of the village. When she told Wamedayin she would be absent for a few days, he patted her arm and said, "I'll miss your help."

Without thinking she blurted, "It seems so silly! Why do we have to leave like this? I don't understand."

Wamedayin smiled kindly. "It is our way. We believe a woman is unclean during this time. A hunter must not be near a woman during this period, or the animal to be hunted will smell the blood and disappear. It is our belief that if a man should drink from the cup of a menstruating woman, or share her food, he would be inviting bad fortune."

Indian Paintbrush sighed. "It sounds like nonsense to me."

Wamedayin was a kind and patient man. "Perhaps it is nonsense to your people. But that is how we believe, and while you live among us you must conform to our ways."

Ashamed, she hung her head. "Yes, I know."

"Instead of being impatient with our differences, think of it as a part of your learning time," he suggested. "You will be among the women of our village who like to talk and you will have ample time to practice our language."

Chapter 25

"Soon I'm going to gather some of the paintbrush flowers so I can sprinkle their essense on Patkima," the young maiden called Ichuri said, giggling. Her fingers darted in and out as she decorated a buckskin tunic with porcupine quills.

"Oh, so that is the brave who has taken your fancy," commented Mazasa, a young matron.

Ichuri nodded, smiling, her dark eyes sparkling. "Yes. He is so handsome and such a good hunter."

"Not as handsome as Utumikwa," declared Tahoma.

"And now we know the object of your love is Utumikwa," said Tahadan, the oldest woman among them. She turned to Indian Paintbrush and asked, "And who is the object of your desire?"

Indian Paintbrush felt her cheeks color, even though she knew Tahadan had only asked her to be polite. There were only five of them living together in the hut. Ichuri and Tahoma were good friends and giggled together endlessly, excluding the others, while Mazasa missed her new husband and complained incessantly. Tahadan was the only one who even acknowledged Indian Paintbrush's presence, kindly trying to visit with the younger woman. But it was difficult, for there was little that Tahadan, a mother of several children and the wife of an honored hunter, had in common with Indian Paintbrush.

Before Indian Paintbrush could answer, Tahoma said, "Oh, what brave would look at her? She's so different."

Indian Paintbrush shamefully lowered her head because she agreed with Tahoma. She knew none of the handsome young men who Tahoma and Ichuri discussed could possibly take notice of her.

Tahadan spoke sharply to Tahoma. "For shame, young woman! That is no way to speak to a guest in our village."

"No, do not scold her," Indian Paintbrush said. "She is only speaking the truth."

Tahadan reached over and patted Indian Paintbrush's hand, and for a few moments the group was silent. Mazasa was the first to speak. "I'll prepare our evening meal."

"We'll help," Ichuri said, scrambling to her feet. Together, she and Tahoma disappeared into the hut, their giggles floating behind them.

"Do not mind them," Tahadan counseled. "They are both foolish girls who can think of nothing but the young braves. You are a very fortunate young woman. Wamedayin has never before shared his secrets with a woman. He cannot make you into a medicine man, but he is imparting great knowledge upon you. That in itself is an honor. You are a lovely young woman, even if you do look different from our people, and you are healthy and intelligent. I feel deep within myself that there is already a brave who has taken notice of you."

When it was time for her to return to the village, Indian Paintbrush walked to the stream to bathe. Her reflection in the water startled her. She had forgotten how red her hair was, and she noticed with irritation the springy curls that had escaped from the thick braids that framed her face. Her skin was disturbingly fair, a great contrast to the darkly rich skin colors of all the people in the village. Accustomed to looking into the large, dark eyes of the Menominee's, she was shocked by the pale blueness of her own. "Tahoma was right," she thought sadly, "I am a strange sight."

She had only been back with Wamedayin a short time when he suggested she spend the coming days helping her adopted family in the rice harvest. "Rice is an important gift from Manitou and the mainstay of our diet. Since you are living among us now, you must learn about everything that is important to our people. I think you must take part in the gathering of the rice, and you may return to me when Nita Anobi no longer needs your help."

She reached Owaissa's hut just as she and her mother were leaving. "I am to help with the rice harvest," she explained.

Owaissa's face burst into a broad smile. "Good! It's hard work, but with extra hands we can be finished sooner."

The three women climbed into one of the canoes, and Owaissa showed Indian Paintbrush how to pole the small vessel slowly through the shallows where the rice grew. Owaissa and Nita Anobi would take hold of the rice stalks, tying the tops in bundles but leaving them alone otherwise.

Before long Indian Paintbrush's back and arms ached with fatigue, newly used muscles screaming in protest. Every so often, as they glided through the water, Indain Paintbrush would catch a glimpse of another canoe with three Indian women at the same task. She was ashamed of her own weakness when she saw the effortlessness with which the other women handled the poles which propelled the canoes.

A sigh escaped her lips, and Nita Anobi turned to look at her. "My, you are exhausted! Owaissa, you pole for awhile. Change places carefully. Indian Paintbrush, you can help me with the tying."

"I'm so ashamed. Other women are able to do the job so easily," Indian Paintbrush apologized.

Nita Anobi continued to tie the tops of the rice stalks together as she said reassuringly, "There is no need to feel that way. It is always hard when you do a task for the first time. Tomorrow you will find it easier." Nita Anobi was right. Though Indian Paintbrush's muscles were sore they didn't ache as violently the following day.

When all the rice was bundled, Indian Paint-brush was sent back to help Wamedayin for a little more than two weeks, then she was summoned again for the final harvesting of the rice. It seemed to Indian Paintbrush that nearly every able-bodied member of the village was drifting in small canoes through the rice plants. This time Nita Anobi showed her how to pull the stalks over the sides of the craft and beat them with a stick to release the husks of rice, but Indian Paintbrush noticed that many of the husks fell into the water instead of the boat. She had no way of knowing that those released husks would settle on the muddy bottom and once again begin the growth cycle.

Indian Paintbrush found this part of the harvest to be easy and comparatively pleasant. The final step was exhausting though; the rice husks were threshed to separate the seeds with husks. Though a bowl of steaming, boiled rice sprinkled with maple sugar was ample reward for the hard work to the Menominees, Indian Paintbrush was not as enthusiastic, turning down her bowl of rice and painfully lowered her aching body onto her buffalo robes. She was contemplating her misery when her exhaustion gave way to healing sleep.

Indian Paintbrush's strained muscles had barely returned to normal when Owaissa found her out in the woods gathering roots and herbs to replenish Wamedayin's supply. "Indian Paint-brush, you're going fishing with us tonight!" her adopted sister said with enthusiasm.

Indian Paintbrush stood and frowned at Owaissa. "Oh, I don't know . . ." she began.

"It's lots of fun. My father has taken me many times, and I know you will enjoy it also. Besides it is my father who made the suggestion. Surely you wouldn't want to disappoint him?" A mysterious smile played upon her lips, and it appeared there was something more Owaissa wasn't telling.

Reluctantly, she agreed, and Owaissa abruptly left, a merry laugh floating back as she dis-appeared among the trees. Indian Paintbrush stared after her adopted sister, frowning slightly. "I wonder what that was all about?"

Despite her early misgivings, Indian Paintbrush was excited about the fishing expedition. She had followed Owaissa and her father, Wakuwa, as he carried a small torch to light their way through the forest to the lake. Darkness was all around, but already the waters of the lake shimmered with the flickering glow of torches fastened to canoes.

As they approached the bank where Wakuwa's canoe waited them, Indain Paintbrush was startled by the appearance of a tall, young brave who stepped from the shadows. "*Poso*, Wakuwa." The Indain spoke in deep, melodious tones. "Have you come for the fishing?"

"*Poso* to you, Taihinca," answered Wakuwa. "Yes. My daughter thought it would be a good thing to share this experience with Indian Paintbrush. Have you met her?"

Taihinca stepped close to Indian Paintbrush and smiled. Her heart beat furiously, and she was grateful for the darkness for her cheeks felt warm. He was looking straight into her eyes, and she returned his gaze.

"*Poso*," she answered.

"You have been the talk of our little village ever since your arrival. I am grateful for the opportunity to see you face to face." He turned to Wakuwa. "I was unable to find anyone to come with me tonight and came anyway on the chance there might be someone extra to paddle my canoe. Since you have your daughter, perhaps you could lend me Indian Paintbrush."

Wakuwa turned to Indian Paintbrush and said matter-of-factly, "You go with Taihinca."

Indian Paintbrush was startled at the turn of events. Taihinca turned and went towards the canoe pulled alongside Wakuwa's, while Owaissa nudged Indian Paintbrush, giggled softly, and ran to her father's side. Indian Paintbrush watched as they fastened a larger torch to the bow of the canoe, then lit it with the smaller torch while they extinguished.

Together Wakuwa and Owaissa pushed the canoe into the water and climbed aboard. Owaissa dipped the paddle into the smooth surface of the lake, and the small craft moved quietly but swiftly away from the bank.

"Why are you standing still?" Taihinca asked,

his own torch blazing in the front of his canoe. "Your sister, Owaissa will have guided her father's canoe to all the fish before we have even left the shore."

"Oh . . . I'm sorry." Indian Paintbrush was confused. She helped Taihinca slide his boat into the water, scrambling awkwardly aboard, then picked up the oar and copied Owaissa's movements. The canoe trembled but remained where it was. She glanced at Taihinca, embarrassed by her ineptness.

"I'm afraid I've never done this before," she apologized, feeling as though she might cry.

"It isn't very hard once you get the idea." He put his arms around her, held his hands over hers, and slipped the paddle into the water, pulling it back forcefully. The canoe slid across the surface easily. From time to time he dipped the paddle into the water on the other side of the canoe, keeping it on a straight path.

"There, see, it's not so hard." His head was beside hers, and she could feel his warm breath on her cheek. He released her hands, letting her propel the boat on her own.

"Take it slow. We'll move along easy in the water until I see the fish being attracted to the light of the torch. Then I'll tell you to stop, and I'll spear the fish."

Taihinca stood in the bow of the canoe, spear held in readiness. It was the first time Indian Paintbrush had really been able to study him. His black hair hung down his strong back, while a beaded headband across his forehead kept his hair pulled back from his face. She could only catch a glimpse of his profile as he turned to scan the smooth, black lake. He had heavy, well-defined eyebrows which accented large, dark, intelligent eyes. His nose was straight, his cheekbones high and broad. His lips pursed in concentration were slightly fuller than most of the Menominees, giving him a generous, pleasant look. Indian Paintbrush thought he was the most handsome man she'd ever seen and wondered why she'd never noticed him before. She did recall some of the unmarried maidens had mentioned his name, but there were many names bandied about when the young girls were together. Indian Paintbrush could link few faces with the names.

Taihinca thrust his spear into the water with a forceful drive and within seconds was holding the spear out to her, a large, silver sturgeon flipping on the end. He released it into the bottom of the canoe and smiled triumphantly at her.

She returned his smile but said nothing. She continued to dip the paddle in and out of the water, propelling them along slowly, and tried not to look at the fish flopping spasmodically by her feet. Instead she watched Taihinca's body as he bent to spear another fish, his movements swift and graceful.

He fished on successfully and soon filled the narrow bottom of the canoe with various types and sizes. "Ah, I see Owaissa and Wakuwa are returning to shore. We shall go in now also," Taihinca said, sitting down to face her.

"You must have a big family to need so many fish," Indian Paintbrush commented.

Taihinca laughed. "Yes and no. There is my mother and father and three brothers, but they are all healthy and able to fish. I will take the sturgeon home to my mother because it's sweet flesh is my mother's favorite, and the rest I will share among the old and sick."

Indian Paintbrush was fascinated by the young brave. He not only was handsome but also thoughtful of his mother and generous to those less fortunate than himself.

"That's very kind of you." A warm feeling came over her.

Taihinca laughed his glorious, hearty laugh once again. "It is too much fish for my family's use, and it would be foolish to let it spoil when others could eat it. Besides that is the Menominee way."

He jumped from the canoe to the shore, pulling the craft onto the beach before Indian Paintbrush even had a chance to climb out. She stood, and he lifted her from the boat, setting her on the bank. With his hands on her waist, their warmth seeming to burn through the buckskin fabric of her tunic, he said casually, "Thank you for your help. I hope I will be seeing you soon."

He released her. Pulling the burning torch from the canoe, he doused it in the water of the lake, strung his catch onto his spear, and strode off, disappearing quickly into the darkness.

Owaissa ran to Indian Paintbrush's side. "What did you think of Taihinca?"

"He is very nice," Indian Paintbrush answered.

Owaissa pouted, asking petulantly, "Is that all you can say about him? This outing was all Taihinca's idea, you know."

"What do you mean?"

"Taihinca wanted to meet you. He knew my father was going to fish tonight, and he asked me to bring you."

Instantly Indian Paintbrush thought of questions to ask Owaissa, but Wakuwa, ready to return to the village, called to them to hurry. Wakuwa's fishing had been successful, too; he had two large sturgeon on a stick which he handed to Owaissa.

"Tell me, Indian Paintbrush, did you enjoy the fishing?" Wakuwa asked.

"It was interesting," she answered politely.

"And of Taihinca—what did you think of him?" Indian Paintbrush thought she saw a glint of mischief in the usually somber man's eyes.

"Well, he seemed quite pleasant. And he was most patient with my awkwardness when paddling the canoe," she said.

"Taihinca is a fine young brave, one of the best hunters in the village. The young woman who marries him will be taken care of well." Wakuwa said this to her as though it was vital information, but Indian Paintbrush couldn't understand how it concerned her.

For politeness sake, she answered, "Yes, I am positive that is so. I am sure there are many maidens who have their eye on Taihinca. He is indeed a fine young man."

"But that is the difference. It is not which maidens desire Taihinca," Wakuwa explained. "It is which maiden Taihinca desires."

Indian Paintbrush found the entire conversation puzzling. It was as though Wakuwa was trying to tell her Taihinca was attracted to her—but that couldn't be. Owaissa and her father must have gotten the wrong impression, because Taihinca had shown an interest in her. But she was wiser in this matter than they. Taihinca had no doubt been curious, and this small rendezvous he had arranged was no more than a means of satisfying his curiosity. There was no doubt in Indian Paintbrush's mind that a handsome brave like Taihinca would find her far lacking in the attributes needed for his wife. There were too many lovely maidens in the village of marriageable age for Taihinca to waste any time with her.

Still, it wouldn't hurt to hope. Owaissa and Wakuwa were right about one thing—Taihinca would be a wonderful husband! Thinking about him made her heart beat faster, and she remembered how nice his hands had felt on her waist.

"See, even father knows Taihinca is going to seek you for his bride," Owaissa whispered into her ear.

"Don't be foolish," Indian Paintbrush protested, though in her heart she hoped her sister was right. "I'm sure he's already promised to a beautiful maiden in the village."

Though she had never noticed Taihinca previous to the evening they went fishing, now he seemed to be everywhere. She passed him on her way to Wamedayin's in the morning, then on her return trip in the early afternoon. She came across him while she was gathering herbs in the woods and saw him when she sat outside her adopted parents' home in the cool of early fall evenings. He greeted her rather formally, but her heart would skip a beat and she knew her cheeks colored. She wished she had more control over her emotions, for she was sure all these meetings were purely coincidental—as much as she hoped otherwise.

Several others noticed the regularity that Taihinca crossed Indian Paintbrush's path, but no one else shared her assumption about coincidence.

"See, I told you Taihinca was interested in you," was Owaissa's happy comment.

Wakuwa nodded somberly and said to his wife, "Soon we will have to speak to Taihinca's parents about our adopted daughter."

Even Wamedayin remarked, "Taihinca seems to have taken a fancy to you. You should be proud. There is no finer young brave in the village, and he will make a fine husband for you."

Even some of the other unattached maidens congratulated her on her conquest. "Ooooh, you are so lucky. Taihinca is so good-looking!"

Ichuri had said to her confidentially, "I would be so happy if Pathima would pay half as much attention to me."

But there was one villager who was not at all pleased by Taihinca's seeming fondness of Indian Paintbrush. A maiden with whom Indian Paintbrush was not well acquainted, confronted her in the hour after dawn at the stream where Indian Paintbrush came to bathe. She stepped from the chilly water, her fair skin covered with goose bumps. She was dressing hurriedly when she heard mocking laughter, and looking in the direction of the sound, she saw Awahtay standing close by, her arms crossed.

Indian Paintbrush had often envied Awahtay. She was the most beautiful of all the Menominee maidens. Her black hair shone with blue highlights and hung in two thick, luxurious braids down her back. Her dark eyes were large, fringed with lashes which cast slight shadows on her high, broad cheekbones, and her skin was a creamy golden color Indian Paintbrush admired. Standing straight and still, gazing at Indian Paintbrush with haughty disdain, Awahtay was regal looking. And Indian Paintbrush had never felt more uncomfortable as she awkwardly dressed under the other woman's unflinching stare.

"Even if Taihinca is so foolish as to marry you, he will be sorry on his wedding night." Awahtay spoke in scornful tones. "Your skin is the color of the underbelly of a fish. No Menominee could be attracted to such an uninviting sight."

Awahtay held her head high, peering at Indian Paintbrush through her thick lashes. She pursed her red lips as though there was a bad taste in her mouth while continuing to berate the other girl. "Your breasts are too round and fat, like a nursing mother, and your nipples are pink. What brave could make love to someone with nipples colored so? Your hips are too narrow, and you will probably be unable to bring forth a child, if you can get pregnant at all."

Indian Paintbrush couldn't argue with Awahtay's cruel assessment because she agreed with it herself. It was always how she felt about her appearance since she could remember.

Awahtay laughed mirthlessly and continued her tirade. "And that hair! True, it is unusual and might attract an unsuspecting male at first glance, but a man who has grown up with silky straight black hair such as mine will soon tire of such unnatural tresses. Look at the way it rebels against our manner of braiding, making unsightly curls all around your face and at your neck. You are truly a misfit in our society."

Indian Paintbrush accepted the insults bravely, brushing the tears from her cheeks. "You're right, Awahtay. Everything you have said is true."

Awahtay was startled by the acquiescense of the object of her abuse and seemed to be at a loss for words—but the silence was only momentary. "Taihinca is my betrothed," she blurted out. "Whatever evil spell you have cast over him will wear off. He'll return to his good sense and see you for what you really are—a spiritless, homely woman, incapable of making a happy Menominee home for him!"

"Your mouth is speaking when it would serve you better to be silent." Taihinca's voice was quiet, but the anger in it was apparent. He put an arm reassuringly around Indian Paintbrush's waist pulling her against his side.

"How long have you been listening?" a chagrined Awahtay asked.

"Long enough to know you have been filling the

air with cruel lies, insulting my future bride!''

Awahtay stifled a cry, hurrying away without so much as a parting glance.

Taihinca turned Indian Paintbrush by her shoulders so she faced him. "Look at me. I did not want to declare my feelings to you at this time, but now it is necessary. I want you for my wife, Indian Paintbrush.''

She gazed into the eyes of the handsome Indian and saw love and kindness there. "I am grateful to you, Taihinca, but you must listen to me. I don't know how much you overheard, but nearly everything Awahtay said was true. But most important was that I am a misfit and could never make a Menominee brave happy—and I agree. Awahtay would be a much more suitable bride for you.''

Taihinca held her chin in his hand so she would have to look at him. "Listen, my wife-to-be, and listen carefully, for we shall not discuss this again. Awahtay and I are not, and have never been, betrothed. It has been mentioned that she and I would be fitting mates because she is the daughter of my mother's brother, and such marriages are encouraged. But never have I agreed to the match, nor have I given Awahtay any reason to think there was a wedding for us in the future. In fact I have already discussed my plans with my father and Wakuwa and Wamedayin. The only one I hadn't spoken to is you. I was waiting for you to get to know me—and perhaps desire me as a husband as I desire you for a wife.''

Indian Paintbrush felt both overwhelmed by his declaration and unsure of her own feelings.

"Taihinca, I am flattered by what you have told me. But there is more for you to consider. You do know I can't recall anything from my past, don't you?'' she asked seriously.

"Yes. I had a long talk with Wamedayin. He

assured me that if you had not remembered by now, chances are you never would. Anyway, it doesn't matter," he assured her.

"But what if I'm already married, and just can't remember?"

Taihinca laughed, little lines crinkling at the corners of his eyes. "Oh, I don't think there's anything to worry about. If you already had a husband, he would care for you at least as much as I do and would never have given up his search for you. He would have found you by now. No, I'm positive there's no husband in your past."

Chapter 26

Indian Paintbrush had difficulty realizing that a wedding ceremony to unite Taihinca and herself was truly forthcoming, but it was obviously so. Her adopted parents, Wakuwa and Nita Anobi, had several meetings with Taihinca's mother and father, mentioning after their discussions that they hoped to have the ceremony before fall turned into winter.

Taihinca no longer visited Indian Paintbrush and she expressed her concern. "Maybe he is reconsidering and has decided it wasn't such a good idea to marry me after all."

Owaissa laughed away her friend's doubts. "No one has explained to you what has to happen now, did they? You and Taihinca must be kept apart until the wedding. Taihinca is being purified."

This explanation only caused her to worry about other matters. She wondered if she loved Taihinca, as she didn't feel she knew him very well. And she also pondered what it was going to be like to be married, knowing she was ignorant as to what he would expect.

One day several older women came to Indian Paintbrush's home, and Owaissa and her father were sent away. The women, along with Nita Anobi, spent most of the afternoon giving Indian Paintbrush instructions on how to be the perfect wife for Taihinca—and so, in this way, she finally received her sex education.

Indian Paintbrush was unfamiliar with some of the words the women used, but she had no difficulty understanding their meaning. Though embarrassed at times, she appreciated the guidance of the older women but was dismayed by the thought she would soon be a participant in what they had been describing.

The day of the wedding was bright and clear with a nip of the coming winter in the air. Owaissa and Nita Anobi had accompanied her to the stream early in the day to help her bathe and wash her hair, then Owaissa had dried, combed and braided her hair, weaving in leather thongs decorated with beads.

Nita Anobi had sprinkled Indian Paintbrush's body with sweet smelling herbs before helping her into her dress. A gift from her adopted mother, it was made of the softened doeskin, hanging with fringe, and decorated with beadwork and porcupine quills. Her beaded moccasins were also new, made by Owaissa of the same soft leather.

"I wish you a good life with your husband, daughter," Nita Anobi said, hugging Indian Paintbrush tightly as a tear escaped from the corner of her eye, slowly making its way down her plump cheek.

Owaissa pressed her cheek against Indian Paintbrush's, tears also filling her dark eyes. "You will always be my sister."

Choked with emotion, Indian Paintbrush didn't trust herself to speak. She was leaving the only family she knew to begin a new life with a man who was nearly a stranger. She was sad and a bit frightened.

"Come," Nita Anobi urged softly, taking her by the hand. "It is time."

The three women walked together to the huge fire where the members of the village were gathered and slipped quietly into place. Across the fire Indian Paintbrush spied Taihinca, surrounded by his family. She couldn't see the expression on his face because of the combination of the evening shadows and the flickering glow of the flames.

The Menominee Chief, an imposing old man dressed in his ceremonial best, stood in front of the fire. He began the evening ritual by telling a story of the Menominee people, a story Indian Paintbrush had heard before at other ceremonial and festival times. He spoke of how the Menominee hunt, not only to provide food for their people but, more important, to have communion with the earth sanctified by the Great Spirit. The land is sacred to the Menominee—the land stands for the tribe.

In times past, Indian Paintbrush had been fascinated by the story, but tonight she neither heard nor understood the words—it seemed as though the Chief droned on for hours. She was startled when she heard him call for the two families to present the betrothed couple, Taihinca and Indian Paintbrush.

Taihinca was escorted to the fire first, introduced by his father to all his relatives and the other members of the village where he had grown up. Wakuwa turned to Indian Paintbrush and said simply, "Come."

She almost felt as though she was walking in a dream as she followed Wakuwa, her eyes fixed on his broad back, and stopped beside the fire. Though she looked at the ground, Indian Paintbrush could feel the heat of the flames and the many eyes staring at her. She knew some of the eyes were friendly and some were not.

In a voice deeper than usual and filled with emotion, Wakuwa stated, "Here is my daughter, Indian Paintbrush. I have only had the privilege of sharing my home with her for a short time, but she will be sorely missed." Wakuwa took Indian Paintbrush's hand into his, held it tightly for a moment, then handed it to Taihinca. At last the couple stood side by side. She was overcome with shyness and couldn't bring herself to glance at Taihinca, but the strength and warmth of his hand comforted her.

The ceremony continued to go on and on. The Chief spoke directly to them, though Indian Paintbrush only digested bits and pieces. She knew he spoke to them about being fruitful. He charged Taihinca to be a great hunter, and Indian Paintbrush to dutifully care for her husband, his home, and their future children.

Finally she heard the Chief declare them husband and wife, and the music and chanting began.

The remainder of the celebration continued to have a dream-like quality for Indian Paintbrush. People gathered around the couple offering good-natured advice and congratulations, but it was as if she could no longer understand the Menominee language—nothing registered. The sound of the drums beat against her ears, and the high whine of the flutes assaulted her brain, while the dancers she usually admired seemed to dart about causing distorted shadows. For a moment there were no well-wishers nearby, and Taihinca leaned over and whispered in her ear, "Let's slip away."

He helped her to her feet, and unnoticed, they stepped back into the darkness. He put his arm possessively around her waist, his hand resting easily on her hip, as he led her to the newly constructed hut he had prepared for her.

It was dark inside, and Indian Paintbrush was unable to see her surroundings. Taihinca cupped her chin in his hand and said, "You have made me the happiest of braves."

Indian Paintbrush's eyes adjusted to the lack of light, and she was able to discern her husband's strong, handsome face. She could see by the happiness shining in his eyes that he was truly pleased she was his wife, and the realization made her feel more comfortable. "I hope I shall always make you happy," she murmured.

With trembling fingers he helped her undress. When she was naked he said, "Please undo your hair."

While she was unbraiding her hair, he discarded his own clothing and stood patiently before her so she could look upon him. It was the first time she could remember ever seeing a grown man unclothed. His muscles rippled under his smooth, bronze skin, and she thought he was perfect.

Taihinca came to her, gently helping her to the bearskins arranged in the corner. Tenderly, his fingers explored her body, creating explosive sensations never felt before. When he lowered his body to thrust himself inside her, despite the first sharp pain, she eagerly accepted him.

When it was over Taihinca murmured, "My

woman," and pulling her within a circle of his arms, they slept.

When she woke before the sunrise, Taihinca was propped on his elbow staring down at her. He smiled and said, "Good morning, my woman." He smoothed her curly red hair which fanned out around her head.

Leaning over her, he brushed his lips against hers, kissed her shoulder, the swell of her breasts, each pink nipple, and the hollow of her stomach. Together they explored each other's bodies, and Indian Paintbrush felt both excitement and love engulf her.

Indian Paintbrush was kept busy as the wife of Taihinca. He was a successful hunter and fisherman, and they often had enough food to share with those who were needy. She gathered the roots and herbs to make tea and flavor their meats, and when Taihinca brought home a deer, it was her job to prepare the skin so it could be used to make clothing.

She had to call on Owaissa to show her the proper procedure she had not learned while living under Wakuwa's roof. Owaissa demonstrated how to scrape the hair from the pelt with a stone bladed knife. When that was done the skin was turned and scraped free of all fat. The pelt washed and smoked to make it flexible, then it was ready to fashion into leggings, tunics, breechcloths, or moccasins.

Indian Paintbrush worked hard at her chores all day and eagerly looked forward to the time she and Taihinca were together in the evenings. Taihinca was gone most of the day—and sometimes for two or three days at a time.

One night she asked her husband, "Couldn't I go

along with you on your hunt?"

Taihinca furrowed his brow and answered, "No, my Indian Paintbrush, it is impossible, for it is against tradition for a woman to join the hunt. Is there not enough at home to keep you busy?"

"I have more than enough to do, Taihinca, but I miss you when you are gone. And I would like to see where it is you go in the forest and share in what you do."

He smiled and hugged her close. "The Great Spirit gave me much blessing when he gave you to me. It is too bad we do not still have a winter camp. In the olden days the tribe would leave the village for the winter months, the old and the sick remaining behind with a few braves to watch over them. They carried small domed wigwams with them that could be easily set up wherever the hunting was good. The women and children were on hand to skin the animals and prepare the meat for cooking or preservation."

"That sounds like a good idea. Why don't your people do it any more?" Indian Paintbrush asked.

Taihinca's face clouded over, and his voice became gruff as he explained, "We have a treaty with the white man. We are to stay within a small area—but it is impossible. The Menominees live by the land, and it is necessary for us to go beyond the boundaries. But to make it less obvious that we are not following the impossible rule, we now leave our families behind when we hunt."

"How terrible! Isn't there some way it can be changed?"

"It is best that we go on as we have been. We do not bother the white man, and he does not bother us."

Indian Paintbrush was troubled by her husband's explanation. "It isn't fair for your people to change their traditions. This is your land! It certainly doesn't belong to the white man, and they shouldn't be allowed to make silly rules and regulations!"

Taihinca chuckled. "It is too bad the rest of your people do not feel as you do. The life of the Indian would be much simpler. But do not fret about such things, my wife. I don't like to see your forehead marred by worry." He gently massaged the crease from her brow with his thumb.

"That's better," he said, as she smiled at him. "I have an idea, dear one. One day soon, we will ride together into the forest, and I will show you some of the places I hunt and fish."

"I would like that very much."

"Let's not talk anymore tonight," he said softly, as he laid her gently back onto the bearskin.

Taihinca was true to his word. One clear, cold winter day, he turned to her as she was clearing away their breakfast things, and announced, "Hurry, Indian Paintbrush. Today you will leave your wifely chores behind and come with me to the forest."

Excitement bubbling inside her, she grinned at her husband. "Truly? Then let's go. There's nothing here that won't wait until evening."

Taihinca helped her wrap herself in a bearskin robe, then put one on himself. "Come," he said, leading her by the hand, "we have a great day ahead of us."

Together they rode on Taihinca's horse through a white wonderland. He showed her the sparkling rivers and streams where he fished for trout and northern pike. He pointed out traps he'd set for raccoon and the places he planned to set traps for bear in the early fall. They rode to the top of a slight hill and looked onto a small clearing through a screen of young pine trees, snow weighing down their slim branches.

"Here is where I felled the large buck I brought home last week. Manitou always provides for our people," he stated proudly.

They sat on a large rock near a swiftly moving stream to eat their noonday meal of smoked fish. "Are you enjoying yourself?" Taihinca queried.

"Oh, yes, my husband, it is beautiful. The snow has made everything look like a dream world."

"It is always beautiful—and always different. You must come with me during the different seasons. In the spring you will see the snow melting to reveal the new green. By summer all the wild flowers are in full bloom, and in fall many of the trees turn color—rich reds, browns and yellows."

Indian Paintbrush sighed deeply. "I'm so happy to be here with you."

Taihinca squeezed her hand. "I'm glad I took the time to do it even though some of my friends made fun of me."

Indian Paintbrush was concerned by this revelation. "What do you mean? Why would anyone make fun of you?"

Taihinca shook his head. "Do not concern yourself with such foolishness. Some of the braves have nothing better to do than tease me about how I choose to spend my time."

It grieved her to think she was the cause of trouble to her husband. "Please, if this trip has made you look bad in the eyes of your friends we should not repeat it."

Taihinca's first answer was a hug, followed by the question, "Are you pleased with our day together?"

"I will count it as my greatest pleasure . . . next to our love-making," she answered, blushing slightly at her boldness.

With his arms around her, his warm breath against her ear and cheek, he said, "I too have received much joy from partaking of the beauty of this land with you by my side. It is said life is to be lived day by day. We must cherish each moment for its own. So why should I be disturbed and give up something that I enjoy because of some idle taunts from men who have never been so fortunate as I?"

Taihinca succeeded in soothing Indian Paintbrush's fears, and they spent the rest of the afternoon riding and reveling in nature's beauty. The sun had turned the sky a deep red with a few scattered clouds casting long shadows across the forest's floor, when Taihinca reined the horse to a halt.

"What is it?" Indian Paintbrush asked. She peered about, but could see nothing alarming.

"There, just ahead." Taihinca spoke with a tinge of fear in his voice.

Puzzled, Indian Paintbrush still couldn't see anything that would upset her husband.

"Stay where you are." Sliding down from the horse, Taihica walked toward a tall, gnarled oak stump. The dead tree had been struck by lightning and burned with only one remaining limb sticking up toward the sky, almost as if to signify its agony.

Indian Paintbrush watched as her husband warily approached the stump. He pulled a pouch from his clothing and began to sprinkle what looked like tobacco on the snow all around the stump. Fascinated by his actions, Indian Paintbrush saw his face was creased by worry when he returned to her.

"What is it? What did you do?"

"It is nothing for you to concern yourself about." He pulled himself up behind her on the horse.

"Please explain to me what you just did. I want to be able to understand you and your people."

Taihinca turned the horse away from the object of his uneasiness, riding silently for awhile. Finally he spoke, "I sprinkled the tobacco on the ground to ward off any evil spirits who might be hiding in the stump."

"But what would that do?" Indian Paintbrush was puzzled by her husband's words. She knew the Menominees believed in evil spirits but had never heard of tobacco being used in connection with them.

"Tobacco is a gift from Manitou. It will ward off any misfortune the spirits might cause."

Taihinca's explanation didn't enlighten her, only bringing more questions. "How did you know there was a possibility of evil spirits being in that stump?"

Her husband was usually extraordinarily patient with her, but now his voice was short, and she could tell he was annoyed by her inquisitiveness. "The tree stump was ugly—out of place among the surrounding beauty and perfection —an obvious spot for evil spirits to dwell. It is nearly dark, we must return to the village."

Indian Paintbrush knew Taihinca had ended the conversation, and any further questions or remarks would be unwelcome. By the time they reached the village, Indian Paintbrush had pushed all thoughts of evil spirits to the back of her mind.

Chapter 27

The winter, which had begun mildly, turned fierce. The snow fell unceasingly for nearly two weeks, making hunting impossible. Most of the villagers remained inside, venturing out only when absolutely necessary. At first, Indian Paintbrush enjoyed the luxury of extra time with her husband.

Even with a fire burning all the time the hut was freezing. In an effort to keep warm they cuddled together under their bearskins—talking, giggling, making love, passing time in the most enjoyable manner.

But as the days went by, Taihinca became restless. He paced back and forth inside the hut, stepping outside from time to time as flurries of snow blew in the door and slowly melted into a puddle.

Taichinca stayed outside one unbearably cold day for an unusually long time. When Indian

Paintbrush pulled her bearskin robe around her and left the comfort of her home, the bitterness of the temperature was a shock, even paintful to breathe. She looked all around but couldn't see Taihinca, but that wasn't surprising with the snow coming down so heavily. Just as she started to turn back inside she saw a dark shape coming towards her.

She was only able to recognize Taihinca when he was but a few feet away. "Indian Paintbrush, you shouldn't be out in this storm," he scolded.

He ushered her inside the hut. Flinging off his robe, he stood near the fire, stamping his feet and swinging his arms. His face was red with cold, his eyelashes wet and stuck together. "Why did you go outside?"

"I was looking for you. You were gone for a very long time."

"I'm sorry. I didn't mean to worry you, but I have felt a nagging concern for my family for the past few days. It was quite strong today and I felt compelled to check on them. Unfortunately, my worries were proven true. My father has been stricken by an illness of the lungs and was sick for several days before he would allow one of my brothers to go for Wamedayin. I greatly fear for him."

"I'm sorry, Taihinca," Indian Paintbrush cried. Seeing her husband so distressed brought great sadness to her heart.

By the following morning, it had stopped snowing, leaving high drifts against anything which had stood in the way. Wamedayin visited their hut soon after a weak sun cast a pale light on the white landscape.

"Come in, dear friend," Indian Paintbrush greeted. "Have a cup of tea with us and warm yourself by the fire."

"I will be glad for a cup of tea, but I bring sadness to your home," the medicine man said.

Taihinca stared at him, his eyes growing moist. "It's my father, isn't it?"

"Yes," Wamedayin stated. "He was too near death by the time I was summoned for the medicine to work. I am very sorry."

Taihinca stood. "I must go to my mother."

"Will you need me?" Indian Paintbrush asked.

"No. I will come for you when it's time." Taihinca pulled his robe round him and went out into the snow, his shoulders hunched as though carrying a heavy weight.

Taihinca and his brothers, though impeded by the snow drifts, built a small hut for their father in the woods. Taihinca returned for Indian Paintbrush and they joined most of the tribe as Taihinca's father was lifted out through the west window of the family home. Carried at the head of a procession, he finally was laid to rest in the hut built for him in the forest.

Indian Paintbrush returned with Taihinca to his family's hut where they remained through the night. Ceremonial drums sounded unceasingly as each family member took a turn recalling the many good things Taihinca's father had done during his lifetime.

"The spirits will listen as we tell about my father's greatness while he is on his journey to the happy hunting ground," Taihinca whispered to Indian Paintbrush.

The next four days members of the family, including Indian Paintbrush, fastened on their snow shoes and trudged over the snow to the hut in the woods, bringing food which they placed inside through the windows. "We must do this so my father will not be hungry on his long journey," her husband explained.

When life returned to normal, Indian Paintbrush realized she hadn't seen Owaissa during the funeral ceremony, even though the rest of her family had been present. After Taihinca left to go hunting, she decided to pay a visit to her adopted family.

She found Nita Anobi and Owaissa busy fashioning new garments from deerskin. They embraced her, welcoming her heartily. "I am so glad you came to see us, my daughter," Nita Anobi said.

"I am glad to see both of you. I was afraid that you might be ill, Owaissa, since you did not attend the funeral of my husband's father," explained Indian Paintbrush.

Owaissa giggled, "It was my time of the month, so I was unable to come."

"Oh," Indian Paintbrush said thoughtfully. She was suddenly puzzled. A flickering thought crossed her mind.

Nita Anobi asked, "What is the matter?"

Indian Paintbrush shook her head and almost smiled. "I just remembered . . . I have not had my regular period since I've been married."

Nita Anobi's round face lit up, her eyes crinkled, and her mouth turned upwards into a grin. "You're going to have a baby!"

Owaissa grabbed Indian Paintbrush's shoulders, kissing her soundly on both cheeks. "Isn't it wonderful?"

Blinking, she peered at her adopted mother and sister and felt bewildered. "Do you think it could be so? Could I really be going to have a baby?"

"Of course, my daughter. You are newly married and you've missed your monthly time. You will soon be a mother."

Indian Paintbrush, trying to grasp the significance of what Nita Anobi had said, found herself

smiling, a warmth flowing through her veins.
"That's wonderfu! Taihinca will be so pleased! Oh,
I can hardly wait for him to return so I can tell
him."

Nita Anobi took hold of Indian Paintbrush's
hands. "It is a happy time, but now you must take
care so you can bear a healthy child."

Immediately Indian Paintbrush was fearful,
knowing nothing about being pregnant. She was
afraid her ignorance could somehow be detri-
mental to the child she was carrying. "Tell me,
what must I do?"

"Eat well, for what you eat feeds your unborn
child, but do not partake of the meat of the rabbit
or the squirrel. The rabbit is too big of eyes. The
squirrel should not be eaten because when it is
frightened it runs up the tree, and the baby's
journey must be downward. Do not stand in doorways, for when your time comes you don't want
the child to linger overlong before he enters the
world. Rest when you become tired. Take care of
yourself and your child will be fine and healthy."

Indian Paintbrush wondered if she could remember all the instructions. Might she do something wrong without knowing it?

Nita Anobi patted her adopted daughter's knee,
adding, "Now, now, you must not be anxious. That
is not good for the baby either."

"There is so much I don't know," Indian Paintbrush moaned. "What about clothes, all the things
you need in order to care for a baby?"

Owaissa answered quickly, "Don't worry yourself. We will help you make the necessary items,
and there is plenty of time."

Indian Paintbrush could hardly remember what
she did the rest of the day. Her head was awhirl,
and all she could think of was the baby. She would
have liked to have gone from hut to hut and spread

her news to all who would listen, but she knew Taihinca must be the first one she told. She could hardly wait for his return.

He was later than usual, and Indian Paintbrush began to worry—perhaps he'd had an accident. When finally he came through the doorway, there was a dejected slump to his shoulders, and Indian Paintbrush knew his hunting had not been successful.

Dinner was ready. A piece of venison left over from a previous kill was sizzling on a plank beside the fire, and rice was steaming in a basket. "Come, sit down and have your supper. I have good news for you."

"I will be happy to hear any good news." He smiled wanly as he cut off a piece of the meat and began to eat.

"You will be especially happy to hear this news," she teased.

He glanced at her curiously, still chewing, and said, "Ummm, then please tell me what it is."

"No, not just yet. You eat your supper—and afterwards I will give you the news." She dished up a bowl of rice for him, sprinkling it with maple sugar.

Taihinca's hunger was greater than his curiosity, and he ate voraciously until his appetite was satisfied. He did glance at Indian Paintbrush from time to time, but she ignored him, eating daintily and smiling mysteriously.

When she had finished clearing away the remains of their meal, he stretched his arms out toward her. "Come, sit by me and tell me your news."

She knelt in front of him and took his hands. "I must look at your face when you hear this. My dear husband, we are going to have a child!"

Taihinca gripped her tightly, almost painfully.

His eyes widened and searched her face. "Is it really true? I have been hoping for this news!"

"Yes, it is most certainly true, I should have realized it sooner."

"When?" Taihinca demanded.

She shrugged her shoulders. "Nita Anobi says the child will arrive in the early summer."

Taihinca threw his arms about her, pulling her onto his lap. He cried a victorious war hoop and squeezed her tightly. "My wife, you have made me the happiest brave in the village." He nuzzled her neck, covered her face with kisses, and soon those light kisses of gratitude turned to passion. He lifted her into his arms and carried her the few steps to the pile of bearskins, and they celebrated their good news with love-making.

At first Indian Paintbrush found it difficult to accept the fact that she was expecting a child. She felt no different, nor could she discern any change in her body. But all at once her breasts became rounder and noticeably heavier, along with a slight thickening at her waist. Taihinca was intrigued by the physical transformation of her body, and every night he would have her stand naked beside the fire and inspect and caress her.

Lifting her breasts in his hands as if to weigh them, he would say, "There will be ample milk for my son." Sliding his hands over her growing abdomen, he would smile ecstatically, mumbling, "My son, my son."

Taking Indian Paintbrush into his arms, he would demonstrate his love and gratefulness by his gentle caresses and tender love-making.

When her stomach bulged blatantly beneath her doeskin tunic, all the members of the village congratulated Taihinca and Indian Paintbrush on their coming child—all but one.

The winter was nearly over with only patches of snow remaining in the shadows and denser parts of the forest. Nearly all the villagers had made temporary camp deep in the woods, since it was the time of year when the Menominees collected their supply of maple syrup.

Taihinca, choosing a stand of trees for him and his wife to tap, demonstrated how to make a gash in the trunk a few feet from the ground. Next he hammered a cedar spout into the gash, and from the spout a trickle of sap ran into a birch bark pail set on the ground. Together they tapped several trees, pouring the sap into large birch bark containers.

Indian Paintbrush was given the task of tending the fire and collecting the rocks which were heated in the fire. Taihinca would lift the hot rocks from the flames with two long sticks, dropping them into the sap and causing it to boil.

At one point Indian Paintbrush left to gather more rocks, and while awkwardly stooping over, she heard a familiar voice call her name. She stood, holding a heavy rock in her arms, and looked around.

"Here I am." A slim maiden stepped into the open, and Indian Paintbrush immediately recognized Awahtay.

"Poso," she said. She hadn't talked to Awahtay since the day Taihinca had scolded her. She had often crossed her path, but Awahtay had always averted her eyes and changed her direction so they would not come face to face.

"I see you are swollen with child," Awahtay sneered.

Indian Paintbrush smiled uncomfortably. "Yes, we are expecting our child to be born this summer."

Though she was beautiful, the young woman stared at Indian Paintbrush with such hate and malice that her countenance became thoroughly unpleasant.

"Do not expect to have a healthy child," Awahtay snarled. "It is not right for a male and female of different races to mate. A bear and a panther do not mate, nor do a raccoon and a rabbit. It is against nature. So it is unnatural for a Menominee brave to mate with a white woman. You will see I am right. The product of your union will be imperfect."

Before Indian Paintbrush was able to respond to Awahtay's vicious remarks, the woman spun around, disappearing into the forest. Indian Paintbrush stared after her, stunned by her words, then casting aside the rock she had been holding, she ran to Taihinca. She was sobbing by the time she reached him, and putting her head against his chest, she allowed the tears to flow unchecked.

"What's the matter? Are you sick? Have you been hurt?" Taihinca asked in alarm.

At first Indian Paintbrush was unable to talk. Taihinca held her, soothing her until she was calmer. "Now, my love, tell me what happened."

"It was Awahtay," she blurted. "She told me it was unnatural for us to mate, and that our child could not be normal." Her tears flowed anew.

"Stop!" Taihinca ordered. ' 'All this crying certainly isn't good for the child. Why do you listen to such foolishness? You know Awahtay is jealous of you and only desires to cause you pain. She is to be pitied. She has let her hateful feelings against you take over her life. None of the braves will want her as she is. No one desires a wife with such bitterness in her heart, knowing she would not be able to create a happy home. There is no husband or child in Awahtay's future. She blames her circumstances on you, but all the village knows she is the cause of her own unhappiness.

"Dry those tears, and tend to your fire. I need more hot rocks if I am to finish preparing our supply of maple sugar."

Indian Paintbrush swallowed hard, drying her tears on the tail of her tunic, and returned to her task, working especially hard in an effort to forget Awahtay's ugly words.

When each family had collected and prepared a year's supply of maple sugar they returned to their homes. Hunters were sent out immediately, and on their successful return a huge feast was prepared—a ceremonial rite in honor of Manitou. Before the festivities began, Taihinca turned to Indian Paintbrush and said, "Come, we will take some of our maple sugar to feed the spirits of my ancestors."

Indian Paintbrush watched as her husband reverently offered small amounts of the sugar to his departed relatives. In other memorial huts for departed Menominees, she could glimpse other members of the tribe going through the same ritual as her husband.

It was nearly dark when they returned to the village where the celebration had commenced. Before Indian Paintbrush and Taihinca partook of the feast, Taihinca offered her a bit of the maple sugar. "Eat this now in honor of Manitou."

The next morning, Indian Paintbrush woke before dawn with an annoying ache in her lower back. Crawling out from under the bearskin coverings, she stood up and felt a tearing within herself, a wet stickiness flowing down the inside of her thighs. An agonizing pain reached from her back to her pelvis, causing her to bend over, a groan escaping from her lips.

"What is it?" Taihinca asked, kicking back the covering and leaping to his feet. "Is it the baby?"

"Something is wrong," Indian Paintbrush gasped. "The baby is coming—and it's much too soon!"

"Lie down. I'll go after your mother. She'll know what to do." He helped her back onto their bed.

"Please hurry," she panted, as her body was again wracked by pain and she drifted into unconsciousness.

Voices woke her. "I don't think we can take her to the birthing hut," Nita Anobi said. Indian Paintbrush tried to speak, but only a moan came out.

"Stay quiet," her adopted mother urged. She felt a cool, damp cloth being placed on her forehead.

Wamedayin spoke. "Drink this." She sipped a bitter tasting drink which was held to her mouth. "This will check the bleeding."

Another pain grabbed at her insides, and she felt as though she were being torn apart. Mercifully she again drifted into a state of unconsciousness. At times she could hear recognizable voices—but nothing they said mattered to her.

"She's lost too much blood."

"Here comes the baby."

"Too small."

"A shame! He seems perfect in every way."

"He's not even going to take a breath."

Then all was quiet—and she drifted into an untroubled sleep.

Chapter 28

Indian Paintbrush rested on the bank of the small stream. The pungent odor of smoke from the village cooking fires hung heavily on the crisp, early morning air. The wild flowers were beginning to bloom, and near her feet was a scattered bouquet of purplish blue flowers with fringed petals and tiny white blossoms. Across the brook, growing beside clumps of goldenrod, were bright red buds of her namesake, Indian paintbrush. The branches, which had been bare all winter, were now thickly covered by new, green leaves, and birds were chirping from the treetops. Happy children's voices could be heard also—but Indian Paintbrush remained oblivious to all sights and sounds.

Her thoughts were absorbed by the death of her infant son, never even seen by her because he had been sent on his journey to the spirit world long before she had regained consciousness.

Wamedayin had told her she had been delirious with a fever for five days after she gave birth. Since then, Indian Paintbrush had remembered what Awahtay had said to her, mulling it over in her mind again and again.

When she had first opened her eyes Wamedayin had knelt beside her, holding a cup of herbal tea to her lips, urging her to drink. Knowing her baby was dead, tears stung her eyes, and she cried, "Why? Why did my son die?"

The medicine man patted her sympathetically. "He was already dead before he was born."

"I don't understand!"

"Something went wrong—it happens sometimes —he came too soon. But you are healthy and will have more sons."

Indian Paintbrush turned her head to hide the tears from Wamedayin. She didn't care about other sons; her arms ached to hold the one she'd lost. There was an emptiness in her heart.

Though Taihinca was also disappointed, he seemed more concerned for Indian Paintbrush's health. It was difficult for her to understand why he wasn't suffering more, since all she could think of was her tiny, dead son.

While she sat alone, she wondered if Awaytah had been correct—maybe it was against nature for Taihinca and herself to mate. Perhaps there could never be a healthy child from their union. If so, the love they had for each other would be a curse instead of a blessing.

"There you are! Why are you sitting here all by yourself?" It was Owaissa, who squatted down beside her adopted sister, peering into her face. "Are you ill?"

"No, I'm fine," Indian Paintbrush said listlessly.

"You must come and help us with the planting." Owaissa held out her hand to Indian Paintbrush.

Walking along beside Owaissa, Indian Paint-brush remembered she had intended to help with the planting when she left her hut, but her head had been flooded by sadness from the tragic loss of her son. She really didn't remember walking to the stream, or sitting beside its bank. Wasn't it enough to have no memory of her life before she came to the Menominees? Was she also going to be plagued by more lapses of memory?

She had pushed herself, working harder and longer than necessary, and now she was so weary she could barely prepare Taihinca's evening meal. Now that the days were warmer she was cooking outside, and leaning over to stir a pot of stewed meat, she didn't notice Taihinca approach.

"Are you ailing once again, my wife?" he asked.

Indian Paintbrush pushed a strand of red hair away from her eyes and frowned. "I must be a sight—you're the second person who has asked after my health today. I am quite well, thank you, just tired."

She dished up Taihinca's supper, setting it before him without comment. She ate her own portion quickly, ignoring Taihinca's questioning glances, then disappeared inside the hut, undressed and stretched out on the bed.

Later, when Taihinca lay down beside her, she turned her back, pretending to be asleep. She ignored the hand which gently stroked her shoulder, and after a time he sighed and turned away.

She was sorry but couldn't make herself acknowledge him. She felt something was missing within her—something that had been taken away along with her dead son. She loved Taihinca and didn't want to hurt him, but she didn't want to make love with him. She might get pregnant again and have another baby that would die.

In the morning Indian Paintbrush was shamed by the hurt in her husband's eyes, but she could say or do nothing to reassure him, her own feelings in a turmoil. No one understood why she mourned so excessively for her baby. Brief sympathy had been extended along with the suggestion she have another child right away. Why couldn't anyone see that a second baby could not replace the one she had lost?

And if Awahtay was correct, each child she carried would be born dead—and she couldn't bear to lose another one.

Poor Taihinca! Her troubled emotions had affected the physical side of her love for him, and she couldn't bear to have him touch her, afraid of another pregnancy. If only she could explain to Taihinca in a way he could understand. But how could she expect him to understand when everyone else kept recommending a second pregnancy as a solution to all their troubles?

Hard work was the path she took to quiet her troubled mind. After completing her own chores, she offered her services to the ill and elderly, and by bedtime she didn't have to feign fatigue, barely able to keep her eyes open.

But she didn't deny Taihinca when he approached her, permitting his touch, neither responding nor participating. After a few unsuccessful attempts to overcome Indian Paintbrush's unresponsiveness, Taihinca gave up.

The summer sun was already warming the inside of the house when Taihinca woke Indian Paintbrush by shaking her shoulder. She blinked and frowned. "Is something wrong?"

"No, nothing at all." Taihinca was smiling broadly. "Get up quickly. I have a surprise for you!''

She dressed and prepared breakfast with Taihinca prodding her on. ''Hurry now. Don't waste any time.''

''What is this surprise?'' She was beginning to be annoyed, since he would give no hint, an enigmatic smile playing on his lips.

When breakfast was over and the hut straightened to her satisfaction, she put her hands on her hips and stared at Taihinca. ''All right, now I'm through. What is this surprise of yours?''

''We're going to spend the day together. We have not gone riding together since way before . . . a long time. I remember how you liked it, and I have found a beautiful spot I want to share with you.''

''That does sound nice . . . but I planned to help Nita Anobi decorate a friendship bag this afternoon . . . and I should check on Siboka. He was very ill yesterday.''

Taihinca took her hand and led her outside. ''I've already spoken to your mother, and she agrees that a day's ride will be good for you. As for Siboka, I'm sure his wife can care for him as she has done in the past.''

Indian Paintbrush raised no further protest, following meekly behind her husband to where the horses were kept. Taihinca helped her onto the back of his horse and easily settled himself behind her. A feeling of exhilaration and lightness settled over her as the animal trotted into the forest, and she relaxed against her husband, welcoming the warmth for the first time in weeks.

The surrounding beauty of the forest charmed her immediately. She had always appreciated the varied shades of green of the pine, spruce, oak, birch, and other trees. Taihinca guided the horse to a stream which trickled over a rocky bed, eventually joining another that was wider with water rushing against the sides of its banks. Taihinca continued to follow it. They rounded a bend, thick berry bushes and a clump of birch trees blocking the view ahead.

The horse carefully stepped his way around the obstruction, and Indian Paintbrush gasped at the vista before her.

A thick carpet of verdant green moss covered a rolling hillock where massive rocks were scattered about as though a giant had casually tossed them. More rocks were stacked in the stream bed, causing the water to fall over them in a shimmery veil. Tiny purple flowers grew in the shadows of the trees, almost hidden by curly fronds of lacy ferns. A golden butterfly danced, alighting softly on a delicate blossom, floating gracefully to land on a wavering leaf.

"Taihinca, it's breathtaking!"

He slid from the horse and helped her down. "I knew you would be delighted by this place." He led her to where the waterfall cascaded over the rocks, and when droplets splashed on her face, she laughed.

"That is the first time I've heard the sound of your laughter in a long time," Taihinca said. "It is a sound I have been longing for."

He put his arms around her and kissed her. At first she was rigid, then, as though the sunlight filtering through the trees had effortlessly melted her reserve, she tasted the sweetness of his lips, pressing herself against him. Passion engulfed her.

Barely aware of Taihinca releasing her from her garments, she was only conscious of the rapturous sensations caused by his lips and fingers on her love-starved skin. He gently lowered her onto the soft, mossy bank, and she pulled him to her hungrily, welcoming him eagerly with her body.

Their passion was limitless, the act of love a flaming release.

When it was finished, Taihinca cradled her in his arms. He smoothed a spray of tangled curls from her forehead, tracing her profile with his fingers. Kissing the hollow of her throat he breathed huskily, "I prayed it would be like this."

She ran her hand across his smooth, bronze chest. It was as though this was the first time she had ever touched him so, her fingertips tingling with a fresh awareness. "I'm so sorry for the way I've been. I don't know what's been the matter with me," she said meekly.

He touched his forefinger to her lips. "Shhh! It is over now, and we can put it all behind us." He kissed her slowly, sensously, savoring the taste of her.

Pulling away from her, Taihinca raised himself on an elbow and grinned, a mischievous sparkle in his eyes. "Let's bathe in the waterfall."

After he helped her to her feet, she glanced at her pale nakedness and asked shyly, "But what if someone should come?"

"No one will," he assured her, leading her carefully down the mossy bank, guiding her through the outcropping of rocks and into the water. The cool, clear stream reached to their waists when they stepped under the gentle cascade of water.

It flowed gently over their bodies, and they gamboled about like children, laughing and splashing. When they tired, they sat on the rocks, resting and admiring each other's bodies. Taihinca fondled and caressed Indian Paintbrush, and she nuzzled his ear while running her hands down his smooth back. Their desire again aroused, he scooped her into his arms, lifting her from the water, and carried her to the cushiony spot on the mossy bank. Their lovemaking was gentle and prolonged, an act of beauty and promise.

Afterwards, when they realized the shadows had lenghtened and the air was cooler, they dressed. Standing hand in hand, they gazed at the waterfall. "This will always be our special place," Taihinca said. "I've visited here before. I've made tobacco offerings to Manitou and to all the rocks and trees about us, and even to the waterfall, to influence their forces to reunite us. And you will see, my wife, today you have conceived, and another boy child will be born to us. This one will come at his appointed time and will be healthy and grow up to become a great hunter."

Chapter 29

Taihinca's prophecy was correct. Indian Paint-brush knew she was again with child by the time of the annual wild rice gathering, this time recognizing the signs herself without consulting her foster mother.

She and Taihinca went together to gather rice. He would let her pole the canoe through the rice stalks for short periods, then trading jobs, let her beat the bundled stalks she pulled into the boat.

When they had gathered enough to satisfy their needs, Taihinca would not allow her to participate in the back-breaking chore of threshing; instead, he did it. Indian Paintbrush had argued, "Taihinca, please, the other braves will laugh at you doing women's work. I can do it. I promise to stop when I tire."

But Taihinca was adamant. "There is no need for you to make promises, for you will not do the work. I care not what the others think. I will do everything in my power to care for my unborn son.''

No one dared insult Taihinca, the only slur heard being directed at Indian Paintbrush. When her nemesis, Awahtay, passed by, kicking her moccasins to stir up the dust, Indian Paintbrush glanced up from her beadwork. The girl was standing directly in front of the sun, outlined brilliantly with her face in shadow. Indian Paintbrush shaded her eyes and squinted.

Awahtay was staring at her, her black eyes filled with hate, her lips set in a thin bitter line. "How can you humiliate a great hunter like Taihinca? It is unfitting for him to do women's work. And it is also for no good purpose. You will never be able to bear a healthy child for Taihinca. One of these days he will come to his senses and be free of your spell."

The woman spun around and disappeared, sending up another flurry of dust. Indian Paintbrush's stomach did a flip-flop of fear, her skin turning clammy.

"Was that Awahtay?" Owaissa stepped over to Indian Paintbrush, who nodded her head, not trusting her voice.

"What nastiness was she up to now?" Owaissa asked, sitting down beside her adopted sister.

Indian Paintbrush sighed. "She is criticizing me for letting Taihinca help with the threshing of the rice, though everyone surely knows I do not control my husband nor have any desire to do so. But worse, she says I will not be able to have a child for Taihinca." She brushed away a single tear.

Owaissa hugged her sister. "Pay no heed to that one. She is no longer right in her head and is to be pitied."

"Dear sister, I am worried. I do so want to have

a baby for my husband."

"And so you shall."

The summer drifted into fall. The days became shorter and the nights were chilly, with a hint of frost in the air. Indian Paintbrush had started to have an uneasy feeling someone was watching her. When she went to the stream for water she thought she heard a soft footfall, but when she turned around she only saw a fleeting shadow.

Dipping her bark container into the water, she was startled, as she often was, by the sight of her reflection with its fair skin and bright red hair. Now feeling so much a part of the Menominee village, she no longer wondered about her background.

She felt something—or someone—behind her, and suddenly the tormented face of Awahtay appeared in the mirrored surface beside her own. The young woman's eyes blazed with hatred.

Beginning to turn, she caught sight of Awahtay swinging a heavy tree branch toward her, then her head exploded with pain. There was darkness— then nothing.

She tried to open her eyes, but the lids seemed to be stuck, and her head throbbed from the effort. Someone moaned from far off—and she realized it was herself.

"Indian Paintbrush?" It was Taihinca's voice.

Painfully she lifted her eyelids enough to see through the lashes. The world whirled about in an unfocused fuzz. She blinked several times until her eyes finally adjusted and she saw Taihinca sitting beside her.

A broad smile crossed his face, and he lifted her hand to his lips. "Thank the Great Spirit! Finally you are awake! You've been lying there so quiet

and still for three days. I must go after
Wamedayin and tell him you are finally
conscious."

"No . . . wait. What happened? I don't quite remember . . ." she said.

"A dead branch fell from a tree and struck your
head. Some of the women discovered you and
carried you back to the village."

While Taihinca spoke the image of Awahtay's
face appeared in her mind—and she remembered
what had really happened. Before she could tell
her husband, Awahtay's face disappeared to be
replaced by another. It was familiar, a face much
like her own, though masculine. Many faces
crowded around the boy's: a lovely woman with
hair a shade lighter than hers, along with other
young women. She instinctively knew they were
her family. Their names flooded her memory:
Willy, her mother, Jessie, Dora, Desdemona. Tears
stung her eyes as she suddenly ached for them.

"You are in pain! I must get Wamedayin to care
for you," Taihinca said, worry clouding his face.

"No, please." She clutched his arm. "I must
think."

Reluctantly he remained in his place, holding
her hands and watching her. Indian Paintbrush
was unaware of him as memories sped painfully
through her mind, bumping against each other in
a jumble. She knew it would probably be a long
while before she could sort them all out.

Taihinca squeezed her hand, and she returned to
the present. Worry was etched on his face, and she
smiled in an effort to reassure him. "My husband,
I have something important to tell you, but it must
be a secret. No one else must ever know."

"I will promise anything you desire. I am so
relieved you are awake and seem to be well. What
is your secret?"

She lowered her voice and whispered, "I know who I am. I remember what happened. I remember so much my head hurts from the remembering!"

Taihinca's smile faded, his eyes clouded, and his mouth set in a grim line. "Now you will want to return to your home. How can I live without my Indian Paintbrush? And what about my unborn son? Perhaps your family will not be willing to accept a child with Menominee blood."

Indian Paintbrush raised herself, reaching her arms out to her husband and hugging him tightly. "My dear Taihinca, I shall never leave you until the day I die!" They clung to each other for a moment, Indian Paintbrush placing her hands on Taihinca's bronze cheeks and gazing deeply into his dark eyes.

"Taihinca, I do not want anyone to know my memory has returned. You must never tell."

"I have promised," he reminded her, "but I do not understand."

"Your people have accepted me, but I believe it is because they feel sorry for me because there is nowhere else for me to go. I know Awahtay is not the only one who resents my presence. If the village realizes I now know who I am, and where I came from, they will force me to return to my former home."

Taihinca nodded his head. "Perhaps you are correct. But your family . . . don't you want to see them again?"

"I would like to, of course, especially my mother, but it isn't a good idea. You see, my father was murdered by renegade Indians when I was two years old, and my mother suffered terribly because of his death. She loved him dearly.

"When he was gone she was unable to keep the family together and had to give up my three older sisters. Though she never spoke much about it, I know she has very bitter feelings toward Indians, and I don't believe she could accept our marriage. So, though I would dearly love to see her, it wouldn't be fair. You can see that, can't you? After all the time that has passed since my disappearance, she surely thinks I'm dead and is probably accustomed to the loss by now. If I went to visit her now she would expect me to stay, and I couldn't do that, and she would have to go through the pain of losing me all over again. No, I think it best to leave things as they are."

Taihinca pondered his wife's words. He remembered stories told by the old ones of a brave of bad seed who had caused problems, broken the laws of the tribe and was banished, later teaming up with other rebels and misfits. The great leader, Half-face, who had become a legend after his death, had kept a watchful eye on the troublemakers. He'd reported regularly the band's infamous crimes: pillaging and murdering the white man and Indian alike. There had been no news of the renegades in the last few years—hopefully they were dead, killed by an avenging band.

A question came from Taihinca: "Tell me, do you remember how you came to be with the men who our people found you with? They were not the same Indians who killed your father, were they?"

"No, surely not. They were young men, and none of them had the look of your people, nor dressed in the same manner. It was a terrifying experience— and now I can remember the tiniest of details— but it almost seems as though it had happened to someone else. It is like an incident in a story I once read."

She described the events of the day she was taken from her home. "My mother had gone to a neighbors to borrow a cup of sugar and I was alone in the house, lying on the floor reading. I heard nothing unusual, but when I read, I wasn't easily distracted." She remembered how often her mother had had to call her in order to attract her attention when she was engrossed in a book.

Indian Paintbrush continued. "A shadow fell across the page and I looked up to see a tall Indian standing with his legs apart, hands on hips, a ferocious leer on his face. And you must remember, my love, except for stories of an Indian friend of my father's, the only other Indians I knew anything about were the ones who had killed my father. Of course I was terrified. I started to scream, but the man clamped his hand over my mouth and grabbed by hair, pulling my head back until I thought my neck would break.

"Another Indian appeared from nowhere, and together they picked me up and carried me outside to their horses. I remember kicking and hitting, but my blows went unnoticed. They slung me like a sack of flour over one of the horses, one of the Indians leaping up and holding onto me while they galloped away into the woods.

"They called back and forth to each other as they rode further and further from my home. I was horribly uncomfortable, and just when I thought I couldn't stand any more, they stopped.

"I was dropped to the ground and started to scream, but they simply ignored me and built a small fire. I just sat there and cried. When it was dark and the Indians seemed to be asleep I decided to run even though there was no moon and I could hardly see. Tree branches hit me as I stumbled over the rocks. When I heard the Indians shouting and knew they had discovered my escape, I ran even faster.

"I tripped and tumbled and hit my head—and

that's all I remember until I woke in Wamedayin's hut."

Taihinca smoothed his hand across Indian Paintbrush's brow, a strange expression on his face. "Tell me . . . what is your name?"

"My name is Indian Paintbrush—and always will be. My mother called me Wilhelmin, but there no longer is a Wilhelmina. That part of my life is over, as much as when I couldn't remember it. Now my life is with you and with our family."

"You give me great joy. But I can't help feeling you may have regrets about not seeing your family once again," Taihinca said.

Indian Paintbrush took hold of Taihinca's hand and squeezed. "My dear husband, I would love to see my sweet mother's face once again. And I have a twin brother, Willy . . . and three sisters . . . but I know it is best for all concerned to leave things as they are."

Taihinca frowned and gazed thoughtfully at her, his face lighting up with a smile. "I have an idea! When you have recovered from your head wound, before the first snow, we'll see if we can discover your old home. We can view it from afar, perhaps catching a glimpse of your mother and brother."

"Oh! Wouldn't that be wonderful? I could see them without them knowing!"

"Now I must let Wamedayin know you are awake." He tried to rise, but Indian Paintbrush wouldn't release her hand.

"Remember," she pleaded, "do not mention I have regained my memory."

"I have promised."

She let him go.

Wamedayin was pleased with her recovery. "You had us all worried, Indian Paintbrush, but you now are mending swiftly. The wound on the back of your head has nearly healed, and you should be back to normal in a few days. Continue to rest." He mixed her a bitter mixture of herbs and watched her drink it.

She closed her eyes, faces from her past crowding her mind's eyes, and fell asleep to dream of her family of long ago.

Chapter 30

The sun had not yet risen when Taihinca and Indian Paintbrush stepped outside their hut. The village was still, no smoke curling skyward.

"Come, we can slip away before anyone is even awake." Taihinca's breath clouded as he spoke.

The reason for their journey had been told to no one. To their families they had merely mentioned a hunting trip, because they could not foretell the length of their absence.

Taihinca helped his wife onto the horse and secured the pack with the few items they would need. Tucking the bearskin robe around her tightly to ward off the early morning chill, he pulled himself up behind her. They rode toward the area where Indian Paintbrush had been found.

The sky was filled with ominous, black clouds as they reached a small clearing. Indian Paintbrush walked around, shaking her head. "I don't know. This doesn't seem familiar at all. Remember, I was here at night and nearly out of my mind with fear."

"I didn't expect you to remember," Taihinca said. "And I'm not even sure we'll be able to locate your home. But you do remember your mother's farm was but a few miles from the place called Woodlake. We will look for some homes near there, and perhaps you will begin to recognize something as we get closer."

They spent the night curled together under the bearskin robe in a makeshift shelter Taihinca had constructed to ward off the threatening rain. At dawn they breakfasted on boiled rice with maple sugar and a bit of smoked fish.

Indian Paintbrush peered at the dark sky and suggested, "Maybe we should turn back."

"A little rain will not harm us."

By afternoon Indian Paintbrush knew she was in familiar territory. They rode to the edge of the forest, peering through the trees at a man-made clearing.

"There! That was my home," Indian Paintbrush whispered excitedly, pointing to a small building on the other side of an overgrown field.

Taihinca helped her down from the horse and they circled the perimeter of the clearing, staying within the shelter of the trees. "Something is not right," Indian Paintbrush said. "There is no smoke coming from the chimney."

"It appears deserted," Taihinca commented. "There are no animals about, the barn looks empty, and all the gardens are dry and full of weeds."

Indian Paintbrush tried to swallow the lump which had formed in her throat and blinked back her tears. "What could have happened?"

Taihinca reached for her hand. "Let us take a look around."

They walked with caution across the field toward the house. It was obvious Taihinca's assumptions were correct—no one lived there anymore. The front door was ajar, and Indian Paintbrush stepped inside filled with fear. She was instantly overcome by an overwhelming sense of loss and put her face against her husband's chest and sobbed. He patted her back, murmuring sympathetically.

After a few moments he raised her head. "I think your people moved away by their own choice— you see, they left nothing behind."

She gazed around through damp eyelashes. The house was bare, a film of dust covering the floor.

"Judging by the garden and field I would guess they have been gone since summer," Taihinca commented.

A sigh escaped her lips. "Mother surely thinks I'm dead, so perhaps she has gone to be with my sisters. I hope she is happy wherever she is."

Taihinca put his arm around her. "Come, we will now return to the village. You are now only Menominee. There is no longer a girl called Wilhemina. You are Indian Paintbrush, wife of Taihinca."

Indian Paintbrush managed a smile and felt her unborn child stirring within her for the first time. The sorrow in her heart was gone, replaced by great joy. She felt love and admiration for her tall, strong, handsome husband. Realizing the wisdom of the Menominee's philosophy to cherish each moment for its own, she smiled at Taihinca once again, filled by happiness for what she possessed.

Indian Paintbrush never told anyone that Awahtay had attacked her. The woman obviously was consumed with guilt and fear, for whenever she and Indian Paintbrush met, Awahtay would avert her eyes and change her direction. Awaytay hadn't expected Indian Paintbrush to survive, and it was obvious she was fearfully waiting for her victim to expose her.

But Indian Paintbrush had no intentions of revealing the information. She felt no animosity toward Awahtay—merely pity. Awahtay's cheekbones jutted out above her hollowd cheeks, her once beautiful eyes now haunted and underlined with dark shadows.

Because her days were so full of happiness and anticipation, Indian Paintbrush seldom even thought of her former enemy. Though at times feeling a tug of worry for her unborn child, usually she felt smothered in warmth and well-being.

Taihinca often assured her their baby would arrive at the proper time—alive and healthy. To insure it he intended to participate in the Grand Medicine Dance in the name of his unborn son. He explained a little of what that entailed. "I've never felt the need to dance the Grand Medicine Dance before, because my guardian spirit always guided me well. But now I am moved to join in the ceremony."

The members of the society would all meet in a large, mat-draped lodge. The men would dance until overwhelmed by wondrous ecstasies, and cowrie shells endowed with magical powers would be thrown at all the intitiates. "And when I'm hit by one of the shells, I'll fall into a trance—a state between life and death—and the magic will fill my spirit and I will rise with a new life, abundant health and vitality. Nothing will be able to touch me—or my son."

Taihinca was always to believe that the Grand Medicine Dance had a great part in the successful delivery of his healthy son, who Taihinca proudly named Shoawa. Indian Paintbrush was filled with love and tenderness when the baby first nursed at her breast. The infant was perfect, but she was amazed she could find no likeness of herself in the child. He resembled the other babies in the village —except, of course, his black hair was silkier, his sturdy body showed every sign of being stronger, and his dark eyes sparkled with much more intelligence.

Indian Paintbrush seldom thought of the family she had left behind. Her life with the Menominees was full and satisfying, and her love for Taihinca expanded and matured through the years. She watched Shoawa and his three younger brothers grow tall and handsome, her heart bursting with pride.

When Shoawa reached the age of manhood, Taihinca told Indian Paintbrush it was time for their son to seek a guardian spirit. At breakfast the next morning, Shoawa was offered a bowl of rice and a lump of charcoal. His three brothers, sensing the importance of the moment, were unusually subdued, peering curiously at their parents and Shoawa.

Without hesitation Shoawa picked up the charcoal and rubbed it on his face. Taihinca rose from his place and without a work walked outside. Shoawa, eyes straight ahead, followed his father.

The three younger boys stared after them for only a few moments, then the quiet was broken as they began eating, laughing and talking. Indian Paintbrush shut out their youthful noise as she thought of her first born and what was about to happen as he made the giant step into manhood.

Taihinca had explained the ceremony to her many times before. He and Shoawa would walk in the forest until they discovered the right place, where together they would build a shelter. When it was done, Taihinca would leave Shoawa and return to the village.

For the next four days the youth would fast, sitting patiently as his strength ebbed, until a guardian spirit came to him. From that moment on, the guardian spirit would protect him for the rest of his life. When Shoawa finally returned, he would be a hunter and a warrior.

The girls in the village also sought a guardian spirit in much the same manner. Owaissa's daughter, Luatehaw, had recently had her first menstrual time and had gone to a hut outside the village, fasted, and awaited the appearance of her guardian spirit. The divine aid she sought would be used to assure good health, a strong and prosperous husband, and many children.

One day Awahtay disappeared from the village, and her bloated body was found several weeks later floating in the shallow water of one of the many fingers of the lake.

Indian Paintbrush lived a long and happy life within the Menominee village. When Wamedayin died and a new medicine man was chosen in his place, Indian Paintbrush became the only one left in the village able to speak the white man's tongue.

White men settled all around, and soldiers came to enforce the 1854 treaty made between Chief Oshkosh and the Wisconsin governor. The treaty, which limited the Menominees to a small area of land, had been mostly ignored since its inception, and several times Indian Paintbrush was called upon to renegotiate with the white man.

Her hair was white, though still thick and unruly with curls framing her face. The Army officers with whom she spoke supposed she might be an albino because of her light blue eyes and fair skin—a strange apparition in her heavily beaded

deerskin tun;ic always worn on special occasions.
The soldiers were in awe of her because of her
superior command of their language and
considered her to be a female shaman, endowed
with divine powers. Neither she, nor the elders of
the Menominee village, did or said anything to
clear up the misconception.

Several times Indian Paintbrush successfully
explained the necessity for the men of the tribe to
hunt and fish in areas away from those allotted
by the treaty, assuring the soldiers that the Menominees would not encroach on the rights of
the white settlers in any way. Indian Paintbrush
soon became a legend in the local Army posts.

She was happy to be able to assist the people
who had sheltered her and become her own, but
deep within her heart she was sad. She knew that
as the years passed the white man would become
more demanding, and eventually the Menominees
would be forced to exist only in the small area
originally designated to them. She was often
reminded of the story told by the elders of the
tribe.

When Chief Oshkosh met with Wisconsin
Governor Dodge, he was given a top hat. When he
placed it on his head, he commented, "Don't I look
awful? This is the way the white man's law fits the
Indian."

Indian Paintbrush knew that in future times the
Menominees would be forced to change their life
style, causing great pain and frustration. And
when she thought of this, she was downhearted.
Though she and Taihinca would not be affected,
she knew that her children and grandchildren
faced a future of insurmountable problems

BOOK IV

Will Vradenburg

Chapter 31

He was called Willy—a tall, skinny boy, mostly knobby knees and elbows, dressed in ill-fitting, rough clothing, his cheeks and upper lip barely covered with down. He had left home without telling anyone his intentions, knowing he would never be able to convince his mother of his need to be out on his own. And there was that promise he'd made to her when his twin sister had disappeared. "I'll never leave you," he'd said. He felt a twinge of guilt when he remembered, but at least he'd left a note explaining his leave-taking. After all, she did have Mr. Cromer to take care of her.

Though his sisters still called their stepfather Mr. Cromer, Willy had a true affection for the man who had married his mother and had found it easy to fall into the habit of addressing him as Pa. He couldn't really remember his own father who had been killed by Indians when Willy was only two.

Packing his clothes in a carpetbag, along with

half a loaf of bread and some thick slices of ham, he left in the middle of the night, headed for Hill City, and was soon able to hitch a ride with a farmer heading south. His first few weeks on his own were spent as a hired hand on a cattle ranch in Nebraska, but it was too much like the work he did at home, with none of the ensuing warmth. On the evening of one pay day he just took leave of the ranch, hoofing it to the nearest Union Pacific station.

He hadn't decided whether to head east or west when the choice was made for him by the station master. "First train a comin's headed west," the man snapped, obviously wanting no part of a young man who didn't even know where he wanted to go. It was only an hour's wait until a snorting, chugging train staggered to a halt to take on fuel, water, and a handful of passengers—one of whom was Willy.

The train ride was a new and exciting experience. When the train started, it heaved and lurched, nearly throwing everyone out of his seat, and sparks from the locomotive flew in through an open window, once burning a hole in a passenger's clothing. But watching the scenery whisk by made the trip worthwhile. As the days passed Willy was happy it was early summer, so he could hang his head out the window, away from the malodorous unwashed bodies around him.

Sleeping sitting up on the hard seat was not a problem for Willy, who could sleep anywhere. He felt sorry for the few women aboard, being exposed to the worsening stench while having to sleep unconcealed from curious eyes.

Eating was an adventure in itself, since there were no facilities for dining on the train. Passengers traveling shorter distances brought food with them. Others, such as Willy, had to depend upon townspeople selling sandwiches, cold chicken, and drinks at whistlestops, or take their chances in the station lunch rooms in the larger towns.

In most places the train would stop for twenty minutes, barely enough time to order, pay for, and try to eat one's meal before the boarding bell was rung. And sometimes it was a real race when Willy suspected the lunchroom owners had made a deal with the trainmen to leave early. The bell would be sounded after ten minutes, so that food that had been paid for was left uneaten, only to be resold to the next crowd. It happened but once to Willy, after which he was careful to order only what he could snatch from his plate and carry back to the train.

As the days passed he realized one lady in his car was traveling as far as he was. He'd noticed her from the moment she boarded the train, for she was the most beautiful creature he'd ever seen. Glancing at her whenever possible, he found her as breathtaking as the scenery.

Her hair was the lightest yellow, piled high on her head in an unbelievable array of falling curls. Perched atop this astounding hairdo was a magnificent hat adorned with a huge feather of dazzling blue. Willy wondered what kind of bird it had come from.

Her dress was the same shade of blue, made of a shimmery material he'd never seen before. A dangerously low cut neckline barely contained her pale, full bosom, and he tried not to stare at it too blatantly when glancing her way. Her waist was so tiny he knew he could fit both his hands around it easily with room to spare.

It was her face which fascinated him the most. She had the fairest of skin—the color of milk after the cream was skimmed from the top—except for

prominent cheekbones which blushed the faintest
of red. Her eyes were a cool, light blue, accented
by dark, long lashes. Often holding a lacy handkerchief to her dainty nostrils, Willy knew she was
protecting herself from the onslaught of the overpowering rankness of the crowded car. Her lips,
full and pouty, were colored a bright red, and her
fingers were adorned with colorful rings set with
sparkling gems. Despite the heat, she always
seemed to be cool, calm and composed.

Many of the male passengers had tried to strike
up a conversation with her, but she had discouraged each of them with an icy stare.
Therefore Willy was completely surprised when,
as the train was nearing Reno, Nevada, the
beautiful woman slipped into the seat next to him.
Her voice was the most melodious he'd ever heard.
"Excuse me, young man, but may I inquire as to
your destination?"

Embarrassed by his voice cracking, he stammered, "I hadn't really decided, ma'am." The
musky aroma of her perfume enveloped him, and
he found it difficult to even think.

"Perhaps you would consider going on to
Virginia City with me. I will be in need of a strong
young man to help with my luggage and various
other duties during my stay. You look exactly like
the sort of person I need. What do you say?"

"Well . . . ah, ma'am, I don't know . . ."

"You'll be well paid for your efforts, of course!
Allow me to introduce myself. I'm Crystal
Brouilette. Perhaps you've heard of me?"

"No, ma'am," he said, his heart pounding in his
ears. "I mean, no, I haven't heard of you, but yes,
I'd be honored to work for you." He stuck his hand
out to shake hers as he introduced himself. "I'm
Willy Van Vradenburg."

She took his hand and clasped it tightly.

"Pleased to make your acquaintance, Will. I'm a singer and I have an engagement in the Piper's Opera House in Virginia City. I think we'll get along just fine!"

"Yes, ma'am," agreed Willy. Why he'd be willing to do anything for this gorgeous creature—whether he was paid or not. Hallelujah!

Chapter 32

They changed trains in Reno, Crystal supervising Willy as he helped unload the several trunks and valises. He couldn't even guess what could be in them all—surely no one had use for that many clothes—and he couldn't help but compare it with his own small wardrobe which fit quite nicely into his carpetbag.

The V. and T. Railroad which they boarded for the fifty-two miles to Virginia City was a bit different from the previous train. The seats were woven straw which was supposed to afford a sense of coolness, but Willy decided the coolest place on the train was the privy, where he could see the train track racing by when he looked in the hole. When he sat, a blast of air cooled his bare behind, and he found it a surprising, rather refreshing experience.

The train made an unbelievable climb up the mountainside, the view both breathtaking and often frightening, because the tracks were perched along the sides of rugged cliffs. They went through a four mile long tunnel, and while riding in the dark, Miss Brouilette slipped her hand into his. Willy squeezed it reassuringly, trying to act like the protective male she obviously thought him to be. With her small form pressed shivering against him, he did indeed feel brave and strong.

The first good view of Virginia City was afforded them when they pulled into the station. The town was perched high above them. The business district was on either side of the main street, and houses of every imaginable size and style dotted the side of the mountains. It was surprising to find a town of such proportions in the middle of nothing but barren and unyielding rock mountains.

But there wasn't much time for gawking. The minute the train stopped Miss Brouilette ordered him to oversee the unloading of her trunks. From the corner of his eye he could see she was being greeted by several prosperously dressed gentlemen.

"Will," she called in her honey tones, "these kind sirs have provided that wagon over there for my belongings. You see that everything is loaded carefully and have them taken to the International Hotel and I will meet you there later. Have the trunks carried to our rooms."

The driver of the wagon was a surly fellow who grunted out one syllable answers to Willy's questions. It was futile for Willy to try and learn anything from him, so he sat back and eyed his surroundings with awe.

The ride from the depot to the main thoroughfare, C Street, was up such a steep grade that Willy wasn't sure the horse could pull up such a heavy load. The driver didn't seem the least concerned, just holding the reins casually and spitting a stream of yellow tobacco juice over the side of the wagon. The horse lowered his head, the muscles in his neck bulged, and wonder of wonders, the wagon's wheels began rolling and creaking their way laboriously to the top of the hill. The driver guided the horse to the left into the biggest mess of traffic Willy had ever seen!

There was every kind of wagon, carriage, and cart drawn by horses and mules. The foot traffic was even more astounding! Pedestrians of all sizes and shapes filled the boardwalks on both sides of the street, darting with abandonment in front of the wagon with no regard for their personal safety as far as Willy could tell.

He spied Indian families and one or two Indians in full regalia, complete with feather head dresses. He saw a Chinese person dressed in pajama-like clothing, complete with a single pigtail dangling down his back, scurrying from one store to another. There were miners dressed in working garb and speculators of one sort or another in fancy clothes the likes of which Willy had never seen before. A number of women were doing their daily shopping, housewife types in simple dresses trailed by various numbers of children. Glamorous ladies, dressed in fancy outfits with parasols twirling over their heads, daintily lifted their skirts as they too made the dangerous dash across the crowded, dirty street. Here and there a small boy could be seen darting in and out as he ran down the boardwalk, a dog chasing along at his heels.

From the doorway of each establishment barkers and pitchmen called out, telling of their wares—from hot tamales to snake oil! It was the busiest main street Willy had ever seen, every other sign advertising a saloon or gambling hall.

The delicious aroma of frying food was inter-
mingled with the smell of tobacco, horse manure,
exotic perfumes, wood smoke, and other odors not
so easily identified, both pleasant and not so
pleasant. The assault of his senses nearly made
him dizzy.

He figured he'd seen everything when the driver
mumbled, "That's the hotel."

Willy gasped and stared. The International
Hotel towered above the corner of Union and C.
"Wow!" He counted the rows of windows,
realizing the edifice was six stories high!

"Hey, kid, I ain't unloading these trunks by
myself!" The driver nudged him with his elbow
before he could climb down off the wagon.

"Oh . . . sorry." Willy jumped to the street. A
small hand cart was resting on the porch, and the
driver motioned to Willy to bring it beside the
wagon. The baggage then was piled onto the cart.

"Well . . . take it on inside, boy. I got other things
to do."

Pushing and pulling, Willy was finally able to
maneuver the cart through the huge swinging
doors. The lobby was the largest single room Willy
had ever seen, and gaped at the luxurious surroundings—settees upholstered in red velvet,
walls trimmed with gilt, a huge crystal chandelier
hanging in the center. He realized the man behind
the rich mahogany desk was beckoning to him.

"Mr. Vradenburg, Mr. Vradenburg, sir."

"Yes. That's me."

"Miss Brouilette has requested you join her as
soon as possible in her room. It's suite number
202." As Will started back towards the luggage
cart, the hotel man called after him, "No, no, that
won't be necessary. The luggage will be taken to
her room."

"Oh, well, thank you." Willy felt awkward and

dumb as he bounded up the carpeted staircase.

The door to room 202 was slightly ajar and Willy could hear voices from inside. He tapped lightly and Miss Broilette called, "Come in."

Upon entering, he saw the two elegantly attired men were perched on a small, satin covered settee while Miss Brouilette held court from an ornately carved chair. "Oh, it's you, Will . . . finally. Come here." She held her hand out to him.

Willy went to her side, and she clasped her hand. "Gentlemen, this is my man, Will Vrandenburg. Will, I'd like you to meet Mr. Habok, the proprietor of the International Hotel, and Mr. John Piper, the owner of the Opera House."

"Pleased to make your acquaintance," Willy said, bobbing his head. He felt out of place amid such grand surroundings and in the company of such well-dressed men, when he was still in his dirt-caked shoes and travel-stained clothing. He was well aware that he was dirty and smelly and he longed for a bath. Miss Brouilette also had been in the same clothing for several days, but she appeared clean and unruffled.

It was as though she had read his mind, for she said, "Gentlemen, if that's all, I'd like to bathe and rest before my performance this evening."

They murmured polite goodbyes, Mr. Habok adding, "And don't forget, you and Mr. . . . ah . . . Vradenburg are to be my guests for dinner tonight in the hotel dining room."

After they left Miss Brouilette rose from her chair. "Now, Will, come help me with my bath. The water has been poured and yours is ready for you in your room. When I'm through you can tend to yourself." She motioned toward another door which led from the sitting room.

He couldn't believe his ears. Help her with her bath! Goodness! He didn't know anything about a

lady's toilette. He was sure the next few minutes
would bring the end of his job, and he meekly
trailed along behind her.

The hip tub was decorated on the outside with
painted roses and curlicues, the inside filled with
soapy bubbles. Miss Brouilette turned her back to
him and said, "Hurry and unfasten me. I can't
wait to soak myself!"

He couldn't control the shaking of his hands as
he undid the fasteners. She lifted her skirts and
began to struggle to pull her dress over her head.
"Help, Will," her muffled voice commanded
through the voluminous folds of cloth.

Trying hard not to look at her lacy underskirt,
he pulled the dress off, but he was forced to put
his modesty aside when he was obliged to lift
less than five of the delicate garments over Miss
Brouilette's head. Embarrassed, he shut his eyes.

Miss Brouilette began to laugh. "My, my, dear
Will, I do believe you're uncomfortable!"

"Yes, ma'am," Willy gasped, peeking at her.
Sakes alive—there she stood in a lacy camisole
top, her bosom barely covered, silky bloomers
halfway down her milky white thighs, and black
stockings rolled just under her dimpled knees. To
be frank, he not only was uncomfortable—he was
astounded! He'd never seen women's underthings
anyplace but on a clothes line, and the ones he had
seen had been plain and utilitarian. He could
hardly believe this beautiful, fragile female, who
was nearly a stranger, was standing before him
practically in the all together!

"I'll . . . ah . . . just be going now, ma'am," he
croaked, backing toward the door.

"Not so fast, Will. I guess I'd better explain what
your duties are. First, please do not all me 'ma'am'
anymore, since it makes me feel old. And don't call
me Miss Brouilette either. We shall be on much

more intimate terms than that. From now on you may call me Crystal!

"And as to your duties—I don't care to have a silly little female servant around, but I do still need the services a personal maid would provide. That is where you come in, Will. You will help me undress and dress each day, and assist with my bath. You will be my escort to dinner and to the opera house each night and home again, unless I give you other instructions. The rest of the time you may do as you please.

"Another thing—you have to do something about your wardrobe today. There are several men's clothing stores right here in Virginia City, and Mr. Habak has agreed to arrange credit for me. As soon as I've bathed and settled down for my nap, you are to wash and then go down and see Mr. Habak, and he will direct you where to do your shopping.

"Now, help me into the tub and scrub my back." She stepped out of the remaining garments and stood in naked splendor before him.

He'd never beheld such beauty in his whole life. He tried not to stare, but that was impossible, and he knew his mouth was hanging open. It was like a wonderful dream. He was feeling emotions he'd never even imagined, and he wondered if he were in love.

There was an amused smile on Crystal's lips as she reached for his hand. "Much as I enjoy such open admiration, do try and control yourself. Help me into the tub."

He was silent, for what could he say? There were no words in his mind, only the rush of strange and wonderful feelings. He helped Crystal step into the bath, watching her smooth, voluptuous body disappear into the bubbly water.

"Pick up the sponge and soap my back."

Gingerly, he massaged the silky skin, finding it difficult to breathe. After a few moments, she sighed. "That will do, Will. Go ahead and get yourself cleaned up and tend to your shopping. I'll expect you back here by six o'clock to wake me and assist me with my dressing."

He was grateful to escape. Shutting the door, he gulped some air and crossed the sitting room to the room Crystal had indicated was his. He was amazed to find it was every bit as large and luxurious as Crystal's, and a bath similar to hers was awaiting him. After shedding his clothes he slipped into the tepid water. It was pure heaven. He scrubbed himself with the fragrant soap and sponge, dunking his head and washing his hair.

Clean and refreshed, he toweled himself dry and put on a pair of overalls and a clean shirt from his carpetbag. He brushed his damp hair and peered at his reflection in the mirror over the dresser. "I look like a durned hick!" he exclaimed. But at least he was now a clean hick.

Chapter 33

Willy dashed into the hotel lobby, glanced at the clock hanging over the front desk, nodded to the clerk, and juggling his parcels bounded up the stairs. It was five of six, time to awaken Miss Brou —Crystal—it was difficult to call her by her first name, even in his mind—and help her dress. The thought alone turned his cheeks fiery hot. Oh, if only he could control himself!

Bursting into the sitting room of Crystal's suite, he dropped the packages onto the settee. Taking a deep breath, he shoved open the door of her bedroom. "Ah . . . Crystal, it's time for you to wake up!"

She wiggled, yawned and stretched, the sheet slipping down to reveal the soft, roundness of her magnificent breasts. Willy tried not to stare but felt blood rushing to all parts of his body. When she opened her eyes, she coquettishly fluttered her eyelashes, before slowly covering herself.

"Good evening, Will," she greeted. "Poor boy, I keep forgetting how sweet and naive you are. Do forgive me, but I assure you, you will soon be used to my ways. If it makes you more comfortable, turn your back and I'll get up and slip into some lingerie, then you may help me with the rest of my clothing."

He did as he was told, but the vision of her bare loveliness danced before his eyes while he listened to her padding softly about the room along with the whisper of her undergarments slipping over her skin.

"Turn around; it's safe," she said. Crystal was sitting on the edge of the bed, pulling the sheerest of silk stockings over her shapely calf and fastening it with a lacy, beribboned garter.

Standing, she placed her hands on her hips, tilted her head from side to side and inspected him from head to toe. "Yes, indeed, your new clothes improve your appearance greatly. You are every bit as handsome as I'd imagined! Now, bring me my red taffetta dress out of the wardrobe, and the big pile of petticoats. While I'm dressing you can tell me all about your shopping spree."

This time he found it easier to help with all the fasteners. While fumbling at the task, he told her of the sights he had seen during the afternoon and of the clothes he had purchased. He continued his tale while she brushed and arranged her unusually light blonde hair into a spectacular upswept arrangement of pompadours and spit curls.

"There are so many people! And they all seem to be out on the streets! Did you know there are a hundred saloons in this town?"

"And we're 6200 feet above sea level, isn't that something? The first silver strike here was in 1859! But everyone I talked to say this is a banking town, not a mining town. And I did see a lot of banks . . . but if they're going to call it by what it's got the most of, it would be better labeled a saloon town!"

Crystal listened while applying mysterious lotions and creams to her face.

"One of the storekeepers told me Mark Twain used to live here! He was a reporter on the newspaper. Did you ever read any of his stories?

"They have something I've never heard of here. Mr. Squire, the bootmaker, said the red light district is right up the street. He said that's where the 'calico queens' live. What was he talking about?"

Crystal paused in the middle of coloring her lips with carmine rouge, her color-stained pinky held in midair. "You truly haven't had much of an education, have you?"

"Oh yes, ma'am, I attended school right up to the last grade. My mother used to be a school teacher, and she always said an education was most important."

"No, no, that's not the sort of education I was referring to. I mean educated in the ways of the world. I guess it's going to be up to me to take care of that part of your learning . . . you *do* know about sex, don't you?"

Once again Willy's face burned from embarrassment. "Sure, I do," he muttered. His stepfather had explained about how husbands and wives made babies—and of course he had a few discussions with his friends on the subject.

"Well then, Will, a calico queen is just another name for a prostitute, or a lady of the evening, as they are sometimes called. And the red light district is where they live and do business, called that because they usually burn a red lamp in their window as a means of advertising their trade."

Not used to hearing such topics discussed

freely, and certainly not by a lady, he knew his face remained crimson. "But, that's sinful, isn't it? Why don't the lawmen put a stop to it?" he asked.

"Sinful it may be, but if they chased away all the calico queens the lawmen would have a lot more problems than they do now. When you have a town as isolated as this one is, and with as many single men as there are here, a red light district is as needed as a neighborhood grocery. Maybe even more so. As long as the calico queens are around to take care of the miners' appetites, the wives and daughters of the town are fairly safe from the attacks of sex-starved drunks."

"Oh," was all Willy could think to say.

"Now that that's taken care of, tell me what you bought besides what you're wearing."

Willy glanced at his newly purchased outfit and was pleased with his appearance. At Maher and Company he'd bought the ready made suit he had on and another one, both complete with vests and two crisp white dress shirts. He'd visited two boot-makers without success, neither having shoes or boots in his size. At Mr. Squire's he'd been lucky. A pair of boots, crafted for a miner shot dead in a ruckus a few days earlier, fit him like they'd been made for him. At John Lee's general merchandise store he'd purchased new underwear, socks, hand-kerchiefs, and string ties to go with his suits.

But his favorite purchase had been made at Jacob Morris' Dry Goods. There he'd been fitted with a soft, leather-fringed jacket and heavy duty trousers, also buying some everyday cotton shirts. He'd never owned so many clothes at once in his whole life!

"Thank you very much, Crystal, for everything."

"There's no need to thank me, Will. You must be outfitted properly since you'll be in my company much of the time, and you'll earn everything you

receive from me. What you purchased today will
do until you get to a tailor and we can have some
clothing specially made."

"Oh no, ma'am, I don't need anything more,"
Willy protested.

"You certainly do!" Crystal argued. "I'm going
to have to look at you every day, and I don't want to
be bored!" Toilette complete, Crystal stood,
smoothed her skirts, patted her hair, and turned
to face Willy. "Tell me, how do I look?"

"Beautiful, ma'am! Absolutely beautiful! You
could be a fairy princess!" Willy complimented
her with conviction, for indeed, she was breathtaking. The deep crimson of her dress contrasted
becomingly with her pale, smooth skin. The
neckline was dangerously low, her magnificent
bosom threatening to escape, nipples barely
covered by the shimmery material. Short, puffed
sleeves uncased her upper arms, but her plump,
white shoulders and a great deal of her smooth
back were exposed. The waist was nipped in, with
yards and yards of red taffeta making up the skirt,
one side of which was caught up with a huge
matching velvet bow to expose the many ruffles of
her top petticoat. Sparkling diamonds decorated
her ear lobes, throat, and fingers.

"Thank you so much, Will. Now if you'll offer
me your arm, you may escort me to dinner."

Chapter 34

Willy's eyelids were heavy, and he couldn't suppress his yawns while he waited for Crystal outside of her dressing room at Piper's Opera House. He'd stepped outside to make room for the hordes of admirers who had rushed backstage to greet Crystal after her performance. The men spilled out of the doorway, jostling each other, trying for a better look or the chance to exchange words with the celebrity.

Crystal's debut had been thrilling to Willy. Her voice echoed throughout the huge hall as she sang a variety of songs in her seductive manner, each piece being greeted with loud applauses, stomping, shouted hurrahs and piercing whistles. Proud of his assocation with the beautiful and talented star, he'd viewed the premiere from a box secured by Crystal with a clear view of the stage and the capacity crowd. Everyone was dressed in all their finery for the occasion.

The opera house was a three story wooden building, and it seemed to be filled with every citizen of Virginia City who could afford the price of a ticket for Crystal's opening night. Willy wondered if there was anyone left to attend the rest of her scheduled performances.

Willy's drooping eyes flew open when he heard Crystal say, "It's time for you to escort me home!"

Crystal slipped her gloved hand into the crook of his elbow and with her free hand blew kisses to the men who still clamored around her. "Goodnight, kind sirs! I do hope you shall return to hear me again soon!" She whispered to Willy, "Quick, Will, let's hurry to the carriage. I'm bone tired and my face aches from smiling so much."

Back in their hotel suite, Crystal pointed out a bottle of champagne and two wine glasses waiting on the chiffonier. "Pour us each a glass, Will, and let's celebrate!"

When he handed Crystal a full glass she said, "Let's toast my opening night. I do believe it was a success!"

"Yes, it certainly was! Everyone loved you and I thought you sang like an angel, ma'am."

"Will you please cease with the ma'am business? Just call me Crystal. Drink your champagne and relax."

The bubbly liquid was another new experience for Willy, and he slowly sipped it, enjoying the new and different taste. After the third glassful he felt a bit lightheaded, his tongue seemed thicker and he found it difficult to enunciate properly.

"I see we've finished the bottle," announced Crystal when Willy poured the last few drops into her glass. She drained it dry, stood up and grasped Willy's hand.

"Come along, Willy. It's time for you to fulfill

your duties as my hired man," she said, leading him into her bedroom.

He helped her undress, commenting, "I think I'm beginning to catch on how to do this."

"Uh huh," she murmured while leaning against him as he pulled the dress over her head.

Standing in her undergarments, she held out her arms to Willy. "Come to me."

Taking a tentative step toward her, he felt her arms encircle his neck and her softness yielding against him. The musky scent of her body and perfume enveloped him as her lips pressed against his.

All that followed was like a beautiful dream. Naked, lying in bed with Crystal, he had never possibly imagined the ecstasy he'd experienced after the teasing and tantalizing, then finally completely possessing the voluptuous body beside him. After exciting him to the limit, Crystal had utterly fulfilled him.

As they rested in each other's arms, Willy whispered into Crystal's delicate ear, "I love you . . . please marry me."

Crystal ran her fingers over his lips. "Shhh! Don't bother your head, my dear. You merely feel like this because it's your first experience, but we can't get married. I'm much too old for you."

"That doesn't matter one bit," Willy protested.

"It will one of these days. But I don't intend to marry for a long, long time. I enjoy my career as a singer and it isn't compatible with married life. Be patient, dear Will, someday there will be the right woman for you."

"No, no," Willy argued, "you are the only woman in the world for me."

"Dear, sweet boy, let's enjoy what we have for now. One of these days everything will be changed.

Go to sleep now, and please don't wake me before noon. Then you can show me the town." She kissed him affectionately on the lips and snuggled closer.

For a long time after Crystal's even breathing told him she was asleep, he stared into the dark. He couldn't believe his good fortune, but somehow he would have to convince her to marry him. He knew his strong feelings for her could be nothing but love. It was what all the poets described—there could be no mistake!

The following days were filled with excitement. He trailed after Crystal when she visited the various shops, ordering hats and a new cape from Mrs. Arend's Millinery Shop, jewelry from Chatelain's, a gold dress from Mrs. Smith-Gray, a teal blue one from Mrs. J. Schwartz, and new petticoats and other unmentionables from Mrs. Nuttall. She commissioned a portrait from Miss Nell Wright and went for hourly sittings each afternoon.

Crystal insisted Willy take dancing lessons from Mr. Gosse so he would be a presentable partner for her, since she had already received several invitations for galas and balls in her honor. Grudgingly, he went to Mr. Gosse's twice weekly. Crystal had him order several new hats from James Daley, the hatter, and he was measured at the tailor for two more suits.

Many nights they ate in the elegant dining room of the International Hotel, but they also visited the other restaurants of the area such as Allen and Chumound, J.H. Bornhodt's, Mrs. Steele's, John Show's, the Grand Central, the United States, and the Fizmier and Armbrust. After dinner, four nights a week, Crystal performed at the Opera house, and attending each performance, Will was never bored.

The evenings she was free they attended parties and balls given in her honor in some of the huge mansions perched high on the steep hillside. There was the Savage Mansion, the Piper home, Mr. Morgan's place, the Kenny and Spaulding house—but most impressive was the Castle which belonged to the superintendent of the Empire Mines, Robert Graves.

When they arrived at the front of the Castle they were greeted by footmen who helped the guests from their carriages. Willy was amazed when he discovered the doorknobs were actually made of solid silver—and he noticed he wasn't the only guest who was impressed!

On the afternoons Crystal did not require his company, Willy wandered up and down "C" Street. He entertained himself by drifting in and out of the various saloons and gambling houses and watching the proceedings. Some of the most flamboyant characters seemed to be only interested in playing cards and gambling, winning and losing with equal frequency. There were two or three of these gamblers who Willy got to know and he noticed they were more successful than the others. He could easily wile away an afternoon watching them play out their hands with expert skill.

His favorite was a stocky fellow with raven black hair and a bushy, walrus moustache hiding his upper lip. Willy knew he was called One-Eye Blake because of the black patch which rakishly concealed a blind eye.

"Hey, kid," One-Eye called to him one day, "sit in on a hand."

"Me, sir?" Willy peered behind him, hoping One-

Eye had been addressing someone else.

"Yeah, you, kid. We could stand some fresh blood. Old McIntyre here needs to rest . . . ain't that right, McIntyre? I think he's into us for way too much by now. He's gonna have to beg for his job back at the mine in order to pay what he owes us as it is." The man called McIntyre pushed his chair back and got up, looking relieved to be excused from the game.

"Set yourself down, kid."

"I don't have much money," protested Willy, "and I haven't ever played before."

"Don't matter—you been watchin' long enough to know the rules. Your lady friend will honor your debts if you lose—I'm sure of that. Deal him in, Henning."

Reluctantly, Willy dropped into the chair and fanned out his cards. He didn't really remember too much about the afternoon. He won a little, lost a little, learned how to play their style of cards, found he did so quite well. The swirl of cigar smoke circled around the game table, and the players downed enormous amounts of whiskey with seemingly little effect.

It was nearly time for Willy to meet Crystal when One-Eye said, "Young fellow, you did yourself proud. You'll have to sit in with us again one of these days." Willy knew he was being dismissed.

One-Eye turned to the other gamblers and said, "Think I'll go on up to Spiro's Saloon and see what kind of action is going on there."

Willy began to look forward to his free afternoons and would search out One-Eye. Sometimes he was invited to join in, but usually he just watched. And there were times One-Eye wouldn't be a participant, but instead be propped back in a chair against the wall, relaxing.

"Set yourself down, lad," he would say, passing on tips to Willy on the fine art of being a card shark, the best way to bluff through a mediocre hand, how and when to call another's bluff, and clues to discover a cheat.

As Crystal was schooling Willy in the fine art of love-making, One-Eye was taking care of Willy's education as a gambler.

Chapter 35

Crystal Brouilette's engagement in Virginia City was such a huge success that John Piper signed her up for a four week extension. Some of the local, prominent business men began inviting her out to dinner, thus relieving Willy of that responsibility.

Willy had mixed emotions about this new development. Though he liked having his evenings free —Virginia City was an exciting place to roam at night, and One-Eye Blake seemed to enjoy Willy as a sidekick—he had painful twinges of jealousy when the various gentlemen came to pick up Crystal. He could see their lustful looks as they gazed at her luscious, exposed cleavage and tantalizingly clothed body.

Often she returned to the hotel long after Willy but always bid each escort goodnight at the door. Once inside she would invite Willy to her room where he would try to keep his feelings under control. After all, while the other men could only dream of possessing her, he was sharing her bed nearly every night.

At least that's what he thought—until One-Eye brought up the subject one afternoon. "Your lady friend's doing a bit of cavorting with James Callahan, ain't she?"

James Callahan was one of several mine owners who had entertained Willy and Crystal in his mansion. Will knew there was no Mrs. Callahan, and pondering over what One-Eye was hinting, he realized Crystal had been seeing Mr. Callahan nearly exclusively for the last week or so.

Willy's face must have revealed his sudden jealous feelings because One-Eye cautioned, "Hey, boy, don't get all riled up—ain't hardly worth it. That gal has covered a heap of miles and you're just getting started. There's a lot more ladies around. Try a young one next time."

Willy felt tears stinging his eyes. One-Eye spoke as though it were all over between him and Crystal. Could it be? Was he so naive that he hadn't noticed Crystal's feelings had changed toward him? Had she ever really cared for him at all? Though he had professed his love for her, she had never expressed her feelings toward him, and he'd just assumed she returned his love. She certainly acted like she cared for him when they were together in bed, but maybe it wasn't the same for her as it was for him.

"I thought she loved me," Willy said.

"Lady like that don't love nobody but herself. She's been paying for your services, ain't she?" One-Eye emptied his glass of whiskey and wiped his bushy moustache with a thumb. "I know you ain't a drinking man, but maybe this is a good time to start. Hey, Charlie, give the kid a shot."

The whiskey burned going down and had a

harsh taste, but he drank it anyway. "I don't know what to do, One-Eye. Crystal gave me a job, and I have to be grateful to her for that. But I sure don't want to be a miner . . . what else is there?"

"Listen, kid, you got a talent for the cards. You've been making money right steady, and you'll get along just fine. So why don't you have another drink, march yourself on up to that hotel, pack up your duds, and tell that fancy lady farewell?"

With the second drink fortifying him, Willy found he no longer suffered from a broken heart. In fact he felt better than he had in his whole life and was ready to tackle the world on his own.

Back in the hotel room he found Crystal sitting at her dressing table. He perched on the edge of the bed and stared at her, for once with a discerning eye. For the first time he noticed tiny wrinkles at the corners of her eyes and mouth, and without her makeup, her skin was colorless—almost unhealthy. And her bosom sagged when unsupported by her corset! Why hadn't he noticed before?

"It's about time you got here, Will," she snapped. "You almost made me late for my dinner engagement with Mr. Callahan."

"That's what I want to talk to you about, Crystal. Seems like you've been seeing a lot of Mr. Callahan lately. Maybe you better get him to help you dress, since he's already taken over the escorting part of the job. I'm not too keen on the idea of sharing you in bed."

Spinning around on the stool Crystal smiled coquettishly at him. "Why, Will, dear I do believe you're jealous!"

He realized he was seeing her as she really was for the first time. Her fancy clothes and the make-up had mesmerized him, and the sexual mysteries she had revealed to him had clouded his vision.

"I was jealous . . . but I'm not anymore. I want you to know I really do appreciate all you've done for me, but it's time for me to go out on my own." He was glad he hadn't drunk any more whiskey because as it was he was having a difficult time putting his thoughts into words.

Crystal's face darkened with fury, and she threw her silver-handled hairbrush at him; her aim being poor, it banged against the wall behind the bed. "You ungrateful pup!" she shrieked. "All that talk about love was nothing more than that—just talk! Here I thought you were grateful, when all the time you were planning to desert me—after I gave you the very clothes on your back and more money in your pocket than you've ever seen!"

There was nothing for Willy to say. He just stood there, wondering how he'd been so taken in by such a shrew.

She composed herself and took a deep breath, swelling her bosom. "For your information, young man, I was going to give you your walking papers anyway. Mr. James Callahan has invited me to be a houseguest for the duration of my stay in Virginia City—on the sole condition that you are no longer in my employ. So everything has worked out for the best. If you'll be so kind as to pack your belongings and vacate the premises, I'll be most grateful. You'll find your wages atop the chiffonier in your room."

Chapter 36

Willy found cheap lodgings at Mrs. Cavanaugh's boarding house, where hearty meals were provided for an extra $7.00 a week. Her place was on South C, so he had but a short walk to be in the midst of all the activity of the main street. After only a few days on his own as a gambler, he quickly realized he would have no trouble making a living.

The single miners enjoyed a game of cards on payday, even though they usually lost, having combined their card playing with too much liquor. Men from the mines and the mills below C Street would stop at the Chung Kee China store on D Street for a Chung Kee Liner which was a beer and two shots of whiskey for twenty-five cents. Usually staying for seconds, by the time they reached the C Street saloons and gambling houses their judgment was so diminished that they were easy prey for the professional gambler.

The episode with Crystal had changed Will into thinking of himself as a man—there was no longer a boy called Willy. And though he didn't relish the idea of separating the hard working miners from their money, he knew if he didn't, someone else would.

Will learned a lot about the men around the card table. They all belonged to the Miners' Union of the Comstock, the $2.00 a month dues being withheld from the men's pay. One of the benefits of the union was they only had to work eight hours a day for their $4.00, which wasn't so bad since California miners only received $2.00 a day for ten hours of work.

From the outside all the mines looked alike; the large buildings had changing rooms for the miners and sheltered the mining equipment. It was unbelievable to Will, but he'd been told that the Ward shaft went down 2725 feet before it was stopped by excessive water and heat, and another shaft, called the Combination, was said to be the deepest, going down over 3000 feet. After taking a tour of one of the mines, Will was mighty grateful to be making his living by another means.

Will's life settled into a regular routine. Besides becoming friendly with the miners, he'd also become well-acquainted with several of the business people in Virginia City. His new life was enjoyable as well as profitable.

Crystal only crossed his path once more before her singing engagement ended and she departed for another city. They came face to face in a general merchandise store where she acknowledged him coolly, immediately returning to her perusal of a new shipment of woman's lingerie. Though he had thought he was completely over his infatuation, his knees became shaky and his heart thumped wildly in his chest.

His infatuation didn't completely cool until winter, but unfortunately it also heralded the end of his prosperous sojourn in Virginia City.

While tramping through the snow late one Sunday afternoon, after finishing a sumptuous chicken dinner topped off by a delicious pumpkin pie at Charlie Ching's Virginia Restaurant on his way to the Delta Saloon next door, he spotted a diminutive female figure struggling with a heavy valise.

He approached the woman and discovered she was the young wife of Harvey Dewar, one of the miners he knew. Though he only knew Mrs. Dewar by sight, he was sympathetic toward her being married to the huge, brutish man. Unlike most of the married miners, Harvey spent most evenings glued to a bar stool, drinking up the major portion of his salary, growing meaner and more belligerent with each drink.

It was Will's policy to vacate any premise Harvey Dewar occupied as the man would antagonize everyone in sight until eventually he would cause a noisy brawl. Harvey was an enormous, brawny man who usually came through his fights unscathed, leaving many bloody noses, black eyes, missing teeth, and battered bodies in his wake. Rumor had it that he continued his battles at home with his helpless wife.

When he reached her, Will could see that recently she had been the victim of her husband's fists. Her light brown hair straggled down from a hat that had been hastily pulled onto her head, and tears welled from large brown eyes, one of which was swollen an unsightly blue-green. A bruise also was discoloring one bulging cheek, distorting an otherwise pretty face, and split and bleeding lip made it difficult for her to talk.

"Oh, dear, I hoped no one would see me." A hand flew to her face in an unsuccessful attempt to hide her wounds.

"Excuse me, Mrs. Dewar, perhaps I can be of some assistance." Will took her valise from her. "Allow me to introduce myself, ma'am. I'm Will Vradenburg. It appears you need some medical attention; please allow me to take you to a doctor."

"No, no," she protested. "I can't—nobody else must see me like this. Besides, I don't have any money."

"Where are you headed? At least I can carry your bag."

Tears flowed down her cheeks. "I don't know. I just had to get away from Harvey."

"Come along with me to Mrs. Cavanaugh's. She's a kindly woman, who's bound to have a room available, and she'll tend to your wounds. When you're feeling better, you can decide what you want to do."

She started to murmur something about no money but he interrupted. "Don't worry, ma'am, I'll take care of it."

They started toward his boarding house, but after only a few steps she fell against him, almost collapsing into the snow. He scooped her into his arms, carrying her and the valise the short distance to Mrs. Cavanaugh's. His landlady greeted him at the door.

"Goodness, Mr. Vradenburg, who have you there?" The plump woman wiped her hands on her apron and opened the door wide as Will carried his burden inside.

"It's Mrs. Dewar. That monstrous husband of hers has given her a nasty beating, and she's run away from him. I discovered her on the street."

Mrs. Cavanaugh had been a widow for several

years, her husband having been killed in a mining accident. Will had enjoyed her motherly ministerings toward all the boarders and knew she would take charge and care for the battered Mrs. Dewar.

Directing him to place the injured woman on the sitting room settee, she then sent him into the kitchen to fetch a basin, a tea kettle of hot water from the stove, and some clean cloths. When he returned, he found Mrs. Cavanaugh had stipped Mrs. Dewar down to her undergarments, exposing even more ugly bruises on her fragile body.

"Men who beat their wives should be horse-whipped," declared Mrs. Cavanaugh. "Put those things down and I'll see what I can do for the poor child."

Indeed, Mrs. Dewar looked barely out of her teens. She moaned a bit while Mrs. Cavanaugh bathed her. Turning to Will, Mrs. Cavanaugh said, "You mustn't be embarrassed, Mr. Vradenburg, but I believe it is necessary for me to undress her the rest of the way, and I'll need your assistance. See if she's got a nightgown in her bag."

When Mrs. Dewar was completely unclothed, Will exclaimed, "Good Lord, the man is a monster!" Mrs. Dewar's pale body was covered with fresh welts, as well as older bruises. One of her small, pink-tipped breasts was tinted blue, and her stomach and buttocks were covered with ugly marks.

The battered woman was tended to without fully regaining consciousness, though low moans escaped from her swollen mouth while they dressed her in the cotton nightdress they had found in her bag. Mrs. Cavanaugh suggested, "Carry her upstairs to the room next to yours and keep an eye on her until she wakes. I'll prepare some chicken soup."

Will followed his landlady's instructions,

tucking Mrs. Dewar into bed as gently as possible.
He watched over her until it was dark, and finally
lighting the lamp next to her bed, he noticed her
eyelashes flicker.

She groaned, "Oooh, where am I?"

"Mrs. Dewar, remember me? I'm Will
Vradenburg, I met you out on the street. You're
now in Mrs. Cavanaugh's boarding house."

"Yes . . . it's coming back to me." Fear was in her
eyes, and she grasped Will's arm. "Does Harvey
know I'm here?"

"No, don't worry—only Mrs. Cavanaugh and I
know. But don't you think you should report your
husband's treatment of you to Sheriff Emmitt?
He *was* the one that did this to you, wasn't he?"

"No! Please don't tell anyone! The sheriff can't
help me. I'm Harvey's wife, and he can do
anything he wants to me." She shuddered. "But I
can't stand anymore! He was out the whole day
drinking, and he began hitting me as soon as he
walked in the house. I think he would have kept it
up until he killed me, except he passed out. I
packed what I could and left." She buried her
head in the pillow, crying softly.

"Please, don't cry anymore, Mrs. Dewar. We'll
take care of you."

The next few days Will seldom left Mrs. Dewar's
side. At night he returned to his own room to
sleep, leaving his door open so he could rush to
her if she cried out.

On the third day she sat up in bed and requested
her hairbrush. "I must be a sight!"

"No, you're not. Considering what you've been
through, Mrs. Dewar, I think you're most attractive," he assured her. "If you could turn your head
a bit, I'll brush the back of your hair for you." Her
brown hair, hanging nearly to her waist, was
tangled from her stay in bed.

While he brushed, she talked. "I don't know how I can ever thank you. I'd be ever so happy if you would call me Laura. You and Mrs. Cavanaugh have been the kindest people I've ever known."

With some encouragement from Will, Laura told him the pitiful story of her life. She was born in Kansas, the first of eleven children. Her father was a farmer, barely scraping a living from the soil for his large family, and her mother was sickly. Laura cared for the babies as each one came and did most of the housework.

Harvey Dewar had stopped in their town, meeting her father in the saloon. After several rounds of drinks her father had bragged about the capabilities and beauty of his sixteen-year-old daughter, and Harvey had immediately offered a large sum of money for her purchase. Her father, who seldom had any cash, agreed readily. Pleased with Laura's looks, Harvey paid the agreed-upon price, and the transaction was made.

That very night, Harvey took the girl with him. A justice of the peace was awakened and they were promptly married. The beatings didn't start until they had been married a year, one of the beatings causing a miscarriage.

" . . . and thank God, I've never been able to get pregnant again," she breathed.

When her hair was brushed, it hung shimmering silkily over her shoulders, and the winter sunlight which came through the window cast golden highlights on the light brown locks. Her bruises were fading, her lip was nearly healed, and a pink glow had returned to her cheeks.

A rush of feelings came over Will for the woman he'd been caring for out of compassion, and he reached a tentative hand toward her shoulder. "Laura?"

"Oh, Will, I'll never be able to repay you for all

you've done for me," she murmured, and her arms reached out for him.

Gently he took her into his arms. She offered him her lips, and he kissed her—almost shyly. When she pressed her body against him, he could feel the softness of her small breasts against his chest, and his passion rose, though he tried to control himself, fearful of her reaction.

"Help me take off my nightdress, Will," she whispered.

His heart soared as he lifted the gown over her head. Her eyes held the invitation he'd hoped for, and he shed his own clothes quickly.

Eagerly touching her cool skin, he felt her quiver with anticipation. Their love-making was sweet and gentle, building to a grand and glorious climax.

Afterwards they lay silently in each other's arms, Will tracing patterns on her smooth white skin. He was surprised at how different the sweet loveliness had been from the frenzied coupling he'd experienced with Crystal.

"Laura, I love you," he whispered. "You are a beautiful, wonderful woman."

She brushed her lips against his chest. "I love you too, Will." But he felt the wetness of her tears on his skin.

"Whatever is the matter? Did I hurt you?" He lifted her chin and was troubled when he saw the sadness in her eyes.

"No, of course you didn't hurt me. I'm crying because there's no future for our love. I am Harvey's wife, after all."

"Don't say that! I'll take you away from here, and we'll go somewhere faraway and live as man and wife. No one will ever have to know."

She shook her head. "No, Will, it will never happen that way. I know Harvey too well—he'll never let me go.''

But the next day Will began making plans. He withdrew all his money from the Nevada Bank, asking Mr.s Bigelow, the bank's agent, to keep the transaction secret.

On his way back to the boarding house he ran into One-Eye. "Hey, Will, where've you been? I've missed you!''

Will didn't know if he should confide in his friend, but before he made up his mind, One-Eye said, "I can see by your face it's true what they've been saying.''

"And what's that?'' Will asked.

"Rumors have been flying ever since Harvey Dewar's wife ran away. People are saying you've been hiding her, and Harvey's been all over town threatening to blow off your head. And I can tell by your expression that it's true—you *do* know where Harvey's wife is.''

"Wait a minute, One-Eye. I'm taking care of Laura, all right, but she was half dead when I found her wandering the street. That brute of a husband had beaten her within an inch of her life!''

"That don't surprise me none, but it don't change nothin'. Once he gets his courage up with enough alcohol, he's gonna be gunning for you. If I was you, I'd hightail it outta town on the first train!''

"Thanks for the advice. I may do just that.''

Back at the boarding house he found Mrs. Cavanaugh, Laura and Sheriff Emmitt waiting in the parlor for him. Laura threw herself against him, her body shaking.

"See, Will, I told you it wouldn't work!'' She pressed her face against his chest while he put his arms around him protectively.

"What's goin' on?'' He glanced from Mrs.

Cavanaugh's worried face to Sheriff Emmitt's which was set in stern lines.

"I hate to do this, Will. Mrs. Cavanaugh told me all about Harvey's bad treatment of his wife . . . but I'm afraid he's gone and sworn out a warrant against you for wife stealing. I have to go by the law, Will. But I won't arrest you if you'll pack your bags and get out of town, and I'll just pretend I couldn't find you in time."

"Fine, we'll do it. Get your things packed, Laura, and we'll leave right away."

The sheriff stared at his boots and cleared his throat. "I'm afraid I can't let you take her with you, Will."

Will frowned. "I love Laura! Of course she's going with me."

"No, she isn't. I can't allow it. Get upstairs and pack, Will, and I'll be escorting you to the station myself." He stepped over to Laura and pulled her away from Will.

"You can't make Laura go back to that monster—he'll kill her!" Will shouted.

"She doesn't have to . . . and I'll see to it that Harvey doesn't lay a hand on her. But you've got to get out of town!"

Will could tell by the determined set of the sheriff's jaw that he wasn't about to change his mind. He stared desperately at Laura who was now within the circle of Sheriff Emmitt's arm.

"Hurry, Will, go pack. It's the only way," she urged quietly, her eyes glistening.

He bounded up the stairs. While he packed he sought desperately for a solution to his problem, but there seemed to be none. He carried his two valises down to the sitting room. "Sheriff, please at least let me tell Laura goodbye."

"Okay, Will, but hurry. The train will be leaving soon and I want you on it."

Will crossed to where Laura sat stiffly in a chair. "What will become of you?"

"Please, don't worry about me, Will. Mrs. Cavanaugh says I can stay here, and she will ask around and help me find a job in one of the stores or restaurants. I'll be all right."

She put her arms around him, kissed him, and murmured, "I'll never forget you, Will."

He was unable to speak, and tears blurred his vision. He spun on his heels, picked up his bags, and headed for the door without looking back. "Come on, Sheriff, let's not miss the train."

Chapter 37

The next five years Will wandered from mining camp to mining camp. He had polished his gambling techniques and was accomplished enough to live in high style.

The heartbreak of leaving Laura finally faded, the memory of his love only occasionally haunting his dreams. He romanced a few rouged, ruffled, and slightly rumpled dance hall girls, along with a haughty, but slightly naughty middle-aged widow, and had a dalliance or two with plump, kindly calico queens.

He learned to respect the prostitutes of the frontier towns. Most of these women mothered the lonely cowboys and miners, made the scroungiest of men bathe before granting their favors, and tamed the rowdiest of the roustabouts, making them toe the line. But none of his conquests managed to touch his heart.

In 1893 he found himself in the tiny hamlet of

Hecla, in southwestern Montana, a mining town which clung to the wall of Zion Mountain. The mines were located even higher up the mountainside, and the miners, with the aid of hand cables, pulled themselves up the steep slopes and lowered the ore down in buckets. The veins were rich with silver, lead and copper.

Will probably wouldn't have tarried long in Hecla if it hadn't been for the local schoolteacher. He'd first glimpsed her when she walked from the schoolhouse one afternoon.

Wrapped as she was in a heavy shawl to protect her from the chill fall wind whipping down the mountain, he could tell she was of the same small stature as Laura. As she approached him at the side of the road, he tipped his hat and greeted her, "How do you do, ma'am. Bit nippy today, isn't it?"

Surprise was in her large brown eyes as she stared at him. "Yes, it is a bit chilly." But she resumed her fast step toward town.

Questioning the local business people he learned her name was Blanche La Mont, and she was in charge of the education of the twenty-two children of Hecla.

Making it a point to be near the schoolhouse when Miss La Mont was leaving offered Will the opportunity to greet her nearly every day. On one particularly cold and blustery afternoon with rain just beginning to spit from threatening clouds, Will watched until the last child bounded down the schoolhouse steps. He entered the school, banging the door behind him.

Miss La Mont peered up from her desk, a mixture of surprise and pleasure appearing on her face when she recognized him. "Mr. Vradenburg," she greeted primly, "what can I do for you?"

Will could tell she was flattered by his attention. Over the years he'd acquired a polished manner which never failed to impress the ladies. He put his hat on the scuffed desk, aware she was admiring his curly, dark hair. Told often enough that he was handsome, he was quite self-assured. He smoothed his neat moustache with his thumb, smiled broadly, and allowed his eyes to flicker over her face. He knew he was making her nervous.

"I've been attempting to make your acquaintance, Miss La Mont. I'm sure you must have noticed." His voice was nearly a caress, and the object of his attention squirmed in her chair.

"Is that what this is all about?" she asked.

Will caught his breath, realizing the young woman resembled Laura even more than he'd imagined. His first instinct was to take her into his arms and kiss her, but he knew he must hold himself in check.

"I would be most pleased if you would call me Will . . . and perhaps I could call you Blanche." She nodded, and he added, "Perhaps I could escort you home, Blanche."

"I certainly can't prevent you from walking along beside me, now can I?"

"And if you have no other plans, I would consider it a privilege if you would be my guest for dinner this evening."

Dipping her head, she said, "No, Will, I'm afraid that is out of the question. In the first place, as the schoolteacher, I can't be seen in a public eating house—and especially not in the company of a single man. In the second place, and I suppose most important, I am not allowed to have gentlemen friends."

Will laughed. "That's the most archaic nonsense I've ever heard, Blanche. Who says you can't have gentlemen friends?"

"Unfortunately, sir, it is only too true, archaic or not. It's written right into my contract, and if I'm to keep my job, I must follow the rules set up by the school board. After all, I agreed to the stipulations when I took the job. So you see, you are really wasting your time!"

"I don't feel it's a waste of time, my dear. Somehow we'll manage to become better acquainted. You mentioned rules—are there more silly rules you must follow? Make me aware of all of them now, so I know what I must work around."

Blanche blushed as she explained, "The other rules only apply to me personally."

"Come on, tell me what they are, now that you've aroused my curiosity."

"They are rather embarrassing. I mustn't loiter in the icecream parlor . . . I can't smoke cigarettes or dye my hair, and . . ." she paused, looking down at her hands.

"Go on," Will urged.

"I have to wear at least two petticoats!"

Will slapped his knee and guffawed. "What a bunch of garbage!"

"Unfortunately, sir, you are not a member of the Helca School Board." She rose from her chair and put her shawl around her shoulders. "And now, sir, I must be heading home."

Will was not easily discouraged. He waited patiently each day across the road from the schoolhouse until the children were gone, then he would enter and greet a flustered Blanche La Mont. He soon found himself doing chores he hadn't done in years. He chopped wood for the stove, nailed a loose door back onto the outhouse, and rearranged the desks in the classroom. But the process of developing a friendship was slower than Will desired. Miss La Mont expressed her gratitude politely, but just as politely refused to grant him any courting privileges.

After two frustrating weeks, Miss La Mont asked Will to carry a stack of books for her to her rooming house. "I want to mend them this evening," she explained apologetically.

"Certainly, my dear," he said, gathering the books under his arm. "But don't you think it's time I received some sort of favor for all the work I've done for you?"

Miss La Mont blushed a becoming shade of pink. "Sir, I've already explained to you that it is impossible for me to have a friendship with a gentleman—no matter how much I might want it."

Will opened the door for her with his free hand and ushered her through. Once they were down the stairs and headed along the road, Will winked and said, "No one needs to know you have me for a friend, do they?"

"That is nearly impossible in a small town like this," Miss La Mont argued.

"Oh, I don't know," Will said, grinning. "As the old saying goes, 'Where there's a will, there's a way.'"

In the time it took to reach her rooming house, Will had extracted a reluctant promise from her to meet him for a picnic that coming Saturday. And Miss La Mont suggested the place—an isolated area sheltered by pine trees, a quarter of a mile from town.

Chapter 38

The colder weather was making their weekly rendezvous more difficult. Will had taken to packing along a heavy buffalo robe to wrap around them both as protection against the rain or the snow flurries, which came often during their picnic lunches.

Under the shelter of the robe they had learned more about each other and shared a few tender kisses. Will had made a few attempts to caress her body, invariably thwarted by Blanche's admonishment to "Stop before things get out of control." Will respected her virginity, realizing marriage was the only way he would ever be able to enjoy the delights of her body.

He made the decision to propose—partly because of the inclement weather and partly because of his own need to physically express his growing love. But on the day he planned to reveal his intentions, Blanche didn't arrive at the usual time, causing Will to become a bit worried.

When she finally did arrive, she ran to him, her body shaking and her face streaked with tears. "Oh, Will," she cried, "I can't ever see you again!"

He held her close. "Why is that?"

"I was called before the school board! Somehow they found out about us! I have to stop seeing you immediately or I'll lose my job!"

He smoothed her hair, which was coming loose from it's bun, and held her close. "There, there, my sweet, it isn't that bad!"

"Oh, but it is, Will. Though I tried not to, I think I've fallen in love with you." Her crying began anew.

"There really isn't a problem then, my sweet Blanche. We'll be married, and you won't have to have a job."

"I can't marry you, Will! I just can't!" She was nearly hysterical.

"Blanche, I don't understand what the problem is!"

"I have to be a schoolteacher. I promised my father on his death bed that I would always be a teacher. He scrimped and saved and denied himself in order to send me to teacher's preparatory school, and I can't break that promise, don't you see?"

"No, I don't see," he protested. "If your father were alive today, he would understand. The love between two people is precious and should never be denied."

She pulled away from him, bowing her head. "I'm sorry, Will, but that's the way it has to be." She stood on tiptoe, kissing him lightly on the lips, then gathering her skirts, she ran towards town.

"Wait, Blanche," he cried after her, "you can't

leave like this. Let's talk some more. We'll work it out some way."

"No . . . no . . . no . . ." floated back to him, as she fled into the distance.

It was happening to him again—he could hardly believe it! Every attempt he made to see her thereafter was thwarted. Finally, realizing she wasn't going to allow him any opportunity to try and change her mind, he packed and left Hecla for a warmer climate.

Will concentrated on gambling, moving from town to town as the fancy took him. He returned home in the spring of '95, staying a week and then traveling on. Every so often he popped in on his family unexpectedly, including his nieces and nephews in various parts of the country.

His gambling took on a different form, as he turned to speculating in oil and land, becoming exceedingly wealthy. He was remembered by his grandnieces and nephews by the post cards he sent from the glamorous resorts he frequented, along with expensive gifts he gave them on his infrequent visits.

And he helped his mother financially until her death, fulfilling his boyhood promise to always take care of her.

BOOK V

Desdemona Diana

Chapter 39

"Minnie, please come into the kitchen right away. Surely you're through primping by now—I need your help!" The whiny voice grating on Desdemona's ears belonged to her foster mother, Myrtle Foss. She had to be grateful to Myrtle Foss for the home she and her husband, Hiram, had provided the last ten years for herself and her sisters, ever since their father had been killed by Indians. Now that Myrtle and Hiram were not in the best of health, Desdemona had felt obligated to stay and help them out, especially since Jessie had married and moved to South Dakota, taking Eudora with her.

But, oh, how she hated being called Minnie. Myrtle Foss felt the name Desdemona Diana was much too frivolous for a young girl, immediately changing it to Minnie. Now nearly everyone used Minnie, with the exception of Desdemona's real mother, Mary.

Even Desdemona's fiance, Julius Bailey, called her Minnie. It wasn't quite so hateful coming from him, since he seemed to infuse it with a certain lilt, an affectionate tone which kept it from sounding so dreadfully plain. By this time tomorrow she would be Mrs. Julius Bailey, and they were moving to Minnesota. She guessed she could put up with the name Minnie for the short time that was left.

She took one last look in her mirror and was pleased with her reflection. "I am Desdemona Diana!" Curly, dark brown hair glimmered with red highlights, piled high on her head with wispy curls framing her heart-shaped face. She knew she was attractive—with large blue eyes thickly fringed with dark lashes, a nose perhaps a shade too short and uptilted, but lips full and red enough to look as though they had been rouged. (Never would Myrtle Foss have allowed rouge in her house.) Desdemona wasn't tall but had a good figure. And since she earned her own money working as a nurse for Dr. Higgins in town, she purchased the material for her clothes, decorating all her dresses with lace and ribbons.

She had learned to close her ears to Myrtle's remarks about it being sinful to waste so much material on one dress, that the colors that were more suited for a dance hall girl's costume, and that Christian folks might mistake her for a fancy woman. Desdemona enjoyed wearing her pretty clothes despite her stepmother's remarks.

It was through her job as a nurse that Desdemona had met her future husband, Julius. He had no sooner arrived in town when he had an acute attack of appendicitis and stumbled into Dr. Higgins' office, crazy with pain, minutes before Desdemona had planned to leave for home.

Dr. Higgins diagnosed the stranger's problem,

and he was immediately helped into surgery. She had neither the time nor interest to notice much about him while she assisted the doctor in removing the infected appendix.

When the operation was successfully completed, the unconsious patient was taken to a recovery room with a bed in the back of the doctor's office.

Relaxing with a cup of coffee Desdemona had prepared in the utilitarian kitchen, Dr. Higgins said, "Well, Minnie, looks like you'll be busy the next few days tending to Mr. Bailey."

"It does appear that way, doesn't it?" Desdemona agreed good-naturedly. That was Dr. Higgins' way—he never asked her to do anything, just presumed she would.

The physician stood, putting on his suit coat. "I have to stop by Mr. Tate's near your place before I go home, so I'll let Mrs. Foss know you'll be nursing a patient for a week or so."

Desdemona smiled. "Thanks. I'd appreciate it if you'd also ask Myrtle to pack a few clothes for me, too."

"Sure. Well, I'd best be on my way. Mrs. Higgins isn't going to be happy that I'm late for supper again, but I know I'm leaving Mr. Bailey in capable hands. Goodbye now, Minnie."

After the doctor left, Desdemona found an apple that would have to suffice for supper, then she moved a large, overstuffed chair beside her patient. She had ample time to study Mr. Bailey as she dozed on and off beside him through the night. He had sun-streaked hair, parted on the side and combed back from his face, and she guessed he spent a good deal of time working outside because his face and hands were a golden brown while the rest of his body was pale. His broad forehead caused her to assume he was intelligent, while his mouth seemed sensitive.

She had to laugh at herself, making decisions about the man solely on his appearance. But she liked the way he looked and she hoped his personality would prove as nice as his appearance.

Sometime after midnight, Desdemona pulled a blanket over herself and fell into a light sleep.

She was awakened when the patient said, "Excuse me, miss."

She immediately sat up and noted the sun was streaming in the window. "How are you feeling this morning?" Desdemona inquired cheerily, placing her palm on his forehead.

"I . . . ah . . . need to . . . you know . . . go to . . ." Mr. Bailey stammered.

Desdemona smiled knowingly. "Yes, of course." She pulled a chamber pot out from under the bed. "Here, let me help." She carefully pulled the blankets away from him.

Mr. Bailey's surgical gown did not reach down to his genitals, and he hastily covered himself with his large hands. "No! No! I'll do it myself."

"There's no need for you to be embarrassed— I'm a nurse. My name is Desdemona Van Vradenburg, I assisted Dr. Higgins with your surgery, and I am in charge of your care."

It was obvious her explanation did not put Mr. Bailey at ease. "If you would step outside, I'm sure I can . . ."

"I don't think you'll be able to sit up without help," Desdemona persisted.

Mr. Bailey was adamant. "I know I can do it myself!"

Desdemona turned her back, but whirled around, hurrying to Mr. Bailey's side when he let out a painful groan. "See! You *do* need my help." Expertly she assisted him so he was able to relieve himself, then quickly covered him.

Dr. Higgins poked his head in the doorway. "Hello there, Minnie, and how's our patient this morning?"

"He seems well, and how are you this morning, Doctor?"

"Fine, just fine. I brought some groceries from Mrs. Higgins and the clothes Mrs. Foss packed for you. You'll find everything in the kitchen. I'll check my handiwork and change the bandages while you freshen up and fix breakfast."

When Dr. Higgins had departed, Desdemona propped up Mr. Bailey as carefully as possible so he could eat the meal she had prepared. He didn't make a sound while she shifted him about, but she could tell he was in a great deal of pain by the grimace on his face. "I'm sorry, but this way you can feed yourself, and I'm sure you would prefer that."

"Oh, yes, ma'am," he said.

Desdemona set a tray across his lap and cut the ham slices into small pieces as well as the biscuits smothered in gravy. "I hope this will satisfy you. I'm afraid I didn't have much to work with," she said as she poured him a cup of coffee.

She sat in the chair eating her breakfast as he ate his. As Desdemona took away the dirty dishes, Mr. Bailey commented, "Thank you, it was very good, Miss . . . ah . . . I'm sorry, but I can't remember your name."

"It's Desdemona," she said.

The man frowned. "I thought I heard the doctor call you something else."

"Yes, you did . . . Minnie. I sort of have two names, but I prefer Desdemona. I'll explain it all to you sometime. . . perhaps."

She returned to the room with a basin of soapy water, a sponge and towels. "What do you have in mind to do with all that?" asked Mr. Bailey, blue-grey eyes large with alarm.

"It's time for your bath," Desdemona said in her most professional tone.

"Oh, no, you're not giving *me* a bath!"

"Yes, I am! In fact, I'm going to give you a bath every single day until you're able to get out of that bed and go home."

Mr. Bailey pulled the blankets up under his chin, and Desdemona laughed. "Oh, come now, Mr. Bailey, it isn't all that dreadful. If you'll just relax, you might enjoy it."

"Never!"

"Come on, don't be so difficult. Let's ease you on to your side and I'll do your back first. You can take care of your private parts if it bothers you so much—but I can assure you, Mr. Bailey, you haven't got anything I haven't seen before."

"My name is Julius," he said, as she soaped his back.

"All right—Julius."

Besides being extremely modest, Desdemona discovered Julius had other idiosyncrasies—he only liked a pat of butter on his oatmeal, he didn't care for milk or sugar, and he didn't like his sheets to be ironed but preferred to have them put fresh from the line onto his bed. Desdemona agreed with him wholeheartedly about the sheets; to her, ironing them had always been a terrible waste of time and energy, but unfortunately she'd never been able to convince Myrtle Foss.

While caring for Julius she found out a few other things. He'd been a fairly successful plasterer in his home state of Vermont, and after saving a nest egg, he'd decided to start anew somewhere else, only planning on stopping over in Woodlake. "But now, since I've met you, Desdemona, I've decided to settle here—for a little while, anyway," he explained.

Desdemona knew Julius' recovery was nearly complete when one morning, while she damp combed his hair, he suddenly grabbed her, and losing her balance, she fell across his chest. "Careful, you're liable to reopen your incision!" she scolded, trying to pull herself away.

But his muscular arms held her tightly, and it was a surprise when he pressed his lips against hers, kissing her soundly before releasing her.

She righted herself immediately. Repinning her apron which had come unfastened at the corner, she scolded, "Julius Bailey, shame on you!"

"Ah, come on Desdemona, didn't you kind of enjoy it?" he teased, his eyes twinkling with amusement.

"Very unseemly behavior for a patient towards his nurse." She turned her back so he couldn't see the smile tugging at her lips.

"Wasn't it the proper behavior of a man towards the woman he loves?" Julius asked quietly.

Desdemona didn't trust herself to speak; instead, she busied herself tucking the stray strands of hair back into her neat pompadour.

"Turn around, Desdemona," Julius commanded. "I have an important question to ask you and I'd like to see the expression on your face when I do."

Desdemona took a deep breath and turned to face her patient who was propped up on his elbow. "Yes, what is it?"

"Desdemona Van Vradenburg . . . Minnie Foss . . . or whatever name you choose to call yourself . . . would you consider becoming Mrs. Julius Bailey?"

Desdemona didn't even hesitate before she answered, "Yes, I'd be honored to be your wife."

Julius' mouth dropped open and his eyes

widened in surprise. It was obvious he didn't believe his ear. "Truly? Are you sure? I figured you'd show some kind of reluctance. I never thought in a million years you'd say 'yes' just like that!"

"What's the matter? Do you want to take your offer back?" Desdemona teased.

"Oh, no, I'm holding you to your answer. I can't believe I'm so lucky!"

"Maybe you're not so lucky," Desdemona said, shrugging her shoulders. "You hardly know anything about me."

"I know everything I need to know," Julius said, reaching for her hand and pressing it against his smooth-shaven cheek. "I've learned more about you in this week you've been my nurse than most men find out during a long courtship. I knew you were beautiful from the first time I set eyes upon you, and now I know you're kind and gentle. I know you can cook because I've eaten your food three times a day. Whiling away the hours, I've discovered you are a good conversationalist. I know you're a sensible person. And most of all, my dear . . . I've come to love you."

Desdemona had no response for this declaration of love. She only smiled. She didn't feel like she'd been smitten by Dan Cupid, but Julius Bailey was handsome and pleasant, and at age twenty-nine, he seemed ready to settle down. Marrying would be a means of escaping the Foss household, and by now she had certainly put in enough time repaying her foster parents. And to be perfectly frank, now that she had reached the age of twenty she was beginning to worry she would end up an old maid. She'd already turned down proposals from several eligible farmers, but the thought of being a farmer's wife had been even a worse prospect than remaining single.

Julius Bailey was definitely the answer. He wouldn't ever make a fortune as a plasterer, but he did have dreams for the future. Desdemona felt she would never be sorry if she married him.

Julius reached for her. "Come on, sweetheart, give your husband-to-be another kiss."

"Only one. You mustn't get too rambunctious—consider your stitches!"

No sooner had Julius fully recovered than he was urging Desdemona to marry him as soon as possible. She knew he was surprised when she readily agreed, even going a step further by suggesting a simple ceremony in town without unncesssary trappings.

"I had expected you to want all the folderol," Julius commented.

Desdemona just shook her head. "The less commotion our wedding causes the better. Neither of us can afford to waste money."

Myrtle Foss certainly had something to say about Desdemona's plans. "Why on earth do you have to be in such a hurry? It isn't fitting for you to marry without your family present. What kind of a wedding will it be without a man of God to say the words? I don't understand what you see in that blue-bellied Yankee anyway. Why couldn't you have settled for one of the nice, young men from around here? You don't realize what a chance you're taking marrying a stranger. We don't know anything about his people. Oh, well . . . what more could I expect from such a silly girl like you!"

As usual Myrtle's arguments didn't affect Desdemona one bit. She had long ago learned to tune out her foster mother's incessant chiding, knowing there was little she could do to meet with Myrtle's approval.

The short engagement reached an end, and one

afternoon, Julius Bailey was ready to fetch her and her belongings and have them married by the judge. It had been a cold winter, and on this first day of February the ground was still covered with snow. Julius was coming for her in a horse-drawn sleigh, and the picture of them gliding over the glistening snow danced romantically in Desdemona's mind as she went into the kitchen to see what Myrtle wanted.

"Here I am, Myrtle. What can I do for you?" Desdemona asked gaily. Even Myrtle's sour countenance couldn't dampen Desdemona's spirits on this special day.

"Oh, I see you're already dressed for your wedding," Myrtle said. "I don't suppose you'd consider drying the dishes for me?"

"Of course, I will," Desdemona answered with a smile.

"Too bad you wouldn't let us give you a proper wedding. Being married by a judge isn't the same as being united by a minister of God," Myrtle muttered, splashing her hands around in the dish water.

Desdemona ignored her foster mother and continued to dry the dishes.

Myrtle took a deep breath and scrubbed at a greasy pot furiously. "Minnie, I believe it's my duty to speak to you concerning another part of marriage." When Myrtle didn't continue, Desdemona glanced at her foster mother and was surprised to see the older woman was blushing.

"What I meant to say is, there's . . . a wife has a duty she must fulfill to her husband that isn't commonly discussed among women. It's a physical function, and though it's unpleasant, it's necessary for the procreation of children. In the Bible it says we must cleave unto our husbands,

and when we marry, two become as one. And what
this is, well, ah . . ."

Desdemona couldn't suppress a giggle when she
realized the woman was trying to explain the
sexual side of marriage. Taking pity on Myrtle, she
interrupted. "It's all right. You don't need to
worry about it, since I already know about such
things. You forget I've been a nurse for these past
two years, and Dr. Higgins explained everything to
me a long time ago. After all, Myrtle, I've had to
bathe sick men and tend women during childbirth.
I'm afraid the human body holds no further
secrets for me."

"Well! I had no idea Dr. Higgins would expose a
genteel young lady to such things!" Myrtle was
genuinely shocked.

"I wouldn't have been much help as a nurse if
the doctor had to worry about offending my so-
called gentility!"

"Still . . . he should have had some consid . . ."

"Remember, I've already had to care for my
future husband after his appendectomy. I bathed
him from head to toe."

Desdemona was immediately ashamed of
herself when she noticed Myrtle's face. The poor
woman was horrified, and for a moment Desdemona was afraid she was going to faint.

"Myrtle? Are you going to be all right?" She
guided the woman to a chair. "Remember, it's my
duty to keep the patients clean," she explained.
"Mr. Bailey wasn't the first man I'd bathed, and
since I plan to continue working after my
marriage, I'm sure he won't be the last!"

Myrtle's head was swimming. She'd had no idea
what Minnie's job as a nurse had entailed. Now
she felt as thought she'd failed as a mother. She
should have discussed the duties of a nurse with

Dr. Higgins before she'd permitted Minnie to work for him. And she'd always considered the doctor to be a learned man of propriety! Well, it just proved once again that appearances were deceiving.

It was a blessing Minnie was getting married. If it was common knowledge that Minnie had been familiar with men's bodies, it was no wonder she'd had no luck capturing a local boy for a husband. All this time she'd thought it was Minnie turning away prospects, and instead it must have been the other way around. Thank heaven for Julius Bailey —he obviously wan't smart enough to realize Minnie's occupation wasn't suitable for a young lady of good breeding!

Chapter 40

Julius Bailey gazed upon his sleeping wife's countenance. After nearly nine years of marriage and two children, Julius thanked his lucky stars for the good fortune he'd had to marry Minnie Foss. She was still the most beautiful woman he'd ever seen. She was particular about her appearance, and after the birth of their children, had worked religiously to regain her figure.

Though Minnie was tiny, appearing fragile, she was a strong woman, both in body and spirit, and had continued working as a nurse right up to the birth of their first child, Roy. She managed their household well and kept her husband's spirits buoyed even though he had difficulty finding enough work in Minnesota.

Friends of theirs, Charlie and Harriet Weaver, had written to describe the pleasures of their new home in a small California community called Delano, and urged them to move west also. Julius had tentatively suggested they accept the

Weaver's invitation and was surprised by the
enthusiasm with which Minnie accepted the idea.

From time to time she still tried to get him to
call her Desdemona, and though he had made the
effort when first married, he soon found it
impossible to remember. She had been introduced
to him as Minnie, and everyone, with the exception
of her mother, called her Minnie.

Sometimes he was amazed by Minnie's ability to
cope with crises and accept the tragedies of life.
When her sister, Wilhelmina had disappeared, she
had, of course, gone to her mother and offered
support, but she'd shown no outward signs of
distress. It was the same when Roy and their
daughter, Beulah, were born. Both labors were long
and difficult, but Minnie had suffered them
silently. And after each confinement she was
quickly back on her feet. When the children were
ill she tended them carefully, showing no outward
signs of worry.

The day came to leave for Chicago where they
would board a train for California. Minnie had
packed all their necessary belongings and clothing
into trunks and valises, selling or giving away
everything else. Minnie had slept peacefully
through their last night in their home while Julius
had tossed and turned, worrying how his family
would fare on the long trip ahead. He also
wondered whether he could find the necessary
work to support his family, but Minnie never
seemed to worry. She seemed to have complete
confidence in both their abilities to cope with all
new situations.

Julius leaned over and kissed her cheek.
"Minnie, it's time to get up!"

Minnie rubbed her eyes and smiled, stretching
and climbing out of bed. Her large, blue eyes
twinkled. "Good morning, Julius. Isn't it exciting?

What an adventure! I can hardly believe it—clear across the country on a train. Our children will remember it the rest of their lives!"

She hugged him tightly. "It's so wonderful!" Reaching for her clothes, she said, "We'd better not dilly dally, because there's lots to do. If you'll wake the children and see that they bathe and dress—their clothes are out—I'll fix breakfast and pack our lunch."

The trip to Chicago went well, though it was hard to tell who was more excited—Desdemona or the children. Beulah, a plump, pretty little girl, with dark hair like her mother's, was bubbling over, chattering non-stop, pointing out the sights along the way, and asking questions about everything.

Roy, who was thin and tall for his age, was more reserved, but he squirmed and craned his neck, peering here and there and revealing his fascination for all the new surroundings.

The hustle and bustle of Chicago was overwhelming. By mail they had made prior arrangements to sell their horse and buggy and were met at the railroad station by the purchaser. Once the business was transacted, Julius bought their tickets to California, the luggage was loaded into the baggage car, and before long they boarded the train.

"It's beautiful!" Desdemona exclaimed. They had purchased accommodations for the sleeping car due to the length of the trip and found it beautifully furnished with plush upholstery and ornately carved wood. They had just settled into their places when they heard the cry, "All aboard!"

This was to become a familiar signal as the train made many stops and starts for water, fuel, food, and more passengers. Soon they also became accustomed to the noise of the train as it heaved into motion with a hoot and a hiss, immediately followed by the accelerating clickety-clack of the wheels on the rails.

When the train jerkily started, it almost threw them out of their seats causing gales of laughter from Desdemona and the children, though Julius managed to keep a stern countenance as he clung to the arms of the chair. When the train picked up speed they all watched the scenery slipping past their windows.

"It all goes by so swiftly," Desdemona gasped.

"The train is a wondrous invention," Julius agreed.

Dinner time was first announced by Beulah exclaiming, "Mama, I'm hungry," and secondly by a black porter playing a melodious tune on chimes he held in his hand.

"Dinner is being served in the dining car. First call for dinner."

When the porter had gone to the next car, Beulah asked, "Can we go eat now, Papa?"

"Certainly," he said. Along with a few of the other passengers the family made their way down the narrow aisle. When they passed from one car to the next they were shielded from the outside by accordian-pleated vestibules of steel and elastic.

Upon entering the dining car, Desdemona whispered to Julius, "Look, my dear, it's absolutely elegant!" The car was crowded with tables covered with the best Irish linens and set with bone China dishes and Sheffield silver. The chairs were upholstered with red plush, mohair seats.

A white-jacket waiter seated them and gave Julius and Desdemona each a large menu with a drawing of the dining car on the cover. Desdemona glanced over the many choices listed and whispered, "The meals are only seventy-five cents each, much less expensive than I expected!"

They spent several minutes studying the menu.

Dinner

Blue Points on shell	Cream of Barley Soup
Broiled Fresh Salmon,	Sliced Cucumbers
Shrimp Sauce	Boiled Ox Tongue, Sauce
	Piquante

————

Roast Beef au Jus	Loin of Veal
Young Turkey, Cranberry Sauce	

————

Mashed Potatoes	Browned Sweet Potatoes
New Beets Spinach	Asparagus on Toast

————

Sweetbread Saute, Petis Pois
Minced Ham with Eggs
Queen Fritters, Maderia Sauce

————

Roast Spring Lamb, Mint Sauce

————

Fresh Lobster	Cold Ham
Chicken Salad au Mayonnaise	

————

Sliced Tomatoes	Dressed Lettuce

————

Apple Pie	Peach Pie
Rice Pudding, Vanilla Sauce	

————

Assorted Fruit	Batger's Orange Jelly
New York Ice Cream	Assorted Cakes

————

Bent's Water Crackers	Edam & Roquefort Cheese
French Coffee	
Meals . . . .75¢	

"My, I don't know how they do it," Desdemona said, her admiration increasing when the meal was served. Every item was piping hot, served elegantly, and best of all, delicious! Even the children, who were often picky eaters, had no complaints.

"I had no idea train travel would be such a grand experience," Julius said between bites.

Later Beulah and Roy had already fallen asleep in their seats when another porter came into their car and lowered the angled overhead panels. Desdemona and Julius held their sleepy children in the aisles while their seats were folded back, and the car was turned into separate little bedrooms right before their eyes.

After the children were bedded down, Desdemona found herself unable to suppress a few giggles while struggling to undress inside the curtained booth. The voluminous material of her traveling suit and her ruffled petticoats made the task difficult, but once they were all settled in their places for the night, the steady rhythm of the train lulled them quickly to sleep.

The Baileys made the acquaintance of various fellow travelers who boarded and disembarked at different stops along the way. The scenery changed radically as they progressed westward, the route closely following the Oregon and California trails taken by earlier settlers and finally arriving on the outskirts of San Francisco, where they changed trains for the trip to central California.

Delano, their destination, was a small town surrounded by farms and ranches, the uncultivated land colorfully abloom with wild flowers. There were bright orange California poppies, buttercups, lupine, lemon drops, tiny purple lilies, white fields of birdseye resembling snow, and

Desdemona recognized scatterings of the brilliant Indian paintbrush.

The Weavers were waiting for them at the train station. After exchanging hugs and kisses, the Baileys and their belongings were piled into two wagons and driven to the Weavers' home one mile north of the Southern Pacific Depot.

When Harriet Weaver pointed out their house to Desdemona, she was delighted with it, clapping her hands and exclaiming, "Harriet, it's absolutely beautiful!"

The two story house was surrounded by large shade trees and a white, picket fence and was decorated with fancy trimwork, with a small balcony over the large, front porch. Some of the Weaver children awaited them on the steps, while Charlie's mother and father and the two oldest children were watching from the balcony.

After all the Weavers had an opportunity to greet the Baileys, Charlie said, "Now, if you'll follow me, I'll show you where you'll be staying."

He led the family through the kitchen and out the back door. Nestled in between a large vegetable garden and a grove of fruit trees covered with blossoms was a cabin. "This is where we lived when we first arrived in California. It's small, but there's a front room, kitchen, and two bedrooms, and you're welcome to live there just as long as you like."

"Mama, Mama," Beulah squealed, "it's a doll house!"

Desdemona could already envision the windows draped with curtains created by her own hands. "This will suit us just fine!"

"I'll give you a hand bringing the trunks around, Julius. Harriet will have dinner on the table in about twenty minutes," Charlie said, heading for the front of the house.

Julius hugged Desdemona. "Don't despair, Minnie. I'll build us a fine house as soon as I can."

"Oh, Julius, don't fret about it. I'm happy to have a roof over our head. This will be a nice home for us. Let's go inside and take a look at our little doll house, children."

A while later, during their first meal eaten in Delano, Charlie asked Julius, "What kind of work did you plan on looking for?"

Julius shrugged. "I don't rightly know, but I'm certainly willing to try anything. Plastering has been my trade up 'til now."

Charlie scooped a second helping of mashed potatoes onto his plate and handed the bowl to his son sitting next to him. "There ain't much call for plastering around here. I 'spect you'd be better off in another trade. If you like, you could give me a hand in the store." Charlie owned a hardware store and plumbing shop, and also sold buggies, wagons, and farm implements.

"Inside work isn't for me," Julius commented, turning down another piece of chicken as it was passed in front of him.

"How are you with a hammer and nails?" Charlie asked. "We could sure use another good carpenter around here. Old man Wallace is getting old and can't begin to do all the jobs he's offered."

Julius answered modestly, "I do right well building most anything."

"Julius is a good carpenter!" Desdemona added proudly.

"Then I'd say it's all settled. You come on down to the store with me in the morning and take your pick of tools. I'll spread the word, and you'll be in business in no time!"

Soon Julius had plenty of work, and in time he purchased a lot on Fremont Street. Working evenings and on the weekends he built a large one story home for Desdemona, as promised. It had several bedrooms because Desdemona and Julius both hoped for a large family.

When the house was completed the family moved in. Desdemona busied herself with home-making and caring for the children when they weren't at the local grammar school.

At Charlie Weaver's invitation Julius joined the local branch of the International Order of Odd Fellows, and soon Julius and Desdemona became a popular couple in the community, entertaining and being entertained often.

In 1890 a baby girl was born to them, and they called her Flossie. She was an adorable, chubby child with merry, dark eyes, and her birth was an especially happy occasion for Desdemona and Julius.

"I had almost given up hope," Julius said, admiring his newest daughter as Desdemona sat in the rocking chair by the bed, nursing her.

"Maybe we'll fill up all our bedrooms yet," Desdemona said.

"That's what I always hoped for, but you know I'm happy with what I have—a beautiful wife and three healthy children."

Flossie's birth was Desdemona's introduction to Dr. Hildreth. When the doctor discovered Desdemona's nursing background, he began calling on her for help. She considered herself fortunate, for despite whatever diseases swept through the town, her own family stayed healthy. As she tended to those less fortunate, she doused herself heavily with good cologne, truly believing the practice shielded her from all germs.

When a grateful patient gave her an accordian, she was surprised to find she had a natural apptitude for playing the instrument. Enjoyable evenings were spent with family and friends, Desdemona playing the accordian and Julius the harmonica, for singalongs.

One such evening, when friends had gathered to celebrate the Bailey's anniversary, Harriet Weaver called for "Love's Old Sweet Song." On the last note Julius lifted the accordian from Desdemona's arms and set it in the corner. "Friends," he said, "I want you all to know how fortunate I've been all these years to have Minnie as my own dear, sweet wife."

The name Minnie still grated on Desdemona's ear, but since Julius had fallen into the habit of calling her by that name, all of her friends in Delano only knew her as Minnie. Deep inside she still thought of herself as Desdemona, but she smiled sweetly as he leaned down to kiss her on the forehead.

"As a token of my love I have a gift I want to bestow on my sweetheart. Roy, give me a hand." With the help of his son, Julius brought a large package into the room and put it on the floor.

"My goodness, Julius, whatever could it be?" Her hands trembled as she untied the ribbon which encircled the wrapped package. She didn't dare hope it could possibly by the one thing she secretly wanted, knowing it was far too expensive.

Casting the paper inside she squealed with delight. "Oh, Julius, it's exactly what I've been wanting!" It was the latest model sewing machine.

She stood on her tiptoes and hugged her husband, giving him a resounding kiss. Taking hold of Beulah's hands she danced a jig with her daughter. "My, oh my, oh my, I'll have the best dressed young ladies in all of Delano!"

The Bailey family continued to be hardworking,

healthy, and happy. Roy graduated from the eighth grade of Delano grammar school, immediately going to work for a local rancher. Two years later Beulah finished school and the following week made a surprising announcement at the breakfast table.

Visibly nervous, Beulah began, "Mother . . . father . . . I hope you aren't going to be too upset . . . but, well . . . I've got a job at the post office."

"Why would we be upset? I think that's wonderful news," Desdemona said, feeling proud of her daughter.

In a quiet voice, Beulah added, "In Kern."

"What was that you said?" Desdemona asked.

Beulah raised her voice, enunciating carefully. "I said my new job is in Kern."

Kern was a small town just outside of Bakersfield. "Why you can't work there," Desdemona argued. "That's much too far to ride your bicycle back and forth."

Beulah looked down at her hands and sighed. "Mother, I don't plan on coming back and forth— except on weekends, of course. I've taken a room in a very nice boarding house."

"Beulah Belle Bailey! You are much too young to go off and live by yourself in some boarding house. Tell her she can't do that, Julius." When she looked to her husband for agreement, Desdemona knew it would be forthcoming, but she was in for a surprise.

"Minnie Bailey, I'm surprised at you!" he chided. "You raised your children to be independent just like you. Are you going to stand in Beulah's way now that she's ready to go out on her own? I think our Beulah is grown-up enough to take care of herself!"

It was quite a speech and it caused Desdemona to stop and think. Julius was right, of course.

Desdemona had raised all three children to think
for themselves and to make their own decisions. It
would be unreasonable to stand in Beulah's way.
Desdemona hadn't hesitated an instant when Roy
had announced his plans to move out, only
questioning him about the details of his job and
pay and living accommodations—then she'd
helped him pack.

Desdemona leaned over and kissed her
daughter's cheek. "I'm sorry, dear. Your father is
right as he so often is. I'm proud of you. What can
we do to help?"

She saw Beulah for the first time as a grown
woman. She wore her thick, dark hair piled high
atop her head in an effort to add inches to her
short stature. She had a buxom figure with a tiny
waist, all the latest styles flattering her.

Desdemona knew all the young men had
certainly discovered Beulah long ago. Her
daughter's weekends were always filled with
bicycle rides, picnics and dances. But she had
been waiting for Beulah to announce her engagement—not employment in another city.

Chapter 41

The turn of the century was coming, and Delano made big plans to herald in the year 1900. The celebrations had begun before Christmas with private dinner parties held in many homes. All the fraternal organizations held festivities, and huge balls were planned in many different locations for New Year's Eve.

Desdemona was pinning the hem on the elegant ball gown she'd created for Beulah who had come home for the gala event. She spoke through the pins held between her lips. "Have you finally decided which young man you're going to choose as your escort for New Year's Eve? If you wait too long to decide, all the bachelors will have asked other girls, and I'll have slaved over this dress for nothing!"

Beulah laughed at her mother's remark. "Don't fret, Mama, I told Lance John I would go to the ball with him, but I promised dances to all the others!"

"Don't you ever think about getting married? After all, dear, you *are* nineteen and some of your old beaus already have chosen other girls to be their wives. You don't want to be a spinster and work at the post office the rest of your life, do you?"

Beulah sighed. She and her mother had had the same conversation many times before. "Oh, mother, you say spinster with such distaste! It might not be so bad to stay unmarried. I enjoy my work at the post office, and I like being independent. I'm certainly not going to marry just anyone to settle down to a life of drudgery!" She'd seen enough of her married friends and watched her mother's life to know that being a wife meant a great deal of hard work. It would take a very special man for her to give up the enjoyable life she now had.

"But, dear, some of your young men would make very suitable husbands," Desdemona argued.

"Oh, Mother." Beulah rolled her violet-blue eyes. "I really can't see myself spending the rest of my life with any of the boys I know. That's what they all are—just boys! They're awkward and hard to talk to and will probably all be farmers! I want someone who I can love and respect. And I don't want to be stuck in Delano, or Kern, for the rest of my life. I want to travel and have fun. The man I marry will have to be exciting and handsome!"

Desdemona shook her head and sighed. She would never have admitted it to Beulah, but her daughter had thoughts quite similar to her own at the same age. But she had been fortunate because Julius had come into her life. It wasn't likely Beulah would find a Prince Charming.

*   *   *

The new dress was a great success at the parties and dances Beulah attended that night. She went to bed at dawn on the first day of 1900—with aching feet and three more marriage proposals on her scoreboard.

Chapter 42

Desdemona put down the letter she had received from her sister, Eudora. "And what's the news from South Dakota?" Julius asked. He'd brought the letter home when he came for his noon meal.

"It's not so good. Eudora's husband, Roscoe was killed in a gun battle—he was the sheriff, you know—and Eudora is very upset and doesn't know what to do."

"What a shame! How old are her two girls now?" Julius asked.

Desdemona figured for a moment, then said, "Hazel must be seven and Vera three. You know I love living in California, but times like these I wish I lived closer to my family." She stared at the letter before her, thought for a minute, then an idea came to her.

"Julius, I know what we should do! Let's invite Eudora and the girls to come out here with us! We have plenty of room. Oh please, say you like the idea! A change of scene would be so good for her, and Flossie would enjoy her little cousins. It could be just for a visit, but then again maybe she would like to stay. Oh, do agree, Julius."

Julius chuckled because he had never denied her anything she had ever asked for, and she knew it. "Of course you can ask Eudora and her children to come and stay with us, but don't count on it too much. Remember you invited your mother and your sister, Jessie, to visit, and no one has ever taken you up on it. Perhaps Eudora will have decided on some other course of action before she hears from you."

"She'll want to come! Don't leave until I get a letter written and you can drop it off at the post office on your way back to work." Desdemona was already on her way out of the room to fetch paper, pen and ink.

Picking up his fork, Julius continued eating his lunch. There was no point in reminding Desdemona that the job he was working on was at the opposite side of town from the post office.

Desdemona was right about Eudora. In July of 1900, on the hottest day of the year, Eudora and her red-headed daughters arrived at the train station. Desdemona met them with a horse and wagon and was delighted by the large amount of luggage her sister had brought with her, for it appeared Eudora planned a long visit.

"Here I am, Eudora," Desdemona called, running to her.

Eudora was wearing a two-piece dress, her hair in a fashionable pompadour in front and hanging long down her back. She had changed a great deal since Desdemona had seen her last, for she still had been a youngster when she'd left for South Dakota with her older sister, Jessie. At thirty-eight she was a handsome woman, taller and plumper than Desdemona, but the signs of her recent tragedy were apparent in the dark smudges under her eyes.

The sisters embraced, and Desdemona had to stand on tiptoe to kiss her sister on the lips.

"Hazel, Vera, this is your Aunt Desdemona," Eudora said.

Desdemona knelt down beside the girls. "Hello, Aunt Desdemona," Hazel murmured shyly, while the younger child hid behind her mother's skirt.

"Hello, you two darlings, I'm so happy you are here. Your cousin, Flossie, is waiting at home, very anxious to finally make your acquaintance. Let's find someone to help us load your baggage into the wagon, and we'll by on our way."

During the short ride to the house, Desdemona explained to her sister how no one called her Desdemona anymore. "But you know how I've always hated Minnie, and if the girls would like to call me Aunt Mona, I certainly would be pleased."

The addition of Eudora and her girls to the Bailey household filled most of the empty bedrooms. But within six months they were empty once again. Eudora married a Mr. Knuckey after a whirlwind courtship which had begun almost immediately following their introduction, but Eudora and the girls, along with Mr. Knuckey, continued to be frequent visitors to the Bailey home. Vera would perch upon the small red stool behind the parlor door and listen to her Aunt Mona play the accordion as the other grown-ups sang the popular songs of the day.

Vera loved summer best when all the children were home for vacation and she had playmates. But when September came and the older children were back in school, she had difficulty keeping herself occupied, sometimes just wandering down to the depot, to sit and watch all the activity.

The September Vera turned six she thought she too would be going to school, but her mother disappointed her by saying, "Not his year, you're still too young!" She didn't cry until she was outside and under the protective overhang of the weeping willow in the front yard. She had to face another long, lonely year by herself, and she stretched out on the cool grass and sobbed.

One Friday afternoon Eudora shoved Vera out of the house. "Must you always be underfoot! Go outside and play. Mother is busy."

Her mother was always busy. Vera walked down the dusty road toward the train depot—maybe something was going on there. As she approached the station she spied her Uncle Julius who was loading his wagon with furniture from a freight car.

"Uncle Jule, Uncle Jule," she cried.

"Why, hello there, Vera. How are you today?" he asked, while positioning his load on the wagon.

"Fine. What are you doing, Uncle Jule?" Vera kept her distance from the two large horses hitched to the wagon.

Julius walked around the wagon to where his niece was standing and lifted her high into the air. "I'm picking up a load of furniture for some new folks in town. Would you like a ride back home?"

"Uh uh, I just came from there. I think I'll stay here and watch what's going on."

"Whatever you say, honey." He put her down. "I'd better get going now. See you soon!"

Vera watched her uncle climb onto the wagon seat. He lifted the reins and was beginning to sit, when a train engine on the next track blew its whistle. The horses lunged forward, bucking and kicking, jerking the lines in Julius' hands and yanking him from the seat. As he fell head first between the wagon and the horses, the team charged forward, and the wagon wheels rolled over him.

Vera screamed in horror, while the men started shouting and running from every direction toward Julius.

Vera stared at her uncle. He was lying still, one leg jutting out from his body at an impossible angle, blood soaking his sleeve. She knew she had to get home and tell her mother, and she began running as fast as her legs would take her in the direction of her house.

Bursting in the front door, she shouted, "Mama, Mama, Uncle Jules . . . I think he's dead!"

Eudora threw down her mending and ran to Vera. "What are you talking about?"

"The train station . . . Uncle Jules' wagon . . . the horses ran away . . . the wagon ran over him!"

"Oh, God!" Eudora gasped. "Stay here, Vera! I'm going to the station."

By the time Eudora reached the depot, Dr. Hildreth and some men were lifting Julius into the back of the wagon, and Eudora's heart sank as she saw her brother-in-law's limp body.

"Doctor," she gasped, "is he . . ."

"No, no," Dr. Hildreth assured her, smiling kindly. "He's unconscious, but the worst of his injuries seems to be a broken leg. We're taking him home now."

"I'll go with you," Eudora announced, climbing into the wagon without waiting for permission.

Desdemona was surprisingly calm when she heard the news. "I came to see if I could help," Eudora said.

"Thank you. Please run inside and turn the covers down on our bed," Desdemona directed in professional tones. "You men can carry him this way."

Eudora admired the way her sister worked beside the doctor, assisting in the setting and bandaging of the leg, the break being above the knee.

"A bad place for a break," the doctor commented. "Let's have a look at this arm."

A minor wound, the doctor cleaned it, applying antiseptic, and Desdemona dressed it. "Why isn't he regaining consciousness, Doctor?" she asked, with a tinge of worry in her voice. "Is there something else wrong?"

"Now, now, Minnie, you know that despite the seriousness of the fracture, it certainly isn't mortal. Julius is most fortunate, and he certainly has the best nurse around to care for him. Your husband will be up and about in no time," he assured her. "I'll stop by in the morning and check on him. Just try and keep him comfortable. He may be in some pain when he wakes up, but you know what to do in that case."

Desdemona walked the doctor to the door, Eudora following along behind. "If you don't need me anymore, Minnie," Eudora said, "I'll go on home. I left Vera by herself—poor thing saw the accident and she's worried sick—and it won't be long before Hazel comes home from school. If you want me to come back . . ."

"No, no, that won't be necessary. Flossie will be home soon and we can manage. Thank you for coming." Desdemona gave Eudora a quick hug, and hurried back towards the bedroom.

When Flossie came into the house calling for her mother, Desdemona stepped from the bedroom, holding a finger to her lips as she quietly shut the door. "Shhh. Your father's had a dreadful accident, and we must let him rest."

"What happened? Is he going to be all right?" The plump girl's eyes opened wide.

"He was run over by his wagon. His leg is broken, but the doctor says there's nothing else wrong."

Flossie prepared a simple supper and Desdemona left her patient long enough to eat it. "How is father doing?"

Desdemona sighed and toyed with the food on her plate. "I'm worried. I think he should have regained consciousness by now."

"Oh, dear, do you think we should get the doctor?"

"No, there's nothing he can do, and he's supposed to come by in the morning."

"Try to eat a little, Mother. Don't bother about anything—I'll clean up in here."

When Flossie had finished with her chores she joined her mother at Julius' bedside. "Has there been any change?"

Desdemona shook her head. "No. He hasn't moved!"

There wasn't anything Flossie could think to say. Her father's face was drawn and pale, his eyelashes not even flickering. Mother and daughter kept their vigil by Julius' side all night.

Dawn was beginning to lighten the room when Julius' eyes fluttered open. He gazed at Desdemona, his lips lifting slightly into a smile. "Minnie," he breathed. His eyes shut, a strange hissing sound escaping from his slack mouth.

Desdemona leaped to her feet, leaned over him, and felt for his pulse. "Julius!" she cried. "Oh, no! Please, dear God!"

"Mother?" Flossie questioned fearfully.

"He's gone." Desdemona sighed, leaned over and kissed him on the lips, then pulled the sheet over him. Flossie threw her arms around her mother and sobbed.

After a time, Desdemona gently pushed her

daughter away. "Flossie, try to pull yourself together. I need you to go after Dr. Hildreth, and then please tell your Aunt Eudora. Ask her to come by later today to help me with the funeral arrangements. And see if Mr. Knuckey will ride out to the ranch to tell Roy. And we'll have to send someone for Beulah, too."

Trying to be as brave as her mother, Flossie blinked back her tears and nodded her head. She covered her mouth to hold back the sobs until she was out of the house, then crying, she ran towards the doctor's house.

The funeral was held Sunday at the Bailey home. It was one of those hot September days when the heat settles oppressively over everything. Every window and door in the house was open wide in an effort to coax the nonexistent breezes inside. Their faces shiny from perspiration, everyone was obviously uncomfortable in their dark, heavy clothing.

The body was laid out in the parlor, surrounded by potted palms and ferns. The I.O.O.F. choir sat in a row of kitchen chairs behind the casket and sang several songs including, "Lead Kindly Light" and "I Must Tell Jesus."

Most of the women cried and sniffled throughout the service, and after the eulogy, when the choir sang "Nearer My God to Thee," there was hardly a dry eye in the house—excepting Desdemona's.

Julius' widow sat straight, facing ahead and looking beyond the body of her husband. On either side of her were the children, openly crying. Desdemona put her arm around Flossie and patted Beulah's hand, then glanced over Flossie's head at her son, Roy. Tears ran down his cheeks, and she smiled comfortingly at him.

The last song the choir performed was "God Be With You 'Til We Meet Again" which was the undoing for all those who had managed to somewhat control their emotions. Even Desdemona wiped the corners of her eyes with the lace-edged handkerchief she'd clutched in her hand throughout the service. When the last note died away, Desdemona led the procession of mourners past the open coffin to bid Julius Bailey a last farewell. After the mortician closed the casket, the pallbearers carried it to the black, horse drawn hearse, to be taken to the cemetery for burial.

Chapter 43

"Oh, my dear, dear sister, I know exactly what you're going through! Whatever will you do?" Eudora was wringing her hands, her eyes brimming with tears.

Desdemona found herself becoming the comforter, even though she knew Eudora's visit had been intended as consolation to her. "Eudora, please, pull yourself together. I'm doing fine under the circumstances."

"But how will you ever manage? How will you pay your bills and support your family? I'm not in any position to give you any financial help—and you and Julius were so good to me when I lost my first husband!" Eudora wailed.

"You mustn't fret. After all, Beulah is twenty-one, has a job and will help us if need be. And Dr. Hildreth has already promised to recommend me for any nursing jobs which come along. Also I've decided to rent out some of my bedrooms."

Eudora's eyes were round with surprise. "Who will you rent to—strangers?"

"I'm going to go to the depot and put up a sign. There are lots of railroad men who would enjoy having a clean room and home cooked meals, I'm sure."

"But Desdemona, what will people think? Strange men living right here in your house!"

"Frankly, Eudora, I really don't care what people think. It seems a good way to support myself and Flossie, and I'm certain I can continue to conduct myself as a lady."

"But . . ." began Eudora.

"Don't bother to say anything else. I've made up my mind."

A procession of railroad men and other bachelors lived a part of their lives in the Bailey home, some for a short time, others for several years. The income from the boarders and her nursing provided Desdemona with a good living for herself and Flossie.

On July 2nd of 1906, Beulah married a young railroad man named Harry Hoffman, the happiness of the day only clouded by the illness of Eudora. Her sickness had been diagnosed as dropsy which lasted for six months and ended with her death. At that time Hazel was fourteen and Vera ten, and they lived with their stepfather, Mr. Knuckey, who later sent them to a Los Angeles school of nursing, from which they both graduated as registered nurses. Hazel spent her entire life in the profession, while Vera worked for a time, then retired and married.

Desdemona's son, Roy, married a widow named Jennie and continued ranching and farming, raising sheep, cotton and other crops.

Chapter 44

"Mother," Flossie said, "I have something very important to discuss with you."

Desdemona looked up from her sewing at her sixteen-year-old daughter. Flossie was quite attractive, her thick, dark hair arranged in a large pompador framing her face. Blue, laughing eyes sparkled, and dimples danced in her plump, pink cheeks when she smiled. She was dressed in her usual costume of dark skirt and starched white blouse which set off her small waistline and most generous bosom.

"Yes, dear, what is it?"

"Mother, please put down your sewing and listen carefully."

Desdemona was surprised by her daughter's serious tone. Flossie was seldom serious. "Go ahead, Flossie. I'm listening most attentively."

Flossie clapped her hands and danced a hop and a skip. "Oh, Mother, it's so exciting! Grace Mitchell and I are opening a little store!"

"Oh! My goodness, that is certainly interesting news. What kind of store would you two girls know how to run?" Desdemona chose her words carefully. She could almost hear Julius telling her not to throw a wet blanket on youthful enthusiasm, reminding her yet again of her own independent nature.

"We're going to sell homemade ice cream, bread, pies, cakes and candy . . . maybe even cigars and stationery and magazines, too. We've even thought up a name for it—the Bon Bon Shop."

"That's a catchy name. Where is this store going to be?"

"Over on Eye Street. Grace Mitchell's father is painting it for us right now."

"My, it certainly sounds as though you two girls have thought of everything. Where did you plan to get the money to buy your supplies and furniture?" Desdemona hoped her practical question wouldn't burst Flossie's bubble, but obviously Desdemona hadn't given her youngest child credit for her initiative.

"Remember, I got a hundred dollars when Papa died? Well, I took it out of the bank. Grace also had some money saved, and her daddy's loaning us the rest. We'll pay him back right away, as soon as we start making a profit. I have to go now, Mama. Grace and I have a million things to do!" Pecking her mother on the cheek, Flossie fairly skipped out the door.

The Bon Bon Shop was an immediate success, which was no surprise to Flossie or Grace. It had one of the best equipped soda fountains for miles around. Flossie insisted on absolute cleanliness, and when she wasn't waiting on customers, she could be found scrubbing equipment, mopping the floors, or wiping down countertops, tables and chairs.

One busy day Flossie put her hands on her ample hips and smiled as she looked over the shop. It was the first time she had had a moment to rest; it seemed that every young man residing in Delano had been in to order something. She had been kept busy making their concoctions and bantering with her customers in her usual good-natured manner.

Grace had already left for a date with a young man whom Flossie suspected would soon become her partner's husband.

The bell on the front door jingled, announcing a new arrival, and Flossie smiled warmly at Lloyd Hamlin as he sauntered over to the counter. "Good day, Lloyd. What can I do for you?"

"If you want the honest truth, Flossie, you can close up this place, and run off with me and get married," Lloyd teased.

Flossie knew he was more serious than not. She had many suitors but Lloyd was by far the most persistent, and though she favored him over all the other men, she didn't let him know it. He was tall, handsome, and he had a seriousness she admired, but she was not at all interested in giving up her independence yet.

"Oh, go on with you, Lloyd—you probably say that to all the girls," Flossie retorted.

Lloyd fixed his light blue eyes on her. "No! As a matter of fact, I've never said such a thing to anyone."

Flossie chose to ignore this. "I've got some fresh strawberries—how about a nice soda or milk shake?"

"Nope, think I'll just buy a magazine and go sit in the corner until you close. You wouldn't turn down a ride home, would you?"

Bestowing a warm smile on Lloyd, Flossie said,

"No, of course I wouldn't. I'd be much obliged."
She would be glad for the ride but she wasn't too
happy to have Lloyd sitting there for the next
hour. He blankly turned the pages of a magazine
but kept his eyes on her.

When two young men who were regular
customers came in, she turned her attention to
them. "Hi, Frank . . . Michael."

Frank, a short, redheaded fellow, reached
across the counter and patted her hand. "How's
the most beautiful girl in town?"

"Hey, quit flirting with her. Don't you know
Flossie's my best girl?" the curly headed Michael
said, jabbing an elbow in Frank's side.

"Don't you wish!"

"Come, come boys, there's enough of me to go
around," Flossie bantered good-naturedly.

"There sure is," Michael said, wiggling his
eyebrows. "How about making us a couple of your
famous milk shakes."

"Be glad to—what flavor would you like?"

The young men stated their choices, taking seats
at the table closest to the counter. Throughout the
silly exchange Flossie had felt Lloyd's disapprov-
ing stare, and when she stole a glance in his
direction, sure enough he had a dour look on his
long face. She smiled at him and winked, but he
glanced hastily at the open magazine before him
and shuffled the pages.

Flossie returned to her task of shaking the glass
milk shake container with vim and vigor, well
aware that most of her male customers ordered
milk shakes mainly to watch her make them. Long
ago she'd noticed that Grace, who was not nearly
as well endowed in the chest, had far less requests
by the male clientele for milk shakes. But Flossie
ignored the goggle-eyed fellows who watched her
with such interest.

Not so Lloyd. He coughed and squirmed in his chair, and when she glanced at him, she was surprised to see his sun tanned face had turned a deep purple. If it bothered him so much, he should go elsewhere. After all, he didn't have any claim on her.

On the way home in Lloyd's truck, he let her know exactly how he felt about her job and her male customers. "I think it's absolutely disgusting the way those buffoons ogle you. If they want that kind of entertainment, why don't they go to a burlesque show in Bakersfield! I don't see why you put up with it! It's . . . well, it's demeaning!" Lloyd sputtered.

Flossie knew he was jealous and felt a certain pleasure from such knowledge. "Oh, Lloyd, it's harmless. They don't mean anything by it."

"I don't know why you have that shop anyway. Women aren't supposed to work!"

Flossie burst into laughter. "Oh, that's very well for you to say! I need the money. Remember, my mother and I support ourselves, and the shop is doing very well. I'm even putting some money in the bank!"

Lloyd parked the car in front of her house. "You wouldn't have to worry about money if you married me."

Patting him gently on the arm, Flossie said, "Lloyd, if I wanted to get married, I'd certainly choose you . . . but I'm not ready for marriage. I like my job and everything that goes with it! Thanks for the ride." She opened the door and jumped out, slamming it behind her. Leaning in the window she added, "Bye now," and blew him a kiss.

Though she had many invitations from male admirers for excursions on free weekends, she preferred to go with her mother down to Kern to visit her sister, Beulah, and her sister's husband, Harry. She was crazy about her tall, handsome brother-in-law; he was more fun than any of the fellows she knew—even Lloyd, who was too serious to have much fun.

One hot Saturday, when Desdemona and Flossie were staying at Beulah's, Harry called to Flossie through the open screen door. "Hey, why don't you come outside and give me a hand in the garden."

"Are you crazy, Harry? It's too hot!" She was sipping a glass of iced tea.

"Be good for you to get on out here and work off some of that fat," he taunted.

"Fat!" she squealed. "Are you calling me fat?" She stood in the doorway, one hand on her hip, her full glass in the other one.

"Yes—fat! You can tell who the chief taster of all the goodies is at the Bon Bon Shop," Harry continued to tease.

"Harry Hoffman, you are a beast!" Flossie shrieked, running out onto the lawn. She reached up and pulled open Harry's shirt collar and dumped the tea and chipped ice down his back.

"Oh, so that's how it's going to be, is it?" He turned the hose he held and sprayed her full force.

She screamed in surprise and mock horror, soaked to the skin. Actually the cool water felt good on such a miserably hot day, but she stamped her foot on the sodden grass and glared at her brother-in-law. "You've ruined my hairdo! I'm never speaking to you again!"

She started up the front steps to go inside but was stopped by Beulah. "Oh, no you don't! I just scrubbed the floor yesterday, so you're not coming in here and dripping all over it."

Flossie scurried back down the stairs, dodging

the spray Harry was aiming at her again. She ran around the back of the house and discovered a large tin bucket, filling it from a faucet by the kitchen door.

Staggering under the weight of the full bucket, she crept up behind Harry who was watering a flower border. "Hey, Harry, watch out," she cried, heaving the water right into his face as he turned around.

"Why you little brat!" He tried to squirt her with the hose again but she ran out of the spray's reach around the corner of the house.

She took off her soggy shoes and stockings and went on bare feet into the house. Peeking out the kitchen window she could see Harry creeping cautiously around the side toward the back door, bucket in hand. Confident she was nowhere around, he filled the large container.

"Flossie," he called. "Come back outside. I don't have the hose anymore."

Searching the kitchen, Flossie found Beulah's mop pail under the kitchen counter. She filled it in the sink and carried it to the back door.

"Here I come, Harry," she hollered, flinging open the door and pouring the water on her brother-in-law. Throwing his bucketful at her at the same time, the water splashed all over Beulah's highly polished kitchen floor.

Unfortunately Beulah came through the swinging door between the kitchen and dining room at that exact moment.

"Flossie Bailey!" she screamed.

"I didn't do it," Flossie said. "It was Harry!" She pointed an accusing finger at Beulah's husband who had just stuck his grinning face inside the door.

"Oh, oh," he cried, spotting his wife.

"Harry! You know how hard I worked on this

floor. Look what all your tomfoolery has done!"
Beulah crossed her arms and tapped her foot
impatiently.

"Don't you fret, darlin'," Harry cooed. "Flossie
and I will fix it up just like it was, won't we,
Flossie?" He winked broadly at her.

Flossie agreed quickly, "Yes, Beulah, we sure
will."

When they were both down on their hands and
knees wiping up the mess, Harry looked over at
her slyly and said, "It was worth it, wasn't it, Sis?"

Flossie couldn't help giggling. "Cooled things
off for awhile, anyhow."

They had all stayed up late that night sitting on
the kitchen chairs out on the back lawn to enjoy
the evening breeze. Flossie and Desdemona hadn't
been in bed more than a few minutes when they
were startled by the clanging of the town fire
alarm. Going to the door of the spare bedroom,
Flossie saw Harry go out the front door.

Flossie and Desdemona pulled wrappers on over
their nightgowns and joined Beulah who was
already standing in the living room. When Harry
came back inside he said, "There must be a fire in
Delano—the fire engine is headed in that
direction." Delano had no fire department of its
own, so whenever there was a big fire the Delano
volunteers couldn't handle, they would send for
Kern's fire department.

Desdemona clutched Flossie's arm. "I hope it
isn't our house."

Flossie was shocked to see how pale her mother
was—as if the blood had drained from her face.
"Mother, my goodness, why would it be our
house? There are a lot of houses in Delano?" But it
was unusual for her mother to imagine the dark

side of anything and Flossie had a sense of uneasiness, too.

Desdemona sighed. "I don't know . . . I just have this terrible feeling in the pit of my stomach."

"Oh, Mother," Beulah said, "I'm sure it doesn't mean anything. Being disturbed by that loud fire bell is enough to make anyone sick."

"If it'll make you feel any better, Mother," Harry suggested, "we can sit up until the firemen return and ask exactly where the fire was."

Desdemona reached up and patted her son-in-law's cheek. "Oh thank you, Harry. I know I won't get any rest until I know for sure one way or the other."

"We're probably wasting our time," Beulah complained, "but come on, let's go into the kitchen and have a snack."

In the wee hours of the morning, after eating a whole peach pie and drinking two pots of coffee, they heard the fire truck rumble down the street. Harry walked to the fire station a block away, and the three women waited his return.

Flossie immediately knew Harry's news was bad by the look on his face. Before he could say anything, Desdemona jumped from her chair. "It was my house that burned, wasn't it?"

"I'm afraid so," Harry said, quietly.

"Were they able to save anything?" Beulah asked.

"No, it burned clear to the ground."

"Oh, Mother," Beulah wailed, "all of your beautiful things are gone!" She rushed to Desdemona and put her arms around her.

"Tell me . . . " Desdemona asked, "was anyone hurt? Did all my boarders get out all right?"

"Yes, yes, everyone is safe," Harry assured her.

Flossie rolled her eyes. "It was probably one of

the boarders who started the fire—probably old Mr. McIntrye did it with one of his smelly cigars!"

Desdemona held up a hand. "Now Flossie, we'll never know what caused it, most likely—and it wouldn't change anything if we did. The house is gone and that's all there is to it." She sighed. "Julius built that house for me."

Tears streamed from Beulah's eyes as she clung to Desdemona. "Oh, Mother, it's so awful! Whatever will you do?"

"Now don't worry about a thing, Mother Bailey," Harry interjected. "You and Flossie can make your home here with us."

Flossie grinned at her brother-in-law. She knew he meant what he was offering—but, Oh boy, wouldn't they drive poor Beulah wild? "Don't you concern yourself with me, Harry," she said. "I'll stay with friends in Delano. After all, I have to be near the Bon Bon Shop."

Desdemona patted her son-in-law's hand. "Thank you ever so much, Harry. I shall accept your kind offer for the time being, but only until I can find a job and save enough to rebuild my home."

Beulah frowned. "I don't want you to go to work, Mother! We'll take care of you."

"Don't forget, daughter, I'm a practical nurse, and a very good one at that. And I enjoy helping those less fortunate than myself. Besides, I couldn't stay here very long. I'm too used to taking care of myself."

Flossie knew her mother couldn't be persuaded to change her mind, but Beulah continued to try. "But Mother, I don't think it's good for you to be around sick people at your age—after all, you might catch something."

"Oh, posh," exclaimed Desdemona, "I'm not all that old—and besides, I haven't had a sick day in my life! I douse myself good with cologne and the germs stay away.''

Desdemona worked as a practical nurse in Kern until she saved enough money to rebuild her home in Delano. Once done, she again rented extra rooms to boarders.

Grace Mitchell married just like Flossie expected and was no longer interested in the ice cream parlor, so Flossie bought out Grace's share of the partnership and continued to run the Bon Bon Shop on her own.

Still spending a weekend every month or so with Beulah and Harry, one night Flossie decided to visit them quite late, but when she arrived she found they had already retired for the evening.

Tiptoeing into the house, she quietly set up the cot she usually slept on. Fishing around in the pitch black linen closet she had to select the sheets by feel alone.

In the morning she was awakened by gales of laughter from Beulah and Harry.

"What's so funny?" she asked, raising herself sleepily from the cot.

"You certainly are using classy bedding, young lady," Harry retorted.

Looking down she saw she had mistakingly used Beulah's finest damask linen table cloth for a bed sheet!

Chapter 45

"You certainly don't need my permission to get married again, Mother," Flossie declared.

"I wasn't asking for your permission, dear. I merely wondered how you would feel about it," answered Desdemona chuckling. "After all, Mr. Smith has lived here for the past year, so you've certainly had an opportunity to get to know him."

"I like him, Mother—you know that—he's a very nice man. But how do *you* feel about him? Do you love him?" Flossie asked. Desdemona had surprised her daughter by her announcement. After all, her mother was fifty-two, and Flossie had never really considered the fact she might remarry. Flossie now looked upon her differently —as a woman rather than a mother—and realized Desdemona was quite attractive. Her once dark hair was now white, and she wore it in a short, curly manner which gave her a young appearance, only laugh lines showing beside her still vibrant blue eyes. Flossie was envious of her mother's trim figure. Always pleasingly plump herself, the tasting of her own goodies in the Bon Bon shop hadn't helped.

Smiling pensively, Desdemona explained, "When you reach my age, Flossie, you look for other attributes in a man as a potential husband— whether you love him or not isn't really important. I had love with your father, but honestly I didn't love him when I married him—that came later. Now there are other considerations more important to me, such as companionship and security, and I think John Smith can provide these. He's a kind, gentle man, who's been left a widower twice . . . and he's lonely, just as I am."

"Oh, Mother, I never imagined you were lonely!" exclaimed Flossie. "You're always so busy, and you have so many friends!"

"That's not the same as having someone to share everything with at the end of a long day."

"I guess I understand, Mother." Flossie knew her mother certainly wasn't marrying Mr. Smith for his looks. Though John Smith was near the same age as Desdemona, he looked older. A thin man with prominent ears, he wore glasses to correct the vision of slightly crossed eyes. He worked steadily as a carpenter for the Edison Company, always paid his rent on time, was clean and tidy, and seemed pleasant enough as far as Flossie could tell. And though Flossie thought her own beau, Lloyd Hamlin, with his tall ruggedness, was the handsomest man she'd ever laid eyes on, she knew everyone did not share her opinion. Perhaps, seen through her mother's eyes, homely John Smith appeared handsome and debonair.

So, on a warm spring afternoon in April, with Flossie as her attendant and a wedding party consisting of her son Roy and his wife Jennie, her daughter Beulah and her husband Harry, their two little girls, Genevieve Mona and the baby Flossie, and John's daughter, Amy, Desdemona became Mrs. John Smith.

Flossie ran the Bon Bon Shop for nine successful years, while Lloyd Hamlin continued to pursue her even after all her other beaus had given up. Lloyd proposed at least once a week and Flossie kept putting him off.

"I really do care for you, Lloyd, and if I was thinking of marrying, which I'm not, you'd certainly be my choice. But I'm just not ready yet," was her usual answer.

Lloyd came into the Bon Bon shop most evenings around closing time, helping Flossie lock up, then driving her home. One evening, expecting Lloyd momentarily, Flossie noticed the definite smell of smoke.

"Do you smell anything?" she called out to the family sitting around one of the front tables. She set aside the broom and peered around the room.

The woman at the table began to scream, "Fire, fire!" Then there came the sound of breaking glass as the woman, her husband and their two children fled from the shop.

Flames burst through the storeroom doorway and licked at, then seemed to devour the paneled wall. Realizing she could do nothing to fight the fire, Flossie opened the cash register and emptied it into her purse. Looking back one last time, she could see the fire had already engulfed the back of her little shop, and it didn't look as though the fire department could possibly save anything.

As people began to gather outside, the volunteer firemen arrived and fought desperately but vainly to save the shop.

Flossie stood by helplessly, watching the fire

destroy her livelihood. She felt an arm slip around her waist and she gazed into Lloyd's worried face. He didn't say anything, just held her as she buried her face against his chest.

After crying for a few minutes, she wiped the tears from her eyes with Lloyd's handkerchief, and squeezing his hand, she said bravely, "Could you take me home now, Lloyd? It's too depressing here."

At the house Flossie invited Lloyd inside. Sitting around the dining room table she told the news to her mother, and her mother's husband of two years. Desdemona poured them all a cup of coffee. "You do have quite a bit of money in your savings account, don't you? Is it enough to start over?"

Flossie smiled. "I have six hundred dollars— that's more than enough to begin again." She leaned against Lloyd's broad shoulder and patted his hand. "But I don't think I will."

"No?" Desdemona said with surprise. "I thought you loved your ice cream store."

"Uh huh, I did. But I think it's time to do something different." She glanced shyly at Lloyd. "If you still want me, Lloyd, I think it's the right time for us to get married."

Lloyd, obviously astonished, stared at Flossie in open-mouthed, wide-eyed amazement.

"Of course, if you've changed your mind . . ." Flossie began when Lloyd kept his silence.

Usually stoical, Lloyd's facial expressions were quite limited. But for the first time since Flossie had known him, his whole face smiled, and his words tumbled out in rush, "No . . . I mean, yes . . . of course we'll get married . . . soon . . . whenever you say!"

Lloyd had a small ranch on the outskirts of a hamlet called Pond, and after their marriage he and Flossie moved out there. The house was far more primitive than what Flossie was used to—there was no inside bathroom, just an outhouse in the yard—but she didn't complain. She enjoyed being Mrs. Lloyd Hamlin.

One evening when they finished dinner—they had been married less than a month—Lloyd told Flossie he needed to discuss something important with her. Flossie couldn't help but feel nervous, since Lloyd rarely talked much about anything. He was certainly a kind and a most loving husband, but he was the stereotypical 'man of few words.' She wondered if perhaps there was something unsatisfactory about her as a wife.

"I've always wanted to raise cattle," were his first words and Flossie began to relax. "I was wondering . . . that is . . . if perhaps you might be willing . . . I'd certainly pay you back as soon as possible . . ."

"My money!" she squealed with relief. "You want to borrow my money!"

"Yes . . . to buy cattle."

"Of course! Take me to town in the morning so I can withdraw it from the bank. I'm so happy that's all you want!" She hugged Lloyd around the neck and kissed him soundly.

Unfortunately his cattle raising venture was a failure, and he turned more successfully to farming and breeding sheep. In time their family was increased by two daughters, Huberta and Betty.

Flossie never let Lloyd live down the fact that she had given him her six hundred dollars and he'd never repaid her. "Oh, say," she'd tease, "when are you going to be able to pay back that money you owe me?" Lloyd would always pretend he didn't hear her and go about his business.

The two little girls soon caught on to the family

joke and would ask their father, "Do you still have Mommy's money?"

Every Christmas Lloyd would present Flossie with a practical gift, something useful for the house. One year it was a washing machine with a wringer; another time the gift was a much appreciated indoor bathroom!

But, one special Christmas, years later, after Lloyd was financially successful, he presented Flossie with a large gift box. She couldn't help but notice the logo printed on the lid was of one of the better dress shops of downtown Bakersfield.

"What on earth?" she asked, looking towards her husband for a clue. But he only stared back at her, the usual unreadable expression on his face.

Flossie untied the velvet bow and lifted off the top. Pulling the tissue paper aside she gasped in disbelief. She lifted out her gift, crying out as she realized it was a luxurious, full length mink coat.

Slipping it on, she savored the elegance of it. "Oh, Lloyd, it's absolutely gorgeous. I've never had anything so beautiful! Thank you, thank you, thank you."

"Fit's does it?" he asked.

"Oh, Lloyd, it's a perfect fit."

"That's to fully pay back the six hundred dollars," he explained with a straight face.

Desdemona had ten wonderful years as Mrs. John Smith, until John was stricken with stomach cancer and died.

Again a widow, Desdemona continued to rent out rooms, enjoyed visits from her children, grandchildren, and eventually great-grand-children. She died of bronchial pneumonia when she was eighty, still the very feminine, but extremely independent, woman she'd been her entire life. Desdemona Diana died as Minnie Smith—the name she hated was written on her death certificate and carved on her tombstone.

BOOK VI

Angus Henry Hoffman
and
Beulah Belle Bailey

Chapter 46

"No, no, they're burning! Mama, Papa, help them, someone help them!" The red-headed boy screamed out in the night, tears flowing down his freckled cheeks. Miss Moss, the superintendent of the Hollygrove Orphanage in Los Angeles, stepped into the dormitory, having heard his cries from her office. Her newest charge had awakened each night since his arrival, always screaming from nightmares.

She glanced at the other boys sleeping in the nine cots and was grateful to see they all were still asleep.

"Angus! Angus!" she whispered harshly. "Hush! It's only a nightmare. You're a big boy now! You must learn to be quiet." She held the boy's skinny shoulders, patting him sporadically until he calmed down. She resisted an unusual urge to pull him against her bosom; his wet, slightly dirty face might soil her stiffly starched uniform. Besides, though the child was only four, his future was so bleak that he might as well learn immediately that no one was around to pamper him.

A week before Angus and his two sisters had been brought to the orphanage by Mr. Wright, the social worker, who hadn't much information about the children, only that they had lived with their grandmother in one small room. The grandmother worked as a janitor, and the children were left alone for long periods of time. Neighbors, feeling the grandmother's care of the children was inadequate, had reported the case to authorities. The room where they lived was dirty and overcrowded and the children appeared undernourished. The grandmother had hardly protested when Mr. Wright had taken the children; in fact, Mr. Wright confided to Miss Moss that he thought the old woman seemed relieved by the turn of events.

The oldest girl had contributed the only other pertinent information for the orphanage records. She concurred that the old woman was their grandmother, and she had brought them all out to California on the train from Chattanooga, Tennessee, after their parents had been burned to death in a house fire. The girl had identified herself as Eleanor, usually called Ella, and she was eight years old. Her younger sister was Adeline, or Lena, and she was six, and the boy was Angus Henry. The three children had stood in Miss Moss's office wide-eyed and frightened, dressed in clothing which had once been expensive but was now torn and soiled.

As was the policy of the orphanage, the girls were put in one part of the building and Angus in the other. It was a procedure that simplified the operation of the insitution, but Miss Moss knew the separation of the boy from his sisters made the transition even more difficult. But she accepted no blame for this—she was merely the superintendent and didn't set the policies.

Once Angus was quiet Miss Moss left the room.

He wasn't asleep, but he squeezed his eyes tightly to keep the tears from spilling out. He knew Miss Moss was angry because he cried every night, but he couldn't help it. The nightmare frightened him. Even now, with his eyes closed, he could see the flames consuming the big, white house, the people running back and forth. He could feel the heat from the fire even though he was standing barefoot in the damp grass, clad only in his nightshirt. But worst of all were the horrible screams echoing in his brain.

He knew his dream was caused by something that really had happened—but all he could remember was the dream. Whatever had happened had taken his mother from him. Oh, how he longed to climb into her lap, nestle his head against her soft bosom, feel her cool arms around him, and smell the sweetness which clung to her. But he knew she was dead. He tried not to think about her because when he did his throat ached and there was a tightness in his chest and tears stung his eyes. He was the smallest boy in the place where he now lived and he didn't want them to think he was a baby.

Angus wished he could see Ella and Lena, but even when he was herded outside with the rest of the boys, the girls were never there. As the days passed he began to realize that the girls weren't allowed in the playground at the same time as the boys.

Once he caught a glimpse of his sisters when he was standing in line waiting for his weekly check-up by Mrs. Stalmer, the nurse. But he was afraid to step out of place because he knew that the big black man who bathed them every Saturday night also administered spankings to anyone who broke the rules, and he didn't want to take a chance on that.

He was reunited once with his sisters when their grandmother came to visit—at least everyone said she was his grandmother. He really couldn't remember anything about her except she was the one who had brought them on the long train ride and they had lived with her for a while until that man had taken them to the orphanage.

The visit wasn't very satisfactory. The whole time his grandmother had held him tightly with his face pressed against her bosom, and Angus had been afraid he might smother. He tried to turn away from the sour smell of perspiration, talcum powder, cheap perfume, and alcohol which emanated from the old woman, but when he wriggled she only held him tighter.

He wanted to talk to Lena and Ella, but when his grandmother finally released him and backed out of the room sniffling into her handkerchief, Miss Moss entered and quickly sent them back to their separate areas of the orphanage.

His days all melted into a blur. They were awakened and put to bed by the sound of a bell. He did kitchen chores and kept his part of the dormitory clean. All the boys played marbles and ball in the play yard, and they ate simple, tasteless meals. Each Saturday night the big black man bathed each boy and Miss Moss wiped them dry with a towel.

Christmas arrived, but the only thing which differentiated it from any other day was each boy received an orange and a nickel. Not remembering previous Christmases, Angus didn't even miss the presence of a decorated tree.

Tucking his nickel under his pillow, he dreamed of the treasures he would buy. When he awoke in the morning, he slipped his hand under the pillow —but the nickel was gone! Leaping from his cot, he threw the pillow to the floor, yanked the blanket down and search all over his bed. Squatting, he peered underneath the bed but only a few dust balls decorated the bare, wooden floor.

Tears blurred his vision when he stood, but he noticed one of the older boys had a smirk on his face as he jingled coins in his pocket. Angus knew the boy had stolen his nickel, and though angry, he knew it would be foolish to confront the thief who had a reputation as a bully and was known for beating up younger orphans.

The next news concerning his sisters came from one of the bigger boys. He was twice the size of Angus, though only a year or two older. Angus knew his name was Peter, though he seldom spent any free time with Angus, usually chosen by the big boys to play in their rougher games because of his size and good coordination.

"Hey, Angus," Peter called, pausing briefly on his way out to the yard, "your big sister got taken out of here."

"Was she adopted?" Angus asked, flooded by a mixture of emotions—happiness for his sister, yet sadness because he'd lost the chance to see her again.

"Heck no! People just come and take kids outta here to work for 'em!"

Angus had questions to ask, but Peter had run off to join a ball game in progress on the opposite side of the playground.

The dull routine finally was changed when Angus was enrolled in the Castellar Street School the September he was six. He walked with the

other children from the orphanage the four blocks
to school. When they were joined by the girls
Angus searched desperately for the face of his
beloved sister, Elia, but to no avail. Distraught, he
tugged at the sweater of the nearest girl.

"Please," he gasped, "do you know what's happened to my sister, Ella Hoffman?"

The girl turned from her group. "Ella? Yes, I
knew Ella."

"I thought I would see her on the way to
school."

The girl tentatively touched Angus' skinny
shoulder with a chubby hand. "She was taken out
of the orphanage by someone way back in July."

"Carrie! Hurry up!" One of the girl's friends
called out to her.

The girl patted Angus and ran off with pigtails
swinging behind her. The boy blinked back tears
and stumbled blindly in the wake of the children
now nearly half a block ahead of him. He'd never
felt so alone. He was the only one of his family left
in the orphanage, and he could hardly think of
anything else as he ran to catch up with the others
now disappearing inside the school.

Angus had little recollection of his first day of
school. Sitting dumbly on the hard seat of the desk
which nearly dwarfed him, nothing said by the
teacher had sunk into his numb brain.

By the second day he'd recovered sufficiently to
pay more attention to his surroundings. The
teacher, who seemed old and wise to Angus, was in
reality quite young, anxious to mold and guide the
youngsters in her class.

She began her instructions by introducing the
alphabet, and Angus found himself fascinated. The
little red-headed, freckle-faced lad became the
teacher's most eager student. Listening anxiously
and absorbing all her directions, he was soon

reading. Along with this newly acquired skill came happiness—an emotion not experienced in his immediate past.

He looked forward to each new day. With his reading ability increasing quickly, his teacher loaned him books to take back to the orphanage for the weekends. Soon Angus was crouching in a corner of the play yard with his freckled nose in a book whenever possible.

His short term of bliss was interrupted when he was herded for the first time along with other boys into the parlor of the orphanage, where they were lined up against the wall. Sitting across from them on settees and assorted chairs was a variety of strangers. The orphans were obliged to stand at attention while they were examined by the visitors. The first time he underwent this inspection Angus was so frightened he stared straight ahead with eyes unfocused, barely aware of those who passed in front of him.

During future line-ups, Angus came to realize the children who were chosen inevitably were the sturdy ones. Angus was grateful for his short stature and slight build for the first time in his life. He was able to resume his reading cheerfully, only slightly disturbed by the weekly inspection. For who would be foolish enough to choose a puny lad like himself?

Chapter 47

Three years passed quickly and uneventfully. Angus religiously went to school, sopping up every scrap of knowledge offered. He stood in line each Friday to be inspected, but he'd been passed by so many times he no longer had any fear of being chosen. The people who came seldom gave him a second glance.

One Friday in September of 1893, when Angus was eight years old, he stood placidly between two squirming boys while several folks surveyed the line, pausing now and then to take a closer look. The boy next to Angus mumbled under his breath, "Watch out for the old biddy what's comin' now. She's old lady Speer, a real witch. She picked me once. Brought me back inside a week. Ate too much she said. She's mean as hell—stingy, too. Hope she don't take a notion to try me again!"

But it wasn't Angus's neighbor Mrs. Speer had her eyes on. The formidable woman stopped squarely in front of Angus.

She was short and very stout, the seams of her dress strained by her girth. Afraid to look at her face, Angus focused on her ankles which bulged over the tops of her shoes. Her veins, knotted like thick, purple cords, showed through her heavy stockings.

"What's your name?" she demanded in a raspy voice while yanking his head up by his chin. Her thick fingers were rough and cold against his skin.

He had to swallow a huge lump before he was able to croak out, "Angus Henry Hoffman, ma'am."

"Are you a good boy, Angus?"

"I think so, ma'am."

"Fine! I think I'll just take you home with me!"

Angus's heart sank. He wasn't overly fond of the orphanage, but he certainly didn't like what he had just heard about Mrs. Speer. Life under her roof probably would be as miserable as that at the orphanage.

Suddenly he realized Mrs. Speer was still talking to him. "Excuse me, ma'am?"

The woman's tiny pig eyes snapped darkly from the folds of wrinkled fat. "You'll have to learn to pay better attention, boy!"

Angus felt the blood rush to his face. "I will, ma'am."

"I was telling you I have a surprise for you—your sister, Lena, lives at my house. You'll be glad to see your sister, won't you, boy?"

His heart did a joyful somersault. "Oh, yes, ma'am!" That exciting bit of news put a new slant on things. He could put up with anything Mrs. Speer dished out if he was near his sister.

While Mrs. Speer made arrangements for Angus's release into her custody, he was sent to gather up his few belongings. Then he joined Mrs.

Speer who was waiting for him in a horse-drawn wagon outside of the orphanage.

His head barely reaching above the hub of the wagon, he had to scramble to pull himself up into the seat. Mrs. Speer sat impatiently watching him struggle, making no offer to help, merely grumbling, "Hurry up!"

It was a long, bumpy ride to the Speer's ranch, way out into the country and finally turning onto a road Mrs. Speer called Verdugo. As they finally neared their destination, Mrs. Speer informed him the twelve acres was mostly planted with fruit trees, though they also raised vegetables and chickens.

The house was a one story, wood frame building consisting of three rooms plus kitchen and pantry. It was in the kitchen that Angus caught his first glimpse of Lena, who was on her hands and knees scrubbing the wooden floor.

Mrs. Speer put her big hands on her padded hips and snapped, "Aren't you through with that floor yet, Lena?"

"No, ma'am," Lena said in a tiny voice. But when she looked up and spied Angus, a smile spread across her sweet face, and Angus grinned back. His sister hadn't changed much. He didn't realize she was painfully thin for a ten-year-old, and he didn't notice how red and raw her hands were.

"Hi, Sis," he cried exuberantly, dropping his small bundle of clothing and starting toward Lena. He was halted midway by Mrs. Speer's fingers clamping tightly on his shoulder.

"Enough of that. You two will have plenty of time to visit when the chores are done. Angus, put your things away there in the pantry."

He tucked his few belongings onto an empty spot on the shelf. Later he would discover that the

narrow room, lined with shelves, would be outfitted with a pallet on the floor to become his
bedroom. He turned back into the kitchen hoping
to exchange a few more words with Lena, but
again was halted by Mrs. Speer who shoved her
fist against his bony chest.

"You high tail it outside, young fellow. Mr.
Speer's got plenty of work for you to do. Head
straight out and you won't have any trouble
finding him."

Angus peeked around Mrs. Speer's bulky form
trying to get another look at Lena, who was busily
scrubbing, her skinny shoulders sharply angular
in her thin cotten dress.

"Git!" Mrs. Speers ordered, and Angus ran out
the back door, barely missing a blow from the
woman's big hand.

Once the door slammed behind him he slowed
down. He was afraid to meet Mr. Speer. What if he
were meaner than his wife? It took every bit of
courage he could muster to walk across the yard.
He spied a bent over figure shoveling out the
chicken coop, and taking a deep breath, he said,
"Excuse me, sir."

"Eh? Speak up, lad," the man said as he
straightened himself.

"Mrs. Speer said I was to come out here to help
you, sir."

Mr. Speer towered over Angus, reminding him
of a scarecrow. He had large bony wrists which
hung out from rolled-up sleeves, and his overalls
seemed to be a size too large. Brown hair escaped
in thatchy patches from under a straw hat. He was
an ugly man with monstrous ears and nose and a
huge slash of a mouth that opened to reveal long,
yellow teeth. But Angus wasn't alarmed by his
ugliness—instead he took heart because Mr.
Speer's grey eyes glimmered with a kindly light,

and his voice was gentle when he spoke. "You must be the new one from the oprhanage. What's your name, son?"

Angus told him. Mr. Speer then had Angus take over the cleaning of the chicken pen, explaining that the debris was to be collected in a wheelbarrow and turned into the soil of a nearby garden patch.

Mr. Speer worked him hard, and Angus was happy to hear Mrs. Speer's coarse voice call them in for dinner. Copying Mr. Speer, he washed under the water pump. The wonderful odors coming from the kitchen set the juices in his stomach churning and his mouth to watering. He couldn't believe his eyes when he saw the food waiting on the table.

There was a platter of fried chicken, a tureen of fluffy mashed potatoes with big globs of butter melting down the sides, gravy made with cream, tender yellow ears of corn, a big bowl of steaming spinach, and a plate of golden biscuits. He'd never seen so much food set out for so few people!

"Quit your gawking and take a seat, boy," Mrs. Speer commanded. "We can't wait all night."

"Yes, ma'am." Angus slid quickly into the one empty chair.

Mr. Speer blessed the food and Mrs. Speer dished surprisingly generous helpings onto everyone's plates. The food was delicious, the best Angus had ever eaten. When Mrs. Speer asked if he'd like seconds he remembered the boy who said he'd been returned to the orphanage by Mrs. Speer because he ate too much. Angus didn't think he wanted to be returned just yet, so he declined the offer—besides, his stomach was the fullest he could ever remember.

When everyone had finished, Mrs. Speer stood. "Angus, help your sister with the dishes." She and

Mr. Speer disappeared into the living room.

Angus and Lena threw themselves into each others arms and hugged and hugged. His sister, after too short a time, untangled herself. "Come, Angus, we must hurry. She'll be checking on us soon, and it won't do us any good if she catches us dillydallying. We can visit while we work."

Lena hustled around the table, scraping and stacking plates, while sending Angus into the kitchen with the serving platters. He wasn't able to ask her any questions until she had her hands stuck into the dishpan full of suds.

"What's it like living here?" Angus asked as he gingerly retrieved a dish from the hot rinse water and began to dry it.

"Shhh! Not so loud," Lena hissed. "She might hear you."

"What does it matter so long as we're working?" Angus whispered.

Lena frowned. "Mrs. Speer doesn't put up with frivolity."

Angus wasn't sure what that meant so he was quiet for a moment. Finally he said loudly, "The food's real good, anyhow."

Lena pushed a wisp of hair back from her forehead with the back of a wet hand. "Please, don't be so loud! The food *is* good . . . and that's about it. You'll have it a little better anyway—he's not as mean as she is."

Angus giggled. "She is a monster, isn't she?"

The door between the kitchen and dining room swung open and the dreaded Mrs. Speer burst through. "What are you damn little bastards up to in here? Aren't those dishes done yet?"

Lena threw her arms up in front of her face just as Mrs. Speer's heavy hand hit her against the side of the head. Lena cried out with pain, while Angus stared with his mouth open and his eyes wide with horror.

"And you'll get the same, you little bugger, if you don't get back to work!" the woman shrieked.

"Yes, ma'am!" Angus hastily grabbed the dish towel he'd dropped and began polishing a glass.

Mrs. Speer disappeared through the door, and Angus released the breath he'd been holding. Whispering, he asked, "Are you all right, Lena?"

His sister turned her tear-streaked face toward him. "That wasn't anything," she said bravely.

"I never heard a lady curse like that!"

Lena grinned through her tears. "You just wait until she really gets mad—she can turn the air blue!"

The children quietly finished the dishes and put everything away. When the kitchen was straightened, Lena warned, "You better go to bed now, Angus. We have to get up real early."

"But I haven't even been able to find out anything . . ."

Lena hugged Angus around the neck and brushed her lips against his cheek. "Goodnight." And she disappeared through the swinging door.

He would have liked to have followed her, but instead he went into the narrow pantry that was to be his bedroom. He discovered a thin blanket roll in the corner and placed it on the wood floor. After taking off his shoes and overalls he stretched out on the makeshift bed. His muscles ached, and the floor was hard, but his mind was occupied with the experiences of the day. What kind of life was it going to be living with the Speers? Mr. Speer was tolerable—but that Mrs. Speer! Poor Lena! How dreadful to be constantly under the old woman's watchful and cruel eyes. At least Mr. Speer appeared to be a kinder taskmaster.

Finally Angus fell into a deep, undisturbed sleep, but before dawn he began to dream. It was a fearful dream, with an even uglier Mrs. Speer chasing him, shouting profanities echoing through the chambers of his mind.

"Hell fire and damnation, boy, are you deaf as well as dumb? Get up, and get up *now!*" A hefty kick to Angus's rib cage made him realize he was no longer dreaming. He scrambled to his feet, rubbing his eyes with balled fists.

"Get yourself dressed and washed up. I expect to get at least an hour's work out of you before you have to go off to that dang blasted school. So hurry it up. You'll find Mr. Speer already outside, and he'll tell you what to do."

Angus's ears perked up at the mention of school. Maybe things were going to be all right after all! He hurried fast enough to please even Mrs. Speer. Washing was no more than a few splashes of water from the outside pump. Then Mr. Speer showed him how to feed the livestock and milk the cow, his early morning tasks.

When he brought the bucket of milk into the house, he was brusquely ushered to the table. There he ate his fill of hot oatmeal, two fried eggs, a slice of ham, and biscuits served with thick ham gravy. The food almost made up for everything else.

It was a three mile walk to Tropico school, but Angus fairly danced along the way. Lena was more sedate, though her step was perky by necessity, in order to reach the schoolhouse on time. Many children joined them as they drew nearer, and Angus was fascinated to discover that many of the dark-haired, dark-eyed boys and girls spoke another language. Angus made up his mind he would make friends with some of them and learn to speak as they did.

Tropico school was as wonderful as Castellar school had been. He was an outstanding student and one of the top achievers. But Mrs. Speer didn't care at all about his schoolwork, only berating him for the time spent away from his chores.

The weeks sped by. When Angus wasn't in school he was kept busy by Mr. Speer—tending to the chickens, irrigating, cultivating and picking. Once he helped Mr. Speer plant some strange looking trees along the edge of the property. "I never saw any trees like these before," Angus commented as he hurried along behind Mr. Speer, filling in holes with dirt.

"Them's eucalyptus trees," Mr. Speer grunted. "They'll grow real tall one of these days—make a fine wind break."

Except for the time spent in school, Mr. Speer kept Angus busy, even Saturdays and Sundays. The boy worked from before sunrise until night-fall. But Angus counted himself lucky, because as he had guessed from the beginning, Mr. Speer was reasonable and kind. Angus felt sorry for his sister, because Mrs. Speer not only made excessive demands, she was also cruel. She seemed to enjoy hurting Lena. The woman would kick his sister whenever she wasn't working fast enough, and Lena had black and blue marks on her arms and legs from the abuse. Angry to see how Lena was mistreated, Angus wished he was big enough to do something about it.

Once Angus was the target of Mrs. Speer's wrath. He was out in the chicken yard collecting eggs when the fearful woman walked by, giving him a kick for no good reason. Impulsively he reached out and grabbed her fat ankle, causing her to lose her balance and fall down hard into a pile of chicken manure. Angus laughed heartily.

Mrs. Speer pulled herself to a standing position, her face nearly purple as she glared at him. Angus choked on his laughter and began backing away, but Mrs. Speer snatched a loose board from the fence and smacked him hard, knocking him to the ground. Covering his head with his hands, he curled into a ball. She hit him again and again, until she finally tired of it and cast the board aside.

At the dinner table Mrs. Speer related the incident to her husband. "And I gave the impertinent whippersnapper a grand whipping!"

Angus didn't think 'grand' was the proper adjective for the beating he'd suffered at her hands. The aches and pains and bruises lasted for a full two weeks, reminding him constantly of the need to stay as far away as possible from Mrs. Speer.

In May, before school recessed for the summer, Angus had a terrible shock. When he and Lena arrived home from school, Angus went out in back, as usual, and began his chores. Mr. Speer came to him, and with a strange expression in his eyes, said gruffly, "I have to go to town. Get your work done just like I was here."

"Yes, sir," Angus said, puzzled. It was unusual for Mr. Speer to go to town this late in the day.

He didn't think anything more about it until supper. When he was called to eat, Mr. Speer was already sitting at the table. "You made good time," Angus commented.

Mr. Speer nodded his head but didn't look at Angus. The boy slid into his chair. Mrs. Speer brought out the food, set it on the table, and sat in her place. The chair Lena usually occupied was pushed tight against the table.

"Where's my sister?" he asked.

"Hush, boy!" Mrs. Speer snapped. "She's come to no harm."

Angus felt cold all over. "Where is she then?

Why isn't she eating with us?"

For the first time since he'd sat down Mr. Speer raised his eyes to him. "I took her back to the orphanage."

"Why? Why did you do that?" Angus shouted.

Mrs. Speer brought a heavy fist down hard on the table top, causing the dishes to jump and rattle. "That's no concern of yours, boy! Now hush your mouth so we can eat in peace."

For the first time at the Speer's, the food tasted like cardboard. All he could think about was Lena. She must not have known she was being returned to the orphanage or surely she would have told him. It was going to be so lonely without her—but for her sake he was glad. Now she wouldn't be kicked and hit by Mrs. Speer anymore.

Tears came to his eyes when he thought about Lena, and he wondered if he'd seen her, or his other sister, Ella, ever again.

Chapter 48

Summer sped by. Angus didn't mind the work he was doing for Mr. Speer; it was hard but varied, and he liked being outside all the time.

And finally he was beginning to grow. The hearty meals Mrs. Speer prepared still left him hungry, but he found a way to have a bedtime snack which took the edge off it until morning. The milk was kept in pails in the pantry, and every night before stretching out on his pallet, Angus would cut a thick slice of bread and dip it into the milk, skimming the cream off the top. Fortunately, Mrs. Speer never caught him at it.

When Mr. Speer peddled his fruit at the market in Los Angeles, Angus helped load the wagon and often was allowed to ride along. Each trip was exciting. Angus was amazed by the large number of people in the city, everyone traveling in horse and buggy or on horse-drawn streetcars, and were all in a hurry. And it was noisy all the time—

different from the sounds of the country.

One day, in the middle of summer, Mr. Speer received an exceptionally good profit from his fruit. He purchased several pounds of nuts and took them, along with his unsold fruit, to the orphanage. While Mr. Speer was handing out his gifts, Angus looked around for his sister. Unable to find her, he asked one of the girls he had known if she knew anything about what had become of Lena Hoffman.

"I remember you! You're Ella and Lena's brother, aren't you? My, you've certainly grown, but I would've recognized the red hair anywhere!"

"I guess I have. But can you tell me where my sister is?"

"Of course, there wouldn't be any way for you to hear," the girl said.

Angus was feeling anxious and a bit perturbed. "Hear what? Please, tell me what you know."

The girl was obviously pleased to be imparting the information. "Both your sisters were discharged from the orphanage just last week. The trustees declared your sister Ella old enough to fend for herself and care for Lena.

A million questions popped into Angus's brain, but before he could ask, Mr. Speer called to him.

"One moment, sir," he answered. But while he turned to head toward Mr. Speer, the girl had left and joined a group of her friends.

On the way home Angus pondered what he'd learned. He wondered if he'd still been a ward of the orphanage if he would have been discharged along with his sisters. How was Ella going to make a living? She was barely fifteen. Would he ever see them again?

Fortunately he was kept too busy to worry about the girls. September came, school began again, and Angus was fully occupied.

He was delighted to see all his friends. On the way home the first day, Manuel Ledesma asked him to stop off at his house as he'd done many times the year before. Angus could almost hear Lena warning him not to, but she wasn't here this time to stop him. After all, what could it hurt? He would only stay a few minutes.

Manuel led him into the kitchen of his large adobe home. "This is my mother, Senora Ledesma." Manuel's mother was young and beautiful, her black hair braided and coiled over her ears, and her large, dark eyes sparkling with friendliness.

"*Mama, te presento mi amigo*, Angus."

"*Con mucho gusto*," Senora Ledesma said, putting her arm around Angus and giving him a squeeze. She spoke rapidly to Manuel in Spanish and he answered.

Turning to Angus he said, "My mother only speaks Spanish. She wanted to know if you were the orphan who lives at the Speer's ranch, and she also wants you to sit down and have a snack with us."

"Oh . . . I don't know . . . I'm supposed to come right home after school . . ." Angus answered.

Manuel laughed. "But now you must eat a little with us or my mother will be insulted."

Angus was easily persuaded—especially when he smelled the warm flour tortillas Senora Ledesma heated and served buttered and rolled. He gulped down two, then stood. "Ah . . . muchas gracias, Senora. But I have to get going now. I'll see you tomorrow, Manuel."

He ran the rest of the way home to make up for the time he'd wasted, but when he reached the Speer's lane his heart sank. Mrs. Speer, binoculars dangling from a leather strap around her neck, was waiting for him. She boxed his ears with her fists until his head rang.

"Let this be a lesson to you, boy. You come straight home from school each and that means every day! You better do as I say because I'll be watching for you with my binoculars!"

Because there were only a few houses between the Speers and Tropico school Mrs. Speer had a fairly clear view. For awhile Angus came home without tarrying as directed. But when he realized that every Tuesday afternoon Mrs. Speer entertained friends and didn't watch him and that on Thursdays she regularly went out and didn't return until long after he was home from school, he took advantage of this knowledge. On those days he visited with his firends after school, and in this way he soon learned how to speak Spanish since it was spoken almost exclusively in these homes.

Though Mr. Speer must have been aware of Angus's regular tardiness on Tuesdays and Thursdays, he never mentioned it to either Angus or Mrs. Speer. Angus was grateful to the man but never spoke of it, afraid that if he made any kind of issue of the kindness, Mr. Speer would feel obliged to put a stop to it.

There was another boy who became a special friend of Angus's—Kimwood Peters. The two boys were attracted to each other because of their mutual desire to achieve, and they were probably the only two boys in the whole of Tropico school who enjoyed the time spent within its walls. But their mutual brightness was all they had in common. Kimwood lived with his wealthy parents in a large home with many material possessions. His house was in the opposite direction from school so Angus was unable to accept any of Kimwood's invitations.

The only time the boys were able to visit was a
few minutes before and after school and during
lunch recess. As they got older, they devised
another means of communication. Writing notes
to each other they signed them with secret Indian
names—Kimwood called himself Great Eagle, and
Angus was Strong Bear.

The only time the boys got into trouble in school
was due to this passing of notes. Kimwood had
just written an answer to a question asked by
Angus. He'd folded the slip of paper and was
handing it across the aisle when Professor Roberts
stepped from his desk, and taking one great stride,
snatched the note from Kimwood's hand.

Standing between the horrified friends, he
unfolded the paper with a flourish. "Now we shall
see what is so important that our two young
scholars must put pen to paper during a history
lesson."

Professor Roberts cleared his throat and read
aloud. "Greetings Great Eagle. Have you come to
any conclusions as to the discussion of yesterday?
Your friend, Strong Bear."

Professor Roberts raised one shaggy eyebrow
and peered from Kimwood to Angus, who wished
he could disappear.

The professor continued reading, " 'Greetings
Strong Bear, I will tell you my honest and true
feelings at the noon recess. Most honorably, Great
Eagle.' "

The professor paused again. There was a giggle
at the back of the room. "I wonder which of you is
Strong Bear, and who is Great Eagle. Would either
one of you care to reveal your identities"

Angus knew his cheeks were bright from embarrassment. He could see his friend's face was
also flushed. "N. . . no, sir," he stammered.

"What a shame! Here we have had two such

illustrious personages in our class this entire semester—Strong Bear and Great Eagle—and all the time we thought you were plain, ordinary Kimwood Peters and Angus Hoffman." By this time the girls in the class were tittering and the boys were guffawing and slapping their knees.

The laughter was allowed to go on for a few moments before Professor Roberts frowned and raised a hand for silence. "That will do. Kimwood, Angus, I will see you at my desk at the beginning of the noon recess. Now we shall take up where we left off in our lesson."

Angus could hardly keep his mind on the lesson, fearful as to what their punishment was going to be. He hoped his teacher would administer whatever he felt necessary without sending word home to Mrs. Speer. Though she wasn't interested in any of his achievements academically, he knew she would be more than delighted to mete out punishment for any infraction of school rules.

The hand on the classroom clock finally reached twelve. The rest of the class was dismissed, and with great fear and trepidation, Angus followed his friend to Professor Robert's desk.

"I'm sure you boys are well aware that what you've done is wrong. As far as your punishment is concerned, I believe the humiliation you experienced before your classmates is enough. I'm sure you will have to bear some cruel teasing when you go into the school yard. Let it serve well to remind you the time you are in the classroom is better spent on the subject being presented than on fanciful pursuits of your own. Have I made myself clear?"

Both boys gasped a "Yes, sir!" The professor excused them, and they grabbed their lunch pails and ran from the room. Outside they congratulated each other on their good fortune, ignoring the taunts of the other boys who gathered around them.

While Angus's mind was stimulated at school, his body was responding to the hard work and good food at home. He quickly changed from a skinny lad to a well-muscled youth and reached his full height of five feet eleven by the time he was in the eighth grade.

One of Angus's proudest achievements was winning a spelling bee, outspelling the entire school, even the ninth graders. All the children and the teachers had congratulated him heartily and he couldn't contain himself when he reached home, bursting into the house and calling, "Mrs. Speer, guess what?"

Mrs. Speer answered in an unusually kindly voice. "Oh, Angus, you're home already?"

Sticking his head into the living room he saw there were two other ladies there with Mrs. Speer. "Oh, excuse me, I forgot it was Tuesday."

"No, no, that's quite all right, dear," Mrs. Speer simpered. "Ladies, this is my latest ward, Angus. Say hello to the ladies."

Angus obliged with a "How do you do?"

The women looked him over and smiled. "My, my, such a big boy," one of them said. "Must be quite a chore keeping that one fed."

"Such gorgeous red hair!" another exclaimed.

Mrs. Speer dismissed him. "You can go now, Angus, I'm sure Mr. Speer has something for you to do."

He stepped from the room but heard one of Mrs. Speer's guests say, "Oh my, it is so truly charitable for you to take in these homeless children, feeding and clothing them and seeing they receive a proper education."

Angus snorted in disgust. She only fed him so he

could work, and he had but two pair of overalls and two shirts to his name. The only reason the woman let him go to school was because it was expected, but he still wished he'd had the chance to tell her he'd won the spelling bee!

Mrs. Speer showed her true colors at the evening meal. When everyone had received their portions, Angus said, "I would like to tell you what happened today at school."

"I'll tell you something, boy," the woman snapped. "I don't care one thing about you or that school. If I had my way you wouldn't even go to school! It's nothing but a waste of time as far as I'm concerned. That foolishness takes you away from the chores you could be doing around here."

"Why don't you let the boy tell you his news?" Mr. Speer urged gently.

"I don't care nothing about his news," Mrs. Speer declared and jammed half a boiled potato into her mouth.

"Then *I'll* tell you," Mr. Speer persisted. "Angus won the spelling bee over all the students in the school. That's an achievement to be proud of!"

"Humph," Mrs. Speer sneered. "And what, pray tell, is the boy ever going to have to spell? I tell you both that book learning is wasted on the likes of him. Look at him, will you—see those muscles? A laborer is all Angus is ever going to be. Now, forget all this foolishness and finish eating!"

Angus and Kimwood often discussed their futures and their ambitions. "As soon as I've graduated, I'll be going on to a university. You know, as smart as you are, Angus, you ought to try and talk the Speers into sending you to college."

Angus laughed and ran his fingers through his auburn hair. "You wouldn't even suggest such a thing if you knew Mrs. Speer. The only reason she lets me go to school is because her friends think she's generous for doing so. She gripes constantly about the valuable time I'm wasting."

"But, Angus, if you could make her aware of how well you do scholastically perhaps then she might understand . . ."

Angus interrupted. "No, Kimwood, I'm afraid it's a lost cause."

"What will you do? Surely you don't plan on working for the Speers the rest of your life."

"No, I don't."

Kimwood frowned. "What do you have in mind?"

"I'm not really sure, yet. But I do know I won't be with the Speers much longer."

Chapter 49

"Your good overalls will do just fine," Mrs. Speer declared. That was the answer Angus had expected when he asked if he could have a suit for his ninth grade graduation ceremony.

He'd asked Mr. Speer first, who had answered, "Certainly, boy, I don't see any reason why we couldn't get you a suit." But when the old man had added, "But you'll have to ask Mrs. Speer," Angus's hopes had been dashed. He already knew what Mrs. Speer would say long before he ever got the courage to ask her.

Angus had been chosen to give the valedictorian speech, but he wasn't going to humiliate himself by standing in front of his classmates and their families wearing his patched and faded overalls that were several inches too short. Mrs. Speer's stinginess pushed him to make the decision he'd been considering for months.

That night, after Mr. and Mrs. Speer had gone to

bed and the house was quiet, Angus packed his pitiful few belongings in an old valise he had found tucked away in a corner of the pantry. Then he filled the rest of the bag with food. He pried up a loose floor board and fished around until he found the can which had been protecting his meager savings over the years. It wasn't much because he hadn't had many opportunities to earn extra money—but then again there had been no opportunities to spend any either. So every penny he'd ever received was hoarded for his escape. He emptied the contents of the can into his pocket, picked up the valise and slipped quietly out the back door.

He'd never been outside so late before. There was a little sliver of moon that didn't illuminate much of anything, but there were stars and more stars—their beauty nearly taking his breath away. Though the road ahead was pitch black, he took one step after another with the assurance of someone who had walked the same way hundreds of times before.

Wanting to put plenty of distance between himself and the Speers before daybreak, he marched along with a quick and lively gait. The night was far from quiet—a lonely coyote howled, answered by the bark of a dog, and crickets and frogs and night birds orchestrated their own harmony. Angus paid little attention; he was too busy thinking about his future.

By the time he reached Los Angeles, weary and foot sore, he'd made two important decisions. From that day foward he would call himself Harry Hoffman, and what probably would affect his future the most, he would change his birth year to that of his older sister—1881. As the sun came up over the Los Angeles basin, fifteen-year-old Angus Hoffman   became   nineteen-year-old   Harry

Hoffman.

When he applied for work at a box factory, near what is now called the North Broadway bridge, he was readily accepted by the foreman. The muscular young man was hired on the spot. He would be working six days a week, and wonder of wonders, he would earn three dollars at the end of each week!

Tired as he was, he worked hard his first day, and when it was time to leave he stopped one of his fellow employees. "Excuse me, but could you tell me a good place to find cheap lodgings?"

The burly man looked him over, his eyes lingering on the battered valise Harry was carrying. "Ran away from home, eh?"

Harry wasn't sure how he ought to answer, but the man clamped a hand on his shoulder. "Never mind. Ain't none of my business anyhow."

At a hotel the man had recommended, Harry rented an unfurnished room for a dollar a week. For a long time he slept on the bare floor until he could afford to buy a couple of blankets. For his meals he worked out a deal with the owner of a nearby Japanese restaurant—for the sum of two dollars paid in advance, he was able to eat twenty-one meals.

Things seemed to be working out well, and in order to keep them that way, Harry carefully avoided the downtown market area where Mr. Speer came to sell his fruit.

For entertainment the resourceful young man visited different churches where he could enjoy excellent music for a small token offering. On special occasions, when he'd scrimped enough for the price of admission, he attended local theaters. And so a year passed with Harry at the box factory.

One afternoon he met a man named Lorenzo

Sherwood, who had unsuccessfully applied for a job. Harry liked the looks of the earnest fellow and offered to treat him to supper.

"Thanks," Lorenzo said, "but I must go home. My wife probably has supper waiting for me. Say! That's an idea—why don't you come home with me?"

Harry shook his head. "No, I wouldn't want to upset your wife by being a surprise guest. Maybe another time."

"Oh, hey, come on. Lena is a real sweetheart—it won't bother her at all."

Harry perked up at the mention of the name Lena. "I have a sister named Lena. I'm afraid I don't know what happened to her . . . or my other sister for that matter."

Lorenzo tilted his big shaggy head to one side and said, "What was your name again?"

"Harry . . . Harry Hoffman."

"Interesting," Lorenzo said thoughtfully. "My wife's last name was Hoffman."

Harry grabbed Lorenzo's upper arm. "Really? Tell me what she looks like? Did she ever live in an orphanage?"

Lorenzo's grin was as wide as Harry's. "First, my wife looks enough like you to be your sister— and it sounds like she very well might be. And yes, she did live in an orphanage. The only thing, Harry, is she told me her brother's name is Angus."

"Yahoo!" Harry shouted. He tightened his grip on Lorenzo and danced a jig. "You're married to my sister! Come on, let's go there right now!"

Lorenzo led him to a small frame bungalow. Flinging the door open wide he cried, "Lena! Come quickly! I have a surprise for you!"

Harry's mouth gaped open. The skinny little girl he remembered had blossomed into a lovely young woman. She wore her dark hair in a roll around her head with curls escaping onto her forehead. Her hour glass figure was demurely clothed in a high-necked blouse with long sleeves and a full skirt.

"Angus!" she cried in disbelief. "Can it truly be you?" She held her arms out to him.

They hugged each other tightly. Tears of happiness spilled from Lena's eyes. "Oh, Angus, I didn't think I'd ever see you again. How on earth did you ever find him, Lorenzo?"

"Purely by accident." Lorenzo laughed. "I promised your brother a meal, Lena. Do you think you could dry your tears long enough to put supper on the table?"

Lena dabbed at her eyes with a handkerchief and smiled brightly at her brother. "I've got a big pot of beans on the stove and a loaf of fresh bread. I'll dish it up right now. And while we're eating I want to hear everything that's happened to you since I last saw you."

By the time they had finished eating and the dishes were cleared away, Harry had told his sister about his life with the Speers after her return to the orphanage. "And when she wouldn't buy me a suit for graduation, that was it—I knew I had to leave. I was so afraid they were going to find me, the first week or two I spent a lot of time looking over my shoulder. But I'm sure the Speers have some other poor orphan child slaving for them now. But that's enough about me! Tell me what happened to you—and to Ella."

Lena sat back down in her chair and began, "Not long after Mr. Speer brought me back to the orphanage, Ella, who'd also been returned, was declared old enough to be discharged, and since I was her sister, they sent me along with her.'"

Harry nodded his head. "I heard that had happened. So tell me, what did you do?"

"I wasn't the least bit worried. In fact I was so happy to leave that old orphanage, but we had only walked about two blocks when I realized Ella was crying.

"I asked her what was the matter and she said, 'I don't know what we're going to do . . . where we're going to sleep tonight.' And it hit me then. Here we were—two young girls with no money and no home—and I began to cry. Only I didn't cry in a quiet, ladylike fashion like Ella—I howled! I was convinced we were going to starve to death, or be attacked, or killed by monsters. With each horrible fate I imagined, I cried even louder.

"Ella tried to quiet me but I didn't even hear her. Naturally we attracted a great deal of attention, and fortunately the first one who questioned us was a kindly policeman. Ella explained our predicament, and he listened sympathetically, suggesting we seek refuge at the Sacred Heart Convent which was close by.

"The sisters at the convent were of a more charitable disposition than the administrators of the orphanage, and they took us in without question. They kept us clothed and fed and treated us kindly, and that's where we lived until we married."

Harry asked, "Ella's married, too?"

Lena answered, "Oh, yes, indeed . . . long before me, actually. She married one of the men who made regular deliveries to the convent."

"I was working as a gardener for the convent, and Lena was the prettiest flower there," Lorenzo interjected. "After we married I was offered a better paying job as the gardener for a large home on Bunker Hill. I worked there for a while but my employer died and his widow moved back east, and that's why I'm looking for another job. I heard there are lots of jobs available in the oil fields in Bakersfield, and they say the pay is good, too. I guess I'll just have to head on over there."

"Could I go with you?" Harry asked.

"Sure, if you want to. But what about your job at the box factory?"

Harry shrugged his broad shoulders. "It's a good enough job, I guess, but I don't want to stay there the rest of my life. And I think it's just about time I tried something new."

"Great! I've a horse and wagon out back. I'll give the wagon a once-over and we ought to be able to leave this weekend."

It was too bad that Lorenzo couldn't have given the horse a once-over too, since it was a marvel the horse could move the wagon at all! And it wasn't because the load was so great, since neither Harry nor Lorenzo had much in the way of possessions. The animal was the most pitiful specimen Harry had ever seen. Though he was no judge of horse-flesh he had enough sense to recognize Lorenzo's horse was long overdue at the glue factory. But despite the horse's sway-back, prominent ribs, and moth-eaten coat, Harry had to admit he certainly lived up to his name, Champ.

Champ pulled and heaved with his stringy muscles bulging until he'd hauled the wagon with its two riders to the top of the summit.

"I never thought he'd make it," Harry said in wonderment.

Lorenzo, standing beside his horse, patted him affectionately on the flank. "There's a lot of miles left in him yet."

"I certainly hope so." Harry peered at the road ahead which wound down the other side of the mountain toward their destination.

"It'll be a cinch. It's downhill all the way," Lorenzo assured him.

"I don't know. Poor Champ looks plumb tuckered out." Harry could almost see the horse's heart beating feebly within the sunken chest.

"A night's rest, and Champ will be as good as new!"

Harry hoped he was being a worry wart and his brother-in-law's bravado was well-founded.

Champ was still standing when Harry and Lorenzo woke the following morning, having slept on a grassy knoll near a stream. Harry didn't think Champ looked any better than he had the night before, but Lorenzo was unconcerned. After eating more of the food Lena had packed, they hitched up the horse, climbed onto the wagon, and continued their journey.

Halfway down the mountain, the wagon lurched to the side. "Whoa," Lorenzo shouted, but it was an unnecessary command. Champ wasn't going anywhere—ever again. The horse's legs buckled, and he keeled over, pulling the wagon onto its side and dumping out the contents, including Harry and Lorenzo.

Both men quickly scrambled to their feet. "Now what are we going to do?" Harry asked of no one in particular. He began to gather his belongings which were scattered on the road.

He didn't even bother to look up at the sound of an approaching wagon, until he realized it stopped. A farmer with a load of produce gestured toward the overturned wagon and the dead horse. "Looks like you fellows have had a bit of trouble."

"Yes, sir, that we have," Lorenzo agreed.

"Where you headed?"

"Bakersfield."

"That's where I'm going. Hop on up, and I'll give you a ride."

Chapter 50

Lorenzo got a job in the oil fields the day they arrived, but Harry went to work at a lumber yard. It was located near the railroad station, where Harry became intrigued by the activity. He began hanging around the trains during his lunch hour and any other free time. He was fascinated by everything and questioned every worker who would take the time to talk to him.

"Hey, young fellow," the yard foreman called out to him one day. "Would you like a job?"

"Yes!" Harry said without hesitation.

The foreman laughed. "Don't you think you better find out what kind of job I'm offering? Might not be to your liking."

"Any job on the railroad would be to my liking," Harry answered honestly.

"Okay. You've got it. It's just filling coal tubs, but if you work hard, I'm sure you'll be doing something else before long."

Harry quit his job at the lumber company and started his first position with the Southern Pacific Transportation Company. Though he didn't know it then, it was the beginning of a forty-six year relationship.

As the yard foreman had predicted, Harry's work quickly expanded. He was still shoveling coal, but he also wiped engines and helped the machinest and boiler makers. By the beginning of the following year he was promoted to running a small engine used to haul cars from the yard to the storage area at the round house and to move tenders. And he was also an engine spotter.

Summer began with a vengeance. Harry found the high temperatures nearly unbearable. Confined as he was while driving the shop engine, he felt the heat even more. Though he never took any time off, he felt sick to his stomach nearly every day.

One of the supervisors approached him at the end of one particularly arduous day. The temperature had risen over a hundred and was several degrees above that in the engine cab. Harry had become so ill he had fled the engine to heave up his lunch behind a fence. He felt weak and light-headed the rest of his shift.

"Hey, Harry, would you consider a transfer to Oxnard?"

"Oxnard, where's that?"

"Little place located north of Los Angeles, on the coast."

The promise of cool sea breezes was enough, and he accepted instantly.

Harry was pleased to find Oxnard considerably cooler than Bakersfield. The town itself wasn't much to see. Situated on a broad, flat plain, the boundaries of the town covered less than a dozen acres surrounded by farms.

Harry soon became aware that the raising and processing of sugar beets was the main industry of the community. Nearly every issue of the newspaper, the Oxnard Daily Courier, contained a front page story concerning the Oxnard sugar beet factory, the paper keeping that industry constantly in the forefront. Harry also noticed that many of the ads in the paper were for the sale of implements used for the cultivating and harvesting of sugar beets.

Later Harry found out that many farmers also raised grain to feed the horses that worked the beet fields.

One fact soon apparent to any new arrival in Oxnard was the excessive number of saloons for such a small town. Harry attributed the imbalance to the fact that many itinerant workers were attracted to the area to work in the fields and the factory, but since Harry didn't care for the taste of alcohol and the saloons tended to ward rowdiness late at night, he avoided them.

On his first day in town Harry looked for a place to live and discovered a beautiful new hotel on the far side of the park in the center of town. The building had inviting verandas running around the outside, but without asking, Harry knew the Oxnard Hotel charged more than he was either willing or able to pay.

A smaller and far less appealing place, called the Colonia Hotel, only charged one dollar a week. There were several other places of lodging, but after looking at each one carefully he observed the same rowdy types who frequented the saloons lived in these places. He returned to the railroad yard and tossed his bedroll and valise into an empty boxcar on a side track. It wouldn't be much different than sleeping on the floor as he had in

Los Angeles. And the price was right! The next morning he made arrangements with the proprietress of the Wolff Restaurant to take his meals there for four dollars a week.

The majority of Harry's daytime hours were spent working in the railroad yard where he became good friends with Mr. D.J. Corn, the Southern Pacific agent. Much of his free time he spent studying, learning anything he could about locomotive mechanics.

The Oxnard weather agreed with him, and he felt healthy and energetic. He was able to work hard at his job, study at night by lantern light, and still seek other diversions.

While out walking on a Sunday afternoon, Harry discovered a band concert was being held in the park in the center of town. Many of the local families were gathered to hear the music, sitting on blankets and carriage robes spread over the grass. Harry settled himself on the ground, stretching out his long legs, and listened drowsily to the music, fascinated by the interesting architecture of the bandstand—it was of Chinese design, resembling a pagoda.

An object bounced off of his head, rudely breaking into his relaxed state. Looking around for the weapon, he found a ball laying harmlessly nearby.

"I told you to be more careful, Sammy!" The chiding words came from a young woman who was holding a wriggling youngster by the hand. "I do hope you weren't hurt," she said as she neared Harry.

"No, no! Just surprised me was all." He stood quickly.

Nearly a foot taller than she, he peered down on a head of golden curls. She tilted her heart-shaped face and gazed up through her thick lashes at

Harry.

"I'm so sorry," she purred. To the boy in a much harsher tone, she ordered, "You apologize right now!"

The child mumbled, "Sorry," snatched the ball from Harry's hands and ran off.

"I don't know you, do I?" the young woman asked, open curiosity on her pretty face.

"We can change that situation immediately, ma'am. Allow me to introduce myself. I'm Harry Hoffman, a railroad man." He offered his hand.

The young woman grasped his with both of hers. "Delighted, I'm sure. My name is Isabel Kimball. Come have a glass of lemonade and meet my family." Without waiting for an answer, she pulled him along behind her.

Isabel's family consisted of her father, a florid-faced, heavy-set man; her mother, a plumper, older version of herself; the brother who had beaned him with the ball; and twin boys of twelve or thirteen. Her parents were friendly and invited him to join them. Mrs. Kimball poured him a glass of promised lemonade, cut him a large piece of cake and handed it to him on a china saucer with an ornate silver fork on the side.

Mr. Kimball asked the expected questions—what was Harry's occupation, where did he live, what were his interests, who were his parents? When he got to the last question, Harry was surprised by Mr. Kimball's reaction to the fact that he was an orphan.

"Really?" he asked with great interest. "And you don't have any idea who your parents might be?"

"No, I'm afraid not. I vaguely remember a fire. Then my grandmother, or someone who said she was my grandmother, brought me and my two sisters out here on the train. Evidently she wasn't able to care for us and we were placed in the orphanage," Harry explained.

Mrs. Kimball clucked her tongue sympathetically. "Oh, my, you poor boy!"

Mr. Kimball clapped him on the back. "You certainly seem to have turned out all right despite your adverse beginnings. I admire a young man with spunk!"

Mr. Kimball proceeded to tell him all about his own life, how he'd grown up on an Iowa farm which he'd taken over at his father's death. Feeling a need to strike out on his own, he'd sold the farm, packed up his belongings and his new bride, and headed west. After much searching he'd finally purchased a large farm that had once been part of a Spanish rancho bordering on the Santa Clara river. Now he was considered one of the wealthiest and most successful farmers in the county. He added, "And I don't mind bragging about it because I did it all myself."

The Kimball patriarch monopolized the rest of the afternoon's conversation, comparing farming on the coastal plain to farming in Iowa. Finally Isabel protested, "Oh, Daddy, Harry doesn't want to hear all that boring stuff. He isn't a farmer like you!"

"I'm sorry, young man. I guess I got carried away," Mr. Kimball apologized.

Harry protested. "No, really, I found it very interesting."

Mrs. Kimball reached over and patted Harry's hand. "And you are a most polite young man. Tell me, have you met many people since you've been here in Oxnard?"

"No, ma'am," he answered. "Except for the men I work with, you all are the first."

"Well, then, we'll have to show you some real Oxnard hospitality. Why don't you come on over to our house next Sunday and have dinner with us?" Mrs. Kimball smiled in the same coquettish manner as her daughter.

Harry glanced quickly at Mr. Kimball to see if he was in agreement with the invitation, and since the large man was smiling broadly, Harry accepted. Arrangements were made for a horse and buggy to pick Harry up at the train station to bring him to the Kimball's farm the following week.

Standing, Mr. Kimball announced it was time for the family to depart. Harry helped them pack their picnic basket and gather up their blankets, then walked them to their buggy. Isabel, swinging her ruffled skirts to and fro, half skipped beside him. "Do you know how to ride horseback, Harry?" she asked.

"No, I'm afraid I don't know anything about horses."

She smiled one of her unnerving smiles. "Then I shall just have to teach you, won't I?"

She held out her hand so he could assist her into the back seat of the carriage. With a deliberate fluff of her skirt which revealed her slim, stocking-encased ankle momentarily, she sat down beside two of her brothers.

"Bye, Harry," she whispered, pouting her full lips almost into a kiss.

Harry stood at the edge of the park and watched them ride off, completely enraptured by the flirtatious Isabel. She was absolutely the most beautiful creature he had ever had the good fortune to meet. Of course he hadn't really met any other young ladies, but he didn't take that into consideration.

His head was filled with memories of Isabel's thick array of golden curls and her blue eyes with their fluttery lashes all the next week. By Saturday he was a nervous wreck and wandered the streets. He found a horse auction in progress at T.A. Rice's stable on Savier's Road which kept him diverted for most of the morning until he realized he was hungry and walked to Mrs. Renshaw's store where he indulged himself with a dish of homemade ice cream.

Still restless, he stopped in at the Athletic Club and watched a few men box, then put on the gloves himself. After sparring with another young man, tired and sweaty, he went to a public bath house and soaked in a tub of hot water.

It was nearing suppertime when Harry found himself passing Lehman and Waterman's Department Store. Though shopping was one of his least favorite pastimes, he decided he'd like to have a new shirt to wear the following day. The store being well-stocked, locating the right shirt took little time. He tucked his purchase under his arm and headed for the Wolff restaurant and his evening meal.

Gussied up like never before, he waited nervously in front of the train station for a full quarter of an hour. He had just begun to wonder if he'd misunderstood, or perhaps they'd forgotten, when Isabel arrived with her brother, David, who held the reins of the horse drawn buggy.

Isabel was even lovelier than he had remembered. The blonde curls were caught up with a blue ribbon which matched the color of her eyes. She was wearing a white dress with short sleeves exposing her smooth and creamy skin.

"Hello," she called.

"Hello there, Miss Kimball," he greeted.

Isabel's delightful face puckered into a frown. "Please call me Isabel. We *are* friends, aren't we?"

Harry felt tongue-tied and flustered, a state he'd

never found himself in before. "Yes . . . at least I certainly hope so."

"Climb on up here. We don't want to be late for dinner." Isabel scooted over on the seat to make room for Harry.

Seated beside her, Harry could feel the warmth of her body as she leaned slightly against him when the buggy swayed back and forth on the trip home. She tucked one of her hands in the crook of his arm and pointed out interesting sights as they drove by, but Harry didn't pay much attention to the scenery. His concentration was divided between the softness of her body next to his and the musical tones of her voice.

"Here we are," she called, breaking his reverie.

The house was at the end of a long drive. It was a large, square, two story, frame home—not particularly attractive. Harry later was told by Isabel's father that the house was an exact replica of the home he'd grown up in. Dinner was served in a large dining room at a table with chairs for ten, though there were only seven on this occasion—the Kimballs and Harry.

Harry sat across from Isabel. Mr. Kimball dominated the conversation with talk of the weather, local farming, the latest equipment and animal husbandry. Harry made one syllable comments while he enjoyed his meal, not having had such delicious food since he'd run away from the Speers. But this atmosphere was far more congenial.

He tried not to look directly across the table too often because he found himself lost in Isabel's large blue eyes. It was impossible to concentrate on her father's dissertation while Isabel smiled at him, fluttering her long eyelashes.

When the last fork had been put aside, Isabel spoke. "I want to take Harry out to see the horses." She didn't wait for any comments before leaving her seat to come and stand beside Harry, who rose awkwardly.

"Certainly. Sounds like a fine idea," Mr. Kimball agreed. "Perhaps Harry would like to go riding."

"Well . . . ah . . . I'm afraid I don't know anything about riding," Harry stammered.

"The only way to learn is to climb on," Mr. Kimball stated, "Anything else you need to know Isabel can tell you."

Isabel grabbed Harry's hand and yanked him toward the door. "Oh . . . it was a very good dinner, Mrs. Kimball. Thank you," he called out.

Isabel giggled behind her hand and tugged on him again until she had him running behind her, through the kitchen, past an astonished cook, out the door, clattering down the wooden steps, and finally halting in the dusty back yard.

Harry found himself breathless after the unexpected exertion, and glancing at him, Isabel burst into laughter. Her merriment was contagious and Harry found himself joining in.

"Come on," Isabel urged. "We'll find Julio and he'll saddle the horses."

Julio turned out to be one of the hired hands. He was a middle-aged man who lived with his family in a small house among a cluster on the Kimball property. Isabel explained that most of the help required to run the large farm—or ranch as she called it—lived in the small houses. Since it was Sunday, work was at a standstill.

Harry followed Isabel to the porch of one of the houses where a group of men were sitting in their undershirts. "Julio, this is my friend, Harry." Isabel tossed her golden curls in Harry's direction.

The short, slim Mexican flashed a brilliant smile

at Harry. "An honor," he said with a soft accent. "How may I be of assistance to you and your gentleman friend, Senorita Isabel?"

Harry was slightly disconcerted when he saw Isabel fluttering her long lashes at Julio in the same manner as she had done with him. "Can you believe it, Julio, my friend has never ridden a horse?"

Julio'e eyes didn't leave Isabel's face. "That is certainly hard to believe, Senorita. You want me to saddle your horse . . . and maybe the old mare for your friend?"

Isabel clapped her hands. "Oh, Julio, that would be marvelous. You're sure you don't mind, it being Sunday and all?"

It was obvious Julio saw through the girl's flirtatious subterfuge but he seemed flattered anyway. "No, no, Senorita, it will be a pleasure to assist you and your friend."

"Oh, thank you so much. You're so very kind," Isabel purred. Julio hurried ahead of the young couple, the sound of Julio's friends' laughter following them as they walked toward the barn.

Harry wasn't particularly comfortable on the wide back of the good-natured horse, and he knew he would never choose horseback riding as a mode of transportation or sport. However he was grateful for the opportunity it gave him to be alone with Isabel.

Their ride took them by several other large ranches and farms, and they passed a family traveling in a two seated buggy, plus several youngsters on horseback. It seemed as if Isabel knew everyone, calling out greetings to everybody they met along the road.

The terrain changed from cultivated, flat plains to rolling sand dunes. Isabel, perched gracefully atop her horse, led the way from the road up a narrow trail over a slight embankment, and Harry caught his breath at the panorama before him. Unblemished golden sand stretched as far as he could see, beyond which blue-green waters of the ocean glistened and sparkled, the endless rhythm of the breakers exploding into shimmering white froth. It was the most beautiful sight Harry had ever seen!

The sea breezes which flowed across the Oxnard plain kept the small agricultural community at a comfortable temperature throughout the summer and was a constant reminder of the proximity of the ocean. But Harry hadn't had an occasion to visit the beach previously.

"Climb down," Isabel commanded. She slid easily off her horse and held him by the reins.

Harry clambered awkwardly from his. "It's more beautiful than I imagined!"

"What is? Oh, you mean the ocean? Yes, I suppose it is. Is this the first time you've seen it?"

"Yes. I work all week and I don't have any transportation."

"Well . . ." Isabel walked along the beach quietly, leading her horse, Harry and his horse following along behind her.

Finally she spoke again. "I don't suppose you've really done much of anything interesting since you've been here."

"Not a whole lot," he admitted.

"We're going to have to change that. Now, let's ride some more."

On the way home Harry thought about his young friend. She had told him she was sixteen. He wasn't seventeen yet, though he had told Isabel, and anyone else who'e inquired, that he was twenty. No one doubted his word. And usually he felt like he was the older age, having considered himself an adult for a long time. But now, all of a sudden, in the presence of Isabel, he felt immature and unable to pinpoint the reason.

Isabel had stirred emotions within him he'd never felt before, and he was having difficulty dealing with them. Isabel was a lovable, beautiful girl with a pleasing personality—all the attributes for a wife.

Maybe that was the problem—Harry wasn't in the market for a wife yet. His first priority had to be his job. His career at the railroad was just beginning, and hopefully, by studying diligently and working hard, he would be noticed by his superiors and promoted. But right now he only made enough money to barely support himself, certainly not a wife too.

He was probably worrying needlessly. Isabel was barely out of childhood and probably no more interested in matrimony than he was. Pretty as she was, she no doubt had a whole collection of beaus and merely was attracted to him as a newcomer to add to her conquests. After reaching this conclusion Harry was able to cast aside his concern and enjoy the remainder of his day.

The entire Kimball family taught Harry how to play croquet on the expansive front lawn. When the evening shadows reached out across their playing field, Harry suggested it was time he got back to the railroad station. "I have to be up early tomorrow, you know."

"Oh, not yet," Isabel pleaded. "I was going to play the piano for you."

"I'm afraid you'll have to save it for another time," Harry said. "Give me a good excuse to return."

"Daddy?" Isabel turned her fluttering eyelashes in her father's direction.

"Yes, yes, dear," Mr. Kimball said, clearing his throat. "Next Sunday our family is planning to attend a barbecue at Hueneme by the Sea. We'd like to have you come with us as our guest."

Harry hesitated momentarily and Mr. Kimball added, "Of course, if you have another engagement . . ."

"Oh, no, it's not that, just . . ."

Isabel clutched Harry's arm and glanced at him in her most disconcerting manner. "Harry, please! It'll be ever so much fun. You'll enjoy yourself, you'll see. Say yes, please do."

Harry chuckled. It would be very near impossible to deny Isabel anything she desired. "I'll be delighted to attend."

After arrangements were made for the following weekend, Mr. Kimball, accompanied by his youngest son, drove Harry back to town. Mr. Kimball expanded on the subject of the sugar beet industry and its importance to Oxnard, and by the time they reached the station, Harry felt he knew nearly as much about sugar beets as he did about the railroad. That was an exaggeration, of course, because the railroad was his primary interest in life.

He bid his host goodnight, thanking him for the good meal and eventful day. After clambering into his box car, he lit the lantern and settled down for an hour or two of studying.

Chapter 51

"Harry, I'd like to have a talk with you in private."
Mr. Kimball sounded so serious that Harry
wondered if he'd done something to offend the
older man. Thinking back over the past months he
could think of nothing except the pleasurable
times he'd shared with the Kimball family. They'd
entertained him royally. Besides numerous meals
eaten at the family's home, they had taken him to
several large barbecues at Hueneme by the Sea,
dances in the wharf warehouse, and picnics along
the riverbank. The highlight of the summer was
the trip they had taken on a yacht owned by the
Oxnard Yacht Club, sailing out to the Anacapa
Island where they had been enchanted by its stark
beauty and the sea animals and birds that made
their home there.

When the weather had curtailed outside activ-
ities, the Kimballs invited him along on indoor
excursions. Occasionally he met them at the

Pioneer Hall to view a play, and when the family was invited to the homes of friends, the Kimballs always included Harry as though he were one of the family.

He'd even been invited to spend the night on Christmas eve, so as to join in with the next day's celebration. He presented each of the Kimballs with a small remembrance and had been surprised and gratified by the generosity of the gifts showered upon him. It had been a wonderful day, the only time he'd ever experienced a family Christmas.

It was after a Sunday dinner that Mr. Kimball summoned him, and Harry followed him into his office, a small room next to the parlor with a huge walnut desk nearly filling the book-lined space. Mr. Kimball sat in the chair behind the desk and motioned to Harry to sit opposite. Harry sat on the edge of his seat nervously awaiting whatever was to come.

"Relax, my boy," Mr. Kimball said kindly. "Don't worry, this isn't an inquisition of any kind."

Mr. Kimball paused as if waiting for Harry to speak, but he couldn't think of anything appropriate so remained still.

"Well, then, I guess I should get right to the point." Mr. Kimball straightened a pile of papers in front of him, and Harry realized Mr. Kimball was nervous, too. "Tell me, Harry, what are your plans for the future."

The question surprised him. Though he had many dreams he hadn't really formulated a definite plan. He made an attempt to explain. "I love the railroad and hope to advance and also continue my education. I want to learn all I can about the railroad . . . and other things, too. I'd like to travel and visit other places. Does that all sound foolish?''

"No, no, it doesn't, though it isn't what I'd hoped to hear.''

"Oh?''

"Would you consider settling down around here? Maybe going into business?''

Again Harry was surprised by Mr. Kimball's questions, but instinct told him to answer honestly. "No, I've never even thought about staying here.''

"Oh.'' The older man was obviously disappointed.

"Don't get me wrong, Mr. Kimball. You and your family have been absolutely wonderful to me. Thanks to all of you, I've had a grand stay here.''

Mr. Kimball leaned across his desk. "You sound like you're thinking about leaving.''

"There's nothing positive yet, but there has been some talk about a transfer back to Bakersfield— and maybe a promotion.''

Mr. Kimball sighed. "We'd kind of hoped . . . well, Mrs. Kimball and I thought maybe . . . tell me Harry, what do you think of Isabel?''

Harry felt his face flush with embarrassment. "Isabel? Why, she's a wonderful girl!''

"I guess I'd better lay my cards on the table, because this conversation isn't going anything like I'd planned. I was kind of hoping you'd set your sights for my daughter. You're exactly the sort of man I'd always hoped she'd marry one day, and I really thought you and she were attracted to each other.''

"Any man would have to be blind and crazy not to be attracted to Isabel. But, sir, marriage just isn't in my immediate future. I couldn't support a wife on my salary.''

"I do understand that, but I am prepared to

make you an offer. I can afford to set you up in business—any kind of business you might fancy.''

This was a surprising turn of events! And he was flattered by Mr. Kimball's proposition. ''Mr. Kimball, I hardly know what to say. I'm certainly grateful for your offer . . . but I'm unable to accept. You see the only business I'm interested in is the railroad business.

''And, please, don't misunderstand me, sir. I am very fond of Isabel. She's exactly the kind of girl any man would want for his wife, and I'm sure there are a lot of fellows around here who'd jump at the chance to court her. I'm afraid I've probably been in their way. I'll bow out of the picture, and you'll see, they'll be flocking around in droves.'' Sadly, Harry realized that to be fair to the Kimballs, and most especially Isabel, he was going to have to make himself scarce. He'd grown fond of the entire family, and hard as it would be to give up the warmth he'd shared with them, he had no other choice.

''Isabel is going to be very disappointed,'' Mr. Kimball said.

''But, sir, let me assure you, I never said or did anything that could have led her to believe . . .''

Mr. Kimball interrupted. ''I know you've shown the highest bounds of propriety, but I'm afraid in my enthusiasm for you as a candidate for son-in-law, I've given my daughter some false hopes. She was sure you'd been holding back any romantic gestures in deference to me and Mrs. Kimball, and I agreed with her and promised to have this little talk with you. Unfortunately the conclusion we've reached is not what my daughter and I had hoped for. As I said before, this is going to be very difficult for Isabel to accept.''

Harry stood. ''Sir, I feel I should take this opportunity to thank you again for the gracious hospitality shown me by your entire family. Under the circumstances I think this will be the last time I'll be visiting your home."

"Now that isn't necesssary. You know we all think a great deal of you . . ."

Harry raised a hand and smiled sadly. "Yes, I know, and I'll miss all of you, but this is the best way, I'm sure. I'll try to explain things to Isabel, and then if someone would be so kind as to drive me back to town . . ."

"Certainly, whatever you say."

Harry found Isabel sitting in the swing on the front porch. Though she patted the place beside her, he leaned against the railing. She smiled at him sweetly, her face tilted slightly as she waited expectantly.

"Isabel, I've come to tell you goodbye," he blurted out.

She frowned. "Why? Where are you going? Didn't Daddy talk to you . . ."

"Your father and I did talk, but I'm afraid I've already made other plans."

"Oh," she said in the tiniest of voices. "You don't like me, do you, Harry?" A tear fell from her large eyes and slid down her cheek.

Harry couldn't bear to see her cry, and he knelt down beside her, holding her small hands in his. "Isabel, Isabel, please don't. I *do* like you—I like you very much. You are the most beautiful, delightful, lovely girl I've ever met and I'll remember you always."

She threw her arms around his neck and kissed him full on the lips, the sweet taste of her mouth nearly upsetting his resolve. But he reached up, and untwining her arms, stood and stepped away. "I envy the man who will be fortunate enough to marry you, Isabel. I truly regret that it can't be me."

He recognized the question in her eyes, but he didn't feel he could answer it to either of their satisfaction. Instead he spun on his heels and stepped inside to tell Mr. Kimball he was ready to leave.

Harry spent several restless nights after bidding Isabel Kimball goodbye. Her face haunted his dreams. He constantly wondered whether he had made the right decision. Though he didn't return to the Kimball's home, he was tormented by her unexpected presence on the street, in the park or in a store. She would stare at him without speaking, her lips forming a melancholy smile as she turned away. His heart would ache and he would again wonder about his decision.

His transfer to Bakersfield was a welcome relief, and with the transfer came new responsibility because he was promoted to foreman. In an effort to forget Isabel—at least to the point where her memory would no longer be so painful—Harry worked hard and continued his studies with renewed intensity.

During this period he put in eighteen to twenty-two hours on trips from Los Angeles to Bakersfield. The engines would burn up to twenty tons of coal per trip, while Harry burned up all of his excess energy. He was able to fall asleep as soon as he got into bed, and he slept the night through without dreaming.

Harry studied every free waking moment, and soon, as an expert on the airbrake, was called upon to test and figure ratios on them whenever it was needed. And when the oil burning locomotive replaced the old coal burners, Harry was prepared. He took the examination for engineer, passing easily. Immediately promoted to engineer, he ran freight and passenger trains over the Tehachapi mountains.

He further increased his study, becoming diversified and taking correspondence courses in every subject available. Through his own efforts he was obtaining a well-rounded education. His first love was still the railroad, and whenever possible he conversed with the older railroad men, learning from their experiences.

Isabel faded more and more into the background, memories of the good times they shared coming to mind less frequently. And when they did, he no longer had any doubts about his decision. He knew he's set his course in the right direction.

Chapter 52

To anyone inquiring his age, Harry Hoffman always answered twenty-four though in actuality he was but twenty. It was 1905, and he was still working for the railroad out of the town of Kern, which was slightly east of Bakersfield. He now made enough money to move from a cheap hotel to a room in a small, homey boarding house run by Mrs. Stickler. Her name fit—his landlady was a stickler for rules and regulations to be followed by each and everyone of her boarders.

The tiny woman with the formidable bosom read the list of rules to Harry, requesting his compliance before accepting him as a guest. She finished with " . . . and I expect you to be on time for meals unless you've given prior notification!"

He agreed, amused by her sternness as she peered up at him over spectacles on the end of a pinched, long nose. "Dinner will be served promptly at 6 p.m." The woman turned, her starched apron crackling and her heels striking sharply on the polished wood floor as she marched off in the direction of the dining room.

Harry followed several other boarders through the open sliding doors of the large room. Mrs. Stickler presided at the head of the table and motioned Harry to a chair halfway down. All the places were filled excepting the one directly across from Harry.

Mrs. Stickler lowered her head and pointedly looked at the watch pinned to her bosom, then at the empty chair. She sighed impatiently. "It seems Miss Bailey has been detained. Well, everyone, I'd like you to meet Mr. Harry Hoffman, our newest boarder. Mr. Hoffman is with the railroad."

The various diners nodded and murmured hellos as Mrs. Stickler introduced them. Miss Forsythe, a prim and proper lady of undetermined age, had a rather pretty face but camouflaged it with a painfully skinned back hairdo knotted plainly at the nape of her neck. She was unsurprisingly identified as a school teacher. Sitting next to her was Mr. Herndon, a bank clerk. Then there was a young man who worked in the local grocery, a middle-aged widow who was a personal friend of Mrs. Stickler, a carpenter named Jones, and Mr. Percell, a salesman—the usual assortment for a boarding house.

Mrs. Stickler bowed her head and said a flowery rhymed blessing, and before the echo from her resounding "Ahh . . . men" had faded, the large bowls and platters of food were lifted from their places on the tablecloth, plates quickly being filled with their contents.

"Sorry I'm late, Mrs. Stickler, but there was extra work at the post office." Harry stared at the late arrival. A short, young woman with a perfect hourglass figure had burst through the door and slipped into the chair directly across from Harry.

Harry was able to study her vibrant good looks while the flustered guest settled herself. Her shiny, warm brown hair was arranged in a pompadour across the front and a thick braid wound around the top of her head. Her plump cheeks had a healthy pink glow, her perfectly shaped lips were naturally red, and her fair skin was flawlessly smooth. Dark lashes raised, her startlingly blue eyes met his gaze—and she smiled at him.

Mrs. Stickler noticed the exchange, quickly interjecting, "Beulah, allow me to introduce our new boarder, Mr. Harry Hoffman. Mr. Hoffman is a railroad man. And this is Miss Bailey."

"How do you do?" Beulah said politely, not waiting for an answer before turning her full attention to the waiting meal.

Harry found himself completely mesmerized by the vibrant, diminutive, and extremely feminine woman. Since his experience with Isabel, he'd avoided any other encounters with the opposite sex, busying himself with work and studies. Besides, the women he had noticed hadn't held a candle to Isabel's golden beauty, and he'd nearly come to the conclusion he'd let the most desirable woman he would ever meet slip from his grasp.

But the delightful creature across the table had already changed his viewpoint. He found Miss Bailey utterly fascinating and beautiful in a whole different way than Isabel. Comparing the two, Harry realized Isabel had been little more than a child, her femininity merely beginning to bud. On the other hand, Miss Bailey was in the full bloom of womanhood. Harry focused his attention totally on her while mechanically shoveling food into his mouth.

He had his first understanding of the popular romantic valentines with cupids pictured, zinging arrows into the hearts of unsuspecting young men. At that moment, he felt as though he most certainly had been the target of one of those chubby cherubs and knew this new emotion was what had been missing in his relationship with Isabel—why he'd been reluctant to change his plans for her.

Unfortunately the object of his attention didn't seem to be similarly affected, barely noticing him throughout the meal. Of course the only gems of conversation he was able to offer were such mundane comments as "Please pass the salad."

Actually, Harry's attentiveness hadn't gone unnoticed by Beulah. In fact, the bold young man was making her nervous. Every time she glanced from her plate the new boarder was staring at her, and she could feel his gaze even when she looked away or down at her plate. His scrutiny made her self-conscious, and her usually healthy appetite disappeared. Leaving half her dinner untouched, she pushed her chair back and excused herself.

Hurrying through the dining room doors, she heard another chair being scraped across the floor and Mr. Hoffman say, "Very good dinner, Mrs. Stickler. See you in the morning."

Beulah retrieved her bicycle she'd left propped against the wall and wheeled it down the hall toward her room.

"Please, wait just a moment, Miss Bailey. I'd like to have a few words with you." She could hear the man bounding down the hall behind her.

The warmth of a blush covered her cheeks as she turned towards him. "It will have to be a *very* few words."

Beulah was surprised by how tall he was! She had to tilt her face to look up into his strong jawed, clean shaven face. His dark auburn hair was parted in the middle and combed back in waves on either side, and his large, clear brown eyes gazed eagerly at her from beneath heavy brows. Freckles sprinkled lightly across his broad cheeks and wide straight nose, his huge smile accentuating a dimple in his chin.

"I'm stepping out this evening with a gentleman friend, and I only have a short time to get ready," she explained curtly.

"Oh," he said, disappointment on his face. "I hoped you might honor me with your company this evening."

Mr. Hoffman's boldness didn't set well with Beulah. "As I've just mentioned, I have a previous engagement. Now if you'll excuse me . . ." Holding her chin high, she resumed her way toward the end of the hall.

Mr. Hoffman trotted along behind her "I have to go on a run tomorrow. I'd sure like a promise that you'll save an evening for me when I return next week."

She realized the only way she was going to be free of this persistent young man was to agree. With a deep sigh she said, "We'll see, Mr. Hoffman. Now really, I must be going!"

"Great! I'll be looking forward to it." He'd followed her right to her door and was still talking when she firmly closed it in his face.

She leaned against the wall of her room, covering her mouth to stifle a giggle. Holding out her right hand, the sight of the lovely topaz ring on her finger quickly sobered her. The ring was a gift from the young man she was stepping out with that evening. He was an eligible bachelor from Porterville, and she had been seeing him frequently. Coincidentally, his name was also Harry, and she always had an enjoyable time in his company, for he escorted her to concerts, stage plays, and dances. But she certainly wasn't in love with him.

Shaking herself from her reverie, she rushed to freshen herself for the evening. She was anchoring the final hairpin into her braid when Mrs. Stickler announced her date's arrival. Beulah gathered up her shawl and evening purse and hurried out to greet him as he waited nervously in the vestibule. He shifted his weight from foot to foot, perspiration beading on his forehead.

"I'm sorry I kept you waiting but I was late getting home from work," Beulah explained as she tucked her hand into his arm.

They stepped out onto the porch. Mr. Hoffman, who had been sitting on the porch swing, leaped to his feet and said is a loud voice, "Have a pleasant evening, Miss Bailey."

Beulah felt her face flush, and she answered haughtily without looking in his direction. "I shall, thank you. Good evening, Mr. Hoffman."

Unfortunately for her date, the brief encounter with Mr. Hoffman caused Beulah to compare the looks of the two Harrys during the evening, instead of giving her full attention to the string ensemble they had come to hear. Unfortunate because her escort came off second best. The Harry sitting next to her, seemingly absorbed by the music, was only inches taller than she and had a tendency towards pudginess. His black hair was plastered to his head by some sort of hair oil, and a broad expanse of bulging forehead was exposed by a receding hairline. His small eyes were almost hidden by shaggy eyebrows, his nose was nearly bulbous, and he tended to smile with his mouth shut to hide his crooked teeth with their slight overbite.

She mentally admonished herself for being so critical of her beau's outward appearance. He was the son of a wealthy Delano pioneer and had his own ranch in Porterville. He was kind and considerate, always a gentleman—but a bit on the dull side. To be fair, so were most of her other suitors. All the men she was acquainted with were farmers and ranchers who seemed to be interested only in the fertility of their land and animals.

In an effort to make up for her unseemly thoughts, she forced herself to pretend interest in Harry's comments on the way home, smiling flirtatiously at his attempts at humor and patting his arm from time to time.

This attempt at salving her conscience backfired. Harry reined in the horse, stopping his buggy under a sheltering maple tree nearly a half block away from Mrs. Stickler's boarding house.

"Harry?" Beulah only had time to say his name before he lurched at her jerkily and threw his arms around her, his puckered lips aimed directly at her mouth.

She turned her head quickly, but too late. His wet lips landed on her mouth but slid across her cheek, and she shuddered slightly, pulling away.

"Pardon me for my forwardness, but it's no secret how I feel about you, Beulah. I've been trying to get up the nerve to ask you a very important . . ."

"Oh, Harry, it's awfully late. I'll just hop out right here and now, since I have to be at work early tomorrow morning."

She was out of the buggy before Harry could react. "B-but . . ." he began.

"I enjoyed the music very much. Thank you, Harry. Bye now." Beulah held her skirt and nearly ran the short distance to her boarding house.

Inside, she pulled the lacy curtain on the window beside the front door and peeked out into the night. She watched Harry pass by as he drove the buggy slowly down the street, his shoulders hunched dejectedly. Letting the curtain fall back into place, she almost felt sad. Harry was a very nice person. But goodness, that kiss! And he almost proposed to her! She certainly had no desire to be married to Harry. He'd probably never call on her again, and very honestly she couldn't care less.

The following week, as Beulah went about her daily routine at the post office, thoughts of the auburn-haired Mr. Hoffman popped unbidden into her head. She angrily tried to push them from her brain and might have succeeded except on Wednesday, while sorting the morning mail, she was surprised to find an envelope addressed to her. It was written in an unfamiliar hand, bold and open. She stuffed it into her work apron's pocket, relieved to see that the postmaster had not noticed.

Taking her lunch to a shady spot underneath the pepper tree behind the post office, she pulled out the letter and tore it open. She realized she was blushing even though no one was around as she read, "My dear Beulah . . ." Mr. Hoffman's boldness was irritating.

The rest of the letter was merely a polite and cheery missive which she crumpled into a ball and dropped into her pocket. Who did this Mr. Harry Hoffman think he was anyway? He was little more than a stranger to her after all, and he certainly had no business writing her a letter. She felt irritated the rest of the afternoon.

Much to her annoyance there was another letter from Mr. Hoffman the next day—and everyday until he returned!

Sprawled across the front steps, he was waiting for her one evening when she rode up to the boarding house on her bicycle. "Miss Bailey!" He leaped to his feet and ran to her even before she dismounted.

"How do you do?" she said icily, looking up at the large man towering over her. She felt a rush of mixed emotions—irritated by his brashness but flattered by his obvious interest. And he was every bit as handsome as she had remembered.

"You did remember we have a date this evening?" A huge smile exposed his large, white teeth.

His pompous self-assuredness was maddening! "I'm terribly sorry, Mr. Hoffman. I wasn't sure when you would be returning and I made other plans for this evening."

His smile disappeared as he took her bicycle and carried it up the front steps. "I have another short run to make but I'll be home late Saturday night. Would you honor me with an early Sunday morning bicycle ride?"

"I'm afraid not. I promised the postmaster I would watch his youngest children while he and his wife attend Mass," she said, reclaiming her bicycle from the persistent young man.

She dismissed Mr. Hoffman with a curt, "Thank you," and wheeled her bicycle inside the boarding house as he held the front door open, then hurried down the hallway to her room.

The next couple of weeks Beulah tried hard to ignore Mr. Hoffman—but he was difficult to ignore. At every opportunity he struck up a conversation with her, and whenever he was gone on a train run, she received a letter from him nearly every day.

On a visit to Delano she told her mother about him. "Mr. Hoffman is certainly handsome. But he's so big! He's always blocking doorways."

Beulah was glad she no longer lived at home because this avoided a lot of teasing from her younger sister, Flossie.

Irritated to realize that she looked forward to the letters that arrived regularly from her would-be-suitor, Beulah's heart still skipped a beat whenever she recognized Mr. Hoffman's broad scrawl on the envelopes addressed to her. It was the letters themselves which finally caused her to re-evaluate the young man. She came to realize that underneath the light-hearted, flirtatious tone of the letters, he revealed intelligence.

Finally, giving into Mr. Hoffman's pleading, she consented to spend an evening with him. Almost before she realized it, Mr. Hoffman, who she now called Harry, was actively courting her, and she began to make excuses to all her other beaus, including the other Harry. She kept open the time that Harry Hoffman was in town so she could spend it all with him, and when he was away she continued to receive his letters regularly—though now they had taken on a more tender tone.

There was another aspect about Harry which intrigued Beulah. He carried an aura of mystery about him. Though he loved to hear stories about her childhood, when she attempted to question him about his past, he generalized. Instead of telling her anything about himself he would describe places he'd visited and things he had seen. And he cleverly avoided all her questions. He had a gift for narrating a scene or an incident, so fascinating her by the account that she would forget her original query.

The only concrete information she'd been able to squeeze out of him was that he was approximately the same age as she was. "What do you think? Do I look much older than you . . . or much younger?"

He had also told her that he'd been orphaned as at a young age, lived in an orphanage for a time and then with foster parents until he was grown. He'd worked for the railroad since his late teens. He didn't hide his feelings about his work, obviously enjoying it, and he was enthusiastic about his career and the future of the railroad.

"You seem to be taking quite an interest in Harry Hoffman," mentioned Desdemona, when Beulah visited for the weekend.

"Well, he's certainly more interesting than most of the fellows around here," Beulah mused. "I just wish I could find out a little more about him. He's so close-mouthed about himself."

"Perhaps his past is too unpleasant and he doesn't care to reminisce about it," her mother suggested.

"Maybe, but it's so frustrating! He knows practically everything there is to know about me, and I don't even know his birthday!"

"Let's have another cup of coffee." Desdemona refilled each of their cups. "Is it possible that my daughter has actually been smitten by the love bug?"

"Oh, mother!" Beulah protested, but she could feel the warmth as it rushed to her cheeks. "Well, maybe . . . but please, Mother, don't even suggest such a thing to anyone else, especially Flossie. She would make my life unbearable! And besides, he hasn't really declared himself."

Beulah's mother smiled as she sipped her coffee. Beulah knew her mother was pleased. Harry had come with Beulah several times to visit Desdemona, who eventually told her daughter that Harry Hoffman was the first young man Desdemona had met that she felt had all the attributes necessary to satisfy Beulah. Desdemona liked his friendly personality, always offering a compliment on her appearance and her cooking.

Desdemona had also voiced her opinion that she was pleased by Harry's ambitions. He often spoke of his chances for advancement on the railroad, intending to take advantage of every opportunity which presented itself. Beulah was well aware her mother thought Harry Hoffman would be an acceptable husband for her daughter.

Chapter 53

Harry was pleased with the way his romance with Beulah was progressing. He recognized the fact that despite her initial reluctance, she now enjoyed his company, and he delighted in teasing her, sometimes making her angry. Though he didn't like her to be angry with him, she was even more beautiful when the sparks flew from her eyes and color brightened her cheeks.

Her anger never remained for any length of time. He would hear her trying to sneak quietly past his room early in the morning after an evening when they'd had a tiff. The unmistakable squeak of her bicycle would alert him, and he would call out to her, "Good morning, honey!" She would giggle as she continued on by.

He had also grown quite fond of Beulah's attractive mother and got a big kick out of her younger sister, Flossie. Flossie was a good match for him in the teasing department, and they had some wild

times together, much to Beulah's disapproval.
Fortunately for him, Beulah could never stay
upset with him very long.

The high degree of independence shown by all
three of the Bailey women commanded Harry's
respect. Mrs. Bailey, twice widowed, supported
herself by renting out her extra bedrooms and
taking on nursing jobs. Flossie, with a girl friend,
owned her own successful business, an ice cream
shop. And the love of his life, Beulah, had been
supporting herself since her late teens by working in the post office. It was unusual to find
women engaged in pursuits outside the home, and
because of having to support himself from an
early age, Harry admired the Bailey women all the
more.

Beulah's inquisitiveness was the only flaw in the
romance. She questioned him incessantly about
his past, but he just wasn't anxious to relive his
painful childhood—nor could he see any necessity
to do so. Instead he would discuss less depressing
subjects.

And, of course, there was another important
reason for not revealing details of his past—
there was the problem of his age. Beulah was
twenty-four, and Harry had led her to believe he
was the same age. He was positive that had she
been aware of the fact that he was only twenty, she
would have never passed the time of day with him.
Beulah was clever, and he didn't want to let slip
any information which might lead her to discover
his deception.

Even though Beulah finally seemed to
relinquish her curiosity about his past, Harry was
never completely free from the worry.

But Beulah hadn't really lost her curiosity
about her beau's younger days, though she set the

pursuit of such knowledge aside, knowing it upset him. Foremost in her mind was the realization that she was in love with Harry.

There were times he nearly drove her crazy with his teasing. And even more annoying were the wild shenanigans he engaged in with her sister—anything from practical jokes to food consumption contests. It was enough to cause her to wonder if he was truly as old as he proclaimed to be. But his attributes more than made up for any irritating traits. She was positive Harry was the man she had been dreaming about—the one man for whom she would willingly give up her independence.

Despite his attentiveness—spending nearly all his free time with her—he didn't propose right away, and the delay caused Beulah some unwarranted torment. She wondered if perhaps she had misjudged his attentions. Finally, on an unusually warm winter day spent in the country, Harry finally proved her fears to be groundless. Beulah had finished repacking their picnic basket and started to rise, when Harry reached out and took her hand. "Wait! Let's not go just yet."

"But it's getting late . . ." Beulah began.

"It's not that late, and I have something important to discuss with you."

"Oh?" Beulah frowned. It wasn't often Harry was so serious.

He clung tightly to her hand, and his voice had an unusual quaver in it. "I think you are aware of my strong feelings for you . . . and I do hope your feelings are similar."

"Well, of course, Harry, I . . ."

He touched her lips gently with a free finger. "Wait, please let me finish. Would you do me the honor of consenting to become my wife?"

Joy flowed over Beulah. She was smiling, but her voice was choked with tears when she answered, "Harry, I didn't think you were ever going to ask me!"

Harry's broad face remained solemn. "Beulah, don't tease me, please . . . what is your answer?"

Beulah pulled herself to her knees and threw her arms around Harry, squeezing him tightly. "Oh, Harry, you silly goose, the answer is yes, of course!"

Harry beamed and his blue eyes shimmered with love. "May I kiss you?" he asked timidly.

Beulah's answer was to press her lips hard against his. They felt soft and tasted sweet, and her heartbeat quickened so she could barely breathe. She'd been kissed before, but never had a mere kiss affected her like this!

With reluctance she pulled away from Harry's embrace. "Now I think we must head back."

Harry sighed deeply. "I suppose you're right, but I shall treasure this moment always."

Just before climbing onto her bicycle Beulah turned to Harry and asked, "Harry, I must know . . . why did you wait so long to propose?"

He shrugged his broad shoulders and winked an eye. "I wanted to be absolutely positive that you would say yes."

On July 2, 1906, Harry Hoffman realized his dream when Beulah Belle Bailey became his wife. This marriage resulted in two daughters, three granddaughters, and ten great grandchildren, and a great deal of happiness which lasted until his death—a period of sixty-four years.

Harry successfully kept his true age a secret to the very end, when it no longer mattered anymore, but was merely an interesting curiosity to his descendants.

Epilogue

Angus Henry Hoffman steadily climbed the ladder of success, due mostly to his perserverance and search for knowledge—though he felt it came from the kindnesses afforded him by his superiors on the railroad.

During Harry's career he had four different Presidents of the United States as passengers on his train. He held many offices, including that of president, in the Brotherhood of Locomotive Engineers, this group sending him all over the country to various conventions, often as the featured speaker. He traveled to many states as an expert witness for the railroad in federal court-rooms and published several magazine articles on various aspects of the railroad. And after his retirement, he also served as the expert on trains for movies made by Twentieth Century Fox Studios.

His wife, Beulah, had her dream of traveling to

faraway places come true. Not only did they live in several homes in central and southern California, but they also took trips all over the United States and to Cuba and Alaska.

In the retirement speech Harry gave to his fellow railroad men, he expounded on the greatness of the United States, affording a little orphan boy the opportunity to rise to the place he had on the railroad, making it possible to purchase several homes and send his daughters to college.

Angus Henry Hoffman died February 12, 1970. At his request, his funeral was attended only by members of the family. He had written his own eulogy which was delivered by the minister, and his family found it to be full of amusing messages and anecdotes—such as an admonishment to those who hadn't bothered to speak well of him before his death not to bother at this late date.

The tears didn't flow until Beulah, his wife and companion of so many years, bent over her husband in his casket, kissed him on the lips, and murmured, "Bye, bye, darlin', see you soon!"

Within six months Beulah had joined her husband. Before her death, she gave the gold wedding band she had worn for sixty-four years to her oldest great-granddaughter to wear at her forthcoming marriage.

Upon visiting her grandfather's grave, his granddaughter, Margie Turner, began unraveling the mystery of Harry Hoffman's age when she discovered that the year of his birth on his grave marker was the same as that on his oldest sister's grave. This fact piqued her curiosity, and she began what was to become a consuming hobby—the research of the family geneology. Locating the old records from the Hollygrove Orphanage she discovered Harry's harmless, but interesting, lifelong deception.

BE SWEPT AWAY ON A TIDE OF PASSION BY LEISURE'S THRILLING HISTORICAL ROMANCES!

Make the Most of Your Leisure Time with
LEISURE BOOKS

Please send me the following titles:

Quantity	Book Number	Price
‾‾‾‾‾	‾‾‾‾‾‾‾‾‾‾	‾‾‾‾‾
‾‾‾‾‾	‾‾‾‾‾‾‾‾‾‾	‾‾‾‾‾
‾‾‾‾‾	‾‾‾‾‾‾‾‾‾‾	‾‾‾‾‾
‾‾‾‾‾	‾‾‾‾‾‾‾‾‾‾	‾‾‾‾‾
‾‾‾‾‾	‾‾‾‾‾‾‾‾‾‾	‾‾‾‾‾

If out of stock on any of the above titles, please send me the alternate title(s) listed below:

‾‾‾‾‾	‾‾‾‾‾‾‾‾‾‾	‾‾‾‾‾
‾‾‾‾‾	‾‾‾‾‾‾‾‾‾‾	‾‾‾‾‾
‾‾‾‾‾	‾‾‾‾‾‾‾‾‾‾	‾‾‾‾‾
‾‾‾‾‾	‾‾‾‾‾‾‾‾‾‾	

Postage & Handling ‾‾‾‾‾‾‾‾

Total Enclosed $‾‾‾‾‾‾

☐ Please send me a free catalog.

NAME _____
(please print)

ADDRESS _____

CITY _____ STATE _____ ZIP_____

Please include $1.00 shipping and handling for the first book ordered and 25¢ for each book thereafter in the same order. All orders are shipped within approximately 4 weeks via postal service book rate. PAYMENT MUST ACCOMPANY ALL ORDERS.*

*Canadian orders must be paid in US dollars payable through a New York banking facility.

Mail coupon to: **Dorchester Publishing Co., Inc.**
6 East 39 Street, Suite 900
New York, NY 10016
Att: ORDER DEPT.